My Art & My Stetson

ISBN 978-0-912887-50-0
Library of Congress Control Number: 2020951747

Original Publication 2008: *Os Passos da Glória*, Lisbon, Bertrand
Editora, selected for the 2008 Fernando Namora Award short list.

Translated by David Prescott
Cover and Book Design by Lauren Grosskopf

Pleasure Boat Studio books are available
through your favorite bookstore and through the following:
Baker & Taylor, Ingram, Amazon, bn.com &
PLEASURE BOAT STUDIO: A NONPROFIT LITERARY PRESS
PLEASUREBOATSTUDIO.COM
Seattle, Washington

MY ART AND MY STETSON

A NOVEL BY

Manuel de Queiroz

Pleasure Boat Studio: A Nonprofit Literary Press

CONTENTS

"Glory is no more than the sum of all the misunderstandings created around a new name."

Rainer Maria Rilke
("Auguste Rodin," Oeuvres en prose, Paris, 1966)

To the memory of my brother, Alfredo Queiroz Ribeiro,
also a talented sculptor, also so unjustly forgotten

———————

And to the memory of Lewis Stetson Allen,
my American "cousin"

NOTE TO THE READER

Although this is a historical fiction novel, it is based on real people and facts that have been studied and researched as far as possible through varied sources of information: newspapers from the period, catalogs, articles, essays, personal accounts, photo archives, etc.

All of the titles, references, and quotations from newspapers—with the exception of one (page 313)—are authentic, as are the respective publication dates. The addresses and descriptions of the places where the protagonist lived are also accurate.

Having thus scrupulously respected the facts, the characters, and their circumstances, the author felt free to invent all of the rest, knowing that in a narrative of such characteristics, it is the fictional truth that in the final analysis ends up revealing a new emphasis for the reality that supports it.

I

EMMA VIRGINIA BEACH. Better known as Emma, Emma Beach. But whom the journalists had baptized Annabelle for whatever reason. Miss Annabelle Beach. Chubby, average build, age somewhere between forty and fifty, round, rosy face, turned-up nose, thin, small mouth, with two accentuated lines at the corners, bright blue eyes that are always attentive behind her thick, round tortoiseshell glasses, fine brown hair tied about the neck, with a fringe over her forehead, beige and white striped blouse and a ruffled collar buttoned to the top, full-length skirt disguising the weight accumulated around her backside and hips. Miss Emma Beach, Mrs. Stetson's private secretary. Referred to respectfully by the rest of the house staff as Miss Beach. Even though she sometimes had the impression that the way that some of the Italian estate workers pronounced her name sounded more like *bitch* than Beach. Ah, the subtleties of the English language that a female with the last name Beach was forced to ignore, she had long decided, after overcoming her initial irritation, since the only thing she could do—to ask the author of the quip whether he or she was calling her Miss Bitch instead of Miss Beach—was worse, much worse than doing nothing at all. It wasn't difficult to imagine the response: "...me? Calling Miss Beach, Miss Bitch? No. You misheard Miss Bitch. When I say Miss Beach, I mean Miss Beach. I don't mean Miss Bitch. Do you understand Miss Bitch?"

Miss Beach, in her office, sitting at a desk facing the window, with two shutters and an awning, through which she could from time to time extend her gaze over the vast lawn down below, stretching all around the house and dotted here and there by tall, leafy trees, then smoothly descending to the bottom of the hill where was the Old York Road that led to Philadelphia. Like right now, before leafing through the daily newspapers looking for articles referring to the public announcement that had been made the previous day by Mrs. Stetson to the correspondents of Philadelphia's main papers, taking advantage of a relatively calm moment in the house, since Mrs. Stetson and the Count had just gone by car to Norristown to deal with the marriage license. And now that the preparations in the music room and the Gothic hall were already well underway.

Emma herself had spent the morning of the previous day telephoning the newspapers, telling them that an important announcement was going to be made by Mrs. Stetson relating to the rumors that were circulating throughout the city about her coming wedding to a European nobleman. Yet obviously without revealing any more details than she had to, despite their insistence. It was up to Mrs. Stetson to make the announcement, and not her, as they would soon understand, she insisted. The press conference, if one could call it that, had taken place right there in the garden, in front of the library porch. Mrs. Stetson, with the serenity and presence of mind for which she was well known, slowly read aloud the official notice that she, Emma, had prepared based on the facts that were given to her, in a hand-written note from the Count himself:

> "The engagement is announced of the Count Santa Eulália to Mrs. S. Elizabeth Stetson. The latter is the widow of John B. Stetson, of Philadelphia. Count Eulália, who is about 50 years of age, is a member of one of the oldest and most representative families of Portugal, his ancestors having been for generations hidalgos cavalleiros da casa real of Portugal. One of them, Dom Manuel Pinto Riberio da Fonseca, was in 1404 grandmaster of the Crusaders, the only Portuguese to be so honoured. The Count is a sculptor of considerable note, his works having been placed in various cities of Europe and America. He was the recipient of the Grand Prix of the Paris Salon in 1892."

The announcement had been carefully reviewed over and over after lunch, before they left by car for an outing that had taken place each afternoon since the Count had moved to *Idro*, on the Fourth of July, Independence Day, nearly three weeks previously. The Count had made some additional alterations, mostly relating to the spelling of the Portuguese words and names, which he insisted should all be correctly translated. Unfortunately, it was only later that evening, following the press conference, that he was able to read the version that Emma herself had typewritten and distributed to the reporters, immediately detecting, despite all the revisions, several errors that she could not have avoided, ignorant as she was of the Portuguese spoken and written language.

Such as that in Portuguese the word was *fidalgos* and not *hilalgos*, which was Castilian, a language spoken in Spain, but not in Portugal, an independent country for more than seven centuries. The Count made a point to explain in a nationalist tone that he wore quite well, since for any ordinary American, Portugal and Spain were normally confused as just one country, the Iberian Peninsula or Iberia, located on the other side of the Atlantic, between France and Morocco.... An error that even Emma, who prided herself on her knowledge of history and geography, had a tendency to make, had it not been for the explanations given to her opportunely by the Count. The fact that the name of his illustrious ancestor, quoted in the notice, was Ribeiro and not *Riberio,* as she, certainly by mistake, had written. And that he had been grand master of the Order of Malta and not the Crusaders, in 1704 and not in 1404, as was wrongly stated in the notice. "It's a difference of three centuries, after all, Emma," the Count had said with a touch of irony, curiously not mentioning his age on the notice, which stated "about fifty years of age," instead of his real age, which was forty. "Well, it's ten years difference, Count, which might be little for the history of a country, but for a person's life, it's a lot," she would have liked to reply firmly to his rebuking of her. But she obviously couldn't do such a thing, so as not to embarrass her employer since she was responsible for the alteration. To avoid any gossip or snide remarks about the Count's real intentions, should it become known that she was about to marry a man ten years her junior? Indeed, looking at the two of them no one could tell—but it was true, Mrs. Stetson was ten years older than the Count since he was born in 1868, and she, in 1858, as Emma was able to confirm to her great surprise when she read their birth certificates a few days earlier, along with the rest of the paperwork that she had to gather to apply for the marriage license. That was the most likely reason, although she had not been given any explanation. Nor had she asked her for one, obviously.

As if age was really that important when it came to love, she caught herself daydreaming. And above all, Mrs. Stetson looked so youthful and elegant, as all the journalists kept on stating the previous day, as soon as she had left. After with great brilliance and presence of spirit, it must be noted, having answered all of their questions one by one, fired one after the other, in a tone that was at times aggressive and sensationalist, as only American reporters could: When and where will the wedding take place? When is the Count arriving in Philadelphia? Why hadn't Mrs. Stetson waited for him to make the announcement? Did the Count have a personal fortune, or was he just another fortune hunter? Where could one see his work as a sculptor? Was he really a Count and who had given him the title? What had made Mrs. Stetson change her mind and now prefer a Portuguese Count to the Irish Earl of Clancarcy, who, according to information recently circulating throughout Philadelphia, was to be the fortunate chosen man? And many, many more questions that Emma was unable to recall.

Mrs. Stetson started by explaining that the essential information that the journalists needed to do their job was contained in the notice she had just finished reading and that her private secretary, Miss Beach, would give out to them shortly. Which meant that nothing had been decided as to the date and place for the wedding. As for the Count, he was at this very moment on his way to Philadelphia from Chicago, where he had been detained by his diplomatic functions as Consul of Portugal to the city. In relation to the suggestion that he might be a fortune hunter, she considered this personally offensive, since the relationship between her and the Count was exclusively based on the love and friendship that had united them for quite a long time. Furthermore, although the Count was not a rich man in American terms, neither was he a person lacking in means, since he received a comfortable sum from the rent on the properties he owned in Portugal, besides that which he earned working as a sculptor, which was also considerable. And one should not forget that he also performed prestigious diplomatic functions in the service of his country and his king, as Portuguese Consul in Chicago. About her supposed engagement to the Earl of Clancarcy, Mrs. Stetson had been curt and cutting, saying that she had known the Earl for a long time as the husband of her great friend Belle Bilton, who had recently passed away. And that she had supported him in his pain and suffering over the death of his wife after she herself had gone through the same experience two years previously upon the death of her own husband, but that nothing more than profound and sincere compassion bound the two of them together. Thus anything that could possibly be inferred beyond this was merely pure journalistic speculation without any credit.

Following this Mrs. Stetson went on to ask the journalists to wait a moment, and, without further explanation, went indoors, to then reappear a short while later with two of the Count's works, having made a point of bringing them out herself as a sign of her deep care and admiration for the Count's talent. This was also so evident in the proud and satisfied manner in which she presented the works, being a woman who was normally so reserved in front of strangers. Her whole face lit up into a beautiful smile as she said: "These are two of the Count's works. The oil is obviously original. And this is a photograph of the sculpture with which he won first prize at the *Paris Salon* in 1892."

They were doubtlessly two high-quality works, judging by the positive comments and demonstrations of pleasure exchanged among the journalists. The oil painting was of a bucolic landscape in the north of Portugal, the region where the Count came from; the photograph depicted a beautiful bust of a woman sculpted in marble with the title *Extase Religieuse*, and which, according to those in the know, resembled sculptures by Rodin, the famous French sculptor with whom it had been said that the Count had worked during his stay in Paris, and by whom he had been greatly influenced.

Then Mrs. Stetson, giving in to the insistent requests of the reporters about whether there were other works they could see, asked Emma to go to the library and bring the folder with the photographs of some of the Count's other works. Among these works was the extraordinary statue of Queen Amelia of Portugal, whose husband, King Carlos, and eldest son, had been assassinated a few months earlier. The photograph showed the Queen, magnificent, opulent in a striking tight-fitting, low-necked dress that made her elegant waist, bust line, and hips stand out, sitting in her place as queen, beneath the royal coat of arms of Portugal. Next to the statue of the Queen was the Count himself, wearing a short white jacket, with his elbow resting on one of the arms of the throne, as if preparing to, respectfully, kiss her hand.

The journalists were left speechless on seeing such a grandiose example of the Count's art as Mrs. Stetson then explained that the statue was to be sent to Portugal, where the present king, Manuel II, wished to have it placed prominently in one of the great squares of Lisbon, in homage to his mother. She then took out some more photographs of the Count's works and showed them to the journalists, as well as some photographs of the Count himself in several different poses and outfits. Finally, Mrs. Stetson invited them into the main hall of the house, the Gothic hall as it was known because its impressive ceiling height made it resemble one of the Gothic cathedrals of the old world, where they could enjoy seeing the magnificent bronze bas-relief of Henry Addison DeLand, founder of the city of DeLand, Florida, another one of the Count's pieces, commissioned by Mr. John B. Stetson who also happened to be an unconditional admirer of the Count's work, she insisted on pointing out. The bas-relief was soon to be placed in the Stetson University, which her deceased husband had founded with Mr. DeLand in Florida, she finally explained before concluding the meeting with the journalists.

Almost fifty newspapers, Emma concluded after counting them one by one. That Vinny, one of the house chauffeurs, had brought that morning from Philadelphia, after having strictly followed the instructions that she, Emma, had given him the previous day: to go to the Central Station newsstands and purchase everything there, whether they were from Philadelphia or any other state in the Union. What she had never expected was that he would bring so many newspapers from such different places, like those she now had in front of her, she thought, as she went through the different mastheads to identify the states of origin before separating those from Philadelphia and stacking them on the right side of the desk. Those would certainly have had more complete information than the others, given that they had almost all been represented at the press conference, she thought, thus taking advantage not only of the facts contained in the official notice but also from the photographs and supplementary information that she had provided for them at the end. Except for the date and place of the wedding, which was clearly the information they most wanted. And that information, according to Mrs. Stetson's instructions, had to be kept secret until everything was over so that the newlyweds could avoid being bothered by reporters. Six Philadelphia newspapers, she noted. Almost all of which, as she expected, giving the announcement great emphasis, some even placing it on the front page, Miss Beach was pleased to see as she went through them one by one. *The Philadelphia Inquirer* headlined in capital letters: "MRS. J. B. STETSON SOON TO MARRY PORTUGUESE COUNT," while the Philadelphia *Public Ledger* had a full-length photograph of Mrs. Stetson in a ceremonial outfit, beautiful and elegant, as only she knew how to be given her age, and a two-column article entitled: *"Mrs. Stetson to be a Count's Bride."* The sub-heading explained: *"Hat Manufacturer's Widow will be Wedded to Santa Eulália of Portugal:* HER FIANCÉ IS A SCULPTOR." *The Philadelphia Record,* under the title, "A COUNT FOR MRS. STETSON," carried an article and two photographs, one of a seated Mrs. Stetson, wearing a beautiful hat and white dress, and another of the Count in which he looked like a veritable prince charming who had just come out of a fairy tale, radiating in his elegant Gentleman Knight of the Royal Household uniform, with a chest full of medals, a bicorn hat adorned with a plume of ostrich feathers and that extraordinary upturned mustache, which, according to more than one person, made him look like Kaiser Wilhelm II of Germany. Yet if they asked Emma for her personal opinion, she would say that the Kaiser in no way measured up to the Count, in physical presence or anything else. "Praise the Lord, what a handsome man, what a figure," she sighed while looking up from the *Record,* she who had already passed the age of being interested in men, condemned to a forced and endless celibacy for the rest of her life, but who certainly still had eyes and was able to appreciate the beauty in things and beings. "The intensity of those eyes, the softness of that voice," she continued without being able to stop the shudder she sensed rising up her spine. "And all those good manners, getting up from the table each time a lady stood up," she thought, this time trying to keep to more neutral, less palpable qualities. "That delicate way, those fine manners, whether they were directed at ladies or employees, without ever raising his voice, with a smile always ready to break out on his lips as he spoke; the way he uses his knife and fork when he eats, with his elbows always close to his torso even when he raises cutlery to his mouth; the way he chews, with his mouth closed, speaking only when he finished. What a difference from common Americans, good Lord, only knowing how to eat with their elbows resting on the table, lowering their heads to their plates as if eating from a trough; chewing with their mouths open, still speaking as they put their food into their mouths," she thought before starting to look through the *Philadelphia Telegraph* for another article. Which she found straight away on the second page under the headline: "SCULPTOR COUNT TO WED MRS. STETSON," accompanied by the same photograph of Mrs. Stetson that had been published by the *Record*.

Yes, because the Count wasn't just about breeding, delicacy, and manners, Emma continued, he was much more than that. He was an artist of great merit, there was no question about it, besides being a polyglot who spoke, so he said, five languages fluently, which Emma had some difficulty confirming, since, besides English, she only grasped a few words of French like *oui, bonjour, très bien*, and little more. But there was no doubt that besides his native language, Portuguese, and Spanish, which one could see he easily mastered, the Count's English was excellent, almost without an accent, and that he spoke French, the language he almost always used to communicate with Mrs. Stetson as if it were his own, which was not surprising after all, since he had lived in Paris for nearly ten years. One should also add Italian, which as a Latin language, he could easily understand and speak through its similarities with Portuguese, French, and Spanish.

So nothing like all those stone-broke aristocrats who had spent their time courting Mrs. Stetson ever since they heard of Mr. Stetson's passing. And there hadn't been just a few, recalled Emma, all full of courtesies and good manners, but without any known occupation or incapable of speaking other languages besides their own, and often badly, only interested in finding someone to pay for the restoration and upkeep of the castles they owned in their countries of origin, on top of the vices they had accumulated during a lifetime of idleness: gambling, alcohol, women, young boys, and goodness knows what else. But Mrs. Stetson was far too intelligent and clever to fall for their pleas, and she made this very clear. Only someone like the Count, who besides his title, persona, and good manners, was an artist and a man of rare sensitivity, intelligence, and culture, could truly interest her. And the wedding that was scheduled for the following day would be proof of this, she concluded, while scanning the *Philadelphia Press*, which only had one short item on the third page titled: "MRS. STETSON NOT TO

MARRY AN EARL," obviously referring not to the Count of Santa Eulália, but rather to the Earl of Clancarcy.

It's a good thing this happened, Emma thought to herself, as if were it not for the rumor, Clancarcy, angered by the fact that Mrs. Stetson was going to marry another Count, started to circulate, practically assuring his marriage to her, perhaps Mrs. Stetson and the Count would not have made an official decision by now. Given that it had been the need for a formal denying of her engagement to Clancarcy that had quickened the pace of things, forcing her to reveal the identity of her true fiancé. At least that was the argument that Mrs. Stetson had used with the Count to go ahead with the press conference, thus putting a definitive end to his, her, or both of their hesitations, perhaps? Who knows, concluded Emma, just in time to spot the slim, clumsy presence of a figure in a dark gray suit, walking up between the trees along the road leading to the house towards the front door. A journalist, no doubt, Miss Beach concluded, picking up the last Philadelphia newspaper, the *Philadelphia News,* where a headline on the second page stated: "MRS. JOHN B. STETSON WILL BECOME A COUNTESS." When she looked up, she caught another shape crossing the garden, followed by another, and yet another. "Danger is at hand," she said to herself, placing the pile of Philadelphia newspapers on the shelf next to the desk. Would George, the butler, be capable of carrying out the instructions he had been given concerning any journalists who might turn up? That is, to tell them that he knew nothing about the wedding and that neither Mrs. Stetson nor herself, Miss Beach, her private secretary, were at home? Although she had no desire to interrupt what she was doing, given that it was important to assess and measure the practical results of her work in public relations with the journalists, Emma decided that it was best to go and see what was going on, albeit prepared to intervene only in the case of extreme necessity, if George could not manage to quickly get rid of the journalists, who at that time were buzzing around like flies. And, she, Emma, knew what she was talking about as a good part of her working life had been in public relations, both before and after being employed by the Stetsons over almost ten years ago.

How time flies, she found herself thinking, now in the corridor on the way to the Gothic hall, already able to hear the voices coming from the main entrance door. She still remembered so clearly the day when she had come there for the first time and the extraordinary impression caused by the size of the house, which had been baptized with the name *Idro* by Mr. Stetson, a Russian word meaning calm and pleasant place, as Mrs. Stetson had explained to her at the time. It was only later that she found out that the mansion was a faithful copy of one of the most beautiful châteaux in Touraine, a region of France known for the fact that it contained the Loire Valley, which was famous both for its beautiful castles and its magnificent wines. Mrs. Stetson had had an engraving of this chateaux framed and placed in the library of the house, hanging above her desk, after it had been used as a model for the project for the house, which Mr. Stetson had commissioned from a French architect. But this was only in relation to the outside appearance of course, because the interiors were completely different, having been designed according to the most demanding American standards of functionality, comfort, and convenience, as she had come to note from early on during the first days she had spent with the Stetsons.

Holding back her natural impulse to receive the journalists herself, Miss Beach decided to remain at the threshold of the door leading to the Gothic hall, from where she could perfectly well see and hear the conversation between the butler, on the inner side of the slightly ajar door, and the journalists on the outside. Peeking through the gap between the door and its frame, she could clearly make out among these journalists the head of the reporter from the *Bulletin* standing out above all the rest, with his sticky brown hair with a center part and a loose lock over his forehead and to whom the day before she had given a photo of the statue of Queen Amelia of Portugal.

"…Because we now know almost everything. That the wedding is tomorrow and it will be celebrated by Monsignor Turner from the Roman Catholic Archdiocese of Philadelphia. That breakfast for eighteen people has been ordered and major floral decorations are taking place in the drawing-room. And that Count Eulália has been here for three or four weeks. All we need to know now is the time the wedding will take place so we can be here, you see?" blurted the bold reporter from the *Bulletin*, showing he had done his homework since the previous day's press conference, thought Miss Beach as she worriedly awaited George's answer. How on earth had that journalist found out all that information, which was absolutely true and correct? Emma wondered.

No doubt through the catering firm. Or the florist. Or from both, which was most likely, when not from the Roman Catholic Archbishopric of Philadelphia. And all this despite the many recommendations made to keep the whole event in total secrecy. But what could one do? No one could find offense when a low-paid employee, finding it hard to pay his rent and feed his children at the end of the month, might accept a few dollars extra in return for information of which the confidential nature was difficult for them to understand, she concluded, just in time to hear George reply to the journalist:

"If you are so well-informed why are you taking the trouble to come here and ask? Go and ask the person who gave you all this information because I don't know anything about it. Not about weddings, nor breakfasts, nor anything else. And now, if you will excuse me, I have to close the door to go about my work."

"Hold on, just hold on a minute," said another reporter, a chubby chap. "What is the name of Mrs. Stetson's secretary? The woman who was here talking to us yesterday."

"Miss Beach," answered George.

"Yeah, that's it, Miss Beach. Miss Annabelle Beach. Can't she come and talk to us?" the same journalist went on, at the same time pronouncing her surname Beach as *bitch*, provoking a great deal of laughter among the others and deep annoyance for Miss Beach, added to that which had been caused by the absurd and inexplicable changing of her given name. And which George hadn't bothered to correct. "What a nerve," she complained under her breath, once again lamenting her fate in having such a surname, then turning and hurriedly walking along the corridor, determined to put an immediate stop to that foolishness. Indeed, the best thing would be to quickly find someone to get rid of them before it was too late—before poor George was overcome and gave them the information they were insisting on hearing, she thought as she burst into the music room, where a group of laborers was attempting to assemble a wooden structure of the arch that would be the backdrop of the altar on which the ceremony would be held on the following day.

"Tom!" she shouted out as an order.

"Yes, Miss Beach," replied a burly, broad-shouldered man, his muscles bursting out of his blue overalls, turning his head towards her.

"At the front door, there is a group of journalists who are getting a little fresh and don't want to go away, despite George having told them everything there is to know. I need you to go there and accompany them off the property. You'd better take the rest of your staff with you," she said, pointing to the other three lads who were helping Tom to raise the arch, each of them as athletic and well-built as he, and being watched with some amusement by the florist's assistants, who were in one corner of the room waiting for the boys to finish their work so they could start theirs: decorating the arch and the altar with roses and orchids, Mrs. Stetson's favorite flowers, which had already been laid out in baskets on the floor.

"OK Miss Beach. I'm on to it," replied Tom, unable to hide the fact that he adored that kind of "work."

"But don't take it too far, Tom. Just accompany them to the main road and that's it," said Miss Beach, who was fully aware of Tom's capabilities when dealing with throwing intruders off the property.

"Fine, Miss Beach. Don't you worry," he said, with a look that suggested he had gotten the message, now ushering the others towards the door.

Back in the Gothic hall, Miss Beach did not need to wait very long to hear Tom's loud voice being aimed at the journalists:

"Come on, guys. I think you know all there is to know. Now let's move it because I've got better things to do than to put up with you."

The reporter from the *Bulletin* put up some resistance, talking about freedom of the press and the right to inform people, but Tom wouldn't be moved, stating that all of this was correct but he had orders to throw them out and that they could go quietly or not. And they did, as Miss Beach saw when she looked out of the window of her office some minutes later and saw them all down there on the Old York Road, smoking and chatting as if they were guarding the house. Then she heard the voices of Tom and the other lads, loudly crossing the garden to come back to the music room and get back to work. Before she sat down at her desk to get back to work herself, to return to her studying of the newspapers. Now starting with those from other states, given that the ones from Philadelphia had been seen. And where it would no doubt be more difficult and laborious to find news about an event that was particularly of interest to the inhabitants of Philadelphia, she thought as she glanced at the first copies on top of the pile that she had placed on the left side of her desk. Yet to her great surprise it was not long before she came across some items, although not so deeply developed as in the Philadelphia papers. For example, a newspaper from Kansas City, Missouri, stated: "A COUNT FOR MRS. STETSON, THE HAT MILLIONAIRE'S WIDOW TO BE BRIDE OF HIDALGO." Why would a Kansas City newspaper be interested in a subject such as this? wondered Miss Beach. Is it due to the popularity of the Stetson hats, the most famous hats in the world, and through which the Stetson family had accumulated its vast fortune? Is it due to the announcement that the widow Stetson was going to marry again, only two years after the death of her husband, and to a European noble, after which she would become a Countess? Is it due to the uncertainty as to the future destiny of such a great fortune, suddenly within the reach of a foreigner who, albeit a noble, was always seen as a potential fortune hunter? Indeed, all of this might explain the journalists' excessive curiosity, which was made very clear during the previous day's press conference, about knowing who the fiancé was, what he did, and what his true intentions were, concluded Miss Beach as she flicked through more papers looking for items on the subject, which didn't take long to find. This time in the *Trenton New Jersey Times,* with a front-page news item including a beautiful photograph of Mrs. Stetson, in a white dress buttoned up to the neck and an ermine cape around her shoulders that Emma had never seen before. Probably a stock photo, taken some years earlier, in the time of Mr. Stetson, when Mrs. Stetson had a very intense social life, thought Emma, reading the headline under the photograph: "COUNT IS TO WED. SANTA Eulália, PORTUGUESE CONSUL TO BE BRIDEGROOM. MATCH BASED UPON LOVE."

Emma wished she had the time to sit there calmly reading all the news items full of information and details about Mrs. Stetson and the Count, as she had seen by glancing over some papers, thrilled with curiosity to know what was said about them and the wedding. But she couldn't afford this luxury on the day before such a major event when there were so many things to prepare and guarantee. It would have to wait for later after everything was over and Mrs. Stetson and the Count had gone off on their honeymoon journey, she thought. Because one thing was certain: the event was going to be a news story over the coming days not just in Pennsylvania but also in many other states of the union. That is if from a simple announcement of engagement to be married there was much press coverage, what would the case be if the press suspected that the wedding was to take place the next day and this became a certainty for them? Which was probably already happening even. Indeed, the questions from the *Bulletin* reporter left little room for doubt: they must already know everything or almost everything, she thought. A good thing that Mrs. Stetson had decided to reinforce the security around the property, not just with the gardeners and the house staff, as was initially foreseen, but also with the police and detectives. Of course, if the property had high walls all around it, completely preventing entrance, none of this would be necessary, it would just be a matter of controlling the entrance gates and no more. But with only a low wall, which in some places was only three feet high, there was no other solution but to organize a security arrangement that would act immediately in relation to any attempt at entry, whether from journalists or other people who were curious. At Mrs. Stetson's request, Emma herself had contacted the Philadelphia branch of the Pinkerton Detective Agency, the head of which, Mr. Johnson, on finding out about the task, offered to immediately go himself to *Idro* and on-site, seeing the specific conditions, study the whole security system to be set up the following day. And that was what happened. After walking with Emma around the edge of the property and making his calculations, Mr. Johnson had unblinkingly declared that at least a hundred men were needed to guarantee total security for the property. He could send a unit of about twenty to twenty-five detectives, and the rest of the contingent would have to be mainly made up of police officers. Including a reasonable number of mounted police to patrol the wildest areas or ones which were hardest to access. Added to this police contingent there would have to be all the members of the staff available, including gardeners, farmworkers, and servants. Early in the morning Johnson himself would distribute the men around the property and coordinate and direct the whole security arrangement set up as long as Miss Beach dealt with getting the necessary policemen. Which she did immediately, in Johnson's presence, phoning Chief O'Hara at the Cheltenham police station, to which Ashbourne belonged. O'Hara was a giant, redheaded, freckled Irishman, almost seven feet tall and with whom she had spoken on occasion, one of which was about the security of the property during the funeral rites for Mr. Stetson, shortly over two years ago. And thus was guaranteed a system of security suited to all circumstances, including those being created now through all the press interest shown about the event, Emma thought, satisfied with herself, raising her eyes in time to see a further bulk rushing across the lawn towards the front door of the house.

"How dare they just come onto the property like this without permission," Emma thought in indignation, walking again towards the Gothic hall in time to catch the bold intruder looking in through the half-open door and shouting, in true American fashion, "Hello! Is anybody home?"

To which she replied, panting: "Yes, what can I do for you?"

"Ah! I'm sorry for intruding. But as I didn't see anyone I decided to come here, just to see how the preparations were getting along," answered the man, with his ginger hair sticking out from under the brim of his hat pushed back over his neck, a light-skinned, freckled face, and white shirt with the collars open over his brown linen jacket.

"So who are you? What preparations?" asked Miss Beach, feigning ignorance.

"Kelly, James Kelly, reporter for the *North American*. My friends call me Jim. Pleased to meet you, Mrs..."

"Miss. Miss Beach, private secretary to Mrs. Stetson," replied Emma, unable to hide her irritation, as at the same time she was obliged to open the door and have him enter so that he could not look through the windows and see what was going on right next door in the music room. "How can I be of help, Mr. Kelly?"

"Well, what I really wanted was to interview the bride and groom. Do you think that's possible, Miss Beach?" fired Kelly, to see if it would work, at the same time quickly glancing around the whole hall, probably trying to spot some signal, some indication of the preparations for the ceremony.

"Interview the bride and groom? You've got to be joking for sure. So why do you think we had a meeting with the press yesterday? If your newspaper didn't want to or couldn't be present then it's your problem. Anyway, everything that had to be said was said yesterday. The best thing I can do for you is to give you a copy of the press release we gave out yesterday."

"That won't be necessary, don't worry, Miss Beach. I've got a copy of the press release. So I should conclude from what you say that the bride and groom have gone out and are not at home, right? Which, being true, fully coincides with what some neighbors I have just interviewed told me," he said suddenly fixing his curiosity on the sidewall of the hall giving on to the music room.

"As was stated yesterday during the press conference, the Count of Santa Eulália is at this moment on his way to Philadelphia from Chicago, where he had been held back due to his professional activities as Consul of Portugal. So I can't see how anyone could have seen him leave the house with Mrs. Stetson. But apparently, the neighbors know more about what happens in this house than I do," Miss Beach replied acidly, taking some steps back to close the half-open door of the music room before Kelly could realize the bustle that was going on behind the door.

"Please, Miss Beach. I am just trying to do my job the best I can, and to do so I have to go to all the available sources of information," he justified, while he glared at the door to the music room as if trying to guess what was going on inside. "And the fact is that some neighbors tell me that they saw Mrs. Stetson leave a short while ago by car, accompanied by a gentleman who looked foreign. As indeed they say has happened almost every afternoon for more or less four weeks. They tell me this; it's not me. Well, the description they have made of this man—tall, thin, dark with an upturned mustache in the style of Kaiser Wilhelm of Germany—corresponds perfectly to the description of the Count of Santa Eulália that was given to us in the Portuguese Consulate."

"The Portuguese Consulate?" Emma asked, bemused.

"Yes. According to our sources, he was there yesterday asking for detailed information about how to get a marriage license in Pennsylvania, after having stated that he was going to marry a Philadelphia lady. And also asking about voyages on transatlantic steamers. For a honeymoon one imagines…"

"Well, it seems that you are better informed than I am about the Count of Santa Eulália. I just know what I've told you. On these issues I have nothing to say," she replied, trying to hide her embarrassment about that sudden revelation as to the Count's movements, while at the same time she felt she should acknowledge the efficiency and professionalism of American journalists. What they had managed to discover in such a short time.

"And in relation to tomorrow's wedding can you tell me the time and where it will take place, or at least whether it will be in the morning or afternoon?" he again boldly attacked.

"As was explained yesterday in the press conference by Mrs. Stetson herself, no date has yet been set for the wedding, although it is expected to be soon."

"So you are telling me that the preparations I've just seen in that room, the arch, the flowers, all that hustle and bustle, you're telling me that all of that is not for the wedding to be held tomorrow?"

"I've got nothing more to add to what I have said. And now, if you don't mind, I will accompany you to the door, as I have other things to do," she replied, almost pushing him to the way out.

"Fine, Miss Beach, I also know everything I need to know. See you tomorrow!" he laughed as a goodbye, raising two fingers to his Stetson hat as a gesture of salutation before almost running out to join the other group of journalists camped out down on the Old York Road, near to the main entrance to the property.

After closing the main door, Miss Beach once again crossed the hall to the music room to see how the preparations for the ceremony were coming along: the altar and the portico set up before it were now completely covered in flowers, *American Beauty* roses, and orchids, many of which came directly from the hothouses of which Mrs. Stetson was justly proud, in a combination of tones and forms that seemed absolutely admirable to her.

"What a beautiful arrangement, what extraordinary effects," she could not help commenting, as if by some enchantment all the concerns going round in her head had disappeared—about Mrs. Stetson, about the Count, about the licenses, about journalists, about security services, about the catering and whatever else—and she remained there stopped at the entrance to the door, admiring that masterpiece.

"Thank you, Miss Beach," the head florist responded not without some pride, with a pair of scissors in her hand, making the final touches to the decoration of the floral arch.

"There's no reason to thank me. It's a real masterpiece. I'm sure Mrs. Stetson and the Count will love it."

"That's our greatest desire. It isn't every day that we have the chance to do decorations like this, above all for people of such a high level. Good Lord, a Count and a Countess," the head florist went on. "It's like we are living in a fairy tale."

"Right. And that's why I want to remind you once again of the need to maintain the greatest discretion possible about what is going on. There is a group of journalists out there gossiping and asking questions, so I hope you know how to avoid them when you go out."

"Don't worry, Miss Beach, we won't say a word about this, right girls?" answered the head florist, while the other girls nodded in agreement.

"I trust you. See you later," said Emma as a goodbye, carefully closing the door behind her, unless another snooping journalist might appear.

"Miss Beach! Miss Beach!" She suddenly heard the trombone-like voice of the butler, coming from the kitchen when she was crossing the Gothic hall.

"What's the matter now, George?" she asked, unable to disguise her impatience.

"It's a journalist on the phone, Miss Beach, asking questions. And I don't know what else I can tell him," answered George anxiously.

"I'll deal with it," said Miss Beach, resigned to her position, and to George's great relief, with her walking hurriedly towards the telephone set up next to the entrance to the corridor that led to the kitchen.

"Miss Beach, private secretary to Mrs. Stetson. How can I be of help?" she said, with her mouth close to the base of the phone and the receiver against her ear.

"Stevens, George Stevens, from the *Philadelphia Press*. Miss Beach, we would like you to confirm whether the wedding between Mrs. Stetson and Count Eulália will take place tomorrow or not. And if so, where?"

"Just as was stated in Mrs. Stetson's meeting with the press yesterday, there is no date foreseen for the wedding yet," Miss Beach repeated again, with as much conviction as she was still capable of summing up.

"And is it true that the Count has been in Philadelphia for several days, according to information we have received from the Portuguese Consulate?"

"The information I have is that the Count is at this moment on his way to Philadelphia, from Chicago, where he was detained due to his functions as Portuguese Consul, just as was stated in the same conference with the press," Miss Beach insisted, starting to feel slightly uncomfortable with her systematically going over an official truth that now didn't seem to convince anyone, given the facts that the journalists had gathered in the meantime. But these were the orders she had, and unless Mrs. Stetson changed them she could not say anything else, she thought.

"Where will the bride and groom live after the wedding?" once again challenged the journalist, this time leaving Miss Beach a little more at ease, given that at least in relation to this question she wouldn't have to lie nor give explanations that would convince no one.

"After a journey to Europe, during which Mrs. Stetson will be presented to the Count's family in Portugal, the bride and groom intend to settle in America," she replied, recalling the conversations she had heard from them, both together and individually, about their future plans, and convinced that this reply was not a revealing of any secret, nor did it put the privacy of the couple at any risk. Mrs. Stetson had been clear: "Emma, not one word about the time and place of the wedding. As to the rest, you more than anyone will know what to answer."

"Where in America, more precisely?"

"In the summer they will be here in *Idro*. During the winter months, they may move to Florida, where Mrs. Stetson also has a large estate, or perhaps travel throughout Europe. The Count refuses to leave America, you know? He admires America and Americans too much for that. According to what he told me, and I am quoting, "Here everyone seems to have an aim in life and an incentive to work," finished Miss Beach, proud of her memory for quotations such as that one, which she had heard a few days earlier directly from the Count's mouth.

"Our Chicago correspondent, in a dispatch we received today, says that the Count is going to ask King Manuel of Portugal to release him from his functions as consul so that he may devote himself exclusively to art. The same dispatch states that Count Eulália has been a favorite in high society, with one of his closest friends being Mrs. Field, the widow of the late Marshall Field, the owner of the well-known stores of the same name. What comments do you have about this, Miss Beach?"

"What I can tell you is that the Count of Santa Eulália is not a 'society gentleman', as your correspondent suggests. On several occasions, I have heard him say that although he has to frequent high society, due to his diplomatic functions and artistic activities, it bores him. His great passion is art, particularly sculpture, and nowadays he is an artist of internationally acknowledged merit. But besides art, he has a series of other interests, managing, as few people can, to reconcile his vast cultural knowledge with enjoyment for sports, for example. He is a truly athletic man and a splendid horseman," Miss Beach concluded, unable to hold back a sigh that, as she was talking on the phone, was fortunately not heard on the other end of the line.

"Miss Beach, my thanks for your cooperation," said the journalist as a goodbye.

"My pleasure, Mr. Stevens," she replied before hanging up the phone, then immediately hearing the doorbell ringing insistently. "More journalists," she thought, in a crescendo of irritation and slowing her pace, hoping the butler would answer the door. But no. Fortunately this time it was not journalists, she noted with relief as she saw that the person who was coming in was John, as John B. Stetson Junior was known, the Stetsons' eldest son and who had inherited Mr. Stetson's name, recently arrived from Philadelphia.

II

Paris, 17th of May 1896

BEHIND THE RECEPTION desk, strategically placed in the middle of the entrance hall to the Hotel, Gérôme, the morning shift receptionist, blondish hair, long sideburns and a solid mustache with the tips turned up, occasionally glances, as if intrigued, at the thick brown envelope resting on the inside covering of the desk, there, at barely a yard away, brought by hand extremely early that very morning by a messenger boy from the Portuguese Embassy in Paris.

When he finally manages to finish dealing with a large and noisy group of Spaniards who have just arrived, having gone through the inherent necessary formalities and suitcases and trunks that need to be unloaded and taken to the respective rooms, Gérôme cannot resist once again picking up the bulky object and closely observing the coat of arms printed on the reverse, above the name of the sender—two quarters occupied by lions and the other two with six half-moons, and above a helmet with another lion—exactly the same coat of arms that appears on the three drops of wax that seal the opening, which, for Gérôme, someone who albeit without any great knowledge of heraldry, worked for a few years as a servant in the château of a French aristocratic family, clearly indicates, due to its similarity to other coats of arms he then saw, that the sender of the envelope is someone from the nobility, perhaps even someone with a title, and apparently someone who has sufficient power and influence to have his correspondence sent in the diplomatic bag of his country. Someone whose surname is curiously the same as that of the recipient, who is, in fact, Monsieur Ribeiro, the guest in Room 44, a pleasant, friendly person, but who, due to his activity and his manner of dressing would never be thought of as also belonging to the nobility of his country. It is true that behind that blasé air of being an artist—long, unkempt beard, long hair at the back and over his ears but thinning on top, almost always wearing thick pullovers and loose-fitting corduroy trousers that no one in a position in society, with an activity or a respectable job would wear—Monsieur Ribeiro has a posture, a way of speaking and the good manners that show he is someone of breeding, yet going from this to belonging to the noble classes is some distance. Might Monsieur Ribeiro be one of those people who, having been born with a silver spoon in their mouths, decided to, due to their love for art, or some such thing, to reject the medium from which they came and live an uncertain life as artists or free-thinkers, as he had heard tell about a member of the family of his former employers? The receptionist wonders as, with a polite smile and a slight nod of his head, he greets the two guests from Room 32 who have just given him their key, and then he once again carefully puts the envelope on the inside area of the counter, waiting for the recipient to come down from his room. But Monsieur Ribeiro is an artist, and like all artists, he gets up late, mostly after ten o'clock, when the breakfast service of the hotel closes, and sometimes even later, which means that he often goes without his breakfast, as *Madame* Rouchès, the wife of the owner of the hotel and the person responsible for the meals, is absolutely inflexible as to timetables. And, either he is very mistaken or it is precisely this that is going to happen today, he thinks, looking at the cuckoo-clock on the wall in the entrance hall, at a quarter to ten, and yet there had been no sign of life from Monsieur Ribeiro. In the meantime, some more guests are coming to the reception desk to leave their keys after having had their breakfast when, from behind the counter, a figure rushes towards the dining room in the basement of the hotel.

"Monsieur Ribeiro!" shouts Gérôme, recognizing the guest from Room 44 no doubt from the length of his hair or his original way of dressing, "Monsieur Ribeiro! *S'il vous plaît!*" he insists, then managing to make him stop and turn round.

"Ah, *bonjour* Gérôme. what's the matter?" asks Aleixo, panting, with his eyelids puffy from sleep and his beard and hair in a mess.

"You have correspondence here, Monsieur Ribeiro," explains Gérôme, glancing at the envelope. "It arrived very early this morning."

"*Merci,*" Aleixo thanks Gérôme, coming to the desk to pick up the envelope given to him by the clerk, then rapidly looking at the address and that of the sender before once again rushing off to the dining room, down a spiral staircase near to a windowed wall leading on to the back patio. It is a relatively small room, with the brickwork exposed and the ceiling made of three stone vaults, and in which there are about twenty tables. All around the walls, there are prints of landscapes and historic monuments of Paris. In the middle, hanging from the plaster ceiling, two large chandeliers light up the room.

"*Bonjour* Monsieur Ribeiro. Would you like coffee?" asks the soft voice of Josette, one of the youngest assistants to *Madame* Rouchès, a beautiful young girl from Brittany, tall, blondish hair and bright blue eyes, elegant in her gray serge uniform under her white apron, with her cap and cuffs stiffly starched.

"*Oui, ma petite* Josette. A full cup, please, because I need a good coffee," Aleixo replies with a smirk, sitting as always in the corner table near to the glass door giving on to the garden after slightly nodding a greeting to some of the guests sitting at the other tables.

"So we have a letter from our brother Gaspar," says Aleixo to himself, glancing again at the bulky envelope on the chair in front of him before taking a gulp of the steaming, dark coffee. And what will the content be, after all? The transcript in one of the newspapers from the Minho region or even from Lisbon, of one of his brilliant speeches? A copy of his latest book of poems, veritable pearls of Portuguese poetry that he, Aleixo, so much appreciates? Or more papers, proxy request documents, certificates, and registers in relation to the process of dividing up the inheritance of his father, which would go on forever? That is what he will do next, after finishing his breakfast, he decides after putting half a buttered croissant with raspberry jam to his mouth. Around him several tables had now become free, with only two or three latecomers like him in the room, he notes as he motions to the beautiful Josette to bring him more coffee.

"*Merci*, Josette. You are my guardian angel, my savior," states Aleixo, with a charming smile, after receiving the generous quantity of coffee that the waitress has just poured into his cup, along with the extra brioche that she had snaffled from the sideboard without *Madame* Rouchès noticing—one day I'll make a bust of you, you'll see—he adds seductively. Josette giggles, blushes, and swiftly disappears off to the kitchen.

Nothing like a steaming hot cup of strong coffee to help clear one's ideas, thinks Aleixo, now no longer able to put off opening the envelope to see what it contains. "Newspapers!" he exclaims to himself as soon as he takes the bundle out. Recent issues of the Portuguese newspapers *Século* and *Diário de Notícias,* all from the month of May. And a card on which Gaspar sends the most sincere congratulations "to the great sculptor, the artist who is the talk of Lisbon." Clearly references to his success at the *Paris Salon.* Which his brother Gaspar, who is always attentive and thoughtful, has collected despite his great, many different daily tasks as an influential politician in the Progressive Party and as a lawyer of renown, or also as a brilliant poet and man of letters, recalls Aleixo as he removes the newspapers from the envelope, not noticing that he is the last of the hotel guests who are still in the breakfast room, the tables of which are already being cleared by *Madame* Rouchès and her two young assistants. The newspapers are set out in chronological order: first the *Século* from the 30th of April, then the *Diário de Notícias* from the 4th of May and lastly the *Século* from the 7th and 10th of the same month. All of them complete and folded into four so as to fit into the envelope, he notes before he starts to look for the "Letter from Paris" in the first issue, which he soon finds in the last column on the first page, as always signed with the initials X. C. by the excellent Xavier de Carvalho, who had on so many occasions shown his esteem and personal respect over recent years. And he is extremely moved when he reads the end of the first paragraph, all dedicated to the presence of the Portuguese artists at the *Paris Salon*, underlined in red pencil by the steady hand of his brother Gaspar: "…and Queiroz Ribeiro, with his bronze bust of the Emperor of Abyssinia, the great Menelik, the vanquisher of the Italians." And then he is deeply disappointed. Bust? How could Xavier mistake his medallion of Menelik for a bust? And why is there no reference to his other work on show at the *Paris Salon*, the *Extase Religieuse*, which was indeed a bust, the merit, and quality of which were fulsomely acknowledged by the acceptance committee by placing it in a prominent place in the entrance hall of the Palais de l'Industrie, along with the works of the major artists, those who won awards? Next comes the *Diário de Notícias* newspaper of the 4th of May, with a "Letter from Paris" dated the 30th of April, the day of the preview, also on the front page, referring correctly to his two works and stating that "Queiroz Ribeiro's bust, *Extase Religieuse*, and his bronze medallion of Menelik, denote a conscientious effort worthy of all applause. May he continue to study his extremely difficult art." The following newspaper is the *Século* again, this time from the 7th of May, in which Aleixo finds a further reference to his work on Menelik, now correctly referred to as a medallion, but nothing yet about *Extase Religieuse*. It is necessary to wait until the final newspaper in the pile, from the 10th of May, to finally discover the following explanation: "As we stated in our last letter, the visit we carried out to the *Salon* on the day of the preview was somewhat fleeting. And in the middle of the crowd of 20,000 to 30,000 people—it is difficult to examine things with attention or even take the notes necessary for an article, albeit brief, in broad terms. This was why we have not mentioned the splendid head—*Êxtase Religioso*—that our good friend Queiroz Ribeiro exhibited, and which is now admirably set in the place reserved for the first prizes, that is, in the semi-circle at the entrance, where the works of all the masters are, next to the figure by Falguière." Ah, that's more like it, Aleixo says to himself, sighing with relief.

In one stroke the omission in the previous chronicles is explained and justice is done for his work. Who would have thought it? He, a young and almost unknown Portuguese sculptor, having arrived in Paris a little over four years ago, now seeing a work of his placed in a prominent position in the middle of the giant entrance hall of the Palais de l'Industrie, after that which was only his third participation at the *Salon*, right next to the *Danseuse Nue* by Falguière, the great Jean Joseph Alexandre Falguière, *Grand Prix de Rome*, Medal of Honor at the *Salon*. And at a short distance from the bas-relief by Puech, Pierre Denys Puech, his Master at the Académie Julian over the last three years, also a *Grand Prix de Rome* and Medal of Honor at the *Salon*. Not to mention the works by other less famous, but no less consecrated names such as Gérôme, Becquet, and Ferrary. Might that distinction be a sign that a medal is on the way, as suggested by several people, both known to him and others, who came to congratulate him for his extraordinary triumph on the day of the preview to the *Salon*? Aleixo wonders, without wishing to notice the strict glance cast by *Madame* Rouchès from the other side of the room, looking at the clock above the sideboard, showing a quarter past ten, as she begins to lay the tables for lunch along with her assistants.

It is still too early to know this, given that the prizes and awards will only be announced after the *Salon* closes, at the end of July. But one thing is certain: his work pleased the jury from the Society of French Artists that was responsible for choosing the works for the exhibition and deciding on their layout throughout the many rooms of the *Palais de l'Industrie,* and the firm proof of this is in the place they chose for placing his work. And it was also to the liking of the public, as he himself was able to note by the comments he heard, not only on the day of the preview but over the following days, he recalls, picking up his cup, there to his right, and drinking the last sip of now warm coffee before reading the last sentence in the news item, in which Xavier de Carvalho says that his work "is enough for an artist to make his mark, if our illustrious compatriot were not already considered one of the future glories of Portuguese art."

"My apologies, Monsieur Ribeiro, but we have to clear the table," he suddenly hears the dry and haughty voice of *Madame* Rouchès say near to him, without him having noticed her approach as he was concentrating so much on his reading. "We need to tidy the room and lay the tables for lunch."

"It is I who should apologize for my tardiness, *Madame* Rouchès," Aleixo promptly replies, taking his envelope and standing up.

"Thank you for your understanding, Monsieur Ribeiro," she says, immediately instructing her assistants to start to gather up the remains of his breakfast.

"So, Monsieur Ribeiro, good news?" asks Gérôme loudly and with an air of complicity as he sees Aleixo go by on the way to the elevator.

"Extremely good, excellent news, Gérôme" Aleixo responds to Gérôme's interest with a courteous smile.

Twenty-five past ten, he notes, looking at his pocket watch as he enters the elevator. With a bit of luck, he will still manage to get to Master Puech's class at the Académie Julian before eleven. Not that he greatly wants to, given that he increasingly feels that he has learned all he could learn from him. But anyway, the fees have already been paid and it is necessary to take advantage of the two months and a bit that remains until the end of the academic year, to at least finish what he is working on, he tells himself as the elevator finally reaches the fourth floor, where his room is. It is a relatively spacious compartment, with a bed, a wardrobe, a commode with a dressing table and a desk, upon

which Aleixo unloads the pile of newspapers after taking them out of
the envelope, only then noticing the intensity of the sunlight coming
through the broad window giving on to the street. It's certainly going
to be a beautiful spring day, he thinks, casually looking at the third-
floor window on the other side of the street, where he had more than
occasionally seen the slim outline of *petit evêque*, as António Nobre
was known among the students of the Boulevard St. Michel. Indeed
it was there, in *Madame* Laïlle's Maison, located on the top floors of
no 42, that the poet who wrote *Só* lived for a large part of his stay in
Paris, which is why it is not difficult to imagine the surprise shown by
the many students who frequented the building which also housed the
General Students' Association on the ground floor, seeing his eccentric
figure, with a long cloak and cane. He would be on the way to his
classes, or simply off on one of his lone walks through the *Quartier
Latin*, recalls Aleixo, putting on his overcoat and placing his Fez on his
head, recalling his trip to Abyssinia the previous year, before he steps
out into the corridor.

Outside the temperature is pleasant, but not so pleasant that he can
go without his overcoat, he notes as he goes through the hotel doors
and then briskly walks towards the Boulevard Saint Michel, or the
Boul'Mich, as the students call it in slang. It was there, in the Hotel
Rouchès, at no 32 of the Rue des Écoles, that he stayed as soon as he
arrived in Paris, in September 1892, and there he has stayed until now.
Not that the rent he pays for the room is cheap exactly, particularly
when compared with the amount of the monthly allowance he receives
from Portugal, sent punctually at the beginning of each month by his
brother Luiz, who, being the eldest, has the undertaking of administering their common inheritance. But, after all, it is a *hôtel de famille*,
governed with an iron fist by *Madame* Rouchès, the devoted wife of the
owner, clean, tidy, with a good room service, not unworthy of someone
of his social condition. And above all with an excellent location, right
in the middle of the *Quartier Latin*, only ten minutes to the Decorative
Arts School, which he attended in his first year, and fifteen or twenty
minutes from the Académie Julian and the Fine Arts School, where he
has alternately studied over the last years. However, on several occasions over the last four and a half years, he has thought of moving to a
cheaper hotel or hostel, among the many that existed nearby, he recalls

as he enjoys the warmth of the sun to be felt on that side of the street. Particularly when, besides paying the monthly rent for the hotel and renting a studio, as well as the fees for the Académie, there was little left of his allowance other than that which was strictly necessary for food. But fortunately it was at that time that work also began to appear, which allowed him to reasonably re-balance his finances, he remembers as he passes the impressive facade of the Sorbonne, rising up on his left side, shortly before finally coming to the corner with the Boulevard Saint Michel, heaving with people on the sidewalks, among groups of rowdy students, businessmen in high hats, ladies dressed for a stroll, or office workers and shop girls. Aleixo quickly crosses over to the other side, carefully making his way through the chaos of the lines of carriages and carts, with some omnibuses as well, to then enter the narrow Rue de L'École de Médecine, on his way to the Boulevard de St. Germain.

First the bust of Councilor Joaquim José Cerqueira, a rich and influential man from Viana do Castelo in Portugal, who had made his fortune in Brazil. Then the medallion of Menelik II, a commission that was as unexpected as it was gratifying and that led him to far-off Abyssinia in the Summer of the previous year. No matter how much time goes by, he will never forget the figure of that dry-bodied, dark-skinned, bearded man, impeccably dressed in a well-cut black tailcoat, pearl waistcoat, striped trousers and a *grenat* Fez hat, exactly the same as the one Aleixo is wearing on his head at the moment, whom he saw enter Master Barrias's class at the Fine Arts School. He was introduced as the Abyssinian *Chargé d'Affaires* in Paris, Aleixo thinks as he observes the long, beautiful neo-classical portico of the René Descartes University, with the spaces between the ionic columns allowing him to glimpse the inner patio around which the building was organized. The man spoke up, and in excellent French, albeit with a strong accent, explained that he was there to announce that his government was seeking a sculptor to make a medallion of the *Negus* Menelik II, Emperor of Abyssinia, destined to serve as the mold for the country's new currency, which would obviously entail a trip to the capital, Addis Ababa, for the Emperor to pose for some sessions. From among the students present only he and two other colleagues showed any interest, and they were then asked to appear the next day at the Hotel George V with their portfolios for interviews, recalls Aleixo as he reaches the small Place de l'Odéon, next to the Boulevard de St. Germain, with its impressive bronze statue of Danton, one of the fearful heroes of the French Revolution, in the middle.

He was the last of the three to be received in the suite occupied by Monsieur Amerik, the *Chargé d'Affaires*, who, once informed of Aleixo's nationality, immediately abandoned all the formalities that had surrounded events until then and started to extremely enthusiastically and knowledgeably talk about the relationships between Portugal and the Christian Kingdom of Prester John, as Abyssinia was then known. He then carefully analyzed the photographs of his works, spent a long time looking at the bust *Christus, flet, orat, obit,* visibly impressed, and then at the end, after some moments of reflection, suddenly came out with: "*Mon cher ami,* the job is yours. When can you leave for Addis Ababa?" recalls Aleixo after crossing over to the other side of the street among the intense traffic of the carriages and the omnibuses, not wishing to waste the heat of the sun for even one minute.

Then came that fantastic, adventurous voyage through the Mediterranean on a French ship, passage through the Suez Canal and finally the Red Sea to Djibouti, where he disembarked and then continued on across mountains and valleys, sometimes by camel and sometimes by donkey, to the capital, Addis Ababa. He stayed there for over a month working in an improvised studio in the Imperial Palace, holding several posing sessions in the intervals between ferocious battles against the Italians, commanded by the Emperor himself alongside his generals. After all this Aleixo returned to Paris to get to work, starting from the many clay outlines and drawings he had brought, he concludes, consulting his pocket watch, showing ten to eleven. With a bit of luck he will get to the Académie before Master Puech, who usually only arrives at eleven, eleven thirty, he thinks, hastening his step on the sidewalk along the side facade of the Church of Saint Germain-des-Près, until he comes to the crossroads with the Rue Bonaparte, where there is the main entrance to the church and the *Deux Magots* café, with its tables still almost empty at that time of day, given that its clientele is mainly made up of Bohemians, intellectuals and artists, who normally get up late and only start appearing after lunch. In front of the café he again crosses the Boulevard, then taking the Rue du Dragon until he comes to no 31, where, in the inner patio there is the Académie, a sober and modest building which can only be seen from the street through the narrow, arched passage that leads to it. Having crossed the patio, Aleixo enters the building, going quickly towards Master Puech's sculpture classroom, located on the ground floor at the end of the corridor. Master Puech, just as he thought, has not yet arrived. He goes through the heavy entrance door after a quick glance at the easels lined up along each side of the central aisle, and on which his colleagues are applying themselves to their wet clay works in front of them. On the dais, located at the opposite end of the room, there is only Pierre, the assistant, whose main task is to knead and provide clay for the students during the class and at the end wrap the works in damp cloth so they do not dry before the following day. The room is wider than it is long, and is lit by two large skylights in the ceiling, facing north so that the light remains constant. To the left of the door, lined up against the back wall, are the students' individual lockers. Aleixo opens the door to his, places his overcoat on a hanger and his Fez on the upper shelf, takes out a white coat, which he puts on over his heavy sweater, and then goes as discreetly as possible to his easel, in the third row from the back.

"*Bonjour,* Alexis!" Vladimir the Russian greets him in his strong accent as soon as he sees him arrive at the next easel to his.

"*Bonjour, mon cher* Vladimir," Aleixo quietly replies as he removes the damp cloth from his work. Meanwhile, some of his colleagues at the front, no doubt alerted by Vladimir's booming voice, turn around and greet him, including Helen Mears, the new American student, sitting at her easel at the front and waving to him effusively.

Adieux d'Evandre à son fils Pallas is the subject for the last work for the year given to them by the Master, based on a scene taken from Vergil's *Aeneid,* in which the now aging Evander says goodbye to his son Pallas before the latter goes off to war, recalls Aleixo as he motions to Pierre to bring him some fresh clay. After many living model drawings, outlines and notes, Aleixo decided to place the two figures side by side, with the father moving forward to his son to embrace him, as if trying to stop him from going at the same time as he says goodbye, as he already imagines his tragic end, while Pallas, with his head turned back, spear in his left hand, seems not to be present anymore, such is his desire to give himself to the ardors of war.

"*Voilà votre glaise,* Monsieur Ribeiro," says Pierre, the assistant, as he sets down the box with the clay on the support stand against the wall, then returning to the dais where Master Puech has now arrived in his high hat and black overcoat, which he puts on the back of the chair next to his desk before starting his usual tour around the easels.

Starting from an initial clay sketch, which was no more than two hands high, Aleixo goes directly to the model that he now has in front of him, in which more than faithfully portraying the two characters according to Vergil's description, he is interested in exploring the expression of their feelings at that moment of farewell, not just through the shaping of their faces, but also through the movement he tries to give each of the figures. And looking at them now, from a distance, next to each other, he cannot help thinking about the extraordinary monument *Les Bourgeois de Calais,* by Auguste Rodin, which he had the opportunity to see and appreciate shortly after its inauguration the previous year, on a study trip organized by the Académie to Pas de Calais. Not that his work might in any way be compared to or set on the same level as such an extraordinary and sublime work as that one, far from it. But there is something of the movement and expression that he could appreciate in the remarkable figures that Rodin shaped, of that there was no doubt, he concludes with a touch of pride as he sticks a small piece of clay on Evander's face, then spreading it with his finisher, heightening his cheekbones, slightly sharpening the arches above his eyebrows and making his nose thinner, before stepping back to look at the effect. And then immediately going back and finishing off the previous touch with the thumb of his right hand. The movement "which is a transition between two movements," according to Rodin, which Aleixo heard for the first time from Antoine Bourdelle, Rodin's main assistant during the visit the latter organized at the request of the Académie, and during which he commented upon and explained the several different aspects presiding over the conceiving of a work and the difficulties encountered throughout the over ten years of making it. Which he gazed at over and over again, from all angles and perspectives, completely in ecstasy with its originality, he recalls as he notices that something is not to his liking, however, in the posture of his Evander. Perhaps that right arm, almost touching Pallas's shoulder, too static, stiff, he concludes after taking two steps back for a better look at his work.

"*Très bien, Monsieur Ribeiro!* I see you are making progress," he suddenly hears Master Puech's sharp, hissing voice say at his side, as the latter clinically examines his Evander.

"Thank you very much, Master. I am just trying to follow your teachings," Aleixo flatteringly replies.

"My teachings are of little use to you now, my dear Ribeiro, from what I can see of the direction you are seeking to grant to your work. In which, in my view, one can see lesser concern for details in favor of greater expression. One might say that you are being impressed by the works and style of Monsieur Rodin, isn't that so?"

"I can't deny that Monsieur Rodin's works have affected me a good deal, Master, in their expression and in the movement that he manages to grant to them. In particular the monument to the *Bourgeois de Calais*, which I visited last year during a study visit we went on…"

"Well, that means that I am not very wrong about your preferences, which indeed are absolutely natural in a young man who is taking his first steps in a career that is expected to be long. But be careful, Monsieur Ribeiro, very careful. Auguste Rodin is without doubt a great sculptor, but the path he is following is dangerous, as it is too bold, questioning the fundamental principles and references on which our art is based. And this may lead those who follow him into serious difficulties. Particularly those who do not have the endurance he shows in relation to his detractors. Pay attention to what I am telling you, Monsieur Ribeiro," Master Puech ends, before going on towards Vladimir's easel, without giving Aleixo any chance to reply, as he immediately starts to make observations about Vladimir's work.

What does Master Puech mean by all that? Might he be feeling threatened because Rodin is questioning the principles and references in which he was trained as a sculptor? And which he solemnly considers as being "the fundamental principles and references on which our art is based," as if this were immutable, unable to have any evolution over time? And what difficulties is he talking about? Lack of recognition by the public and the critics? But how can one innovate and be original without questioning the dominant taste? Otherwise art would be no more than an ad infinitum repeating of the same recipes, the same formulas and the same tricks over the centuries, Aleixo concludes, as he again starts to apply touches to young Pallas, removing a little clay here and adding it there in order to make the expression of the mouth stand out more, with the triumphal smile of someone hurrying to go off to war and to the dreamed-of victory. Yes, better without a shadow of a doubt, in its way of expressing the ambiguity of feelings that move the young warrior, now divided between his love for his aging father, whom he is about to leave, and the excitement of war, in which he is about to participate for the first time, thinks Aleixo at the precise moment that the bell marking the end of the morning classes can be heard.

"Eh, Alexis, what was all that about? Between you and the Master?" asks Vladimir the Russian, as soon as they go out through the classroom door. "He seemed angry when he left you."

"Nothing special. He thinks my work is very influenced by Rodin. Who for him seems worse than the very Devil himself," replies Aleixo, as they walk down the corridor to the little entrance atrium.

"What I think is that he didn't like having your work almost next to his at the *Salon*, that sinister mortuary bas-relief that he exhibited this year. And above all yours was more seen and appreciated," says Georges, a French colleague who has in the meantime joined them, now outside in the Académie front patio.

"Ribeiro, my congratulations. Yours are works of great quality. You see if you don't get a medal," adds Aristide, another colleague from Puech's class, who has also caught up with the group.

"Merci, Aristide, but I think you are exaggerating," Aleixo modestly thanks him.

"Exaggerating? Have you read today's *Moniteur Universel*?" now asks Maurice as he joins the others.

"No. No, I haven't," answers Aleixo, increasingly surprised at suddenly being the target for his colleagues' attention.

"Look here, Ribeiro. You are mentioned immediately after Puech and Desca," says Maurice, opening the newspaper and then reading out loud an excerpt from the news item about the sculpture at the *Salon des Champs-Élysées*: "…'l'Extase religieuse', sujet analogue, de Queiroz Ribeiro, une simple figure, est belle et pleine d' expression."

"And if you also have a look at the *Monde*, the *Rives d'Or*, the *Ménestrel* or the *Etandard*, it is the same thing. Praise after praise. I've got them all here," then says Edouard, another colleague who has also joined the group, taking out a pile of newspapers from under his arm, then opening the *Monde* and reading: "…*Monsieur de Queiroz Ribeiro*, *une tête empreinte d'un noble sentiment religieux...*"

"You are indeed embarrassing me, colleagues," replies Aleixo, not knowing what to say faced with that surprising success, he who that morning was not even up-to-date with the news in the Lisbon newspapers, much less the Paris ones, with such prestige as the *Monde* or the *Moniteur Universel.*

"How modest, Ribeiro," comments Aristide mockingly.

"Congratulations, Monsieur Ribeiro," says Helen, the American, the last one to join the group. "The work you exhibited at the *Salon* is magnificent."

"*Merci,* Miss Mears," replies Aleixo, flattered.

"I'm sorry, but I have to be going," says Georges, on his way to the exit from the patio. "Anyone going to Saint-Germain?"

"I am," Aristide immediately replies, joining Georges.

"And me," Maurice adds, followed by Vladimir.

"Not me. I'm going to Montparnasse," replies Aleixo, as they reach the pavement.

"If you want you can keep the newspapers, Ribeiro. They'll certainly be more use to you than to me," Edouard suddenly suggests, and Aleixo thanks him before he bids him farewell and goes on his way.

Who could imagine this? After the excellent critiques published in the Lisbon newspapers, which he received that morning, now it is the French press that unanimously praises his work. And this is added to the acknowledgement he has just received from his colleagues, greeting him in a manner as sincere as it was unexpected. Georges, Aristide, Maurice, Vladimir, Helen Mears herself, all talented people, quality artists, coming like that after the class to congratulate him on his success at the *Salon*, with references to his work that were so full of praise. What greater reward could he have for his efforts, for his dedication to art? Aleixo wonders, as he glances along the shop windows fronting the little shops that punctuate that side of the Rue du Dragon, until he comes to the Carrefour de la Croix Rouge, where a little café with an outdoor terrace occupies one of the corners, the tables lined up underneath an awning, with tablecloths with red and white squares, full of people who seemed not to want to waste even a second of the sun and the pleasant temperature of that beautiful spring day.

It is without any doubt a great, an extraordinary triumph, he thinks, euphoric, before he enters the Rue de Cherche-Midi. The echoes of which have to be heard in Lisbon also. And in the Minho region, of course. Nothing better to do this than to send cuttings from all the newspapers he has under his arm to his brother Gaspar, who will at once see to it that they get to the *Século* and the *Diário de Notícias* newspapers, but also to the *Novidades* and the *Correio da Manhã*. Not to mention the *Aurora do Lima* and the *Comércio do Lima*, which were always aware and interested in relation to anything to do with him. Yes, he couldn't waste this opportunity, as to be recognized in Portugal in the field of the arts there was nothing better than to be recognized abroad first, preferably in Paris, as his brother Gaspar never tires of telling him. Even if such recognition brings the habitual envy of the consecrated local artists, those who had moved up in their careers without ever having left their own soil and who do not like to see new people appear, from abroad, with more open-minded ideas, Aleixo tells himself as he comes to the broad Haussemanian Boulevard Raspail.

But he can handle other people's envy, he thinks; the important thing is to be up to standard with the works, with the commissions that such public recognition might bring him from now on. As might be the case of the statue of the *Most Sacred Heart of Jesus*, which is planned to be raised on the Monte de Santa Luzia hilltop in Viana do Castelo, and which, according to what his brother Gaspar told him in one of his last letters, some influential people in the city would like to have made by him, due to his connection to the city. Or even works of his own initiative, like the one he has been working on for some time, with which he intends to celebrate the recent victories by the Portuguese in Africa, under the command of that extraordinary man and military officer Joaquim Mouzinho de Albuquerque, a work he has already baptized as *Apoteose da Pátria Portuguesa*. The idea came to him a few months earlier, when he read an article in the *Século* reporting how a small detail of Portuguese soldiers commanded by Mouzinho decimated an enormous enemy force of several hundred, if not thousands, of warriors armed to the teeth by the oldest "ally" of Portugal, Britain, capturing Gungunhana, their chief. Despite at the time being very busy with the works he was going to present at the *Salon*, he immediately started to make the first outlines, first in a more realist approach, in which Mouzinho stood out from a group of soldiers and captures the rebel chief, then with a more abstract conception, in which rather than directly showing the events, he would start out from what they revealed—the courage and bravery of the Portuguese. Given that his idea was not exactly to glorify Mouzinho, nor the army, but instead, the Portuguese Fatherland, which with some meager resources has been able to respond to the threats of the major powers that coveted its colonies, he concludes as he arrives at the crossing with the always busy Rue de Rennes, where he can see the old facade of the Montparnasse station at the end.

Yes, the courage and bravery with which the Portuguese glorified their homeland. And then it is inevitable to immediately think about that which made the greatness of Portugal: the sea, the discoveries, the presence of Portugal in the overseas territories in the four corners of the world. To which he began to give shape, first in the charcoal and watercolor which filled a good part of his album, then in a first outline, which he started working on as soon as he finally finished the works destined for the *Salon*, he recalls as he finally enters the Rue Notre Dame des Champs, where, at no 72, on the crossroads with the Rue de la Grande Chaumière, he has his modest studio.

III

WHEN THE CAR went past them, it was already going at a considerable speed, which it gained going down the path leading from the house to the main gates of the property, so all attempts to try to make them stop and get to talk to the driver, or at least identify him, had been in vain. Might it be one of Mrs. Stetson's children? Could it be the Count himself? Or simply one of the drivers who'd been sent to Cheltenham, or even Philadelphia, to deal with some matter? None of them was able to feel even slightly sure about the answer.

Looking for a few seconds at the enormous dust cloud that had formed behind the car, which was gradually getting smaller as it moved along the Old York Road towards Philadelphia, Jim Kelly, a reporter on the *North American*, decided that the best thing to do would be to go straight after the car, as the way that the driver had avoided the journalists seemed at least suspicious to him. And this is not to mention that strange outfit he was wearing, more like that of a racing car driver or an aircraft pilot than an ordinary driver, and that to Jim's mind was simply to hide his identity. And at least he would be doing something more useful and interesting than staying there in the middle of the road, walking back and forth under a blazing sun with no result at all. In a jiffy he ran to his little, two-seater Ford Model T, cranked up the engine, jumped in, banged the door shut, and drove off, touching the brim of his gray Stetson with two fingers as a gesture of goodbye, shouting to his colleagues: "See you later boys! Look after the house for me. I'll be right back."

Half a mile ahead, John Batterson Stetson Junior, the eldest son of John Batterson Stetson and Sarah Elizabeth Shindler Stetson—firmly holding the steering wheel of his white, two-seater Packard shining in the fierce light of the sun, his leather-lined helmet strapped under his chin, his sunglasses with rubber side protectors on, with leather coat

buttoned up to his neck despite the heavy, humid heat of the early afternoon—put his foot down heavily on the gas lest any of those meddling
journalists decide to follow him, something which he couldn't check,
given that the enormous dust cloud that the car raised up as it went by
stopped him seeing anything at all.

All that he wanted at that moment was to get to the center of town
as quickly as possible and, as discreetly and confidently as possible,
complete the uncomfortable and unpleasant mission that his mother
had suddenly thrust upon him. But a mother is a mother, he thought,
and like the good son he was proud to be, he owed obedience to her,
whatever were the missions that she gave him, or in general about the
way that mess of her wedding to Santa Eulália was being organized.
Which did not stop him from having opinions and expressing them
whenever he had the chance, despite feeling hurt about the fact that,
unlike what used to happen until very recently, they were heard less
and less frequently, most particularly since Santa Eulália had settled
in bag and baggage at *Idro*. Up until then, his mother wouldn't make
any move without consulting him, as indeed was her obligation as he
was the eldest son, and since his father's death, was the head of the
family, but from one moment to the next she had started deciding
almost everything on her own. Not exactly on her own, but rather after
consulting with him, with Santa Eulália, her lover, to call a spade a
spade. Even though from the following day on, Santa Eulália would
officially become his mother's husband and thus his stepfather, Heaven
help him, John said to himself in a crescendo of irritation, feeling the
sweat run down his forehead. Indeed, what other name could you give
to a guy who was shameless enough to move into the house belonging
to the woman to whom he was going to be united according to the
sacred vows of matrimony, five weeks before the ceremony would take
place, cohabiting with her, under the same roof, as if they were already
married? Taking breakfast together, going out for a drive together every
afternoon, and, at night, sleeping in the same wing of the house, only
a few yards from each other, John wondered, at the exact moment that
the car left the limits of Montgomery County, indicated by a wooden
signpost at the side of the road and followed, a few yards further on, by
an identical sign indicating the limits of Philadelphia County, yet without this change producing any effect on the level of the road surface,

which was still made of beaten earth with the exception of the tarmac lane reserved for the tramcars.

And one could now see the consequences of his opinions not being listened to, John noted, wiping his forehead with the back of his right hand before undoing the chin strap of his leather helmet and throwing it onto the passenger seat. One could see this in the disastrous manner they had decided to announce the wedding the previous day, calling in the main newspapers of Philadelphia for a press conference in the house gardens, during which his mother, with an official communiqué and all, had revealed her engagement to Santa Eulália, and then when there was the inevitable question from the journalists about when and where the wedding would take place, she kept the truth to herself, while stating that nothing was decided yet but that it would be soon. As if anyone would believe that someone of the status and social position of Mrs. Stetson could publicly, and with pomp and circumstance, announce her wedding without having a clue as to when it would take place. And all this took place as the groom watched the scene from inside the house, pathetically hiding behind the curtains of the windows of his room, being that the official version that was given out during the press conference itself was that he was at that moment on the way to Philadelphia from Chicago, where he had been kept back because of his duties as Portuguese consul to the city. As obviously it wasn't a good idea for anyone to know that the fiancé of the rich Stetson widow, the gallant Count of Santa Eulália, was already living in the house of the woman he intended to marry before the ceremony took place, John concluded, also taking off his leather jacket and throwing it down next to the helmet, unable to bear the heat anymore dressed like that. Ahead of him finally appeared North Broad Street, the main artery of Philadelphia, recently extended from the city limits to there, to the Old York Road, which meant a fully tarmacked road and cement pavements on both sides, allowing not just safer and more comfortable driving on a more regular surface, and thus less bumping up and down, but also the sudden end of the enormous dust cloud that had formed behind the car, and which stopped him, even if he had wanted to, from seeing Jim Kelly's little car, following only a few dozen yards behind.

And what great duties they must be, which allowed Santa Eulália to be absent from his position as Consul in Chicago for four weeks, without there apparently being any consequences, neither for him nor for the position he carried out, John couldn't help thinking as he casually looked at the sets of houses that were gradually appearing on either side of North Broad Street, many still waiting for a buyer, with their brick walls exposed and porticos with white-painted fronts, set apart from the road by little gardens. Because one of two things was true, and one did not have to be a great genius to understand it: either they wanted to keep the wedding in the greatest secrecy, and thus they would hold it first and announce it afterward when everything was consummated and they were on a happy nuptial journey on the way to Europe, or then, in giving prior public notice that the ceremony was going to take place without announcing when, they obviously could not expect to keep it a secret for very long, given the fact of what it was; that is, the wedding between the widow of the millionaire and philanthropist John B. Stetson, heiress to a fortune estimated to be many millions of dollars, to a European count, who was also, whether or not one liked him, a sculptor and his country's consul to Chicago. As from then on all the press would be on the alert and ready not to miss out on the slightest detail of the event, looking for the smallest sign, the tiniest clue that could lead them to what was going to happen next. He himself had explained this to his mother a short while ago, but to no avail, as instead of taking his advice she had preferred to follow that of Santa Eulália, who on this matter, as on many others, obviously had a different agenda, other interests that in no way, or in very little, coincided with hers, he concluded as he came to the line of cars that had formed at the crossing of the road. Closed as always, he noted as he slowed down to top almost touching the back of the car in front. Just to be sure, he resolved to use this occasion to have a quick look behind him, more out of the sake of conscience than anything else, as he was sure that none of the journalists had followed him. So he didn't pay any attention to the little black Ford that was coming from far off and much less to its driver, whose features he could not see nor recognize at such a great distance. For now, he was just concerned about starting off as soon as he could, which fortunately didn't take long to happen, as the train had just appeared on the line, wrapped in an enormous cloud of smoke and coming from the right, then crossing the road at high speed and then disappearing on its way to New York City.

Indeed, because as his mother had been widowed only two and a half years ago, after a marriage of over thirty years, and now being more than mature, mother of two adult children and grandmother of two grandchildren, heiress to a great fortune, in intending to marry a man ten years younger than her, a foreigner, without any signs of great wealth, it was obviously extremely sensible to maintain the greatest discretion and secrecy around the ceremony, revealing it only after it had happened as a *fait accompli*. While he, being still relatively unknown in the USA as a sculptor, despite his relative success in Chicago, had, on the contrary, great interest in having his wedding to her ounced in all of the newspapers in the country. And even having accepted the discretion that she had no doubt imposed upon him, he would, without doubt, take the best advantage of the circumstances to promote himself through her and the marriage, or his name wasn't John, he thought distractedly looking at the little three or four story buildings with shops on the ground floors and apartments above them which were gradually replacing the sets of houses, while on the horizon one could begin to see, the diffuse silhouette of the skyscrapers of the center of Philadelphia emerging through the thick fog that rested over the city.

One only had to see the way he had convinced her to show his works to the journalists during the press conference, both in photographs that he hadn't forgotten to bring for her and by bringing them in procession inside the house to show them his bas-relief of Uncle Henry Deland. It surely had not been his mother, always so formal and dry in her contact with journalists, who had decided of her own initiative to do this but was certainly him, with his undeniable power of seduction and persuasion, who had convinced her into this. But when one looked at it properly, nothing in Santa Eulália's behavior was exactly a surprise for him. One only had to read the report from the detective agency that he and his brother had contracted to investigate into him, he concluded, coming to the Vine Street junction, where there was another level crossing, which was also closed, and he took this opportunity to look back again, just in time to see Jim Kelly's Ford gradually slowing down until it stopped right behind him, and he couldn't help noticing the strange way that the driver pulled his hat down to hide his face when he felt he was being observed. Hadn't he already seen that car at the last level crossing? Could it be possible that after all one of those journalists had in fact followed him without him realizing earlier because of the dust cloud on the road? He wondered as he waited for the train to go past before the raising of the barrier. So what? He thought, finally seeing the train coming, clouded in smoke that billowed out of the engine's funnel, wouldn't the journalists end up finding out everything one way or another? Anyhow, if that guy were, in fact, a journalist there was nothing much he could do about it, as he couldn't see himself speeding around the city streets just to shake him off, he concluded, seeing the train disappear among whistles and more smoke, after slowly passing in front of him. As the guard lifted the barrier rail, he couldn't help but look back once again, at the precise moment that Jim Kelly was also getting ready to start off again. Yes, that face, that red hair sticking out from under his hat....It was definitely one of the guys who had tried to stop his car at the gates to the estate, with some at the side and others further ahead, shouting "When's the wedding?" "What can you tell us about Count Eulália?" "Is the wedding tomorrow morning or in the afternoon?" And he stepped on the gas without answering them and being forced to swerve at the last moment so as not to knock one of the boldest ones over after he had stood in front of the car. Yes, it was that face, that hat, that hair, he now recalled clearly, he concluded, as he saw the full splendor of the tower of City Hall emerging at the end of the street, standing out from among all the other skyscrapers due to its elegance and size. The only thing he could still do was to try to make sure that the Cunard clerk who dealt with him kept his mouth shut, and didn't tell the whole story as soon as he went out the door, he thought as he finally came to the end of the street, with the impressive north facade of City Hall right in front of him, all made out of stone, with masonry work on the windows, portals sculptured with allegorical figures and colonnade at the angles. Moving around the square carefully, as the traffic was rather intense and chaotic at that time, John started to move into the outside lane so he could safely come out into South Broad Street and then, at the first junction, into Chestnut Street, one of the busiest and most elegant streets in Philadelphia, with its skyscrapers, shops, and large department stores, whose storefronts displayed all kinds of articles and products, which John distractedly looked at as the traffic moved in a single compact line, in an amalgam of cars, carriages, and carts, block by block successively passing the different streets, their numbers decreasing as he moved towards the Delaware River at the end. When getting close to the crossing with 6th St. he took advantage of a place left empty by a cart laden with furniture and parked against the curb. Having turned off the engine, he picked up his beige linen jacket that was folded in the back seat, opened the door, and got out, slamming it behind him, not without a quick glance at the other guy, now just parking four or five places away, but not for the moment showing any interest in getting out of the car. Instead, sticking to pulling the brim of his hat a little further forward while sliding down a little in the seat, no doubt waiting to see what was going to happen next. John slowly put on his jacket, adjusted the knot in his tie, and crossed the street towards the entrance of the building in front, with a sign stretching right across the front stating: "CUNARD STEAM-SHIP COMPANY." Now inside, he hesitated a moment before going to the central part of the reception desk, behind which he thought he recognized the clerk who had received him the last time he was there to book tickets for his nuptial journey to Europe just over a year ago, a middle-aged man, middling in height, white shirt, sleeve protectors, visor on his forehead and glasses on the tip of his nose. What was his name? Vernon? Vernon Walters? He asked himself before he walked in his direction. Yes, that was it, Vernon Walters, he confirmed to himself as he went to the desk, satisfied with his memory for names.

"Mr. Stetson, how nice to see you again," Vernon effused, seeing him as soon as he raised his eyes from the stacks of paper accumulated on his desk. "What brings you here?" he added with a glance of complicity as if stating: "as no one can hear us here, the wedding is tomorrow, isn't it?"

"It's a delicate matter, Vernon," John started, lowering the tone of his voice and at the same time looking around to see that no one else was close, "which involves great discretion."

"Mr. Stetson, my lips are sealed," replied Vernon without a blink as he looked in surprise at the five-dollar bill that John discreetly passed to him over the desk, as if thinking: "Uh-oh, so it really is tomorrow."

"I want to book a suite for two people on the *Carmania* for this Saturday."

"This coming Saturday? Well, I have to phone New York first, but I think there'll be no problem, Mr. Stetson," replied Vernon, trying to disguise his excitement, as he said to himself: This Count Eulávia or

Olívia, or whatever he's called, has certainly got to the widow Stetson, that's the truth. And now the two are going to spend their honeymoon in Europe.

"I just need to know the name of the passengers to make the booking," he added, with the most professional and neutral tone that he could gather, thinking, Bingo, Vernon, now he can't get away.

"Well, that's the problem, Vernon. The name of the passengers mustn't be known," replied John, seeing Vernon's falsely surprised look.

"But, Mr. Stetson, there has to be a name, whatever it is, as I'm sure you understand. I can't make the booking without the name of the passengers," insisted Vernon, not facilitating things, determined not to let slip this chance to make Mr. Stetson talk.

"Well, put down Mr. and Mrs. Smith," retorted John, giving him the first names that came into his head.

"You mean that it's true what they are saying about Mrs. Stetson and that Count Eulávia...?" Vernon finally couldn't resist asking the question ready to get confirmation of what he already knew at any cost, and from the most authoritative source on the matter, that being Mrs. Stetson's eldest son, right there in front of him.

"Well, Vernon, I hope I can count on your total discretion on this matter," John replied, passing another five-dollar bill into his hand.

"Mr. Stetson, as I have already said and I say again, my lips are sealed," replied Vernon, not shy about putting the second bill in his pocket.

"Well, I don't know what's being said out there. The only thing I can confirm is that the wedding will take place tomorrow and they want to leave for Europe on Saturday on their honeymoon. But obviously, they do not want to be bothered by journalists. And you, Vernon, know what it's like. Someone of the status and position of Mrs. Stetson, marrying a European count...It's the sort of thing that the journalists will never let go of, not for anything in the world. Indeed, you'll have proof of this as soon as I leave."

"Don't tell me that you were followed here, Mr. Stetson?" Vernon feigned surprise, as he went to his desk to pick up the phone and ask for a connection to the central booking office in New York.

"Betty? Betty, this is Vernon, Vernon Walters from the Philadelphia office," he said quietly, but loudly enough for John to be able to hear, as soon as the communication was made with the Cunard offices in New York, "Hi, darling. I need a suite on the *Carmania* for Saturday. Yes, Saturday. Pardon, Mr. Stetson?" asked Vernon, seeing Mr. Stetson making gestures to him from the other side of the desk. "It's nothing to do with you, honey. Just give me a second to talk to the customer," he added, covering the mouthpiece with his hand.

"Bridal suite, Vernon," whispered John, his hands cupped to his mouth.

"Bridal suite, Mr. Stetson? I don't know if that is possible at such short notice. But we'll try," replied Vernon before returning to his call to New York. "Betty? Betty, thanks for holding; you're a sweetheart. Listen, Betty, do you think it is still possible to book a bridal suite? Yes, it is? Is it the last one? What great luck. You're an angel, Betty. The names? Mr. and Mrs. Smith. First names? Just a second," requested Vernon, motioning to John, who shrugged his shoulders and pointed at Vernon. "Betty? Can you make a note of this?" he asked as he breathed deeply, rolling up his eyes behind his glasses: "Mr. Smith, first name Harold. H-A-R-O-L-D. Mrs. Smith, first name, Zelda: Z-E-L-D-A. O.K., Betty? You don't need anything else? Bye, honey. Have a good day."

"That couldn't be better, Vernon: Harold and Zelda Smith. I couldn't think of anything like it," John remarked, pleased by all this and even smiling somewhat.

"Inspiration of the moment, Mr. Stetson," replied Vernon, looking satisfied. "In fact, they were the first names of an aunt and uncle of my wife's, bless her soul."

"So, how much do I owe you, Vernon?" John asked, suddenly wanting to get out of there.

"Don't worry about that, Mr. Stetson. I'll have the tickets delivered to the house today, along with the bill," answered Vernon, helpfully, pleased about those two five-dollar bills unexpectedly nestling in his trouser pocket.

"In that case, Vernon, I think I ought to remind you once again that one can never be too careful. I wasn't here today, you don't have anyone on the *Carmania's* passenger list for Saturday with any name remotely like mine…"

"Mr. Stetson, you can rest easy as I know perfectly well how to deal with these people," replied Vernon definitively, holding out his small, sweaty hand to John. "I would just like you to give Mrs. Stetson my best wishes for happiness for her wedding to Count Olívia."

"Eu-la-li-a, Vernon. Santa Eulália."

"I beg your pardon, Mr. Stetson. These foreign names are always a little difficult to pronounce," apologized Vernon.

"Don't worry. I'll give your best wishes to Mrs. Stetson. Goodbye Vernon. Thank you for your discretion," said John in farewell, going immediately to the exit door as Vernon raised his hand to the brim of his visor as a goodbye.

Here outside the air was still clammy and humid, without any breeze at all, he noticed as he cranked up the engine and at the same time glanced at the journalist again, who was still there, waiting in his car, as if to say: "The coast is clear, man, you don't need to wait anymore." Then he started off, stopping straight away at the next corner, this time because of a cart that was stopped in the middle of the street in a complicated maneuver of parking at the curb. An opportunity that John used to look behind him, just in time to see the awkward journalist going to Cunard's doors with a crafty look about him: "If I'm not mistaken you're not going to have any luck there, as old Vernon doesn't mess about, particularly when he's got two five dollar bills in his pocket," he whispered under his breath before he started up again towards Independence Park, which stretched north for several blocks from there. To the south was Independence Hall, considered the birthplace of the United States of America, as it was there that the Declaration of Independence had been signed on the morning of the 4th of July 1776, and, years later, the Constitution. John never managed to go past it without feeling a sudden quiver up his spine when looking at the modest two-story brick building with sash windows regularly set along its front and a simple, white-painted entrance door in the middle, and a tower emerging behind its belfry, originally built to house the famous Liberty Bell. He would immediately start to imagine the Congress meeting there, made up of the representatives of the states that would later form the new nation, closed inside those four walls for days and days on end, grave, concentrating faces, debating paragraph by paragraph, word by word, the first version of what would become the Declaration of Independence drawn up by Thomas Jefferson. All of this was while the American troops led by George Washington continued their struggle against the British army to the north. On his left, in Independence Park, John could also briefly see the little pavilion that now housed the Liberty Bell, not the first one, which was commissioned to be cast in London and which cracked as shortly after it was placed in the steeple, but the second one, which was cast in Philadelphia using bronze from the first one, and which, after having been used to proclaim independence on the 4th of July 1776, also ended up cracking a few years later. After it was repaired, it again showed a small crack and yet no one could explain the phenomenon. It was then considered to be the symbol of the freedom that was won by the Americans in their fight against the British Empire. It would be said that the intensity of the chimes announcing the proclamation of independence, as an echo of the voice of a whole people up in arms against their oppressor, was so great that the walls of the bell could not stand up to them and had broken, thought John, proud to belong to a country and people like this, as he turned left into 5th and then continued along Independence Park until he crossed Race Street at its northern end. It was only at that moment that he realized he was unwittingly going towards the Factory, as the family usually called the Stetson Hats Company. Which in the end wasn't a bad thing, as he could quickly go in, check the correspondence and deal with the most pressing matters before returning to work on Friday, he thought as he started to see the immense wall of the different buildings that made up the plant, which stretched north over several blocks with their brick construction and large glazed windows. More or less in the middle, between the third and the fourth buildings, was the main entrance with the administration block above it, where John had the office he had inherited from his father. He parked the car outside the building and walked to the main door, waving to the doorkeeper as he crossed the wide, white marble entrance hall to the broad staircase leading to the first floor. There, in a wide vestibule that gave on to the offices of the administrators, also with marble floors and mahogany-paneled walls with ornate framing, was the blonde Elsie, the secretary, and receptionist.

"Good afternoon, Mr. Stetson, a pleasure to see you," she greeted in her high-pitched voice and heavy southern accent, momentarily raising her eyes from her desk.

"Hello, Elsie. Good afternoon," replied John, going straight to his office, the first one along the corridor.

"Mr. Stetson, I have some urgent messages for you," said Elsie, standing up, lowering her full breast, which was far too tight inside her bodice, over the top of the desk, looking for the piece of paper on which she had written down the messages.

"Messages? Who from?" asked John, his hand on the doorknob, waiting for an answer.

"From a journalist, who won't stop calling, Mr. Stetson. From the *Inquirer*. He says he wants to confirm some information about Mrs. Stetson's wedding to that Count. By the way, Mr. Stetson, congratulations. Here in the office, everyone is very excited about the idea of our boss becoming the son of a real countess," Elsie couldn't resist saying. "No one in town has been talking about anything else since this morning."

"Come on, Elsie, let's not go too far. If this journalist calls again tell him I'm not in and I'm not coming to the office today, OK Elsie?" John finished off, finally opening the door to his office and closing it straight after.

"That's all I need," he thought as he walked across his office to his desk. "They won't even leave me alone at the office." This was a wide and spacious study, also with mahogany-paneled walls and a stuccoed ceiling, with an enormous fleurette in the middle and a frieze all the way round, with a beautiful Persian rug on the floor. On the wall opposite the door, two high windows lit the room, protected from the intensity of the sun's rays by blinds with wooden slats, and in the middle, in a gilt frame, there was John's diploma from Harvard University, dating from 1906. In the left corner, there was a long Empire-style desk, with piles of papers carefully lined up next to the outer edge of the desk lid, between the brass telephone with a wooden cable, connected to the wall by a thick, cloth-covered wire, and the also gilt metal electric lamp protected by a greenish glass tulip. Between the desk and the wall giving on to the corridor, a bookcase, also in mahogany and stocked with bound books, and on the other side an oil portrait of his father, John B. Stetson, sitting on a high-backed, molded wood chair, looking impressive in his black coat, carefully trimmed white beard and hard, inflexible gaze. Opposite the desk, two armchairs upholstered in *grenat* satin.

"May I, Mr. Stetson?" he heard Elsie's high-pitched voice ask from outside the door when he had hardly enough time to take his jacket off and throw it onto the coat rack and sit down in his padded, leather-lined swivel chair behind his desk.

"Come in," answered John grumpily.

"I've brought the mail, Mr. Stetson," she said, walking towards him with a pile of already opened letters. "By the way," she continued, because of nothing, "the man from the *Inquirer* has just called, insisting that it was urgent to talk to you, that it was very important, something about a news item that was going to come out tomorrow about Count Oliva…"

"Eu-la-li-a, Elsie, Eu-la-li-a," John found himself correcting again, immediately regretting it, fed up with always unwillingly being in that irritating role of always calling people's attention to the way they were adulterating Santa Eulália's name. Couldn't his mother at least have found a fiancé with a normal name that was easy to pronounce, like St. James, or St. John?

"Yes, Eulália. I told him you weren't here."

"So what was the news item. Didn't he say?" asked John, somewhere between curious and intrigued. One never knew what these journalists were capable of discovering.

"Something about a voyage to Europe on the *Carmania* next Saturday. He just wanted you to confirm it."

"A voyage on the *Carmania*, on Saturday? Are you sure he mentioned the *Carmania*?" he stated, startled, not wanting to believe his ears. No, no way. It must be something else. How could they know about the trip if he had made the booking only moments ago?

"Absolutely certain, Mr. Stetson. A trip on the *Carmania* on Saturday and something else about Count…Count…"

"Eulália," John helped again.

"Yes, Eulália," repeated Elsie. "that Count Eulália had been in the Spanish Consulate…"

"Spanish?" John found this strange. "Spanish or Portuguese?"

"Yes, Portuguese. I always get the two mixed up. And he said that…"

"That's fine, Elsie. I can see that I have to talk to this journalist to clear up this matter," John decided, foreseeing the worst. "If he calls again pass it to me. And in the meantime tell Mr. Adams to come here."

"Certainly, Mr. Stetson," replied Elsie, going out and closing the door behind her, while John looked one by one through the letters she had left on his desk but was unable to pay any attention to what he was reading, and kept thinking: "Santa Eulália up to his tricks again, that's clear. It was definitely him, it can't be anyone else," he complained under his breath, suddenly pushing the mail away and raising his two hands to his head, with his elbows resting on the top of his desk. No matter how quick he was the journalist would never have had enough time to go to the Cunard offices, get to the newspaper, and phone there several times before he got to the office. He had to have received the information from some other source. And the reference to Santa Eulália and the Portuguese Consulate was really so obvious, he concluded, lifting his head and sitting back, now with his hands resting on the arms of his chair, before he has a ceremonious Adams, the director of the sales department, sent in, after his respectfully waiting outside the door and knocking lightly three times.

"Good afternoon, Mr. Stetson," he greeted in a low voice, after closing the door.

"Good afternoon, Adams. Take a seat," replied John, pointing to one of the two armchairs opposite the desk. "So how are things going? Anything new?"

"Mr. Stetson, if I may…before we get down to business…I would like to personally offer, and I believe I can speak for all the staff in my department…my sincere congratulations on Mrs. Stetson's wedding," poor Adams almost whispered, nervously rubbing his hands together as the words hiccupped out of his throat. "It is a great honor for all of us to work under the orders of someone…. Someone who will soon have such a distinguished noble title in his immediate family…. And from what I could read in this morning's papers, besides the title of Count, Mrs. Stetson's fiancé, Count…Count…Eulália," Adams blurted out to John's relieved gaze, "Count Eulália is also a world-renowned artist and a very important diplomat."

"Thank you for your congratulations, Adams, and please convey my thanks to the rest of your staff, but unfortunately we have no time to lose, as I have to leave very soon. So let's cut to business: How are things going?" John insisted, without any patience to hear any more eulogies for the Count, above all coming from someone as circumspect as Adams.

"Everything is going very well, Mr. Stetson," Adams replied, now somewhat more at ease. "Today I had a meeting with our Midwest agents to prepare our Autumn campaign. And the prospects looks very encouraging, considerably better than what we were expecting."

"Great news, Adams. Great news," said John, pleased, at the exact moment that the shrill telephone bell started to ring.

"Elsie, I'm in a meeting with Mr. Adams and I would like not to be interrupted," John replied dryly as soon as he picked up the receiver.

"I'm sorry for interrupting, Mr. Stetson, but I have that journalist from the *Inquirer* on the line," replied Elsie, between nervous and excited. "I told him you were in a very important meeting and had asked not to be disturbed. Just in case you had changed your mind and don't want to take it."

"Good work, Elsie, good work. But you can put the call through," replied John, covering the mouthpiece to speak to Adams, while waiting for the connection:

"Well, Adams, I'm going to have to take an important call. I'm pleased that everything is going well and I will be here on Friday morning to go over the matter in detail."

"But Mr. Stetson, there are important decisions to make…" stuttered Adams, waving a bunch of dispatch papers that he held in his hand.

"Friday, Adams, Friday," replied John quietly, motioning for him to leave. "Hello? Mr. Stetson?" John heard from the other end of the line.

"John Stetson Junior on the line. Who is this?" he answered.

"Steiner, Max Steiner from the *Inquirer*," was the reply. "Thank you for taking the call, Mr. Stetson. I know you are in a very important meeting so I won't take up much of your time."

"What can I do for you, Mr. Steiner?

"Mr. Stetson, we are putting together an item about Mrs. Stetson's wedding to Count Eulália, which will have major coverage in tomorrow's morning edition. And we would like you to comment on some information on the subject that has come to our newsroom."

"If I can…" replied John, apprehensive and expecting the worst.

"According to sources we consider reliable, Count Eulália was at the Portuguese Consulate on Monday morning, where, after identifying himself as the Consul of Portugal in Chicago, stated that he was going to be married on the following Thursday, that is tomorrow, to a very rich widow from Philadelphia, whose name he refused to give, however. And that after the wedding they would leave on a nuptial voyage to Europe, and then he took advantage of the occasion to request information about the trip. As in the meantime, at a press conference held yesterday, attended by one of our reporters, Mrs. Stetson announced her upcoming wedding to Count Eulália, it was not difficult to conclude that the very rich widow he referred to was none other than Mrs. Stetson. So the first question I would like to ask you, Mr. Stetson, is the following: Can you confirm that the wedding is tomorrow? And in that case, where?"

"Well," John stalled to gain time while he carefully pondered his answer, "as far as I know, Count Santa Eulália is at the moment on a train coming to Philadelphia from Chicago, where he was held up because of his duties as the Portuguese consul, so I honestly don't understand how he could have been in the Portuguese Consulate here on Monday. And much less how he could have said such extraordinary things as those you have just told me. Unless, besides his many other qualities, the Count also possesses the gift of ubiquitousness."

"Our source is from the Portuguese Consulate itself, Mr. Stetson. And we were also told that the Count took the opportunity to ask the consul, Mr. Ernest Sutor, to help divulge his work as a sculptor, mentioning among other things that he won a Grand Prix in Paris at the *Salon*. Curiously, after having agreed to arrange a meeting with artists and art critics for the evening of the day he was at the consulate, he did not turn up, which left the consul and the people he had managed to bring very disappointed, as they were all very interested in meeting the person everyone is talking about in Philadelphia," continued Steiner, leaving John incapable of saying anything for several seconds. No, that was too much, he thought, trying to contain the enormous anger he felt growing inside him. Not content with only in a few minutes ruining all of his mother's, his brother's and his own efforts to keep the wedding and the nuptial journey a total secret, Santa Eulália also had the nerve to take advantage of such a sacred moment to try to promote himself and his work. All of this on the eve of the press conference at which his mother announced their engagement when she declared that he, Santa Eulália, was at the time on his way to Philadelphia from Chicago. That is, making her out to be a bare-faced liar.

"Mr. Stetson…can you hear me?" Steiner went on, finding the long silence on the other end of the line strange.

"I can hear you very well, Mr. Steiner," John finally replied, "but I don't have very much to add to what I have already said. I insist: as far as I know, the Count is now on the way to Philadelphia, and so only he can clarify the matter of this strange power that according to your source apparently allows him to be in two places as far from each other as Chicago and Philadelphia at the same time."

"I'm sorry, Mr. Stetson, but you haven't answered my question. What I would like to know is whether you confirm that the wedding will take place tomorrow? And in that case, where? And also whether you confirm that the bride and groom will go on a nuptial voyage to Europe on the *Carmania* on Saturday?" Steiner insisted, to a further lengthy silence from John. What sense did it make now to try to carry on keeping the wedding a secret, he wondered, feeling discouraged, when the groom himself had, whether knowingly or not, managed to give out all the details, including the nuptial voyage on the *Carmania* that he had just booked?

"No. I can't confirm any of those statements," he finally answered, suddenly more sure of himself, thinking: If Mother wants the wedding to be held in secret, it's not up to me, her eldest son, to go against her will, no matter what Santa Eulália does. "There are still a lot of preparations to make before the wedding can be held. So the most I can tell you is that it will definitely be held this year," he added.

"Well, Mr. Stetson, all I can do is thank you for your cooperation and say until the next time."

"Whenever I can be of help, Mr. Steiner," John said as a goodbye, relieved to set down the receiver and lean back in his chair. How could Santa Eulália have done something like this? And then stand by, as if he had nothing to do with it, and watch all the efforts being taken to avoid at all costs any leak to the newspapers about the details of the wedding and the nuptial trip, whether through the catering team, the decorators and the florists, or through the members of the staff of the house themselves, without saying anything, without making the slightest mention of what had taken place before at the consulate? John wondered. Had he at least told Mother about the situation and she, in order to cover it up, had said nothing? No. That wasn't possible. If that had happened, his mother would have surely discussed the issue with him, John, and with his brother, and they would have decided on other measures to get around the situation together.

"So much time, so much energy for nothing," John said out loud, getting up from his chair and going to one of the windows, thinking about his trip to the city with that ridiculous, uncomfortable outfit he wore on such a hot and clammy day, just not to be recognized by the journalists, driving the car himself instead of giving it to his driver, just not to raise any suspicion among the servants, forced to bribe the Cunard clerk with ten dollars to avoid any leak to the press, and all for nothing in the end, given that two days earlier Santa Eulália had taken it upon himself to spread to the four winds the fact that he would be leaving on Saturday with his bride for Europe on the *Carmania*. Now he could only wait for the *Inquirer* on the next day, that is if other journalists had not also been to the consulate and the news was not known to the other Philadelphia newspapers. And on the landing stage in New York on Saturday, there would be a battalion of reporters with their cameras to cover the event, he thought, looking at the so far still deserted street. His only hope now lay in one name, Vernon, Vernon Walters, and in the greater or lesser conviction with which he could deny the news when confronted with it. As indeed had surely already happened. But Vernon seemed to be a solid guy, trustworthy, character traits that had surely been somewhat reinforced with those two five-dollar bills he had put away in his pocket without protesting. And one had to realize that if the news was denied by Cunard itself, it would lose a lot of its credibility even if it were published, and would become one more speculation among many others. That would be if Santa Eulália had not in the meantime undertaken other similar initiatives, thought John, without really knowing how he should see that type of behavior by his future stepfather: whether due to some ingenuity, mixed in with a lot of ignorance about the rules of how American society worked, particularly its press; or on the contrary, as deliberate and conscious acts by someone who had very personal and non-confessable aims. Or, to put it another way: was Santa Eulália aware that in presenting himself to the Portuguese Consulate in Philadelphia as Consul of Portugal in Chicago, openly stating he was going to marry a rich widow from the city and that they would then go on a nuptial voyage on the *Carmania* to Europe, at the same time asking for information about how to get a marriage license in the State of Pennsylvania, the most natural thing would be that there would be someone ready to reveal everything to the newspapers in exchange for a few dollars? Or had he done it being absolutely aware of the results he would obtain, making the marriage and the nuptial journey public so that he could get the greatest publicity possible for himself and his work?

His mother, who was always willing to forgive him, as he was an artist and as such was not very aware of worldly realities, would obviously fiercely defend the first possibility, but John, knowing what he did about Santa Eulália, had to clearly incline towards the second. It was true that according to the report from the detective agency that he and his brother had hired to investigate Santa Eulália one could not conclude that his actions were generally dishonest or marked out by a serious lack of character. And much less that one was in the presence of a registered charlatan, or of a typical fortune hunter, ready to do anything to get his future wife's money. Because in such circumstances he and his brother G. Henry would have been forced to take drastic measures to end the romance, no matter what price they would have to pay for this. But it was also true that some of the facts in the agency report did not speak very much in favor of himself and his actions. In conclusion, what the agency said about Santa Eulália was that nothing that he said about himself was totally false nor totally true. Or rather, there was always a basis of truth in everything he said, although the facts were often embroidered or touched up to present an image of himself or of his work that was more seductive and interesting.

The investigation had been carried out at the beginning of the year, as soon as his mother had confirmed what they had suspected for a long time; that is, her romance with Santa Eulália, albeit without clearly telling them about any plans for the future. So, at the right moment to obtain information about the character with it still being possible to do something to stop the romance if this turned out to be necessary. Which, in fact, could only be seen as a gesture of prudence of theirs in relation to all that was at stake, and one should not forget that this was a great deal, he thought. And for which mother, if she had not been so overcome by that sudden, unexpected passion, more fitting to an adolescent than to a mature woman, would certainly thank them.

Also because although the clause that his father had included in his will foresaw the possibility of third parties directly benefitting from his inheritance, granting this right only to his rightful heirs, that is his mother, himself, and his brother, he could not stop someone like Santa Eulália being able to gain great influence over her, leading her to spend enormous amounts or even, at the worst, fritter away the whole fortune, as long it was she and not he who did it. So, despite his father's caution, it was still better to be safe, John concluded with his conscience feeling he had done his duty, at the exact moment that he started to hear the factory siren sounding out, a sign that it was five o'clock p.m. and the day's work was over.

"Will you be needing anything else, Mr. Stetson?" he heard shortly afterward from Elsie's shrill little voice as she poked her head through the opening in the door.

"No, Elsie. See you Friday," answered John.

"See you Friday, Mr. Stetson. And I hope everything goes well tomorrow," she added with a knowing smile.

"Thank you, Elsie," he replied, before concluding that he wasn't needed at the factory and that he ought to go home too. Outside, the street had now returned to its earlier calm after the mass exit by the workers, only being interrupted now and then by a late leaver who, on seeing him going to his car, greeted him respectfully, raising his hand to his hat.

Taking Montgomery Avenue and then Germantown, which diagonally cut across the different neighborhoods in the northern suburbs, until Fairmont Park, John reached Broad Street almost without noticing, and then, further on, the Old York Road. All he wanted to do now was to get home, have a good bath, spend a little time with Ruby and especially with little John Junior, who had the gift of making him forget all his worries in a second, he thought, pleasantly imagining the moment of picking him up and walking around the garden with him a little. Then he would dress for dinner at Mother's house, accompanied by Ruby, a ceremonial dinner, as his mother had reminded him that morning, which meant tails, starched shirt, waistcoat and bow-tie for him and evening gown for Ruby, with matching earrings and necklace, as all the guests for the following day's ceremony would be present; and particularly noteworthy would be the famous Mrs. Potter Palmer, the Queen of Chicago, as she was known not only in the U.S. but also the world over, of whom Santa Eulália boasted that he was an intimate acquaintance, forgetting that he had not yet dreamt of coming to America, while John's mother and father were already friends with her and her husband. So that if she really came it would be in the name of that old friendship and not because of him, of that there could be no doubt at all, John concluded, suddenly remembering that before he went home he had to go to his mother's house first to let her know that the mission she had given him had been successfully accomplished and that the trip to Europe on the *Carmania* had been booked under the names of Mr. Harold and Mrs. Zelda Smith. And he could take advantage of the occasion to try to find out whether she was aware of what her beloved fiancé was up to behind her back if he had the chance to do this, given that it wasn't at all convenient to confront him personally on the matter, at least for now, he thought, as ahead, on the left of the road, he could see first the leafy tops of the trees in the garden, then the low stone wall that went around the whole estate and started right there on the crossing with Beach Avenue, which he had just passed. Following this was the crossing with Juniper Avenue, which crossed the estate and led to his own house at the other end, next to Sycamore Avenue, and finally, the entrance to *Idro*, the great mansion of the Stetsons, standing impressive up among the trees. But which he could not see immediately, with it being temporarily hidden by two hay wagons that were slowly coming in the opposite direction, forcing him to stop in the middle of the road with his left arm out, waiting to be able to turn. Thus he was far from imagining what was awaiting him on the other side. Which he could only see when he finally managed to turn left, as several journalists came suddenly rushing to him from both sides of the road, like a pack of dogs, shouting "Mr. Stetson, Mr. Stetson," until they literally forced him to stop, now that he wasn't going fast enough to go faster than them.

"Good evening, Mr. Stetson," said the first one, a tall, thin man with greasy brown hair with a lock hanging over his forehead. "I would like to know whether you can confirm that the wedding between Mrs. Stetson and Count Eulália will take place tomorrow, and in that case at what time?"

"And I'd like to know where you got such an absurd idea," rebuffed

John abruptly, not having a better argument.

"All the information we have gathered throughout the day point to this, Mr. Stetson. Starting with the Count's statements two days ago in the Portuguese Consulate in Philadelphia…" said a fat, short journalist, his face dripping sweat.

"As far as I know the Count is on his way to Philadelphia from Chicago, so I don't know what statements you are talking about," said John, starting to get fed up with always having to give the same answers to the same questions. "Besides the fact that a marriage license hasn't been requested yet, and it is unlikely for this to happen in the near future," he suddenly thought of adding, in the hope that none of them would know that his mother and the Count had been that very afternoon in Norristown, precisely dealing with the license.

"But, the Count said that…" another journalist presented, rapidly cut off by John, now inspired:

"As you will understand, with the people involved, there are many issues still to be solved before the wedding can take place. As you know, the Count is Consul of Portugal in Chicago, so he will first have to find someone to replace him in his duties if it is confirmed that the bride and groom intend to live in Philadelphia after the wedding."

"But in the statements he made on Monday in the Portuguese Consulate, Count Eulália said that the wedding would be tomorrow and that the bride and groom would leave for Europe on Saturday on the *Carmania*," yet another journalist put forward, one that John could easily identify as the one who had followed him to the Cunard offices. But by the sound of the question, it looked like he hadn't gotten anything out of Vernon, or he would certainly been more incisive about the trip on the *Carmania*. Which, if it was the case, would be good news among so much bad news, he thought.

"As I have stated before, the Count has been in Chicago dealing with his duties as consul, so I do not understand how he can have simultaneously been in Philadelphia. But let's move on. What I can tell you is that, just as was publicly announced yesterday in the press conference given by Mrs. Stetson here in the gardens of the house, the wedding will take place on a date to be announced, but almost certainly this year. And now I am sorry but other duties require my presence," he finished, immediately releasing the handbrake and at the same time stepping on the accelerator, not giving them time to react.

"But Mr. Stetson, in the Catholic Archdiocese of Philadelphia they said...." he heard one of them shout, from a few yards away and hidden in the inevitable dust cloud. "I did what they asked me. If they had all done the same none of this would have happened. Now it is too late to do anything, other than reinforce the security around the estate so that tomorrow they don't come climbing in and sticking their noses in other people's business," he concluded as he drove past the front of the mansion, then turning left to park by the entrance on the path leading to the back of the house and to his own house.

IV

Paris, 11th of January 1897

"*ALLEZ, RIBEIRO, DÉPÊCHE TOI!*" Georges shouts to him from the carriage window, with the train already moving, hardly giving him time to hold on to the rail and jump onto the first step of the platform.

"*Bonjour, chers amis!*" Aleixo greets his former colleagues from the Académie, sitting on the first seats on either side of the aisle as soon as he comes through the door into the carriage: Vladimir, Maurice, Edouard, Aristide, and Helen, besides Georges, obviously.

"*Ah, ce sacré* Ribeiro, *toujours en retard!* By this time no one believed that you would still come," says Aristide, motioning to him to sit down in the empty seat in front of him, next to Georges and Helen, as soon as he finishes shaking hands with the whole group as a greeting.

"Would I miss this trip? Not for anything in the world. If I hadn't caught this train, the worst that could happen would be to catch the next one and go to join you," Aleixo answers without a second's hesitation, after having sat down and unbuttoned his thick gray overcoat.

"Well, I am very pleased that you could come, Ribeiro. Bourdelle promised me that he would be there to meet us and accompany us throughout the whole visit," Maurice, the main organizer of the trip, explains from the next bench. This is because, besides his classes at the Académie, he has also been accepted as a student at the studio run by Bourdelle, one of Rodin's main collaborators.

"But master Rodin will also be there, won't he?" asks Aleixo.

"No one knows. According to Bourdelle the Master is completely unpredictable. He might just as well be working all day as having shot off to Paris on the first-morning train on the way to the Dépôt des Marbres studio," Maurice explains, rolling up a cigarette. "In any case, Bourdelle guaranteed me that he was aware of our visit and was pleased about it," he adds, with the tobacco pack open in his hand, and from which he takes out a little piece and distributes it methodically along with the paper, then rolling it up and gluing it with a little saliva.

"*Eh bien, c'est déjà quelque chose!*" comments Aleixo, unable to disguise his profound disappointment at his colleague's reply. A visit by a group of students from such a renowned and prestigious art school as the *Académie* Julian to Rodin's studio and there isn't even any guarantee that the Master himself will receive them so that they can personally present all of their doubts and concerns, hearing the explanations and advice he might give them from his own lips? He wonders to himself, unsatisfied about this possibility, at the exact moment when through the steamed-up windows of the train one begins to see the typical suburban Parisian houses appearing on both sides, lined along the road running next to the train line, now that the Gare de Montparnasse station, with its infinity of parallel lines and moving and stopped trains, has been definitively left behind.

"*Eh alors*, Ribeiro, what have you been doing since you left us? Or rather, since you left the Académie?" Aristide suddenly asks him, watched closely by Helen Mears, sitting by the window, a blue velvet beret tilted to the left and a thick, woolen cape covering her shoulders and breast up to her neck.

"Work, work, and more work," Aleixo replies, smirking, and briefly glancing at his American colleague then looking at Aristide.

"Is that your own work or in someone's studio?" Aristide insists.

"Mine, fortunately. During the summer in Portugal, I received several commissions, which have taken up all my time since I came back to Paris. And which have even forced me to move to a bigger studio, imagine," Aleixo explains.

"That's great. You're a lucky man, Ribeiro. At least compared to us. Work isn't very plentiful around here, isn't that right, Georges?" says Aristide.

"That's true. Lately, there hasn't been anything," agrees Georges, sitting next to him.

"And might we know what these commissions are?" asks Helen, showing interest and again staring at him with her beautiful deep black eyes, leaning forward towards him and awaiting the answer.

"The main one is for a statue of the *Sacred Heart of Jesus*, in bronze, to be set up on a hill."

"Just like the *Sacré-Coeur* that is being built in Montmartre?"

Georges inquires.

"Well, for the moment no one is thinking about building a church or a basilica, but only a statue, which will be placed next to a little chapel that already exists on top of the hill. Although those responsible haven't rejected the idea of replacing the chapel with a more impressive construction," clarifies Aleixo.

"So, where is this hill? In Lisbon?" Helen asks, showing, for an American who only recently came over the Atlantic, a knowledge of European geography that is considerably above the average.

"No. It's near a city in the north of Portugal called Viana. Viana do Castelo. It is a magical place, of extraordinary beauty, a hill covered in extremely dense vegetation, overlooking the sea, and at the bottom, the city and the river are spread over the land. At the top, when it is not very cloudy, one can see a great deal of the northern coast of Portugal, stretching over many kilometers," Aleixo explains enthusiastically.

"Do you have any ideas for your statue yet, Ribeiro?" asks Aristide.

"Yes and no. I've done a lot of studies and sketches, but I still haven't found a solution that is to my total satisfaction."

"*Mesdames, Messieurs, vos billets, s'il vous plaît,*" shouts the ticket inspector, coming into the carriage through the front door.

"*Merci, Monsieur, merci, Mademoiselle,*" he says, face reddish and sporting a bushy mustache, as he returns their tickets to Aristide and Helen, then clipping those of Georges, Aleixo and the other colleagues before he goes on his way to the back of the carriage.

"Are there any others besides that commission?" asks Helen, full of curiosity.

"Yes, there are a few busts. But there is one that worries me above all," he replies, somewhat surprised by Helen's sudden interest in him.

"Really? Why?" she asks.

"Well, if you must know, it's because of the model's great fame," Aleixo replies.

"Oh, yes? So who is it then?" asks Aristide, becoming interested.

"You won't believe this, but it is…no one but…the Queen of Portugal herself," Aleixo replies, unable to hide his vanity.

"The Queen of Portugal herself? Oh, my God, It's incredible, I can't believe it," exclaims Helen in her native tongue, such is her surprise.

"*C'est pas vrai, tu plaisantes…*" then exclaims Aristide. "You are going to make a statue of the Queen of Portugal?"

"It's not a statue. It's a bust."

"Hey, Vladimir, Edouard, Maurice... Did you hear what Ribeiro has just said? He says he's going to make the bust of the Queen of Portugal," Aristide shouts to the others sitting on the next seat.

"The Queen of Portugal? *Il est incroyable, ce Ribeiro.* But how did you get this work?" an astonished Maurice asks him.

"Well, it's a long story," Aleixo replies, playing difficult.

"Long or short, you're going to have to tell it, Ribeiro," Maurice insists.

"Yes. You can't get out of this one," adds Aristide.

"Well, as you insist, it's like this," Aleixo finally condescends after a few seconds' hesitation. "Everything happened during my last days of holidays in Portugal, before coming back to Paris. One afternoon I was in the family home in the north and I receive a letter signed by the secretary to the King, the Count of Arnoso, in which he sends me, in the name of the Queen and in his own name, the greatest congratulations on my success at the last *Salon*, here in Paris. Which was, to my surprise, remarkably well received by the Portuguese newspapers and public opinion in general, with the publication of several articles in which excerpts from the references in the French press were transcribed...."

"It was a remarkable success, without any doubt, Ribeiro," cuts in Edouard, who during the last year's *Salon,* collected and gave a pile of newspapers praising his works to Ribeiro. "Particularly coming from a young, unknown sculptor like you. And above all a foreigner."

"Thank you, Edouard. And then, to finish, Arnoso said that the Queen, who as you know is French, the daughter of Louis Philippe, Count of Paris, had shown great interest in congratulating me personally on my success..."

"*Oh là, là,* Ribeiro, *attention à la Reine...*" interrupts Aristide, chortling.

"asking me if I could come to the summer residence of the royal family in Cascais, on the outskirts of Lisbon, three days later in order to be received by her. And so I went."

"So how did it go? What is she like?" Maurice wants to know. "She is an interesting woman..."

"Interesting in what sense?" asks Georges.

"Well…In all senses…" replies Aleixo mysteriously.

"She's French after all…" remarks Vladimir.

"She is tall, harmonious in build, intelligent, educated, witty…" adds Aleixo.

"*Ah, sacré* Ribeiro, be careful what you get involved in. If you're not careful the king will have you sent to the galleys…"

"So what happened during the audience?" asks Helen, very seriously and putting a stop to her colleagues' silliness.

"Well, the Queen was very welcoming and cordial, starting by revealing great knowledge of art, which is not surprising given that both she and the King had artistic education and are excellent watercolor painters. Indeed the King has participated in several different salons, both in Portugal and abroad…"

"So what about the bust. How did the bust idea appear?" Helen insists, somewhat impatient about all this explanation.

"Then the Queen offered her words of praise and congratulations for the way I had, in her words, honored Portuguese art in Paris, words which obviously moved me greatly. And then I decided to take advantage of the opportunity and asked her to allow busts of her and of her husband to complete my work *Apotheose*, on which I have been working since last year. And to my surprise, Her Majesty said yes, that it would be a great privilege for her, and we immediately arranged a pose sitting for the following day."

"You are a very lucky man, Alexis," says Maurice, at the precise moment that the train starts to slow down, a sign that they are finally approaching Meudon, the little town on the outskirts of Paris where Rodin lives and has his studio.

"Ten twenty-five," Aleixo notes, looking at his pocket watch as soon as he alights from the train, then going with his colleagues along the platform towards the steps leading to the station building up above, as the train line is in a sort of ditch between two very high stone walls.

"And now it's always straight ahead," indicates Maurice when they come outside, after crossing the station hallway, emerging into the little square with streets leading off it in all directions, and where Maurice points towards a narrow, unpaved street that crosses the railway and carries on towards the hill that rises up on the other side. Which they walk up, their noses and ears frozen by a cold, dry wind, as they observe the vines bare of leaves on the left of the road, stretching along the valley of the River Seine until they come to a little two-story inn with a tavern on the ground floor.

"*La voilà, la Villa des Brillants,* in all its splendor," Maurice finally exclaims, stopping next to an iron gate at the end of a stone wall, and pointing his finger towards a long avenue of chestnut trees descending the hill, which they then walk down until they come to a second door, made of wood, behind which there stands a small two-story bright red brick house, the color of which contrasts strongly with the white stone-work framing the windows, with a slate roof with high, narrow dormer windows and a long, smoking chimney, also made of brick, rising high above the eaves. It is a relatively recent construction, which Rodin be-gan renting four or five years earlier to set up not only his studio but also his residence, which is taken care of by Madame Rose Beuret, the only woman capable of putting up with all of his passions and whims, explains Maurice as he goes around the house towards a little stone staircase leading up to the entrance door, which Rose Beuret in person, with her stooping body, gray hair, and aging, worn face, opens to them.

"The Master is not in. He has gone to Paris, but left instructions for Monsieur Bourdelle to accompany you on your visit," she says, inviting them into the small sitting room on the right of the vestibule as soon as Maurice explains who they are and why they have come. They are wait-ing for Bourdelle to arrive, sitting in that austerely furnished little space, where there are only a few chairs and a round table, when Aleixo takes the opportunity to peek through the half-open door at the Master's dining room, dominated by a large canvas on the back wall, and accom-panied by some other smaller ones on the side walls. In the middle, on the table, a small stone torso and a vase with flowers.

"*Ah, les voilà, les élèves de ce sacré Puech,*" he suddenly hears behind him a voice with the unmistakable accent of the Midi area of France, which belongs to none other than the truculent Antoine Bourdelle, ap-pearing at the door, in a white coat buttoned up over a thick sweater, high forehead, hair thinning at the sides, long dark beard. Who then invites them to cross the vestibule to the studio itself, a vast room of five or six meters in height, lit by a long, high window located in the wall opposite the entrance, and full of sculptures of the most varied forms and sizes, some placed on plinths and easels, others on wooden platforms or even small scaffolds, and at which some students are working dedicatedly. The left wall is almost totally made up of very high wooden shutters that open on to a large glassed-off balcony.

"Before we start the visit proper, I would like to give you some information which I think is necessary for you to better understand what you are going to see," says Bourdelle, motioning to them to gather around him. "Does anyone know what work that is?" he then asks, pointing to an enormous rectangular plaster haut-relief placed on a platform opposite the entrance door.

"La Porte de l'Enfer?" chances Aleixo, suddenly remembering the description that Maurice gave him of the famous Porte, made up of two tall, narrow panes, as well as the jambs and the spandrel, covered in small figures, some of which stood out completely from the background and others only partially.

"Correct. This is the latest version of *La Porte de l'Enfer*, brought here from the Dépôt des Marbres studio only a few months ago, as we are working on several figures that are a part of it. And why am I drawing your attention to it? Because it is a fundamental work for understanding the Master's artistic career. It not only synthesizes all the new aspects that he has brought into our art in a sublime manner, but above all because it has acted as a source of inspiration and a starting point for a great many of his most recent works.

"*Excusez-moi*, Monsieur Bourdelle, but for how many years has Monsieur Rodin been working on the *Porte*?" Helen Mears asks in her rather rudimentary French.

"Since 1880, *Mademoiselle*, the year when he officially received the commission for a bronze door for a decorative arts museum to be built in Paris. That is, for almost seventeen years."

"And why hasn't it been cast in bronze and put in the museum yet?" she asks, surprised.

"Well, that a rather more complicated issue, *Mademoiselle*. As soon as he signed the contract to make the Porte, the Master got to work and worked on it intensely, almost exclusively, for four years. In 1884 he considered it was practically concluded, and started the preparations for it to be cast in bronze. But when everything was about to go ahead the building of the museum was suspended. Four years later the project was taken up again and Master Rodin gets down to work again. However, after a short time, he was confronted no longer with the suspending of the project, but with the definitive abandoning of it."

"Meaning that the museum never got to be built? And the door no longer had any use?" Miss Mears continues, unable to believe this and thinking that none of it made any sense: deciding to build a museum, commissioning the decoration for its main entrance door from one of the greatest French sculptors, then suspending everything for four years, then deciding to go ahead with it and then finally definitively scrapping the project. This is too much for her practical American mind.

"Yes and no. It is true that the *Porte,* as the door to the future Decorative Arts Museum, no longer made any sense as soon as the project was abandoned. But given the colossal investment made by the Master in this work, creating the extraordinary set of figures and scenes that can be seen in it and which come directly from his very personal reading of *Dante's Inferno,* as described in the *Divina Commedia,* it would be absurd if this work were not fruitfully used. So many of its scenes and figures have been taken out of the *Porte* and then, after being enlarged and reworked, turned into works that are completely autonomous in relation to their original context. This is the case, for example, of the figure you see here in the center, dominating the whole composition," explains Bourdelle, pointing to the little figure of a naked man sitting with his hand under his chin, suspended from the middle of the spandrel above the door. "This figure started by representing Dante himself, and then gradually took on a more universal dimension, that of a thinker, of a creator, who concentrates deeply, cogitating on his work. Once the making of the Porte was abandoned it was taken out of it and became a completely autonomous work, *Le Penseur,* which you can see further on in its latest version," he adds, pointing to a plaster statue on a platform some meters ahead that is very similar to the other but ten or fifteen times bigger and obviously worked in greater detail: a completely naked man, sitting on a rock, bending over and twisted with his chin resting on his right hand and his elbow on his left knee, his face closed in on itself, thinking, dreaming, cogitating, as if he were doing this not only with his head but with his whole body, such is the force and expression resulting from the whole set.

"*Excusez-moi,* Monsieur Bourdelle, but was it the Master himself who enlarged it from the original version?" then asks Edouard.

"No. One of his students made a first version, still in clay, on which the Master worked after it had been set in plaster, through a series of versions until he came to this one, which he considered the final work. Indeed, the Master likes to work on plaster more than anything else, unlike most of his colleagues, who mainly work in clay, considering that after the form has been set in plaster the work is practically finished," Bourdelle explains.

"Who makes the plaster forms?" Georges wishes to know, with them now walking on.

"They're made here in the studio, and always with recoverable moulds, which, although it means more work, allows one to make as many copies as one wishes. From these copies the Master always makes several versions of each work, which he religiously stores away, allowing him to always come back to any of them if he wishes. This is the case of the piece he has been working on most over recent times, the statue of the writer Balzac. Which you will be able to see in the next room, in its several different versions, corresponding to the different phases it has gone through," he adds, before leading them to a little door at the end of the large room and giving on to a lower, narrower and longer space, lit up by a window along the whole of the sidewall and against which there is a succession of statues of Balzac, some of them showing him naked, arms crossed, enormous belly, misshaped head, legs open, and others in which he is dressed simply in a robe over his shoulders and his legs closed.

"Out of all these versions is there one that can be considered final?" inquires Aleixo.

"Yes. That one there," replies Bourdelle, indicating the last in the series, in which Balzac once again has a robe over his shoulders, enclosing a massive body, head up, and being prolonged by an almost non-existent neck. Which they all stop for a while to look at with greater attention.

"One can't say that there is a great physical resemblance to the writer, at least in relation to the known photographs of him," Edouard ventures, hesitatingly, clearly not liking the work.

"That is precisely where one of Rodin's great originalities resides, *voyons*," replies Bourdelle. "For the Master, sculpture is above all the art of what is modeled, which it is necessary to release from the resemblance or the mere restitution of the model. Translating the truth, the life, the power, and the force contained in a figure by plastic means. And in my opinion, this was precisely achieved in this work, despite what his detractors say.

"What detractors?" asks Aleixo, finding this strange as he looks at the work in raptures, while poor Edouard blushes deep red after hearing Bourdelle's explanation.

"Oh, critics, journalists, even colleagues. I don't know. Not to forget the *Société des gens de lettres de France,* which commissioned the monument. And ended up rejecting it, forcing the Master to return the ten thousand Francs he had already received," replies Bourdelle, moving on towards a different work, placed on a platform a little further ahead, in which two scandalously naked youths embrace and kiss each other on the mouth. "This is another work which was originally in the *Porte—Le Baiser*—made from the group set *Paolo et Francesca,* the lovers from the *Divina Commedia.* As you can see, in terms of language and form it is the opposite to *Balzac.* An early version of this work was presented to the public at the *Salon* about ten years ago, causing a great scandal. Several others followed on until we come to this one, considered to be the final one, which I myself am setting to marble," he adds, pointing to the block of stone from which the heads and part of the bodies of the two lovers are already emerging.

"All of this is truly extraordinary," exclaims Aristide, hitherto very quiet and observant.

"*Un travail absolument fou, incroyable,*" a pensive Georges corroborates.

"Well, my friends, I would very much like to carry on here with you, but unfortunately I cannot; I have to continue with my work. But please, feel free to look at and observe whatever you wish. *À tout à l'heure,*" says Bourdelle, using this pause to go over to his block of stone, which he immediately begins to attack with his chisel and gouge, while the group spreads out around the whole studio looking at the different works, whispering observations and comments about what they see.

"*Alors, Monsieur Ribeiro, que pensez vous de tout cela?*" Aleixo suddenly hears Helen Mears' measured voice from behind him at the moment he is attentively observing one of the many versions of the monument to Balzac, not the final one, but the one in which his robe is open at the front, revealing his bare legs and, good grief, what daring, his private parts, *Honoré de* Balzac's private parts, exhibited in all their ugliness and crudeness.

"*Extraordinaire. Absolument extraordinaire,*" Aleixo replies, a little ill at ease at Helen's sudden approach. "It is far beyond my greatest expectations. Master Rodin is a genius, only comparable to a Michelangelo or a Leonardo da Vinci," he adds, trying to hide his embarrassment about the way she stares at him with her beautiful deep black eyes.

"Out of all the works you've seen, what is the one that has most impressed you?" she continues, still staring at him.

"This *Balzac*, without a shadow of a doubt," replies Aleixo, now staring at her also, before he points to the final version of the statue, in front of him. "After a work like this nothing will be the same in our art. Here are definitively the foundations of the sculpture of the new century that is coming," he declares.

"Well, for me, what impressed me most was *Le Baiser*. What an extraordinary composition, what harmony of forms, what movement, what sensuality," she replies dreamily, eyes wide open, without waiting for the question to be asked. "It contains all of the classical tradition, from the Greeks, including Michelangelo and to today."

"It is also an absolutely remarkable work, without any doubt. With a great boldness of forms. But less innovating, one must agree," replies Aleixo, with Helen now moving on towards *Fugit Amor,* a little further ahead, another work taken from the *Porte,* with the same two lovers, Paolo and Francesca, now dramatically fleeing from each other, while he remains for a good while looking at the last version of *Balzac.* Yes, it is all really explicit, that "movement that is a transition between two movements," according to Bourdelle the essence of Rodin's search, Aleixo says to himself, first observing the position of the hands, of which one can only see the volume, crossed over under the robe in a final attempt to stop it opening, then that heavy, compact body, slightly leaning back, and finally the enormous, proud and haughty head at the top, as if directly breaking out from the trunk. And the face, that fearful, disdainful face, almost taken to the level of a caricature, sunken eyes under prominent arches, stressed by thick eyebrows, short nose, bulbous at the end, half-open mouth, slit between an irregular and poorly trimmed mustache and an affirmative chin, projecting forward. How is it possible for such an extraordinary and innovative work like that one to be rejected by the Society that commissioned it, which is no doubt made up of great names in French Culture, but who are, so it appears, the first to turn out to be incapable of understanding and accepting the personal reading that the artist made of the figure of the great writer Balzac? What made them take such a decision? Conservatism, simple myopia, or something else? Wonders Aleixo as he suddenly notices Maurice at the door to the studio, motioning to them to come over.

"It is almost midday and they are going for lunch. So we have to go," he explains when he finally manages to get the whole group around him, while the several students in the studio start to tidily put down their tools and take off their smocks before going for lunch, just as if they were factory workers.

"*Mes amis,* it was a great pleasure to have been able to receive you here in Master Rodin's studio," says Bourdelle in turn, also coming over towards them after removing his smock. "And I hope this visit has opened up new perspectives for the profession you have chosen. Because do not doubt at all: Rodin and his work clearly show us the path to be followed by our art, sculpture. And I am sure that the new century that is approaching will show this," he adds, as he accompanies them returning to the vestibule.

"Master Bourdelle, in the name of all of my colleagues here present I would like to thank you from the heart for the way in which you have received us and guided us on this visit," says Maurice, holding out his hand to Bourdelle.

"And I, Monsieur Bourdelle, would like you to give Master Rodin our deep admiration for his work," Aleixo hastens to add, with general agreement.

"*Je vous en prie, chers amis,* there is no need to thank us; it has been a pleasure to receive you. And your admiration for Master Rodin's work will be passed on to him, *ne vous inquiétez pas,*" replies Bourdelle, saying goodbye to each of them with a further handshake, as strong as that which greeted them on their arrival.

Outside the weather appears to have changed, with high, heavy clouds rapidly covering the sky, and the wind blowing with increasing intensity, Aleixo notices as they once again walk around the house towards the avenue of chestnut trees.

"Well, Ribeiro, what are your impressions?" Maurice asks him after they have come to the road.

"Words do not exist to express what I feel," Aleixo responds, still not fully recovered and buttoning up his overcoat and covering his face with his *cache-nez*. "When faced with a work of such greatness, one feels crushed, belittled, trifling," he adds, somewhat disheartened.

"Attention, Ribeiro, not everyone can be geniuses like Rodin. Geniuses like him appear once every hundred or two hundred years. The important thing is that each one of us should do their best in the works they produce, using the knowledge they have acquired and all the creativity and imagination they are capable of. The capacity to judge our work is for others, Ribeiro," Georges is quick to reply with conviction.

"As Bourdelle said, Rodin shows us the way, the path to follow. It is now up to us to apply his teaching if we are capable of this. But without ever giving up our own identity, which is what makes us ourselves, unique and different," affirms Aristide as they are approaching the inn they passed when they arrived.

"*Bien, chers amis,* it is almost twelve-thirty," Maurice suddenly interrupts, after looking at his pocket watch. "What about having something to eat here before we go back to Paris?" he adds, nodding towards the tavern on the ground floor of the inn.

"Great idea. I'm starving," Georges immediately agrees, stopping at the door to the establishment.

"Let's go," says Aristide, joining him.

"Unfortunately I can't. I have to get back to my studio early," Aleixo hurriedly says, suddenly remembering the interview he arranged for three in the afternoon with one of the models from the Académie.

"I'm sorry, but neither can I," Helen Mears is quick to add, standing next to him.

"In that case, if you don't mind, we will stay," says Maurice, seeing Aleixo looking somewhat concerned at suddenly being left alone with the American woman while the others, after their goodbyes, go off to the tavern.

"I hope you don't mind me accompanying you, Monsieur Ribeiro," Helen hesitatingly starts as they walk towards the station.

"*Je vous en prie,* Miss Mears. For me it is an honor and privilege to enjoy your company," Aleixo replies courteously, yet unable to hide his discomfort in this situation. He, there in Meudon, all of a sudden confronted with a return trip to Paris in the company of his American former colleague at the Académie, with whom up to then he had never even exchanged more than half a dozen words, but whose presence had always disturbed him, he had to acknowledge. Because she was the only woman in Puech's class, attempting to succeed in a profession that was almost exclusively for men? Because of the reserved and distant attitude she normally adopts with their other colleagues? Or because of the sharpness of some of her rare observations? Wonders Aleixo as they walk side by side along the road in a heavy silence. A disturbing feeling that the successive glances she cast his way throughout the morning, first on the train journey and then in Rodin's studio—out of curiosity, interest, or something else?—only managed to increase, he realizes, as beyond the bend in the road he sees the station building emerge, not very different from the chalets he saw along the road and railway line, very sloping slate roof, red brick walls punctuated here and there by strips of painted tiles and finished off on all four sides by high pediments.

"Five after one," notes Aleixo after looking at the station clock when they reach the ticket office. With luck they will reach Paris before two, which will give him enough time to have a bowl of soup and a sandwich in one of the little restaurants near the station and get to the studio around three, he thinks as he waits his turn to buy the tickets.

"*Le voilà!*" he suddenly hears his American colleague shout next to him, now with the tickets in his hand and then also seeing the train, covered in successive clouds of smoke that the black locomotive ceaselessly emits from its thick chimney, coming ever closer until it finally stops at the platform with a screeching of brakes.

"What side do you prefer to sit on, Miss Mears?" asks Aleixo ceremoniously when they finally manage to find empty seats inside one of the second class carriages, as the train is full of groups of tourists and outsiders returning to Paris after a trip to the Palace of Versailles at the end of the line.

"Next to the window, if you don't mind," she says, moving towards the seat.

"So, Miss Mears…or may I call you Helen?" he asks after they sit down. "Nellie. You can call me Nellie," she answers, looking at him with a very serious expression.

"Nellie? Ah, Helen, Nellie. Like an anagram."

"No, Monsieur Ribeiro. It's rather more complicated than that," she adds, her cheeks suddenly blushing.

"What do you mean complicated?" Aleixo insists, intrigued, at the moment the train gives its first jolt before it starts.

"My real Christian name is Nellie, Nellie Mears," she says after a long silence as if she had been seriously pondering how far it was worth telling a stranger that sort of information, "but as an homage to an aunt who left me a small inheritance, with which I could continue my art studies at the Art Institute in Chicago, I decided to adopt her name as my artistic name, Helen, Helen Farnsworth. To which I only added my surname, Mears. Thus the name Helen Farnsworth Mears. *Voilà.*"

"That's funny. With me it was somewhat the opposite," responds Aleixo. "As my name was very long and complicated I decided just to use the first two surnames, Queiroz Ribeiro, and ignore the rest."

"A name with two surnames?" asks Helen, finding this strange.

"Yes. Six altogether: Queiroz Ribeiro de Sotto-Maior d'Almeida e Vasconcellos," explains Aleixo, finding her amazement amusing.

"Is it normal in your country for people to have so many surnames? Because in the States everyone has only one, or two at the most."

"It's normal for people of certain social classes."

"The nobility. Is that what you mean?"

"Yes. The nobility," replies Aleixo, ill at ease.

"And is it normal in your country for a noble to devote himself to art, Alexis?" she asks.

"No. It isn't very common. I must be the exception that confirms the rule. Traditionally, in Portugal, the nobles either look after the family properties or study law, or have a military career."

"So how did you manage to escape from that cruel destiny, Alexis?" she asks with a touch of irony in her voice, at the moment that the inspector enters the carriage from the front, then going along the aisle clipping the tickets of the many passengers.

"Well, with a lot of stubbornness and persistence. Unlike my mother, my father was always directly opposed to my artistic tendencies from the first signs. And as I showed no interest in Law, he decided to send me to the navy, to make a man out of me, as he said. But after six months I couldn't take anymore and I left, despite his protests. Only after his death, a few years later, was I finally able to devote myself wholeheartedly to art," Aleixo finds himself explaining, not fully understanding what is making him talk so much about himself to a stranger, above all a woman and a foreigner.

"Well, I was much luckier in that regard," she replies after a long pause in which she is absorbed in looking at the long fields on the left bank of the Seine that now and then appear in the background between the houses rising along the railway line. "Despite my family's much more modest origins my parents always unconditionally supported my vocation for art. But it was only with aunt Helen's inheritance that I could finally leave Oshkosh to follow it."

"Oshkosh?" Aleixo asks, amused by the sound of the name.

"Yes, Oshkosh. A little city in the State of Wisconsin, north of Chicago, near to Lake Michigan. Where I was born and lived all my youth," she explains, while he unconsciously finds himself thinking about everything that separates him from her—social background, country, language, continent—but also about the many things that connect them—art, above all, but also a taste for adventure, for the unknown—or else they wouldn't be two foreigners that chance brought together there, in Paris, the capital of the world, coming from to opposite ends of the planet, the South of Europe and North America, with the immense Atlantic Ocean in the middle.

"It also wasn't as easy for me as it might seem at first sight. To come to Paris I had to sell everything I had inherited from my father, and even so, what I receive per month is always too little. What keeps me going is the work that I manage to get, otherwise, I couldn't survive."

"Oh, yes. Those magnificent commissions you are working on, Alexis. the *Sacred Heart of Jesus*. And the bust of the Queen…"

"And fortunately a few others that appear occasionally."

"Well, the truth is that from that point of view I can't complain either, as I was fortunate enough to have received a major commission, right away in my first year at the Art Institute," she says, with a touch of pride.

"Really. How was that?"

"When I arrived in Chicago, it was the time of the preparations for the *World's Columbian Exposition,* a giant exhibition that was held the following year, in 1893, to commemorate the discovery of America by

Christopher Columbus. And the Wisconsin authorities, on finding out that there was a young girl from Oshkosh studying sculpture in Chicago, decided to invite me to make the statue representing the State of Wisconsin to be placed at the entrance of our pavilion.

"A great responsibility for a first commission, Nellie," remarks Aleixo.

"Yes. But the best was yet to come, as Augustus Saint-Gaudens, our greatest and most famous sculptor, liked the work very much. It was called *The Genius of Wisconsin*. And when the exhibition ended he invited me to New York to work with him, at the same time giving me the possibility to carry on with my studies at a school where he taught. And I stayed there for two years until I came to Europe."

"Why did you leave New York if things were going so well there?" asks a curious Aleixo.

"Because I thought I should expand my knowledge and come to see what was being done on this side of the Atlantic. Saint-Gaudens himself encouraged me to do so. In the meantime, alongside my classes at the Académie, I got work at the studio of another American, who has lived in Paris for several years, MacMonnies. Which is where I am going now, as soon as we get to Montparnasse."

"MacMonnies? I don't know him. And I had never heard of Saint-Gaudens until now."

"Obviously. Saint-Gaudens is very famous in America, but almost unknown in Europe, despite having studied in Paris and Rome and having had exhibited works at the *Salon*. Curiously, I received a letter from him a few days ago, telling me that he is thinking about opening a studio here alongside his New York studio. And asking me whether I want to go and work with him. I accepted immediately, of course."

"Well, it looks like we are arriving," he points out, looking through the window at the warehouses and lines that are starting to appear on both sides of the train.

"Already? I didn't notice the time passing because of our chat," Helen replies, surprised and noticing that the train is now entering the station.

"I wouldn't like to appear bold, but as it is almost two-thirty and we haven't eaten anything, I would like to suggest that you come for lunch with me before you leave," chances Aleixo, both of them now walking along the platform.

"Thank you very much, Alexis, but I'm already a little late. I'll get something to eat later on when I arrive," she replies, still walking hurriedly towards the steps leading to the lower floor.

"In that case let me thank you for your pleasant company," he says as they cross the main entrance hall, now on the ground floor.

"I should thank you, my dear Alexis. It was a very pleasant journey. It is a shame it went by so quickly. But no doubt there will be more opportunities."

"No doubt, Nellie. *Au revoir,*" he says, now outside on the sidewalk and holding out his hand.

"*Au revoir,* Alexis," she replies, her gaze lingering for a moment with her eyes wide open and a broad smile, before she turns and starts down the Rue de l'Arrivée towards the Avenue du Maine, while he goes in the opposite direction, along the Rue du Départ and immediately enters one of the many restaurants along the street, similar to those that can usually be found near main railway stations, whether in Paris, Bordeaux, Oporto or in Lisbon. Small, stuffy, noisy, full of people who are always in a hurry to catch the next train, or, like him, having just arrived and starving.

"Too many emotions for one day," he says to himself, sitting at one of the tables by the window, after having taken some spoonfuls of the succulent *soupe à l'oignon* that the waiter has just brought him along with a basket of bread, a dish of *fois gras* and a little jug of red wine. First, that extraordinary visit to Rodin's studio, which he is sure he will never forget for his whole life, and during which he could finally see and understand the Master's work completely. Then the sudden and unexpected journey alone with Nellie, so short, but at the same time so rich in the sharing of common feelings and concerns, thinks Aleixo, unconsciously recalling her gaze and smile when they were making such a long goodbye shaking hands. What could he expect from a woman like her? A simple friendship between colleagues in the same profession, who share common concerns and interests, or something else? He wonders, as he eats some bread with *fois gras,* which he accompanies with some sips of red wine. One would see, during their next meeting. He could invite her to go with him to visit the Musée du Luxemburg, or to take tea in the Bois de Bologne when the spring comes and it starts to be not so cold. Or even—Why not?—invite her to visit his new studio to show her his works, like the bust of the Queen, or the composition of the *Apotheose*. Or the studies he had already made for the statue of the *Sacred Heart of Jesus*, he thinks as he drinks his coffee, which the waiter had brought along with the bill. It is without a doubt a work of great complexity and size, particularly for someone who, like him, intends to make something original and different, both from the artistic point of view and in relation to the way in which the *Sacred Heart of Jesus* is traditionally seen by the Catholic Church, he finds himself thinking, as he now walks hurriedly down the long Boulevard de Montparnasse, wishing to get to the studio as quickly as possible. Yes, to take advantage of the stimulus received by seeing Rodin's works, the *Balzac* in particular, in order to analyze the several different solutions one by one, seeing strong and weak points, and trying to conclude which path to follow, he decides, as he reaches the crossing with the Boulevard Raspail, then carrying on towards the Rue de Notre Dame des Champs, where, at no 121 bis, his new studio is located. The building is considerably better and more recent than was no 71, where his last studio was, and its facade is clad in stone on the ground floor and with bare brick on the other floors between the masonry of the windows. The studio is reached through the entrance hall to the building and is at the back of the patio, being made up of a single division with double headroom, lit by a long side glazed opening facing north, against which, on plinths and easels, are the several works that Aleixo has been working on: *Apotheose*, still in clay, but now in its final size, a bas-relief called *Lisbonne*, which he intends to present this year at the *Salon*, and the last sketch he has made for the statue of the *Sacred Heart of Jesus*. On the opposite side, resting against the wall, are the remaining works that he had brought from the other studio, still in closed wooden crates. At the back, against the wall, a large rectangular work table, with two stools, and a sideboard with glass doors, in which he keeps the sketches for the several works, some in baked clay, others in plaster and some in bronze.

"Five before three," he says to himself, looking at his watch. The model from the Académie whom he has arranged to meet should be arriving at any minute and he still doesn't know exactly what to do, he thinks. Perhaps they will only agree on the working conditions and leave the sitting sessions for a better time when he finally has a concrete idea about the work, he decides as he lights the salamander stove, not even being able to take off his overcoat, such is the cold and damp inside the room. Then he goes to the sideboard to get the several sketches he has made for the statue of the Heart of Jesus, placing them side by side in front of him on the large work table, little pint-sized statues, two hands tall, made without great concern for correctness, deliberately imprecise in their outlines, with the sole intention of giving shape to an idea, to a gesture, to a movement. Then he sits down on a stool and remains there for a while staring at them and staring at them again, first from far off, then from closer, picking up one, then another, looking at them straight on, from the side, from the back, without apparently being able to come to any conclusion about which path to follow, dilacerated by the dilemma of always: How can Jesus hold his Sacred Heart with both hands and at the same time give out blessings to the city stretched out at his feet?

"Three-thirty," he notes, looking at his watch again: the man still hasn't appeared, and he probably will not appear. Just as well, he thinks, no point putting the cart before the horse. When the right time comes he will call for him, he decides, picking up the sketch album which was lying on the left side of the table, and flicking through it, slowly running his eyes over all the sketches he has made over the last months, sometimes in charcoal, others in sepia, and yet others in watercolor, most of which have to do with that statue. In them one can see representations of images of the Heart of Jesus in flames, crowned by a thorn-encrusted cross, along with others in which Christ appears in full-body, holding his Sacred Heart in two hands. Suddenly one drawing among the others calls his attention: in it one can see a tall, thin shape standing over an enormous rock, outstretched hand, bending over, descending the mountain. Yes, perhaps that might be the movement he is looking for, he finds himself thinking: "a merciful Christ, coming down the mountain, at the same time that he, from the heights, blesses Viana, Portugal, the World at his feet," he tells himself, suddenly full of enthusiasm. But what about the Sacred Heart? Where can he place the Sacred Heart, which is what the statue supposedly should be representing above all else? he wonders, as he again picks up one of the plaster sketches in front of him, curiously very similar to the drawing he saw in the album, trying to visualize it, squinting at it, upon the rock overlooking the Monte de Santa Luzia, behind the little chapel. "And…why not? Why not place it…inside Jesus' breast?" he says to himself, like someone who has just discovered gunpowder. Yes, instead of being held in his hands, the Sacred Heart can be set within his divine breast. Why not? Perhaps that will finally be the solution to the dilemma, he concludes, immediately opening a blank page in the sketching album and starting to feverishly draw with the charcoal pencil, one sheet after another, trying to find a shape for that idea in its most varied aspects, details, and viewpoints.

The sun has set on the horizon when, with the studio almost in darkness, his hands frozen and his eyes smarting, Aleixo puts down his charcoal pencil, exhausted but happy. Dozens of drawings are all over the table, purposely ripped out of the block in order to see them and compare them as they are finished.

V

INSIDE, IN THE GOTHIC HALL, it was a Miss Beach, somewhere between surprised and relieved, that received him, after George, the butler, had hesitatingly opened the door to him.

"Ah, John, thank God it's you," she said from the other side of the room. "I thought it might be another reporter. You can't imagine what this has been like. People telephoning, others knocking on the door, or even just coming in without asking. Anyhow, you must have seen them down there on the road."

"*Seen* isn't the word. Literally surrounded by them is more like it," exclaimed John, showing his irritation. "They almost jumped into my car to make me stop."

"What did you tell them, John?" she asked, apprehensively.

"What should I have told them, Emma? The usual evasive talk. The worst thing is that they already know everything or almost everything. Unfortunately, not everyone was able to maintain the necessary reserve, and the result is clear," John complained.

"And tomorrow they'll surely all be here bright and early to see if they can get anything. I honestly don't know what it's going to be like."

"Well, at the moment there's nothing else we can do except trust the police and particularly the Pinkerton detectives. By the way, did you speak to them? is everything ready?"

"Everything is absolutely confirmed, John, both with the Cheltenham police station and the Pinkerton Agency."

"Grand, grand. Changing the subject: Is my mother back from Norristown yet?"

"No. And to be honest I'm starting to get a little worried because of the time for dinner. Which is set for seven o'clock, as you know," she said, looking at her wristwatch, showing almost six.

"What about the guests?"

"No one's arrived either. Mr. and Mrs. Van Steuphyn are coming on the train from New York, which stops at North Station at five, so if there's no delay they should be arriving any minute."

"Do we know anything about Mrs. Palmer?"

"The arrival time at Central Station for the Chicago train was three o'clock, so even with some delay, she should be here by now. And she isn't, which worries me a little."

"You mean that her arrival is absolutely confirmed?" John insisted, somewhat incredulous.

"Without a shadow of a doubt," Miss Beach stated categorically. "We received a telegram this morning with all the information about the journey."

"And is anyone else coming from out of town?"

"Well, we have Mr. Stevens, but he won't take more than an hour to get here from his house, so that's no problem. We have your uncle Edward, who arrived late this morning and is out looking at the hothouses with your grandmother. As for the folks from the Portuguese Embassy in Washington and the Consulate in Chicago, although they are both in Philadelphia they were not invited to the dinner, and will only come tomorrow morning, straight to the ceremony."

"Fine. When my mother arrives tell her from me that the trip on the *Carmania* has been booked. I'll tell her the details later. And now I'm off before it gets too late," he concluded, turning his back at the exact moment that one hears the growing noise of a car engine coming from the upper side of the house.

"Ah, there. That must be them. They are coming down Juniper Avenue so as to avoid the journalists. Which I should have done," exclaimed John, going over to the window next to the entrance in time to see his mother's red Buick drive around the house and then make a 180-degree turn along the track leading to the *porte-cochère*, a large lean-to covered in ivy on the outside, which protected the entrance from the rain and snow during the winter and from the inclemency of the sun in the summer.

"It's her. It's Mrs. Palmer!" Miss Beach exclaimed at his side, in a sudden, enormous wave of excitement, before he realized that this lady with a haughty and serene face, beneath a wide-brimmed hat decorated with flowers and ostrich feathers, waiting very upright in the back seat for Jim the chauffeur to open the door for her, was not his mother and could only be Mrs. Palmer.

"Well, Emma, we have to go and greet her," he said to Miss Beach, at the same time as he fastened his collar button and tightened the knot in his tie before going to the door, which the butler, aroused by the noise of the car, had come to open.

"Mrs. Palmer, it is an honor and a privilege to be able to receive you here at *Idro*, here in this your home," said John, smiling courteously, having rapidly covered the difference separating him from the back door to the car, which Jim had just opened, right in time to take Mrs. Palmer's right hand, protected by a very tight-fitting white kid-glove that stretched almost to her elbow, to help her step out of the vehicle. "I am John, John Stetson Junior. My mother and the Count have gone to Norristown to deal with the marriage license and are not back yet, so I have to do the honors."

"My dear Mr. Stetson, the honor and privilege are mine," replied Mrs. Palmer, looking at him carefully for a moment with her large, dark eyes, while John slightly bowed his head to softly kiss the hand she held out to him. "Allow me to call you just John, which is how I heard about you from your mother, my dear friend Elizabeth, and from your late lamented father, for whom my dear departed Potter also had so much esteem and consideration."

"I wouldn't allow you to call me anything else, Mrs. Palmer," protested John, trying to hide his emotion on for the first time being in the presence of such an extraordinary woman, of whom it was said she had been a regular visitor to kings and queens, such as Edward VII of England, Albert of Belgium and even the Czar of Russia, here, in front of him, tall, elegant, energetic, despite the long, almost twenty-hour train journey she had just taken. "Despite only today having the privilege of meeting you, it is as if I have always known you, Mrs. Palmer, so many times have I heard my father and mother make the warmest references to your good self."

"Thank you, John. So we understand each other," she replied, making a broad smile.

"Did you have a good trip? I hope it wasn't too tiring," he asked, surprised by the apparent youth of her face, almost free of wrinkles, when, according to what his mother had told him in confidence, she was over seventy years old.

"It was excellent, John. I slept a good deal of the time. The train is quite comfortable. It is just a shame it doesn't always keep to the time-table. As indeed happened today. A delay of almost two hours."

"Mrs. Palmer, allow me to introduce Miss Beach, my mother's per-sonal secretary," he said, looking at Emma, at his side, dying of eager-ness at finally meeting Mrs. Potter Palmer, *The Queen of Chicago,* face to face.

"Mrs. Palmer, this is such a great honor," said Miss Beach, panting, her voice fading, at the same time as she slightly bends her knees and lowers her head, as if she were curtseying to a real queen.

"Pleased to meet you, Miss Beach," Mrs. Palmer replied haughtily, glancing briefly around and then taking John's outstretched arm and walking with him to the entrance, while Miss Beach remained behind, guiding Jim and Jessie, Mrs. Palmer's maids, to bring the bags indoors.

"Would you like anything, Mrs. Palmer? A cup of tea, of coffee, a lemonade?" offered John, as they reached the hearth, in the middle of the vast living room between the two wide doors in a scheme arch, giv-ing on to the sitting room and the music room.

"Thank you, John. I will have a lemonade. This stuffy, humid East Coast heat always makes me extremely thirsty. And no matter what they say, there is nothing better than a good lemonade to quench it," replied Mrs. Palmer, casting a curious gaze around the whole room, while John motioned to the butler, George, standing by the door to the kitchen, to deal with the lemonade.

"Mrs. Palmer, won't you sit down?" asked John, standing and lean-ing against the mantelpiece, gesturing to the sofas and armchairs dis-tributed around the hearth.

"No thank you, John. I was sitting for the whole journey," she replied, starting to slowly turn round, her head raised to the very high ceiling supported by long exposed wooden beams, then casting her eyes over the wooden balustrade all around the room on a level with the first floor, and finally coming to the walls lined with mahogany panels on the ground floor, with richly worked framings, and then settling on the three full arches set on columns with capitals through which one had access to the broad, two-flight staircase leading to the upper floor.

"What beautiful Gobelins tapestries your mother has, John," she said with a knowledgeable air, noticing the tapestries decorating the walls of the first landing of the staircase, before coming closer to look at them better.

"These were made over a design after paintings by Watteau. They are signed," John points out, also coming closer, and failing to understand why a lemonade, a simple lemonade, could take so long to be served. And there he was, seeing the minutes go by, worried about everything he still had to do before dinner.

"Ah, that bas-relief. What an extraordinary work, so unusual," Mrs. Palmer suddenly remarked upon noticing the enormous bronze panel decorating the whole length of the second-floor landing. "Is that a family member, John?" she asked, after going up the first flight of stairs in order to have a closer look at that figure of an aging man with a long beard sitting on a garden bench with his legs crossed, his left hand resting on a closed umbrella and right hand, holding a pair of gloves, stretching along the back of the bench, on which a hat was laid.

"No. But it's as if he were. That is Mr. DeLand, Henry Addison DeLand, Uncle Henry, as my siblings and I became used to calling him when we were children. A great friend of my father's, and with whom he created what later became the Stetson University in Florida. Near to a city founded by Uncle Henry himself and which was therefore baptized with his name, DeLand," answered John, hesitating a little before adding, "It was the first work that Count Eulália made for our family, a direct commission from my father. It was finished only a few months ago."

"Ah! So I thought. Indeed, here is the signature," confirmed Mrs. Palmer, raising her monocle to her right eye before spelling out, "Santa Eulália, 1908. It is certainly his style, no doubt. Grand. Expressive. He is an extraordinarily talented artist, Santa Eulália. And I know what I am talking about, John. I have spent time with many artists throughout my life. Some of them at a time when no one had seen their true value yet, like Monet, Pissarro, Degas…or Rodin himself, of whom the Count considers himself—quite rightly—to be a disciple."

"At the moment the Count is busy finishing another bas-relief of the same size, this time dedicated to my father. When it is ready they will both be sent to Florida to be placed in one of the buildings of the Stetson University," added John, relieved on finally seeing George coming from the kitchen with a silver tray on which he carried a jug with lemonade and a glass, followed by Miss Beach.

"I'm very pleased to hear that, John. That means that his work as a sculptor is beginning to be recognized here on the East Coast also, as it already is in Chicago. Where he has received many commissions, some indeed after a suggestion by myself. As is the case of the bust of Marshall Field, of my dear lamented Marshall. Another work that is a great success, very expressive," she replied, not taking her eyes off the bas-relief.

"It appears that you finally have your lemonade down there, Mrs. Palmer," John remarked, pointing to the butler and to Miss Beach, waiting on the first landing of the stairway.

"Ah, perfect," replied Mrs. Palmer, letting go of her monocle before beginning to go down the stairs towards the butler. "Mmm! How cool, how pleasant it is," she added after her first sip.

"Well, Mrs. Palmer, after such a long journey I imagine that you would like to rest a little and freshen up before dinner," suggested John, at her side, finally seeing the opportunity he needed to get away.

"Thank you very much for your attention, John. Indeed I am a little tired," she replied with a sigh, after drinking the rest of the lemonade.

"The cases are all in the bedroom and Jessie is now running you a nice bath, Mrs. Palmer," Emma took the moment to inform her pleasantly.

"Ah, excellent, excellent."

"In that case, Miss Beach will show you straight away to your rooms and I will take the opportunity to take my leave. I hope you have a good stay with us, Mrs. Palmer. We will no doubt see each other later on, at dinner," said John, moving away towards the entrance door, after a slight nod of his head.

"Thank you very much for your company, John. Until later on, then," replied Mrs. Palmer, now on her way to the staircase, closely followed by Miss Beach.

"What grace, what presence of mind, what elegance," thought Miss Beach, with a sidelong glance at Mrs. Potter Palmer, one of the most famous women in the United States of America for over two decades, there next to her, going up the stairs, very upright in her leisure outfit, lilac silk blouse and linen skirt, which go so well with the silver of her beautiful hair, completely visible now that she had taken her hat off.

On reaching the top of the stairs, Mrs. Palmer stopped for a moment and looked down at the impressive hall and then at the gallery that ran all the way round it on the first-floor level, here and there punctuated by different portraits on the walls. Above the fireplace, hanging from the balustrade, an enormous stuffed stag's head, which she pauses to admire for a moment before moving her gaze along towards the door giving on to the main wing containing bedrooms, next to which hung the portraits of Mr. and Mrs. Stetson, she looking straight forward, wearing a beautiful tiara, a soft and harmonious face, haughty gaze, enigmatic smile, frilled white dress with a full skirt and low neckline; he in profile, hair and beard now slightly graying, harsh gaze, austere face, very upright in his half-open black coat, showing his light gray waistcoat, white dress shirt with starched collar and blue plastron with white spots, decorated with the inevitable pearl dress stud.

Beyond the door, there was a long, wide corridor leading to the different rooms. The main guest room, where Mrs. Palmer would sleep, was at the end, next to that of Mrs. Stetson, which was followed by the bedroom occupied by the Count. Already inside, in the dressing room annexed to the bedroom itself, was Jessie, Mrs. Palmer's maid, unpacking the cases, while from behind the bathroom door one could hear the sound of water running, filling up the bath.

"Ah, Jessie!" exclaimed Mrs. Palmer on seeing her maid. "When you finish, come and help me undress," she added, crossing the dressing room towards the spacious bedroom, with a bow window shaded by a white and yellow striped awning.

"What a beautiful view," exclaimed Mrs. Palmer, leaning over the middle window in order to contemplate the large, well looked-after garden around the house, with its tall, leafy trees, revealing the little pond through the leaves, and, further on, the road.

"It is indeed a very fine view," replied Miss Beach from the door to the bedroom, as Mrs. Palmer turned back to the inside, only then noticing the magnificent Empire-style four-poster bed and the beautiful inlaid commode that occupied one of the sides of the room, while the other side was dominated by the fireplace, with two fireside chairs upholstered in flower print in front of it, and a small round table decorated with a beautiful flower vase and some framed photographs against the wall.

"What a nice bedroom, so harmonious. Your mistress has very good taste, Miss Beach," she exclaimed before adding, looking at the clock, "Good grief, it is almost six-thirty. At what time is dinner served?"

"Dinner is at seven, Mrs. Palmer. But as you and the Count are late, I think that it will not be served before seven-thirty, or even eight. But I will send word as soon as I know. And now if you no longer need me, I'll leave you to rest, Mrs. Palmer."

"Thank you very much, Emma," said Mrs. Palmer, before motioning to the maid, who had in the meantime come into the bedroom, to come over.

"Miss Beach, Miss Beach!" She heard George's loud voice shout from downstairs as soon as she entered the gallery over the Gothic hall on her way to the ground floor.

"What's the matter, George?" she asked leaning over the balustrade, signs of irritation in her voice.

"It's the organist, Miss Beach. He has just arrived. He says he wants to see the organ and rehearse for tomorrow."

"And what on earth do you want me to do, George? Send him into the music room," she replied, seeing the butler turn round and go off in the same direction he came from, and then herself continuing down when she noticed the noise of another car coming, like the last one, from the upper part of the property.

"Ah, finally, it's about time," she said to herself, starting to quickly go down the stairs and then, on the ground floor, almost run across the hall to the front door. Which she immediately opened herself, standing for a moment watching the car approach the *porte-cochère*.

"Ah, Ma'am, at last. I was starting to get worried," she exclaimed as soon as Vinny opened the door to let out a sun-blushed Mrs. Stetson, brown skirt and embroidered silk blouse, thin-brimmed hat and closed parasol in her hand, followed by the Count, double-breasted ivory linen suit and straw hat with broad blue band, stepping out of the other side of the car.

"The journey is longer and more tiring than one imagines. And then on the way back we got lost, imagine, such is the confusion of the path along municipal and national roads. Frankly, I do not understand how if Norristown is the capital of the county there still isn't a direct route from Philadelphia to it," complained Mrs. Stetson, raising her hand to her head to take off her hat, which she handed to Miss Beach, along with her parasol. "The Count even felt somewhat ill with so many bends in the road, didn't you darling?"

"According to the great Portuguese writer Eça de Queiroz, my dear José Maria, may the Lord keep him in eternal peace, 'motor vehicles make a horrible noise and give off an abominable smell of petrol.' And I, after a journey of almost four hours inside this one, have to concede that he is completely correct," replied the Count in his grammatically perfect English, albeit with a strong Latin accent, looking with undisguisable contempt at the beautiful black 1907 Mercedes-Benz out of which they had just stepped. "For me, there is still nothing better than a good *charrette*, pulled by two pairs of thoroughbred horses. Faster, more comfortable and above all more tranquil," he added.

"Well, I can see that I'm not going to be able to convince you that the motor car is the means of transport of the future, dear Alexis," Elizabeth replied.

"Perhaps of the future, dear Isabel, but we are talking about the present. And to tell the truth, in the present they leave a lot to be desired. Even such modern and sophisticated models as this one," said the Count, this time in irreprehensible French.

"Well, Emma, before I forget, here is the wedding license which has to be handed to Monsignor Turner tomorrow," said Elizabeth, pointing to a leather folder on the back seat of the car before going towards the front door of the house, this time determined not to carry on the eternal discussion about the advantages and disadvantages of motor vehicles in relation to horses and carriages, an argument she had kept on having with her fiancé since his arrival at *Idro* almost four weeks ago.

"Very well, Ma'am," retorted Miss Beach, going to the car to fetch the folder before herself going to the entrance door after the Count.

"Have the guests arrived?" asked Mrs. Stetson, standing inside the Gothic hall. "Only Mrs. Palmer. I have just taken her to the guest room, Ma'am."

"Bertha has already arrived? Oh, what a shame we were not here to receive her," lamented Mrs. Stetson, slowly walking towards the stairs.

"But fortunately John was here, and he took good care of the matter," replied Miss Beach.

"Ah, good. At least that."

"By the way, Ma'am, he asked me to tell you that the tickets on the *Carmania* are booked for next Saturday. And he will personally tell you all the details later."

"Excellent, excellent, one less worry. Did you hear, darling? The trip on the *Carmania* has been booked. At my request John went personally to deal with the issue," she said, turning back in time to see the Count, standing in the middle of the hall running his hands over his hair as if checking that everything was in place, after having taken off his hat.

"I'm very pleased to hear that, my dear," he replied, once again in French and walking towards her but suddenly stopping when he starts to hear a melody coming from the music room.

"It's the organist. Rehearsing for tomorrow," explained Miss Beach, seeing the surprise on his face.

"But that...that is...Wagner!" the Count exclaimed in horror, standing still in the middle of the hall.

"Of course it is Wagner, my dear Alexis. It is the wedding march from *Lohengrin*," Elizabeth explained, this time in perfect French, no doubt greatly helped by her French ascendance.

"But he isn't going to play this tomorrow, is he?" insisted the Count with disbelief, incapable of hiding his deep dislike at the sound of *Lohengrin*, which he heard reverberating around the ceiling and walls of the Gothic hall.

"That's what I had in mind, Alexis. But if you dislike it so much, it can be changed," replied Elizabeth, disappointed.

"I'm sorry, dearest Isabel, but the simple idea of marrying to the sound of Wagner gives me the chills. To make it worse, this horrible march, which is more like a funeral march than a wedding march," insisted the Count. "No matter what one says, for me, there is still nothing better than Mendelssohn's march. It is more joyful, more subtle, and more romantic."

"But, dear Alexis, Wagner...Wagner is to music what your Rodin is to sculpture...if I may make the comparison. He is the spirit of modernity, announcing this new century. This is the 'work of art of the future', as he himself stated..." insisted Elizabeth despairingly.

"Oh, no, my dear Isabel, allow me to disagree. One cannot in any manner compare the pompous and overwhelming artifice of Wagner's music with the subtlety and expressiveness of the sculpture of a Rodin. That is the true 'Art of the Future'," concluded the Count definitively.

"Well, Alexis, I see that we completely disagree, and so the best thing to do is to nip this in the bud," declared Mrs. Stetson, putting an end to the argument before turning to her secretary: "Emma, please inform the organist that instead of the Wagner march he should start rehearsing the one by Mendelssohn."

"Of course, Ma'am," replied Emma, immediately going off towards the music room, relieved at being able to get away and thus avoid being a witness to that unpleasant difference of opinions between her mistress and the Count on the very eve of their wedding, knowing of the enthusiasm that Mrs. Stetson had placed in the choice of that excerpt from *Lohengrin,* convinced that in this manner she would give a pleasant surprise to her fiancé.

"But my dear Isabel, I in no manner wished to alter your plans," insisted the Count politely.

"The matter is closed, my dear Alexis. You have every right not to like Wagner. Far be it from me to force you to get married to the sound of music you detest, as appears to be the case," replied Elizabeth sulkily.

"I thank you for your understanding, dearest," said the Count, unwittingly beginning to hum Mendelssohn's march, which in the meantime one could hear starting to be played.

"Well, Emma…What time is it?" Mrs. Stetson asked her secretary, who had just returned to the Gothic hall.

"A quarter to seven, Ma'am," replied Emma, after again consulting her watch.

"We will have to move dinner to seven-thirty. That is if all the guests are here. On the subject, is there any news of Mr. and Mrs. Van Steuphyn? And of Mr. Stevens?"

"Mr. and Mrs. Van Steuphyn should have arrived at five at the North Station. The train was probably delayed. As for Mr. Stevens, he still hasn't sent word, but he shouldn't be long, I think."

"I wish to be informed as soon as they arrive. And tell Millie to run me a hot bath and wait for me in the bedroom. And tell Bill to prepare a bath for the Count. As he will also wish to take a bath before dinner, isn't that right, darling?" asked Elizabeth, smoothing things over, before starting up the stairs.

"Yes, darling. Thank you," replied the Count, also going towards the first floor.

"I'll take care of everything, Madam," replied Miss Beach, turning and immediately going towards the kitchen.

VI

Paris, 5th of October 1897

"ALEXIS! ALEXIS!" he suddenly hears Nellie's unmistakable voice calling from outside the door to the studio.

"*Un moment, j'arrive,*" he replies from up on the scaffold, where for several days he has been working hard putting the finishing touches to the plaster of the *Sacred Heart of Jesus,* hurriedly putting away his gouge and serrated knife in his smock pocket and carefully starting to climb down the steps of the ladder one by one.

"*Ma chère Nellie, Nellie, vous voilà finalement.* I have been all over the place looking for you since I arrived," he says with a tense smile as soon as he opens the heavy wooden door, taking her by her two hands at the same time, which he kisses slowly one after the other. "I left messages everywhere: at the Académie, at MacMonnies's studio, and even at your house. But without any result."

"I know, my dear Alexis, I know. I got all your messages, but it was completely impossible for me to come earlier. And it wasn't because I didn't want to, believe me. You can't imagine what these last days have been like for me," she replies, turning her eyes away.

"Has something happened, *ma chérie?*" he asks, staring at her, unable to hide his concern.

"No, Alexis, nothing in particular. Just the arrival of Saint-Gaudens from New York, alone and more depressed than ever, I don't really understand why. All the more so as he has just very successfully inaugurated three works in different cities in the USA: Boston, Chicago, and New York. Indeed, the Boston piece is already being considered by many people as a masterpiece, *un chef d'oeuvre,*" she replies with a slight arching of her eyebrows, without seeming to show that she wants to swap the warmth of the sun on the outside of the door for the humid and cold atmosphere of the studio.

"So what justifies such a depressed state of mind?" asks Aleixo, intrigued and unable to fully understand why someone who, according to Nellie, is considered to be the greatest American sculptor of the end of the nineteenth century can be depressed after having rapidly inaugurated three works in a row, one of which, so it appears, is widely praised.

"I've no idea. But from what I know of Saint-Gaudens he is frequently given to crises of neurasthenia," Nellie responds, sitting down comfortably on the threshold. "The first thing he said to me as soon as he disembarked was that he wasn't at all happy about the result of the work he inaugurated in Boston, *The Shaw Memorial*. And therefore, he still had to make some alterations to it. This is after working on it for thirteen years, and with it having been cast in bronze and inaugurated."

"And how is he going to achieve a miracle like that?" Aleixo asks, finding this strange and sitting next to her, increasingly intrigued by what he is hearing about the surprising and complex personality of Saint-Gaudens.

"As he cannot change the final work, in bronze, which is in Boston, ready and inaugurated, he says he will alter the plaster model. Which he will have sent from New York along with the other pieces on which he is working," she replies, her eyes momentarily shut, the intense sunlight flooding over her smooth face.

"A veritable perfectionist, this Saint-Gaudens of yours. Has he at least found a studio in Paris?"

"It's best not even to talk about that," she says, opening her big, dark eyes. "Since he arrived we've done nothing else but go around looking from one place to the other, from Montmartre to Montparnasse, from Montparnasse to Montmartre. Indeed, if you must know, that's the main reason why I couldn't come here earlier because he made a point of the fact that as his assistant I had to accompany him on all his visits. Until today, when we finally found one he liked."

"Where is it?"

"That's the most curious part in the middle of all this. Because it is very near here, on the Rue de Bagneux, I don't know if you know it."

"The Rue de Bagneux? I know it very well. It crosses the Rue de Vaugirard, on the other side of the Rue de Rennes," exclaims Aleixo.

"That's the one. Indeed it was precisely that route that I took to come here. Incredible coincidence, don't you think? After so much looking it was right nearby that we found what we wanted."

"Well, I'm extremely pleased to know that we are going to be studio neighbors, my dear Nellie. Which means, among other things. that we are going to see a lot more of each other, isn't that right?" says Aleixo happily, putting his hand on hers and then intertwining his fingers with hers.

"Of course, my darling," she replies, nestling her head on his shoulder; he softly kisses her forehead.

"Oh, because of all this I am forgetting the most important thing: Saint-Gaudens wants to meet you, Alexis," she suddenly says, lifting her head.

"He wants to meet me? I am greatly honored. But why? What's the reason?"

"Well, I'm to blame because I couldn't resist telling him about you and about our friendship. That you were Portuguese, that we had met at the Académie, in Puech's class. And then, to my great surprise, he started talking about a Portuguese colleague that he had met here in Paris, at the École des Beaux-Arts, when he lived here at the end of the sixties. And with whom he became great friends."

"A Portuguese colleague. Didn't he tell you his name?"

"Yes. Soares… Soares something…"

"…dos Reis. Soares dos Reis," Aleixo quickly adds.

"Yes. I think that's it, Soares dos Reis," she confirms, trilling the Rs in the name. "Saint-Gaudens was a colleague of Soares dos Reis? Good Lord, what a small world it is. I couldn't possibly have imagined it. A great artist. It's a shame he died so young," comments Aleixo, genuinely surprised at this revelation.

"And from the moving way that Augustus spoke about him, they must have been great friends. That's why he wants to meet you, Alexis, perhaps looking for something in you that reminds him of that Dos Reis person."

"He might be a little disappointed there, dear Nellie. But I will obviously be very pleased to visit Saint-Gaudens one of these days, particularly now that we are going to be neighbors."

"Well, Alexis, it's four-thirty. Soon I'll have to go," she suddenly interrupts after a quick look at her watch.

"Then we'd better go in, even if it's only for a short while. I would really like you to see the plaster of the *Sacred Heart of Jesus*, just as it is now. I've been working on it since I arrived, correcting and rectifying it, but the more I alter it the more doubts I have. And sometimes an outside opinion can help, above all an opinion that is as authoritative as yours, my dear colleague," proposes Aleixo, standing up and then giving her his hand to help her up also.

"Amazing! Absolutely amazing!" she exclaims as soon as she walks through the door, no doubt impressed by the size and form of the statue, there, in the middle of the studio, its almost four and a half meters in height, impressive and extremely white beneath the pale light of the sun coming in through the back window. "*Mais c'est magnifique,* Alexis. *Absolument magnifique!*" she feels obliged to repeat, now in French.

"You think so? You really think so?" he asks, slightly insecure, as she takes a few steps towards the statue to look at it more closely, looking up, looking down, touching the plaster here and stroking it there, as if it were living matter, with skin, muscles, and bones.

"Your Christ is beautiful, Alexis, without a shadow of a doubt," she finally says, after a complete walk around the statue back to her starting point. "The expression you managed to give that face is extraordinary, a perfect symbiosis between the human and the divine, between suffering and compassion. And the subtle movement of the body, that slim and bent body, the tunic fallen to one side, which the right-hand helps to open over the thin breast holding the heart, while the left hand gives a blessing. All of this done with enormous clarity and simplicity of forms. The lesson of Rodin is there, learned and assimilated."

"Ah, but how I suffered to get to this, my God. From the first sketch, which I made a few days after our visit to Meudon, do you remember? The one over there in the cabinet," he says pointing to a plaster statue on one of the shelves of the cupboard, with its doors open and placed against the back wall. She gets it and then looks at it for a long time, at the same time looking at the plaster of the *Sacred Heart of Jesus* from a distance.

"The most interesting thing is that almost everything is already here: the slim, bent body, one hand on the breast and the other one giving a blessing, the posture of the head. All that is missing is the expression, the detail."

"Which was obviously the most difficult part. The face, the expression of the face, the posture of the body, the falling of the tunic...sessions and sessions with a live model in order to get that movement of the cloth that falls naturally over the body. And the hands, those hands, my God the trouble they gave me to get the right proportion and shape. But in the end, things started to gradually come together until everything started to make sense."

"I know exactly what that is like, Alexis. I started to feel it straight away in Chicago, with my *Genius of Wisconsin*. And since then it has been the same suffering over every work, even though my control over the technique and my knowledge of my own abilities is always increasing."

"The most difficult thing for me was getting to the final *maquette*, the one that when it was put into plaster I sent to Portugal, to the committee, remember? From then on, everything was more or less clear and defined, although the step to the final size also presented many doubts and uncertainties."

"Congratulations, dear Alexis. It is a beautiful work. Well, now I have to go. Saint-Gaudens is waiting for me over at the new studio."

"Are you going anywhere else today?" Aleixo says, surprised by all this rush.

"No. But I promised I would go to meet him there and I don't like to let him down."

"It's a shame. I thought we might take advantage of this beautiful sunny afternoon to go for a stroll, around Montparnasse or the Jardin du Luxembourg. After all, we haven't seen each other for almost three months, isn't that right *ma chérie?*" he says, putting his arms around her waist and then kissing her lightly on the lips.

"It'll have to wait until another time, Alexis. But I was just thinking.... Why don't you come with me?"

"Go with you? Aren't you going to meet Saint-Gaudens?"

"Yes. But that's it. You could come with me and then you'd get to know him. He would be delighted, I'm sure."

"You don't think it would be a little rude of me to turn up without any advance warning?"

"Not at all. In the state of mind that Saint-Gaudens is in, it will even do him good to talk to someone else besides me. And I think it's good for you as well. You never know what tomorrow might bring, and he's always got a lot of work, many commissions. And many contacts. Besides that, I'm sure he will like you a lot."

"Well, if that how it is, let's go," decides Aleixo, taking off his smock and then putting on his white linen jacket and his Fez on his head.

"After all this, you still haven't told me how things went in Portugal, Alexis. And in the letters you sent me you also didn't say very much…" Nellie wishes to know, as soon as they come out onto the street.

"Everything went well, thank God. Unlike what is happening here in Paris, there are a lot of prospects in Portugal. Besides a commission for another bust, two greatly important public competitions have appeared. Which I am thinking of entering."

"Really? So what are they?" she asks as they walk past the building where the last studio was, with the sun beginning to disappear behind the buildings on the opposite side of the street.

"One is for a monument in homage to a famous doctor and teacher at the Lisbon Faculty of Medical Sciences, Dr. Sousa Martins. A curious character from what I could understand, given that he was a man of science yet became renowned as a saint due to the way he treated and cured people," Aleixo explains, giving her his arm.

"What about the other one?"

"The other one is a sculpture competition as a part of the commemorations of the fourth centenary of the discovery of the sea route to India by the Portuguese, which will take place in Lisbon next year," he explains after they cross the Boulevard Raspail between the compact rows of hackney carriages, coaches and buses traveling in both directions.

"So what type of commemorations will be held in Portugal? We had the Chicago *World's Colombian Exposition* in 1893, also to commemorate the four hundred years after the discovery of America by Christopher Columbus. And Vasco da Gama isn't behind him in terms of importance, but rather the opposite, isn't that right?" she says, with sudden and genuine enthusiasm, no doubt imagining Lisbon full of new buildings profusely decorated with statues, around lakes with fountains and new, wide avenues like those that were built in Chicago.

"I'm afraid that our commemorations will be considerably more modest, Nellie. As you see, we are not America, we are a small country with few resources," Aleixo makes a point of explaining, curbing the enthusiasm. "Apparently the program has not yet been very well planned out. But it appears that it will basically involve a cortège, a bullfight, some regattas, and shooting events. Besides the building of an aquarium and some other artistic competitions with the theme of the discoveries. As is the case of this competition I have just told you about."

"Well, at least the subject seems to be more interesting and inspiring than the other competition, the monument to that doctor, don't you think?" she says, unable to hide her disappointment about the lack of boldness and ambition of such a program, that it is completely the opposite of the spirit of the acts one intends to commemorate, as they now come to the crossing with the Rue de Rennes.

"That was exactly what I told my brother. But he doesn't think so; he says the most important one for my career is the other one, the monument in homage to Dr. Sousa Martins. Because according to him it will be much more famous and much more talked about given that it is of a figure of nationwide importance, who is very well known and famous, not just among the elites but also among the working classes," replies Aleixo after they get to the other side of the street, where they go into the Rue de Vaugirard and, two blocks further on, the little Rue de Bagneux. More or less in the middle of this street, without anything suggesting it, given that this is an area with a predominance of residential buildings, on the right side there appear three big brick pavilions perpendicular to the street and separated by small patios. Number 3 bis is the third one coming from the Rua de Vaugirard.

"Ah, Nellie, at last, I was beginning to think that you had gotten lost," says the man who comes to open the gate as soon as Nellie rings the bell, with some irony in his voice. He is tall, thin, middle-aged, with a stern face, black hair, well-trimmed graying beard, and a very blue and lively gaze; without any doubt the American sculptor Saint-Gaudens in person, Aleixo concludes, while the other man looks at him with some curiosity.

"Augustus, allow me to introduce Alexis de Queiroz Ribeiro, my Portuguese colleague, and friend I told you about."

"*Enchanté de faire votre connaissance*, Monsieur Ribeiro," the other man replies in immaculate French, greeting him with a warm handshake.

"The honor is all mine, Monsieur Saint-Gaudens," says Aleixo.

"Come in, come in, please, otherwise it will be night soon and we won't see a thing," proposes Saint-Gaudens, pointing towards the door under the large glass panel that runs all around that side of the building.

"I see you speak perfect French, Monsieur Saint-Gaudens," remarks Aleixo, surprised, as they go through the door.

"Didn't Nellie tell you? I'm French on my father's side, despite being born in Ireland. And my father insisted on teaching me his mother tongue from an early age. And besides that I lived here in Paris for many years, which allowed me to perfect this beautiful language even more," he explains, as they walk to the inside of the first room.

"Yes. Nellie told me you studied here at the end of the sixties, at the École des Beaux-Arts."

"Where I was a colleague of your compatriot and my dear lamented friend António Soares dos Reis. With whom I fled to Rome when the Prussian army was about to invade Paris in 1870, on a journey full of adventures and risks. And once we got to Rome we shared the same studio for some time, in the Barberini Palace," Saint-Gaudens recalls nostalgically.

"I would never have imagined it, Monsieur Saint-Gaudens," Aleixo replies, surprised by this revelation.

"It's true. Indeed, it was in that studio, at my side, that he started on and finished the work *O Desterrado*, in Carrara marble which he worked on himself. A magnificent work, one worthy of an exceptional artist, of major quality."

"Did you stay in touch after you returned to the USA?"

"Yes. We exchanged some letters, in which he complained a lot about not being understood by his countrymen in relation to his art and about a lack of commissions from the authorities and powers that be. Until one day I got a letter from his widow, telling me about his horrible end, although without many details."

"A tragedy. A veritable tragedy," says Aleixo, upset.

"I ought to say that for me it was a great shock, one which left me deeply shaken for months. At the time I often found myself thinking that he might have been right: what was the point of this permanent struggle in favor of art and beauty in the face of all the unhappiness and suffering that goes on in this world? Up to what point was his not the best response to all our doubts and worries?" Saint-Gaudens states, distressed and moved.

"What exactly was this terrible tragedy?" Nellie can't resist asking, having been quiet until then, attentively following the conversation between the two men.

"Soares dos Reis put an end to his life with a pistol shot to his head, Nellie," Aleixo explains.

"My God, how horrible! What a sad end! How old was he?"

"Forty-two. Today he would be fifty. One year more than me," replies Saint-Gaudens.

"Still so young," laments Nellie.

"*Bien, chers amis,* enough sadness. Let us move on to more joyful matters. What do you think about this space, Monsieur Ribeiro?" asks Saint-Gaudens, leading them through the first room towards the wide double door giving on to the second one, both with extremely high headroom, which must be around six meters, six meters and a half, lit by the high, long *verrière* that runs around the whole north side of the building.

"It seems excellent to me: good size, good height, good lighting," replies Aleixo, looking around before they move on to the third room, separated from the second by a dividing wall that does not go up to the ceiling.

"Of course, these dividers are to be knocked down so we will have a single wide space. And then we will be able to work on several large works at the same time," Saint-Gaudens explains, after giving two or three hard bangs on the divider separating the second room from the third, to assess its consistency.

"It will be a great space, without any doubt," says Aleixo, looking about.

"Well, now we have seen everything, the best thing is for us to get out while we still have some light," says Saint-Gaudens, for moments, looking at the darkening sky outside through the large glass panel, then turning back to walk to the first room and the exit.

Outside the sun has completely disappeared, but there is still an intense glow that floods the sky from the west, spreading out in tones that successively go from red to orange, yellow, green, and blue until they are fused with the darkness of the night over on the other side.

"What a wonderful evening, Nellie exclaims effusively.

"Indeed," agrees Aleixo, also looking up at the sky, while they wait for Saint-Gaudens to lock the gate to the street.

"So you intend to settle definitively here in Paris, Monsieur Saint-Gaudens?" Aleixo wishes to know as they walk towards the Rue de Rennes through the Rue de Vaugirard.

"No. My intention is to stay until the *Exposition Universelle* in 1900 at the latest. And to see whether in the meantime I can achieve the same recognition here as I have received in the United States, alongside the great sculptors of my generation, like Dubois, Falguière, and Mercié," replies Saint-Gaudens when they finally reach the Rue de Rennes.

"What is your opinion about Auguste Rodin?" Aleixo cannot resist asking him.

"What I know of Rodin is mainly his works from his youth, from the time when I was here. Works with great strength and expression, which take a great deal from the classical tradition and from the Renaissance. I have been told very contradictory things about his more recent works. Some say they are masterpieces, others, monstrous. I have even been told about a statue of Balzac that was rejected by the institution that commissioned it to be made," he answers, stopping in the middle of the sidewalk.

"Which he is going to present this year at the *Champ de Mars Salon*, so it appears. Along with *Le Baiser*, which is another of his works of genius. Nellie and I happened to have the chance to see both of them at the beginning of the year when we visited his studio in Meudon along with a group of students from the Académie Julian," explains Aleixo.

"They are both remarkable works, Augustus. But Alexis likes the *Balzac* more, while I prefer the *Baiser*. Which would be your favorite too, if you saw them, I am sure," says Nellie in turn.

"I will give them my full attention at the *Salon*, where, indeed, I also expect to exhibit a good number of works," promises Saint-Gaudens, at the same time as he hails a hackney carriage that is going past empty towards Montparnasse Station. Having said their goodbyes, he and Nellie get into the carriage, while Aleixo remains standing on the sidewalk for a while, watching them disappear in the intense evening traffic before he carries on his way, on foot, towards Saint-Germain.

VII

IT WAS VERY CLOSE to eight o'clock when Mrs. Palmer, accompanied by her faithful Jessie, finally finished her lengthy personal preparations with a last gaze at the dressing table mirror, twirling her dress from one side to the other and at the same time giving some final touches to her hair with her fingertips. "So much trouble for a dinner, a simple family dinner on the eve of a wedding," she thought as she walked to the bedroom door. But after all, she was Bertha Honoré Palmer, Mrs. Potter Palmer of Chicago, *The Nation's Hostess,* as she had been called since the *World's Columbian Exposition,* and she thus had an image to keep up, whether for a group of humble workers in some factory in Chicago, at a great reception in the White House, or at a dinner as intimate and familial as this one. Which at the outset implied great care over her appearance, starting with her dress and finishing with her hairstyle, and including her jewels.

"Mrs. Potter Palmer's famous jewels," she said to herself as she walked along the gallery above the Gothic hall, as she looked at the other guests downstairs, waiting for dinner to be served, some sitting on the armchairs and sofas in the middle of the room, others standing and conversing in small groups. A dozen, if that many, including the bride and groom, Elizabeth and the Count, whom she recognized immediately right there, under the balustrade, before she started to go down the staircase and stop for a moment on the landing in order to once again appreciate the remarkable bas-relief of which he was the author. Why not commission him to make one of her Potter, her dear beloved Potter, who was at eternal rest? She wondered, surprised at only now thinking of the idea. Yes, a bronze bas-relief, at least of the same size as that one, to be put in the hall of Palmer Castle, her Chicago mansion on Lake Shore Drive. Yes, that would be a fine way of preserving his memory with dignity, in that extraordinary building he had constructed with so much enthusiasm and devotion for her, his Cissie, as he liked to call her. And it would be a little more original than commissioning Santa Eulália with a simple bust, like Delia, the second Mrs. Marshall Field, had done after the death of her husband, she thought.

"Bertha, dearest Bertha! You can't imagine the joy you give us, Elizabeth and me, with your presence!" she hears the Count exclaim, the pleasant Count of Santa

Eulália, with his unmistakable accent, tall, slim, well-tailored black evening dress, irreprehensibly well combed and middle-parted hair, slim mustache, turned up at the ends, walking towards her as soon as he saw her emerge from behind the portico of the staircase. What class, what bearing, what elegance, she thought. Whatever the truth was about his title, there was no doubt that he was a person of extremely correct upbringing. And an artist of great talent, as his bas-relief proved.

"My dear Alexis, the joy of being able to be present and to witness the sacred union of two beings I hold in great esteem and appreciation is all mine," replied Mrs. Palmer, majestic in her elegant dark blue velvet dress, gathered at the waist and low cut, a tight necklace made of successive rows of pearls, diamond earrings adorning her haughty, soberly made-up face, beneath her thick silvery hair, with an arrangement of ostrich feathers on top and a curled lock falling gracefully over her forehead, delicately stretching out her hand to the Count for him to hold and kiss lightly. "Indeed, a union towards which I am proud to also have given my modest contribution," she added, lowering her tone of voice, with a knowing half-smile. Yes, she clearly recalled that cold, windy afternoon when she took Elizabeth and John B. Stetson, who were on a visit to Chicago, to see the exhibition by a Portuguese sculptor that someone had recommended to her in the atrium of the Auditorium Annex, on Michigan Avenue, as they were looking for an artist who could carry out a work in homage to an old friend of John's, apparently the work which she had just appreciated again on the staircase landing. This was made after the long season that Alexis had spent in that house to draw the first sketches, she now recalled Elizabeth telling her. Was it there, when John was still alive, that everything had started? Mrs. Palmer could not help wondering as she looked at her elegant hostess, standing next to the Count.

"Dear Bertha, what a pleasure to finally receive you in this house,"

Elizabeth then exclaimed with a beautiful smile, before kissing her lightly on the cheek. Elizabeth was dazzling in her pale pink silk dress, with a beautiful pearl necklace wound three times around her neck and a magnificent tiara on her thin blond hair, tied in a bun. "I'm just sorry I couldn't be here to receive you when you arrived."

"You were not, Elizabeth, but your son John was, and he received me extremely well. A veritable host," exclaimed Bertha Honoré Palmer condescendingly, nodding slightly to the guests who were keeping their distance, waiting to be introduced to the Queen of Chicago.

"I am pleased to hear that John received you with all the attention you deserve. And which I, unfortunately, could not give you," replied Elizabeth, before turning to the closest guests: "Bertha, allow me to introduce you to Mrs. and Mr. Theodore Van Steuphyn, from New York."

"Mrs. Palmer, it is an enormous honor to finally get to meet you," begins Van Steuphyn, an elderly gentleman, tall, thin, shoulders bending under his slightly worn dinner jacket, thin and rosy face, thick white hair, raising the hand of this illustrious guest to his lips, "we have been devout admirers of yours for many years, my wife and I. Since your extraordinary success during the *World's Columbian Exposition,* to be more precise," he added, before he gives way to his wife, unlike him, short and round in stature, hardly fitting within a too tight moss green satin dress.

"Thank you very much, Mr. Van Steuphyn. Ah, the Columbian Exposition. Good times. How I wish today I had half the energy I had at that time," replied Mrs. Palmer with a touch of pride, as she shook Mrs. Van Steuphyn's soft, sweaty hand.

"And this is John B. Stevens, eminent Philadelphia lawyer and great friend of dear departed John," continued Elizabeth, then meeting, one by one, all of the other guests and family members who had in the meantime come over, keen to be introduced to Mrs. Palmer, the famous Mrs. Potter Palmer, there in flesh and blood, without a doubt, the guest of honor for the dinner and the wedding: her mother, Mary, her uncle Edward Harkness, her daughters-in-law Ruby and Helen, and finally her youngest son G. Henry, given that John no longer needed to be introduced.

"Bertha, my dear friend, once again my sincere apologies for the scant notice with which the invitation was sent," said the Count as soon as the guests dispersed around the room, taking advantage of that brief moment alone with his guest, given that Elizabeth had also moved away for a moment to give orders to the butler about the dinner, "but you cannot imagine what this has been like over the last few days. Things suddenly came on top each other, because of certain rumors that started to go around about Elizabeth and someone else... Indeed, an inappropriate intrigue, the origin of which has not yet been determined. Which forced us to bring everything forward in relation to what we had foreseen. And, obviously, to limit the ceremony to only family and some very close friends. But even so, we wished to invite you... Hoping that you would understand..."

"My dear Alexis, coming from anyone else such an invitation would doubtlessly be considered an insult, Mrs. Palmer bluntly replied, "But coming from you and Elizabeth I can only consider it to be extreme proof of confidence. And of friendship. As one only expects from some-one who is very close to us and held in high esteem. And who does not hesitate to go against all the rules of etiquette when it is necessary. "

"We never doubted for one minute that this would be how you would receive our invitation, my dear friend. Isn't that right, Isabel?" said the Count, turning to Elizabeth, again at his side.

"The important thing for us would be for you to be able to share this so decisive moment in our lives with us," Elizabeth then said.

"Because it is you, and only you, whom we have to thank for the fact that we met each other," added the Count. "Without your generosity and interest in the arts, Elizabeth and John would certainly never have visited the exhibition by an unknown Portuguese sculptor in the atrium of a Chicago hotel. And without this fact, we wouldn't be here today celebrating our engagement."

"All true, my dear Bertha. We owe everything to you. Including the words of encouragement you gave us to prevent us from giving up when faced with difficulties and to help us go on to the end. And neither of us will ever forget that, will we, Alexis?" added Elizabeth, resting her hand on her fiancé's arm.

"My dears, I am very grateful for your homages, but the importance of my contribution is only the slightest, particularly when compared to your courage and determination. Which, lamentably, was lacking to me in identical circumstances. And you may believe that there were many occasions. But at the moment of truth, I started thinking about Potter, my poor Potter, and what my children would say if they saw their mother, their own mother, married to another man. And then I would give up," said Mrs. Palmer, her voice choked with emotion. "For that reason, I admire you both, and you, in particular, Elizabeth, like me a widow and mother of two children, but who was capable of taking her feelings to the ultimate consequences. I admire you and that is why I am here to accompany you both on this last step. And with a touch of envy, I must confess," she added with a saddened smile, to the great surprise and stupefaction of Elizabeth and of the Count, hearing that sudden confession that she also had on several occasions considered the possibility of marrying again. Something about which the American press had indeed speculated over recent years, pointing out several pretenders, such as King Peter of Serbia, the Count of Munster or Prince Charles de la Tour d'Auvergne, among others, but which she had always promptly denied. With which of them might Mrs. Palmer have gone further, to the point of having seriously considered a proposal of marriage, only to give up at the last minute? That was the question that from now on was left hanging in the air.

"My dear Bertha, another reason for us to be eternally grateful to you," replied Elizabeth, relieved to see George, the butler, finally opening the doors to the dining room, at the same time loudly shouting: "Ladies and gentlemen, dinner is served."

"Shall we? the Count proposed to Mrs. Palmer, offering her his arm, while Elizabeth motioned to her eldest son, John, for him to accompany her towards the dining room from the other side of the vast hall, making his way among the other guests. It was a wide, rectangular room with tall windows open over the garden, walls lined with *grenat* damask silk, decorated with oil paintings and watercolors of landscape and hunting scenes above the English style sideboards. In the middle, lit by two enormous chandeliers hanging from the ceiling, a long, wide table, magnificently decorated with a centerpiece of roses and orchids. All around, on the embroidered linen tablecloth, the places were laid in Sèvres porcelain, George II silver tableware and a complete set of four crystal glasses lined up in decreasing order of height.

It was Elizabeth who took personal charge of distributing the guests to their places, starting with John, whom she sat for his last time at the head of the table opposite hers, given that from the following day on this place would rightfully belong to the Count, his stepfather. Elizabeth invited Mrs. Palmer to sit on John's right, and Mrs. Van Steuphyn on his left, while on her right she sat her fiancé and on her left Mr. Van Steuphyn. Her mother, her uncle Edward Harkness, the lawyer Stevens, her two sons, and two daughters-in-law occupied the remaining places on each side of the table.

"So, Mrs. Palmer, what do you say about the accident yesterday night?" cut in the lawyer Stevens as soon as they sat down.

"Accident? I don't know about anything..." replied Mrs. Palmer, surprised.

"The accident involving the *Mayflower*, the presidential yacht. It's in all today's papers. By a hair's breadth it didn't end up being a tragedy with unforeseeable consequences," Stevens went on, to the general surprise of those present, hanging on his words, while the servants, in uniform, began to serve the vichyssoise.

"An accident involving the presidential yacht? Where did this happen?" asked Mrs. Palmer.

"It was last night off Long Island, between New Haven and New London, at about one in the morning," explained Stevens. "It appears there was a thick fog, and so the crew of the *Mayflower* was not immediately aware of the presence of another boat, a schooner, into which the presidential yacht ended up crashing."

"Was the President on board?" Mr. Van Steuphyn wished to know, while the Count was engaged in tasting the white wine he had ordered from Rhode Island specially for the occasion, beneath the hardly disguised critical gaze of Elizabeth, who had absolutely exceptionally been forced to allow such a poison to enter her house, on the pretext invoked eloquently by the Count, that Mrs. Palmer was a demanding appreciator of good wine and it would be extremely bad form to disappoint her by serving only a glass of water or a cup of tea to accompany the meal.

"The President, his wife, his children, and some friends," clarified Stevens.

"Was anybody hurt?" asked John, interested to know.

"Fortunately not. Thanks to the *Mayflower* crew's skill and the fact that the other boat was much smaller and going slowly because of the fog the clash was not very violent. Even so, the schooner broke in two and then capsized and sank immediately.

"What happened to the crew of the schooner?" asked young G. Henry Stetson.

"The schooner's crew was saved shortly after the boat sank," John B. Stevens again clarified, being apparently the only one among the guests who had read the newspapers that day.

"Just as well. And how did the President react to all this?" asked Edward Harkness.

"The President and the other members of his party apparently did not even realize what happened, as they were all asleep," replied Stevens.

"Old Teddy always was a very heavy sleeper!" exclaimed Mrs. Palmer, pleased to show how intimate she was with the Roosevelts. In fact, her sister Ida was married to Fred Grant, son of the famous General Grant and great friend of the President. "According to the First Lady, no matter of state can wake him up."

"So, to the health of President Roosevelt. May he remain free of accidents and always be a heavy sleeper!" the Count proposed with an ironic smile as he raised his glass.

"The health of the President!" the other guests all said as one, including Elizabeth, having no other option but to raise her glass, but disguising the fact she refused to bring it to her mouth.

"*Bon appétit!*" she said, finally starting off the meal as soon as her guests set down their glasses.

"Hmm! What excellent wine, Elizabeth. What aroma, what lightness," Mrs. Palmer suddenly exclaimed, looking at her hostess with her glass in her hand. "*Un vin de Bourgogne? Un Chablis Grand Cru?*" she asked, in an almost perfect French.

"You must forgive me, Bertha, but on the subject of wine, I am completely ignorant. Wine or any other alcoholic beverage. Which, to tell the truth, I totally abominate. Indeed, that wine must be the first to be served in this house for many, many years, only due to Alexis's insistence. Perhaps even never, as my dear departed John also could not stand alcohol."

"I am sorry to disappoint you, my dear Bertha, but this is not a *Bourgogne* and much less a *Chablis Grand Cru*. It is a *Colares Chitas*, a Portuguese wine produced in the region of Sintra, on the outskirts of

Lisbon," the Count immediately cut in, radiant on seeing that a wine from his country, his poor, small country, was being mistaken for one of the best and most well known French white wines.

"My congratulations then, Alexis. I never imagined that such high-quality wines were produced in Portugal," Mrs. Palmer replied flatteringly.

"Mrs. Palmer, without wishing to be indiscreet, what can you tell me about certain rumors that have recently appeared in some newspapers that you are seriously thinking about moving definitively to the other side of the Atlantic?" inquired Van Steuphyn, while the servants, after having taken away the soup bowls, started to serve the *sole normande*, with potatoes cooked in butter sauce and French peas.

"My dear Mr. Van Steuphyn, do not believe everything that appears in the newspapers. I enjoy and feel very good on the Old Continent, where I have been received in the best manner everywhere. But you can believe that my homeland is and always will be America. And my city, Chicago."

"So this means you are thinking of staying here for a good while," concluded Van Steuphyn.

"Unfortunately not, Mr. Van Steuphyn. I have to leave within two weeks. Yesterday I booked a passage on the *Lusitania*. But at the end of the year I intend to be here again," Mrs. Potter Palmer promptly replied.

"The good thing is that with the *Lusitania* journeys between Europe and America have become much quicker and more comfortable. One goes from New York to Liverpool in less than a week," said the lawyer Stevens.

"Ah, yes. The Lusitania is an extremely fast ship. Perhaps the fastest in the world. It has gone far beyond the speed of the Deutschland, which was the previous holder of the transatlantic crossing record," said young G. Henry, as if wishing to show off his knowledge on the subject.

"And it only didn't do so on its maiden voyage because when it reached the American coast there was such a dense fog that it was forced to slow down. I was fortunate enough to participate on the first voyage along with some friends, among the over five hundred passengers traveling in first class."

"Oh, how lucky you are, Mrs. Palmer! It must have been an absolutely extraordinary experience," exclaimed G. Henry, totally charmed by Mrs. Palmer's bearing, as he also took a long sip of wine, watched reproachfully by his mother, seeing her youngest son also being corrupted by that poison.

"It really was a unique experience. Starting with the departure from Liverpool, with over a hundred thousand people waving goodbye, singing *Rule Britannia* as one. And then the excitement of that crossing, as everyone was fully convinced that the German record would be broken. Our Count here is the one who should be quite proud, as, so it was explained to me, *Lusitania* is what his country used to be called in the time of the Romans."

"I see that you are very well informed, my dear Bertha," the Count replied smiling, before taking another bite of that tasteless dry fish called *sole* but which had nothing to do with real sole, the sole caught off the coast of Portugal, thick and tender like nowhere else. "Lusitania was indeed the region occupied by the Lusitanians, which corresponded to a good deal of what is today Portugal."

"And as far as I know, when the builders called the ship the *Lusitania* they intended to pay homage to the great Portuguese discoverers, like Vasco da Gama and Pedro Alvares Cabral. Who gave new worlds to the world. Isn't that what is said, my dear Alexis?"

"My dear, I am truly impressed by your knowledge of the history of my country," the Count again replied, drowning his longing for a good Portuguese sole with a mouthful of Colares Chitas.

"So, as I understand it, within two weeks you will be back in Europe, is that right Mrs. Palmer?" Van Steuphyn asked, taking advantage of the pause to get back to the subject.

"That is true, Mr. Van Steuphyn. My sister Ida Grant, my niece Julia and her husband, Prince Michel de Cantacuzènes, of Russia, are waiting for me in Nice, on the French Riviera, for us to spend the summer together."

"Where you will no doubt see King Edward VII of England again..." insisted Van Steuphyn.

"No. Not on the Riviera, my dear Mr. Van Steuphyn. King Edward always spends the summer between Windsor and Sandringham. It is in Biarritz that I have had the opportunity to spend time more frequently with His Majesty, as he goes there for a season every year, in springtime. Albeit incognito, under the name of the Duke of Lancaster."

"Incognito? How is that possible if he is the King of England?" asked Van Steuphyn, surprised.

"Of course everyone, or almost everyone, in Biarritz, knows who he is. But in introducing himself as the Duke of Lancaster, neither he, nor anyone he comes across, feels obliged to follow the protocol due to a King. And he can thus behave almost like a common citizen and, for example, go for his enjoyable drives in one of the Renaults or Mercedes he has at his service, which he insists on driving himself," explained Mrs. Palmer.

"Perhaps that's why he is so popular in his country, 'Good Old Teddy'," exclaimed Van Steuphyn. "For example, who could imagine his mother, Queen Victoria, doing such a thing?"

"Driving motor vehicles has indeed become one of his favorite pastimes, along with dining with his friends, golf tournaments, and playing bridge. Curiously, one of the drives he goes on every year, at least once, is to San Sebastian, on the other side of the border with Spain, to meet his cousin, Alfonso XIII. Who in turn makes a point of also visiting him in Biarritz, always accompanied by a noisy entourage distributed over several motor vehicles. Which sometimes includes Queen Victoria Eugenie and on other occasions the Princesses, besides an enormous group of friends, who are always very lively in the Spanish style."

"Ah, His Majesty King Alfonso XIII. I had the supreme honor and privilege of being present at his wedding to Queen Victoria Eugenie, some years ago. And of being received by both of them in a private audience a few days later," said the Count, preparing to taste the red wine that one of the servants had just served him. "A beautiful, extraordinary ceremony, held with all pomp and circumstance at the Royal Church of St Jerome, in the presence of representatives of all the Royal Houses of Europe and the governments of all the civilized countries in the world. On the streets between the Royal Palace of Madrid and the Church, a crowd calculated at being of hundreds of thousands gathered to greet the bride and groom. If it weren't for that cowardly assassination attempt which by a hair's breadth didn't kill them it would have been a perfect ceremony."

"What assassination attempt? There was an assassination attempt against the King and Queen of Spain on the very day of their wedding?" asked Mrs. Shindler, surprised, now for moments abandoning the state of dumbness into which she had fallen.

"It is true, my dear Mary," confirmed the Count. "When, after the ceremony in the Royal Church of St. Jerome, the wedding cortège was going along the Calle Mayor towards the Royal Palace of Madrid, a dynamite bomb wrapped up in a bunch of flowers was thrown out of the window of one of the buildings, then exploding a few meters away from the royal carriage."

"Which fortunately missed its target, as both King Alfonso and Queen Victoria Eugenie were unhurt, without a scratch," John was quick to clarify.

"Yes John, that is true. But I was there and I saw with my own eyes that horrible spectacle of all those bodies torn apart by the explosion, the wounded and maimed screaming for help. Fifteen dead and almost forty wounded."

"But why? who would be capable of carrying out such an act of barbarity?" insisted Mrs. Shindler, visibly horrified by the event.

"It was an anarchist belonging to a group that called itself neo-Malthusians. The motto of which is 'do not breed slaves.' Imagine. And in order not to procreate slaves, they attempt to assassinate kings and queens. I will never be able to forget the huge roar that the bomb made when it went off, only a hundred or two hundred meters from me, as I was in one of the coaches in the royal cortège."

"So much hatred, so much fanaticism, good Lord, and what is it all for, anyway?" Mrs. Shindler lamented, before returning to her silence and her *filet mignon* with golden potatoes and vegetables that one of the servants had just served her as if she no longer expected an answer to her concerns but only that the meat should be tender.

"What happened to the man, the anarchist? Did they manage to arrest him?" asked Stevens, the lawyer.

"He went on the run through the streets of Madrid for a day or two, but when they finally caught up with him and he was surrounded he shot the guard who was about to arrest him and then killed himself with a shot in the chest," the Count explained.

"What an absurd business, so inglorious, good Lord," commented Ruby, John's young wife, looking somewhat dully at her plate, as if that vicious assassination attempt had taken away any desire to eat.

"Terrorism has indeed become the scourge of the turn of the century," said John. "If we count the number of kings, queens, and presidents who have been victims of assassinations, most of which have been successful, it is an endless list. Starting with President Lincoln and ending with King Carlos of Portugal, including Empress Elizabeth of Austria, King Humberto of Italy, King Alexander and Queen Draga of Serbia, President Sadi-Carnot of France, President McKinley, and an endless list of noteworthy personalities barbarously assassinated by lunatics or anarchists. Unfortunately without the police appearing to be capable of doing anything to stop it.

"This excellent red wine could easily be a St. Emilion, my dear Alexis, but after finding out that the remarkable white we have just drunk was a Portuguese wine, I am making no bets," said Mrs. Palmer, determined to change the course that the conversation was taking, which was too heavy for her liking.

"You are right not to do so, my dear Bertha. Because this is also a Portuguese wine, from the Dão area, one of our best wine regions, located in the center of the country."

"An excellent wine, without any doubt. It is a shame that the Portuguese wines are not so well known. But, returning to Biarritz, thanks to these meetings between the two monarchs, I had the opportunity to again see an old acquaintance of mine from the time of the Chicago *World's Columbian Exposition,* whose name has a curious coincidence with yours, my dear Count. Except that, unlike you, she is not a Santa, neither in name nor in behavior. I'm talking about Infanta Eulália, the aunt of King Alfonso XIII."

"Ah, yes, Infanta Eulália. I also had the opportunity to meet her during the reception after the King and Queen's wedding, in the Royal Palace," the Count was quick to say, as he prepared to eat another piece of steak, reasonably tender but without any flavor, particularly when compared to a good slice of Barroso veal from his beautiful, lush green Minho area. "And I even chatted with her for a short while, as she seemed rather well informed about America. And in particular about Chicago, a city about which she appeared not to have very good memories."

"To be honest, the city of Chicago also does not have very good memories of her. And I most certainly do not. Although it was Infanta Eulália who represented the Regent of Spain, Maria Christina, mother of the future King Alfonso XIII, who at the time was no more than six or seven years old, at the opening ceremonies for the Exposition in which Spain obviously had a special role, as this was a commemoration of the four centuries after the discovery of America by Christopher Columbus in the service of the Spanish Crown."

"Indeed, Infanta Eulália. Now I recall the whole controversy, which appeared in great detail in the newspapers of the time, about the rude and ill-mannered way that the Infanta behaved at a reception held in your house, isn't that true Mrs. Palmer?" Van Steuphyn suddenly remembered.

"True, Mr. Van Steuphyn. Although Infanta Eulália had been received with full honors due to a queen, nothing seemed to be enough for her. And in fact, one of the high points of her visit was the reception given in her honor in my house. Present at which were the most important personalities from the administration, from the world of finance and from the arts and culture, not only from the United States but from many other countries. Yet it was only after great insistence from her country's ambassador that she agreed to be present, but even so, she arrived an hour late. Merely because when she was preparing to leave Palmer House, which was built by my dear departed husband and at the time was the best hotel in Chicago, she discovered that there was no red carpet laid out at the entrance for her royal feet!"

"Ah, how pretentious, how ridiculous, good grief!" a scandalized Mrs. Van Steuphyn exclaimed.

"And when she arrived she was irritated, hostile, and annoyed. When I began to introduce her one by one to all those illustrious personalities who had come on purpose to meet and greet her, I noticed that she hardly looked at them and much less paid any attention to their names, as if she was making a great effort to be there. Suddenly, less than an hour after her arrival, at the precise moment when, after the champagne and Roman Punch, the supper was about to be served, she turned round and walked out without saying goodbye or giving any explanation, then returning to the hotel beneath the huge storm that had in the meantime fallen upon the city."

"What led her to such a lack of consideration for you and your illustrious guests, Mrs. Palmer?" insisted a shocked Mrs. Van Steuphyn.

"According to what I was told in private later on, she did not like the idea that the reception in her honor was given in the house belonging to the owners of the hotel where she was staying, and then disdainfully and haughtily baptized me the *Innkeeper's Wife*. Probably thinking she would offend me considerably in this manner, when, quite the contrary, I am immensely proud to have married such an innkeeper, someone as enterprising as Potter Palmer, who didn't need protection from his family or his blue blood to mark out a position and become someone in life. Capable of making, among many other things, a hotel like that one," explained Mrs. Palmer proudly, at the same time giving up on the steak and setting her cutlery down on the plate, as if those memories had suddenly made her lose her appetite.

"And so thanks to the contact between the monarchs of Spain and England you came across your old acquaintance again, isn't that right Mrs. Palmer?" insisted the tireless Mr. Van Steuphyn.

"Indeed. I saw her again about a year ago, in Biarritz. And since then we have met somewhat assiduously, mostly in Paris, curiously more at her insistence than mine, one should say."

"Then you have buried the hatchet, Mrs. Palmer?" the lawyer Stevens asked with a smirk.

"Not exactly, Mr. Stevens. Her attitude towards me became something else, something radically different. Perhaps because she noticed the kindly and warm manner in which King Edward receives me. Me, the *Innkeeper's Wife*, from Chicago. Only a few months ago I had the pleasure of dining with him in Biarritz."

"Some reception to honor an illustrious visitor? Perhaps King Alfonso of Spain? Or the Infanta Eulália herself?" Van Steuphyn returned to the attack as the servants began to take away the dessert plates.

"No, Mr. Van Steuphyn. In Biarritz, the dinners are always very intimate, around a table with eight places, only for very close friends. Carefully chosen by Sir Ernest Cassel, one of the King's closest friends, along with an old acquaintance of yours, Alexis."

"An old acquaintance of mine?" The Count found this strange.

"Yes, *Blue Monkey*."

"*Blue Monkey*?" The Count became even more surprised. "No, my dear Bertha, there must be some mistake. I don't know anyone of that name..."

"Yes you do, Alexis. It is the Marquis of Soveral, Minister of Portugal in London. Don't tell me you didn't know he was known as *Blue Monkey*?"

"The Marquis of Soveral? *Blue Monkey*? No, I didn't have the slightest idea," the Count replied with an enormous guffaw. "And so what is the reason for this nickname?"

"It is because of the color of his face, what else would it be? Always bluish, no matter how much he shaves, poor man," Mrs. Palmer replied, also laughing, laughter that quickly spread to the other guests.

"It's true that the Marquis has a very thick beard. But to go on from that to call him *Blue Monkey*…is a little harsh," responded the Count, unable to stop laughing, no doubt imagining Soveral's face, as bony as that of a boxer, with his always bluish beard emerging.

"But apart from that he is a remarkable figure, very highly regarded in the court, with his monocle and Kaiser Wilhelm style mustache. The King really enjoys hearing his stories. Some people even say that he and Sir Ernest Cassel are as close to the throne as were Palmerston and Beaconsfield in the time of Queen Victoria.

"Which is rather surprising, given that he is the ambassador of a foreign country," commented John, somewhat acrimoniously.

"The Marquis of Soveral is indeed an extraordinary figure, a brilliant diplomat who always had the total trust of Dom Carlos, may God keep his eternal soul," explained the Count, turning to John. "And King Carlos and King Edward, besides being cousins, were great friends, were very similar, even in their tastes, in physical appearance and in character. So I am not surprised at that intimacy between the Marquis and King Edward VII, despite the circumstance of him being the ambassador of a foreign country. But one which is England's oldest ally, one should not forget."

"Which did not release Portugal from an unfortunate Ultimatum given by that same old ally," retorted John, not wishing to leave the plaudits for knowledge of history to someone else.

"Unfortunately the minor, selfish interests of countries do not sympathize with historical ties and personal friendships, my dear John. And that sad episode serves to demonstrate it. Indeed, if it were not for Soveral's extraordinary diplomatic skill, after being named ambassador to London precisely at that time, the consequences of this unfortunate episode would have been much worse for Portugal."

"Well, I can tell you that your admiration shown for him is entirely reciprocated, as *Blue Monkey* spoke to me about you in highly glowing terms, both as an artist and as a diplomat," Bertha Palmer made a point of stating.

"The Marquis is too generous a person," the Count retorted humbly, as Elizabeth gazed adoringly.

"I recall him telling me that you had been the victim of a tremendous injustice in Lisbon, Alexis. Something to do with a statue of yours that was not very well received," added Mrs. Palmer.

"Ah, that…At the time it was in fact a very unpleasant situation. But what is done is done…" said the Count, ill at ease, not appearing to be at all interested in developing the subject.

"Well, judging by what the Marquis said, it was much more than an unpleasant situation, Alexis," she insisted, surprised by the Count's reaction. "According to Soveral, King Carlos himself took a personal interest in the subject given the esteem and personal consideration he had for you and for your work. To the point of having commissioned a statue of Queen Amelia to you."

"Which unfortunately only now, a few months ago, was I able to finish, after the barbarous assassination of King Carlos and Prince Luiz Filipe."

"Where is the statue now?" Mrs. Palmer wished to know.

"In Chicago. But I want to see if I can have it shipped to Portugal so it can be placed in a Lisbon square or one of the royal palaces."

"It is an absolutely extraordinary statue, Bertha. You must go and see it," said Elizabeth, glowing with pride.

"Well, I hope that when I come back from Europe there will still be time."

"Let us hope so," replied the Count, while he nodded an order to one of the servants to serve the Port to the other guests. After this he stood up and raised his glass very high:

"This Port wine is an 1868 Vintage, considered to be one of the best of the whole of the nineteenth century. It so happens that 1868 is also, due to a happy coincidence, the year in which I had the joy of coming into this world. And thus it is with this precious nectar that I wish to offer a toast to Elizabeth, my darling Isabel, who has agreed to share the rest of her life and her destiny with me. To Elizabeth's health!"

"Elizabeth's health!" all those present shouted in a chorus, standing up and raising their glasses high, with the exception of Elizabeth herself, slightly blushing and with a glowing smile for her fiancé.

"And I, as the bride's uncle, and in the absence of her father, God keep him in eternal rest, propose a toast to the health of the Count of Santa Eulália, who with his noble ascendency and his remarkable talent as an artist, along with his kindness and generosity, has conquered the heart of my dearest niece Elizabeth. The health of the Count! *Hip! Hip! Hurrah!*" Edward Harkness added.

"Well, it would look bad if I, an old friend of the bride's family, and in particular of her late husband, did not also propose a toast: To the bride and groom!" the lawyer Stevens added lastly.

"This is in fact a divine nectar," said Van Steuphyn, consoled, when the toasts were finally over and everyone sat down.

"It's true! A taste and aroma that are absolutely *exquis*," agreed Mrs. Palmer, after making a slight clicking sound with her tongue. "It is an excellent way to finish off such a delicious meal. My congratulations to you also, my dear Elizabeth. Everything was perfect."

"Thank you very much, my dear Bertha. You are most kind. Now I suggest we retire to the sitting room, where the coffee will be served," Elizabeth said as a conclusion, standing up and followed by the other guests.

VIII

"MR. QUEIROZ RIBEIRO, how are you? Very good to see you," exclaims the Consul with his hand stretched out as he receives him at the door to his office. Elegant and well turned-out as always with a dark-blue, well-cut suit and polished boots, a silk plastron with pearl-pin, with a white handkerchief in his lapel pocket, but Aleixo cannot help noticing, thinner and paler than the last time, as he is led by his host into the room.

"The pleasure is all mine, Consul sir," he replies after the diplomat has indicated one of two green leather armchairs placed either side of the fireplace, while he himself sits on the sofa on the other side.

"You cannot imagine how sorry I am for not having been able to attend the ceremony for your decoration of honor by Emperor Menelik last week at the Embassy. But I have been confined to my house until recently, bothered by a very strong flu as well as some malarial fevers, something which attacks me from time to time," the Consul feels obliged to say as a justification, as he crosses his skinny legs and leans back on the sofa. "However, Minister Sousa Rosa came to my house on Sunday and was kind enough to inform me about everything. A marvelous ceremony, no doubt?"

"Indeed, Consul. And completely unexpected for me, as the work at the origin of this honor was completed and delivered over two years ago. But, so it seems, His Majesty Emperor Menelik made a point of waiting for a previously promised and long-delayed State Visit to Paris to decorate me personally, which for me is obviously an enormous honor."

"An honor that I am immensely sorry not to have been able to share with you personally, believe me, my dear Queiroz Ribeiro, but life is like that, occasionally it has surprises for us."

"I am also sorry, Sir, because of everything that you represent, not just for our diplomacy, but also and above all for our culture. And you may believe that it was with great concern that I learned from Minister

Sousa Rosa of the strong disquiet that kept you housebound, preventing you from being present. However, I am pleased to know that you are totally returned to health," replies Aleixo, as he notices the deep shadows under his eyes, his thin, pale face, his slender, pointed nose, his wide, sunken mouth, showing the yellowing teeth under his thick mustache.

"I cannot exactly say 'totally.' These things always take time to cure, but at least I am not worse, thank God. But, returning to the issue of your honor, I ought to tell you that Minister Sousa Rosa was very favorably impressed by the personality of the Negus, as he is a man of extremely refined education and, as well as this, speaks impeccable French. And even more by the consideration and personal esteem that he appears to have for you, Mr. Queiroz Ribeiro, as is indeed proven by the insignia he chose to award you. Which, according to Sousa Rosa, corresponds to one of the highest orders in the country, with these being his words, 'of a beauty and richness that are difficult to equal'," the Consul makes a point of stressing as he struggles to readjust the monocle on his right eye.

"It indeed is a beautiful insignia, the Grand Order of the Star of Ethiopia," Aleixo proudly agrees.

"And certainly well deserved, given that, according to what Sousa Rosa told me, the Emperor offered glowing praise of you in the speech he gave during the ceremony. Stressing not only your qualities as an artist but also your courage and fearless spirit in agreeing to go off to Abyssinia in the middle of a war against the Italian invader," continues the Consul, also seeming to be thoroughly impressed by the subject.

"Well, His Majesty Emperor Menelik is a person of great kindness and generosity. Because in fact, all I did was go there and do my job the best I could, nothing more," replies Aleixo.

"Come on, Queiroz Ribeiro, let's have no false modesty. It isn't every day that a Portuguese citizen receives such a decoration, especially because of a statue," insists the Consul.

"Not a statue, Sir, a medallion."

"A medallion?"

"Yes. A bronze medallion. That served as the base for coining the currency of the country. And which then ornamented the throne room," Aleixo makes a point of clarifying.

"You mean that to make a simple medallion you had to travel to Abyssinia? Wasn't it possible to do the work here, from some drawings or photographs?" The Consul finds this strange, no doubt not familiar with the particular aspects of the difficult art of sculpture.

"It would be possible, but it certainly wouldn't be the same thing, Consul. Nothing can replace the sittings with a live model, particularly when one wishes to capture the spirit, the character, and the soul of the person portrayed."

"And so, in order to capture the soul of the person portrayed you ignored the risks and sacrifices and went off to Abyssinia without even worrying about the fact that the country was at war with a European power. A real adventure, then?" comments the Consul with a fleeting grimace, a mixture of surprise and mocking.

"It is true. An extraordinary adventure, Sir. Starting with the journey and ending in the sittings with the Emperor, in an improvised studio in the palace itself. Taking advantage of the breaks between the fierce battles against the Italian army," Aleixo recalls with enthusiasm while the Consul looks at him, surprised.

"I can imagine the Emperor dusting off his uniform before taking up his pose. And you facing him, shaping the clay like his curly hair and little beard," says the Consul General of Portugal in Paris with a mocking grin, now suddenly turned into the figure of the famous writer José Maria Eça de Queiroz.

"Well, he always had a good bath after each battle. And only after being washed and perfumed would he be ready to pose," Aleixo replies by the same token.

"In any case, the idea of the sittings between battles is fantastic, worthy of a true adventure novel. Which I would be pleased to write. The artist waiting patiently in the palace for the Emperor to arrive, again returning from a ferocious and horrific battle against the invading army. From which he may as easily return as victor or vanquished, dead or alive," insists Eça de Queiroz with a feverish gaze, as if his imagination as a writer had suddenly transported him to Menelik's palace in Addis Ababa, the capital of Abyssinia.

"They indeed were unique, unforgettable moments," replies Aleixo, starting to see time going by without knowing how to put an end to this conversation and say why he has come before it is too late.

"You know, I also know a little about those lands in the Middle East. In 1869, I and my friend the Count of Resende, who today is my brother-in-law, decided to go to see the inauguration of the Suez Canal," continues Eça, lost in his conversation, as if it were nothing. "And then we visited Egypt, Syria, Lebanon, and Palestine. A journey about which I have extraordinary memories. In fact, it was because of this that I was able to write my novel *The Relic*.

"Ah, yes, *The Relic*, a greatly original and humorous novel. Which I read with great pleasure and amusement," replies Aleixo, unable to hold back a guffaw as he suddenly recalls the unforgettable scene of the exchange of packages when the character Raposão gives the relic to Tia Patrocínio.

"In any case, it is rather surprising that this whole adventure took place from here, from Paris, with neither I nor Minister Sousa Rosa, knowing anything about it," insists Eça, to Aleixo's growing nervousness.

"Well, the medallion was exhibited at the *Salon*, two years ago. Where it, in fact, caused great controversy because of the attacks by some Italian newspapers, unhappy about the overwhelming defeat that Menelik's army had just inflicted on them," Aleixo feels he has to answer.

"You know, that is my fault because I have little patience for those gatherings in which art, more than being the reason for the visit, is only the pretext for all those people to exhibit themselves and be seen," Eça de Queiroz replies with an expression full of disdain.

"Yes, I very well recall having read a curious and amusing article you wrote about the *Salon*, in which you precisely placed the emphasis more on the visitors than on the art. Even describing in great detail not the works, but rather the outfits of two ladies who were strutting around the exhibition space," Aleixo says, reminding him of the article that his brother Gaspar showed him on one of his stays in Portugal, criticizing the lack of interest that in his opinion Eça de Queiroz showed for the fine arts.

"Ah, yes. But that was an article I wrote some years ago for a magazine published in Brazil, in 1894, if my memory serves me well. And, well, the Brazilians, so far away, on the other side of the Atlantic, if I had started to describe, one by one, the over three thousand artworks present at the *Salon*, they would have no doubt thought the article to be a huge, monumental bore," the writer says in justification.

"But perhaps they would have liked to know that among those three thousand there were twenty or thirty by Portuguese and Brazilian artists, among them one by yours truly. And, if you will allow me the suggestion, perhaps they might not have minded very much to read a short description or critical reflection on each of them," Aleixo boldly states.

"Indeed. I am sorry I did not notice those works you are referring to, neither yours nor those of the other Portuguese and Brazilian artists. Otherwise, besides those women whose outfits I described in detail, I would also have at least mentioned the two works by a timid Portuguese sculptor who on his own managed to do what the well-armed Italian army was unable to do: to conquer the heart and soul of the Emperor of the Abyssinians," Eça de Queiroz once again replies with a wide grin.

"To keep them inside a bronze medallion. Which through your suggestive words the Brazilian readers would finally be able to 'see' and understand," finishes Aleixo, returning the joke.

"However, it surely was not to talk about your adventures in the land of Prester John that you came here, isn't that so?" Eça de Queiroz finally decides to change the course of the conversation after a quick look at his pocket watch, showing the hands dangerously approaching three o'clock in the afternoon.

"In fact, it was not, Consul. What brings me here is another matter. It is about sending a work of mine to Portugal," replies Aleixo, relieved at finally being able to say why he is there.

"Really? What work is it?" Eça de Queiroz wishes to know, for moments once again assuming his position as Consul General of Portugal in Paris.

"It is a statue of the *Sacred Heart of Jesus*, which is to be placed at the top of Monte de Santa Luzia, in Viana do Castelo."

"Monte de Santa Luzia? A superb panorama, without equal when one looks down from the top..." Eça de Queiroz recalls, a sudden expression of melancholy appearing in his gaze.

"True. Absolutely extraordinary, unique," agrees Aleixo.

"Was the statue made here in Paris?"

"Yes. From the first clay models to the bronze, which was only finished a few days ago. Now it will go by ship to Lisbon and then to

Viana."

"Then I presume that it is because of this trip that you need the services of the consulate," says the Consul, his shrewd gaze looking at him from behind his monocle. "Indeed it is, Sir. In order not to pay entry duty to Portugal it is necessary to have a declaration from the consulate certifying that it is a work carried out by a Portuguese artist residing temporarily abroad."

"When do you need the document?"

"If possible today, or tomorrow morning at the latest, Consul. I know it is extremely bold of me to come here and ask you this so close to the event, but the truth is that I was only told of the need for the document this morning."

"Well, it is possible to have it done, as long as you can give me all the identification data about the work: description, origin, destination, etc.," replies the Consul.

"It's all here, Consul," Aleixo promptly says, taking a piece of folded paper from the inside pocket of his overcoat and handing it to the Consul.

"Ah, very good. Let me have a minute with the Chancellor to see the best way to deal with the matter," replies Eça de Queiroz, already on his way to the door after a quick glance at the piece of paper. While he listens to the two men exchanging impressions in a low voice on the other side of the door Aleixo casts a glance around the Consul's office, noting the heavy, Empire style ebony desk covered in papers, with two bookshelves of the same wood behind it, full of books and ornaments, then looking at the inevitable Map of Portugal and the Colonies, now yellowed and worn, hanging over the fireplace, where a lively, crackling fire continues to burn.

"Right. Everything is being taken care of. Just a few moments and the Chancellor will bring the document," adds Eça, after closing the door and returning to his place.

"I am eternally grateful to you, Sir," Aleixo thanks him, relieved, at the exact moment that one starts hearing a deafening noise coming from outside in the street. Eça de Queiroz springs up from the sofa to the window, which he opens slightly, indifferent to the icy cold, in time to see a large black motor vehicle parked in front of the building, without its driver showing any signs of wishing to turn off the noisy engine, definitively putting an end to the continuous explosions that shake it and the billows of smoke that come out of the exhaust pipe.

"These motor vehicles are truly infernal machines: they make a horrible noise and they give off an abominable smell of petrol," Eça concludes with finality, after closing the window in horror.

"Yet they say they are the means of transportation of the future, Consul," Aleixo barely has time to add before the sudden, violent coughing fit that for moments brutally afflicts the Consul.

"I apologize, but it must be the smoke from that infernal machine that attacked my bronchial tubes," the weakened Consul makes a point of explaining when the coughing finally calms down. "No matter what they say, for me, there is still nothing better than a good *charrette*, pulled by two pairs of thoroughbred horses."

"My opinion entirely, Consul. It is a faster, more comfortable and above all quieter means of transportation," Aleixo is keen to point out.

"It is like this *metropolitain* thing, or whatever it is they call it. I don't know whether you've heard of it. A train that goes under the ground, imagine. Not allowing the passengers to appreciate the beauty of the streets or of the buildings, or simply to observe the passers-by themselves. All of this so that the passengers, carried in fast, modern moles, can get to their destination more quickly, in a deplorable phobia of speed. And for this enormous ditches are being dug, veritable canals crossing the city from one end to the other, over ten, or sometimes twenty, meters deep, like the one opened here nearby, in the Champs Elysées. I don't know whether you've seen it."

"Yes. I went past it a few days ago. It is a truly giant ditch."

"Which I try to avoid whenever I can, when I am coming from my house, in Neuilly, to the Consulate here. You can't imagine the suffering that all that dust and the deafening noise of the hammers and picks make. Not to mention the constant traffic jams in both directions."

"From what I hear they are working night and day because they want to have everything ready in time for the *Universal Exposition* in two years' time."

"They'll be lucky. No one will ever convince me to ride in that thing, of that, they can be sure," counterpoises the Consul, before succumbing to a further coughing fit.

"Mr. Consul sir, you need to go to Portugal to breathe some fresh air and recover fully from that flu. Here, with this cold and humidity, it is very difficult to cure it," Aleixo cannot resist advising, as soon as Eça de Queiroz stops coughing and sits on the sofa again.

"You seem to be able to guess things. Because it is exactly that which I am thinking of doing as soon as I can," the Consul says, suddenly becoming more lively, no doubt anticipating feeling the amenable climate of Portugal.

"I am very pleased to hear it, Consul. I myself intend to go to Lisbon very soon, in time to witness the disembarkation of my statue. To see if I can exhibit it there before it is definitively transported to Viana."

"Where are you thinking of exhibiting it?"

"In the main thoroughfare, the Avenida da Liberdade, among the trees and nature, so it can be enjoyed in an environment closer to that for which it was conceived."

"Very good. I hope I am there in time to see it, although I do not intend to spend much time in Lisbon. Just the minimum time indispensable for my professional and family business."

"Why? Are you not the Eça de Queiroz who is passionate about our capital city, its streets and people?" asks Aleixo, finding it strange to hear the great writer's sudden lack of interest in the city that was the setting for some of his best novels."

"Me? No, what an idea. For me, Lisbon today is a detestable city, to be avoided carefully. I only go there when I have to. As soon as I get to Portugal what I want is to go and get some country air. Everything except Lisbon," replies Eça, wrinkling his mustache in an expression of scorn.

"But one gets a completely different idea from reading your novels. The Lisbon of *Os Maias, of O Primo Basílio*, is a Lisbon of fascination, of amazement, of permanent discovery..."

"Yes, but that is literature. Perhaps it is the Lisbon I dreamed about all these years at a distance, the Lisbon of my youth, of the time of the 'Life's Losers' group's dinner meetings in the Hotel Braganza, or of the "Cenáculo" group in Batalha Reis's house. Which I kept alive in my head. But which unfortunately is very different from the Lisbon that exists today and we all know: dirty, ill-kept and full of mean, envious and stupid people," Eça replies with increasing bitterness.

"Well, but this year, with the Centenary of the Indies, there are extra reasons of interest for visiting our capital," Aleixo says to smooth things over.

"Yes, we are going to have that irritating bore. A few days ago I received the final program. Four centuries after that glorious page in our history which was the discovery of the sea route to India and the best we can do to commemorate it is a bullfight, a parade, and little else."

"And an aquarium, Mr. Consul sir, over by the Algés neighborhood. Which they are apparently going to call *Vasco da Gama*," Aleixo makes a point of indicating.

"Oh, yes, the aquarium. I was sure something else was missing. Do you intend to stay in Lisbon for the commemorations?"

"Well, at the moment I am involved in two sculpture competitions, and the closing dates are more or less at the time of the commemorations. So even if I don't want to I will have to be there."

"What competitions are they?" Eça de Queiroz wishes to know.

"One is a project alluding to the discoveries, to be built in Belém, as a part of the commemorations of the Centenary. The other is for a monument to Dr. Sousa Martins, to be erected by public subscription in the Campo de Sant'ana, opposite the future School of Medical Sciences."

"A monument to Dr. Sousa Martins? What did he do that was so special to deserve such an honor?" says Eça de Queiroz angrily. "As far as I know no one has yet proposed making a monument in memory of Antero de Quental, or even Oliveira Martins, who indeed are writers of unique greatness. But Sousa Martins? A doctor whose greatest glory was, so it seems, that of treating people with homemade cures and hypnotism and not charging anything for his consultations? Note, I even had some esteem and consideration for the man, with whom I occasionally spent some time, but a statue? Frankly, this is beyond sensible belief."

"I would much rather make a statue of Antero. Or even of Oliveira Martins. But unfortunately, I don't give the orders, they do, Consul," replies Aleixo, at the very moment when the office door opens, letting the Chancellor in with the completed document in his hand, ready to be signed.

"In any case, I am pleased to see that you are committed to keeping your credits to yourself, ready to go into battle and take advantage of all the opportunities that are so narrow art field allows you. But be careful, Mr. Queiroz Ribeiro, very careful with the guardians of the temple, those who look upon us, we who come from the outside, the 'foreign-looking ones' as they call us, with distrust and envy. As if they were afraid that we might steal their place in the sun. And, believe me, I know what I'm talking about," warns Eça de Queiroz with a raised finger, before he sits down again at his desk in order to check and sign the document.

"I appreciate the advice, Sir, but at least up to now, I have had no reason to complain. Fortunately, my works have been well received by the critics and the press in general."

"Another reason to be distrustful, Mr. Queiroz Ribeiro," insists Eça de Queiroz, handing him the document after signing and stamping it.

"Mr. Consul sir, I am extremely grateful for the manner in which you have received me. And for the speed with which you dealt with the matter."

"Not at all. I must thank you for your presence and pleasant conversation, Mr. Queiroz Ribeiro. And for everything you have taught me about the difficult art of sculpture," responds the Consul affably, holding out his hand. "I wish you the greatest success in these competitions down in Lisbon."

"Thank you very much, Consul. And I hope you make a quick and complete recovery," replies Aleixo, crossing the vestibule on his way to the exit.

Outside, a freezing wind now sweeps through the whole street, dragging with it successive cloudbursts of rain. Sheltering in the doorway of the building, Aleixo has to wait for some time before he sees a hackney cab emerging down at the bottom of the street, coming from the Champs Elysées. 'A man of higher stature. A mind of great, of enormous class. A subtle intelligence, served by an extremely vast culture and an exceptional sense of humor', he thinks, after sitting back in the seat in the hackney cab, unable to stop thinking about the long conversation he has just had with the person who is considered by many to be the greatest Portuguese writer of the century. After the several different occasions on which he had come across Eça de Queiroz during his seven-year stay in Paris, that was the first time he had had the opportunity to exchange more than a few words with him, and he did not regret it. It is a pity that the urgency of obtaining the document that brought him there has not allowed him to prolong the conversation a little more, so as to better get to know the distinguished opinions of the illustrious writer who, apparently, was having a particularly loquacious day, he who was known for not always being particularly pleasant and communicative, especially with people he hardly knew. If that were the case, perhaps—who knows?—he would have even been bold enough to ask, as he had so many times thought about doing over these years, about the origin of the surname Queiroz, trying to discover possible ties of kinship. But each time the opportunity arose he always ended up holding back, fearing that the writer might see in his question an allusion, albeit indirect, to the opprobrium of his original condition as a bastard. Even though that condition, carefully hidden by his direct family for a long time, is today—particularly since he became famous as a writer—practically common knowledge given that it is often pointed out as an explanation for the subject matter, seen as immoral, of many of his novels, in which abortions, acts of adultery and incest take place, among many examples of irony and sarcasm. A subject matter that is quite often seen as a form of denouncing the hypocrisy of a society that does everything to hide its rotten elements, carried out by someone who has been put through the mill because of the consequences, forced to live hidden away and far from his parents and siblings until being an adult, only to keep up appearances, recalls Aleixo as they drive along the Rue du Faubourg de Saint Honoré.

It was his brother, Gaspar, who told him the whole story on seeing him one day leafing through a second or third edition of his novel *The Crime of Father Amaro*, which he discovered hidden on one of the shelves of the library when he was about eighteen or nineteen years old. The writer's father was José Maria Teixeira de Queiroz, Delegate of the Royal Attorney in Ponte de Lima and, no one knows through what cunning, managed to seduce a young girl from one of the best families of Viana, the Pereira d'Eça, who nine months later gave birth to a child, who thus became marked for the rest of his life by the shame and infamy of his condition as a bastard, recalls Aleixo at the moment they turn right into the Rue de Monceau.

Everything had been kept in the utmost secrecy until the boy became an adult, even to his own siblings, who were legitimate children of his father and mother, who in the meantime had married, his father also explained to him. The child, born in the greatest secrecy, was raised in the town of Póvoa de Varzim by a nursemaid until the age of five, and then taken to its paternal grandparents' house in Verdemilho, in the district of Aveiro. His grandfather died a short time later and his grandmother five years later, when his father went to get little José Maria and brought him to Oporto, but not to his house to be with his mother and siblings, but to the Colégio da Lapa boarding school, once more away from his family. Then, after finishing secondary school at the age of sixteen, he went to Coimbra to study Law, so that it was only at the end of his course, now twenty-one years old, that he was finally received at home, in Lisbon, where he father had in the meantime been nominated a judge at the Commercial Law Courts.

With a past like this, could anyone be surprised that the man was only able to write about the rottenness and wretchedness of our society, as was the case of that scandalous book that he held, at that moment, in his hands? his father had wondered. A book which instead of talking about the beautiful and good things in this life, in this world, was restricted to telling the story of a debauched and corrupt priest who had seduced a naïve and well-meaning girl, just as the writer's father had done years before with his mother, resulting in a child who would end up being given to a "weaver of angels," that is, killed, murdered, his father had concluded, yet without ever making it clear where and when he had obtained such detailed information about Eça de Queiroz's origins, thinks Aleixo at the moment that the cab, after passing through the Parc de Monceau, with its beautiful, leafy trees now completely stripped of greenery, turned left into the Rue de Villiers, finally stopping at no 32, a red brick warehouse with a double sloped roof, a wide door and above it, on a metal plate, a bronze plaque on which one could read *Fonderie des Frères Thiébaut*.

"*Est-ce que M. Victor est là?*" he asks as soon as he goes through the door to the waiting room to the office, to the right of the entrance gate to the building.

"*Oui, Monsieur,* but he is busy with a customer and may be a while. Don't you wish to sit down while you wait?" replies the receptionist behind the counter, indicating one of the two black leather armchairs furnishing the reception room. But Aleixo prefers to go to have a look round the inside of the vast pavilion, looking for his statue, which he soon discovers, right by the entrance next to one of the sidewalls, standing out due to its size and shape in relation to the other ones which are also waiting for the moment to go on to their destination. First he looks at it from far away, trying to imagine it placed high up, on the granite peaks of the Monte de Santa Luzia, then from closer. How will his work be received in Portugal, first in Lisbon, by a public that is necessarily more learned and demanding, then in Viana, on the Monte de Santa Luzia, where it will be seen much more as an image for worship than as a work of art? It is impossible to know. But he is sure about one thing: during those almost two years that the design and execution of the work lasted in its different phases, he gave himself heart and soul, in almost total dedication, to making of it a worthy representation of the *Sacred Heart of Jesus*, and at the same time an original work of art, full of expression and movement. So at the moment when the work is finally ready to be shown to the gaze of the public and the critics, his conscience is absolutely calm. Now it is up to them, the public and the critics, to judge the merits of his work, he concludes, before undertaking his return to the waiting room, just in time to see Victor Thiébaut ahead of him, going to the exit in the company of a man whose shape, even seen from behind, seems immediately familiar to him: short, stocky, broad, slightly bent shoulders, short gray hair.

"No. It can't be," Aleixo says to himself when the man turns around to say goodbye to Victor, and he can finally see his broad, prominent nose, his long, gray beard, his blue eyes, looking at Victor from behind his monocle.

"But wasn't that...?" asks Aleixo, choked up and unable to finish the sentence, as soon as Victor Thiébaut starts to walk up the ramp to come to meet him.

"Indeed. Monsieur Rodin in person. He has just ordered the bronze for two of his works from us, in several different sizes," Victor is quick to reply.

"What a pity. I would so much have liked to be introduced to him. Last year I went to Meudon to visit his studio, but he wasn't there," Aleixo complains bitterly.

"Yes, well if I had realized you were here I would have been pleased to introduce you. Because he has also shown interest in meeting you,

Monsieur Ribeiro, after having highly praised your work. Now, unfortunately, it is too late. It'll have to keep for another time."

"You don't say? You mean he appreciated my work," replies Aleixo, incredulous.

"Yes I do, Monsieur Ribeiro. It is absolutely true. And he was even more excited when I told him that you were Portuguese, being surprised at how someone coming from such a small and far-off country like Portugal could have made such an expressive work, with such soul."

"Then I didn't miss everything," comments Aleixo, suddenly euphoric about what he has just heard.

"So, Monsieur Ribeiro, do you have the document from the consulate?"

"Yes, I do. I've just come from there," replies Aleixo, searching for the document in the pocket of his overcoat. And which he hands over to Victor, after which the latter accompanies him to the door, saying goodbye with a cordial handshake.

Outside the weather seems to be changing, with the leaden sky and the rain quickly giving way to high clouds, with clear patches, as indeed is very common in Paris, unlike Portugal, where the weather is less unstable and uncertain, thinks Aleixo as he goes towards the hackney, parked outside the foundry, giving orders to the coachman to go on to his studio.

Yes, to the studio, now that he doesn't have to worry about the *Sacred Heart of Jesus* anymore, as all the correct conditions for its safe journey to Lisbon have been guaranteed, he thinks with relief, as soon as the hackney starts off. Which gives him more or less a month's stay in Paris to devote himself entirely to the two competitions which he has decided to enter, after which he also will have to leave for Lisbon to oversee the unpacking of the work and to deal with its public exhibition in accordance with what was agreed with the committee, he recalls as they go down the Avenue de Wagram towards the Place de L'Étoile, where the confusion of traffic is enormous, involving buses, motor cars and carriages of all kinds, forcing the coachman to constantly swerve to the left or to the right so as not to crash into anyone. In the Champs Elysées there is a long line going towards Place de la Concorde, as the enormous ditch opened on its left for the metropolitan railway forces the upcoming traffic to be diverted to the downward lane, which is now reduced to half of its usual width. Having passed the Rond-Point, on his right, on the site where, until a year ago, there was the Palace of Industry, he starts to see the building works for the Grand Palais and the Petit Palais, the only two buildings which, along with the d'Orsay and Invalides mainline railway stations, will remain after the *Universal Exposition*, according to what he read recently in a newspaper article devoted to the issue, the first building destined for major exhibitions and the second for the installing of a major art museum. Already under construction between the two is the new Avenue Nicolas II, thus baptized in homage to the young Czar of Russia, who visited Paris two years ago, and where the main entrance to the Exposition will be located.

Having finally passed through the area of the construction works, the traffic, fortunately, starts to flow much more quickly towards the extremely vast Place de la Concorde, with more than enough space for several lines of vehicles at the same time. In the middle of the square, there is the impressive, unusual and extremely tall obelisk brought back from Egypt by Napoleon as the spoils of war, which Aleixo never tires of looking at and appreciating every time he passes nearby. As they cross the River Seine over the Pont de la Concorde he can still see, now from closer, the works for the Pont Alexandre III, which extends the Avenue Nicolas II to the Esplanade des Invalides, on the other side of the Seine, and then, on the left bank, the "Rue des Nations," where the pavilions of the many countries participating in the Exposition will be built. Opposite, on the right bank, there will be the "Vieux Paris" and the "Rue de Paris," with the cabarets, theatre shows and other places of amusement, as well as restaurants and bars. Yet it is difficult to believe that all of that, plus the metropolitan railway line from the Porte de Vincennes to the Porte Maillot, can be ready in less than two years from then, in time for the opening of the *Universal Exposition* of 1900, given how behind time all those works seem to be, thinks Aleixo at the moment that the hackney cab turns left, to finally enter the Boulevard St. Germain, towards Montparnasse.

Where will he be two years from then, when the exposition officially opens its doors? In Portugal, with a studio set up in Lisbon, recognized and admired for his work, or still in Paris, trying to make it in the difficult French art world, at the same time responding to the commissions coming from his own country? It is a question to which he obviously has no answer, but it is a fact that despite his efforts to try to make his name as an artist there in Paris, through his successful participations at the *Salon* and the contacts he established with some influential figures on the French art scene, the truth is that the results have not been profitable. So, being in Paris, working only on commissions for Portugal, makes increasingly less sense, besides being considerably more expensive. Not to mention the more and more frequent moments of sadness and loneliness that he feels, far from his homeland and family. Of course, there is Nellie, with whom over the last year he has shared unforgettable moments, but in the end what future can there be for that relationship? She is more and more distant, despite the proximity between his studio and that of Saint-Gaudens, and is totally devoted to her work, which increasingly seems to be her true passion, particularly since Saint-Gaudens returned from the South of France, reinvigorated by steeping himself into his French roots, and his works finally arrived from New York to be worked upon again. He himself, also too busy with his several different works, first the *Sacred Heart of Jesus*, now the models for the two competitions, not to mention several other ones he had in the meantime finished. Besides the fact that Paris is necessarily, for both of them, a place of passage, which sooner or later both of them will leave and return to their respective countries. And if he can't see Nellie accepting going with him to Portugal, giving up her career as an artist to start a family with him, much less can he see himself setting off for the United States, exiled far away in a little nowhere in the State of Wisconsin called Oshkosh, or even set up in cosmopolitan New York. So, all things considered, his definitive return to Portugal is probably only a matter of time. Which would obviously be made much easier if he won at least one of the competitions on which he is working, given that such a triumph would give him the financial means necessary to move his studio to Lisbon, besides meaning more commissions, he concludes, looking through the hackney cab window at the wide Boulevard Raspail opening up on his left, at the moment they leave the Boulevard St. Germain.

So now that he no longer has to worry about the *Sacred Heart of Jesus*, he has to put his all into making the models for the two competitions, he concludes. The model for the centenary competition, the delivery date for which is on the first of May, is already rather advanced, with there even being possibilities of taking it with him when he goes to Lisbon. In it one can see a young, fearless, robust, and energetic Vasco da Gama, as up to then he had never been portrayed, at the moment when he confronts the giant Adamastor at the helm of his ship *St. Gabriel,* sailing against winds and storms, in total contrast with the more usual representation of the great discoverer, which shows him in old age, or approaching it, with a tired face, a dull gaze, a long white beard, wearing the thick robes of a conqueror, more suited to frequenting the royal court than for facing the sea in a caravel, he recalls at the exact moment that the hackney stops in the middle of the Boulevard Raspail, then turning left and entering Rue Notre Dame des Champs.

Yet the same is not true of the model for the monument to Dr. Sousa Martins, given the small number of elements he has managed to obtain on the subject. Which even so has not stopped him from starting to work, trying out several different solutions and ideas, even though for him it is increasingly clear that he needs to take advantage of his coming visit to Lisbon to get the most information possible about the doctor, testimonies by people who knew him, news items and articles written about him, photographs and drawings, besides, obviously, a detailed visit to the place where the work will be set, he concludes, only then realizing that as he crossed the city the day declined and it is almost night.

"Five in the afternoon," he notes as he looks at his watch. How is it possible for them to have taken almost two hours since he left the consulate? He wonders, as at the same time he is forced to accept the facts: now there is almost no natural light to do anything in the studio, so the best thing to do is to go directly to the hotel, he decides, immediately giving instructions to the coachman.

IX

Ashbourne, outskirts of Philadelphia, 23rd of July 1908

JIM KELLY LEFT the headquarters of the *North American* in Philadelphia in his small Ford Model T two-seater a little after eight and headed to Ashbourne, after only a couple of hours of sleep on one of the paper's editorial room couches as the previous day he had not been able to finish the article on the wedding of the Stetson widow in time to go home. The first piece to be published by the *North American* about the matter, it shouldn't be forgotten, unlike all the other Philadelphia newspapers, which, following the announcement that had been made two days previously in the gardens of her residence by Mrs. Stetson, had already devoted a great deal of attention to the event in their editions of the previous day, some like the *Public Ledger*, or even the *Trenton Times*, going as far as to prominently publish photographs of the bride. It had been necessary for him, Jim, to personally speak with his Editor-in-Chief and to place the other papers' articles under his nose, so that old Walker could finally decide to assign him to cover what was already regarded in Philadelphia as the wedding of the year. Which had forced him to do in a day the work that the others had done in two, but what did that really matter? Work had never scared Jim and, all modesty aside, it didn't seem to him that he had done so badly in the matter, he told himself with a certain sense of pride at the exact moment he exited North Broad Street to enter Old York Road, after passing a black horse carriage with drawn curtains, proceeding on the shoulder of the road, along the tram tracks. One only had to compare the articles that had come out in the other papers, as he had done that very morning before leaving the office, to realize that his was clearly superior to all the others. In fact, the first to recognize this was Walker himself, who had personally congratulated him as soon as he had entered the editorial room. And he deserved nothing less, he thought with satisfaction, quickly recalling the various aspects in which his article was different from all the others.

Was he or was he not the only one to mention the visit by John Stetson, the widow's eldest son, to the Cunard Steamship Company to reserve tickets for the couple's honeymoon in Europe, on the *Carmania*? And why? Because he was the only one to have gone to the trouble to follow the car that had left the Stetson property earlier that afternoon, despite the suspicions that the driver's behavior and dress had raised among those colleagues of his who were there. Even though the Cunard clerk, no doubt well rewarded by Stetson, had refused to divulge any information about the matter, whether, in reference to Stetson's visit to the firm or to the existence of reservations in the name of the newly-weds, Jim remembered, as he started to see, down the road, the top of the trees on the Stetson property rising on the horizon. And what other paper had published a description nearly as detailed as his about the wedding preparations that were taking place inside the house, in par-ticular in the room where the actual ceremony was going to take place? And why? Because only he had been able to penetrate the interior of the mansion, seeing with his own eyes what others had only been able to discover through third parties in exchange for a few dollar bills, this despite Miss Beach, Mrs. Stetson's secretary, and her best efforts to stop him. And who else had mentioned the Count's wedding present to his bride, a stunning and extremely valuable set of jewels that had been in his family for several centuries? No one else, and why? Because no one else had been able to get the information from one of the florists, at the gates to the estate. And what other source revealed with such certainty and precision that the wedding would be performed that very morning at ten o'clock, by Monsignor James P. Turner? And why? Because none of his colleagues knew the priests from the Archdiocese of Philadelphia like he did, specifically Father Jerke, his friend and confessor for more than twenty years, for the simple reason that none of them was the son of Irish parents, and, as such, a fervent follower of the Catholic, Apos-tolic and Roman faith whenever needed, he concluded as he started to see the walls of the property, far down the road, on the left side.

It was precisely Father Jerke who had confirmed this information to him the previous day, when, upon leaving his observation post right there, at the bottom of the road, he had the fortuitous idea to go visit the Archdiocese, in Logan Square. And it was he who had also told him about Santa Eulália's presence at the Chestnut Hill Church services for the past four or five Sundays, which perfectly matched the information that he had obtained from the neighbors about the observed presence at *Idro* of a man of foreign appearance, of medium stature, well dressed, with a black, upturned mustache in the fashion of Kaiser Wilhelm of Germany, who had for the past month accompanied the Stetson widow on long car rides, almost every afternoon.

"Uh-oh!" Jim exclaimed loudly upon passing in front of the first entrance to the Stetson estate, next to the Juniper Avenue intersection, after noticing the group of policemen and plain-clothed detectives that was standing guard there, closely followed by a number of human shapes dispersed among the trees, along the entire wall that led to the main entrance, where an even larger group completely blocked entry.

"They're not even making any kind of effort to be discreet," Jim whispered to himself while signaling a left turn with his outstretched arm outside the car on entering Ashbourne Avenue to look for a parking spot in the shade.

"Hey, guys, how's it going?" he asked the guards after parking his car nearby and coming to the main gate armed with his notepad.

"We're fine. What about you?" disdainfully answered one of the tall, muscular plain-clothed guards, advancing towards him, light-colored jacket, dark gray pants, straw hat pulled down over his brow.

"So all this means that we're going to have a wedding after all, isn't that right?" Jim came out bluntly.

"Wedding? What wedding? One of you getting married, boys?" he asked, turning to the other guards, who answered with a group laugh.

"I'm referring to the wedding that's going to take place up there, in the large mansion, between Mrs. Stetson and Count Eulália," Jim insisted, not giving in.

"Listen, Mr...Mr...What's your name?" said the guard, suddenly changing his tone and expression, as if someone had placed a finger on some sensitive inner organ.

"Kelly, James Kelly, a reporter for the Philadelphia *North American.*"

"Very well, Mr. Kelly. My name is Johnson, Paul Johnson, and I don't have the slightest idea of what you're talking about. We were given orders to come here to guard the property and to not let anyone in who isn't officially authorized. Now, whether there's going to be a wedding, baptism or funeral has nothing to do with us. And it shouldn't be any of your concern either, don't you think, Mr. Kelly?"

"Well, Mr. Johnson, you were given orders to guard the estate, and I was assigned to come here to cover the wedding between Mrs. Stetson and Count Eulália, and that's what I intend to do, whatever it takes. And to be honest, your presence here is the best confirmation that the wedding will indeed be taking place…"

"Mr. Kelly, Mr. Kelly," Johnson interrupted abruptly, raising his voice, while on the outside, the other reporters started to gather around Jim, "see if you can understand once and for all what I'm about to explain to you. I'll repeat it one more time: I don't know what wedding you're talking about. Our job here is to guard the property and to stop all strangers without authorization from entering. Those are the orders we have and we're going to carry them out without any questions. Do I make myself understood?" he blurted out in a threatening tone.

"I understand, Mr. Johnson. You'll do your job and I'll do mine," Jim answered, placing two fingers on the brim of his *Stetson*, before turning around and going off towards the other entrance.

"Where do you think you're going, Kelly?" asked Terry, the tall, awkward reporter for the *Bulletin*, walking right alongside Jim for a little. "The other entrance is just the same. Those guys are everywhere and they're not letting anyone in."

"That's right. When I got here, before eight, I took a full ride around the property and it's completely surrounded," said another reporter, whom Jim didn't know. "All the gates are guarded and there are men along every wall that surrounds the property. And in the areas that are more difficult to control, they've got police on horseback."

"One of the guards I know told me that counting the police, the Pinkerton detectives, and the domestic staff there are over a hundred men here," added Stevens from the *Philadelphia Press*.

"But who the heck are they afraid of anyway?" asked Jim, suddenly stopping in mid-step. "Of us, the poor journalists that are here? I find that hard to believe. For them to put in so much effort there has to be another reason for sure."

"And why such secrecy, if almost everything about the wedding is already known? All you have to do is read today's papers," replied Terry again. "By the way, congratulations, Jim. The Archdiocese thing was a stroke of genius. I would've never thought of something like that."

"Thanks, Terry. My Irish background had to be good for something, don't you think?"

"Maybe all this secrecy is just a way of spiking up the public's curiosity a bit more," said Stevens, with a pensive air. "And ours, in the process."

"Hey, boys, do you see what I see?" Terry asked suddenly, pointing towards a female form that had just appeared on the other side of the road.

They all turned around at once to see her, standing next to the black carriage that Jim quickly recognized as the one he had passed at the beginning of Old York Road, hesitating a moment before deciding to open her parasol and cross the road towards the main entrance, to which they all ran in a pack, each scrambling to arrive first. What could this woman be doing here, all alone, dressed as if she had been invited to the wedding, but instead of entering the estate comfortably riding in her carriage, as would be expected of someone whose presence was welcome, she had preferred to leave it on the other side of the road and walk the rest of the way? Jim couldn't help wondering as he watched her approach the near side of the road, tall, thin, very erect, wearing an elegant white satin dress decorated with lace, advancing decisively towards the entrance to the estate.

"I want to come in," she exclaimed defiantly in English with a slightly foreign accent.

"You haven't been invited, madam," replied Johnson, as if he had been waiting for her. "What is your name?" he continued as if he had just realized that this was how he should have started the conversation. Yes, since Johnson didn't know the lady's name, how could he know whether she had or hadn't been invited? Jim found himself wondering, while attentively following the scene before him and sticking his long neck above the heads of his colleagues, not wanting to miss a single word of this conversation between the deaf.

"If my name reached the house, the big mansion, you would not dare stop me from coming in," she said, not intimidated by that whole set up of guards and detectives. Which she certainly could not have predicted when she decided to undertake such an exploit, thought Kelly, at the same time as he attempted to identify the woman's accent, which was clearly foreign. Portuguese? Spanish? French? Yes, maybe French, by the way, she stressed her Rs and elongated the last syllables of each word. Subjecting herself to come here, convinced that she wasn't going to encounter any difficulties whatsoever in entering the property and going up there, to the big mansion, to finally achieve her designs, whatever they may be.

"That's what you think, madam," replied Johnson, while the other guards around the scene nodded their heads in agreement.

"If the Count knew that I was here, I am certain that he would tell you to let me in," she insisted, not backing down.

"But he doesn't know, and he won't find out. Today, the Count has more important things to do than to worry himself with you, madam. And now, if you don't mind, we would appreciate it if you cleared the gate," insisted Johnson, motioning her to move away. She bit her lip, looked to one side and to the other, then again to the front, in the direction of the big mansion, before suddenly turning around and walking away on the side, in the direction of the other gate.

"Miss, Miss, what's your name?" asked Terry, walking alongside her, while all the others tried to keep up, trying not to miss anything she might say.

"I can't say my name. I don't want to cause problems for my family," she replied without slowing down, despite the veritable siege the reporters making around her, all in a pack.

"So what have you come to do here?" questions Stevens, from the *Philadelphia Press*.

"I am here because I am a personal friend of the Count's. We met many years ago when he wasn't even dreaming of coming to the United States. And I am sure that if my name reached up there he would immediately receive me."

"In that case why don't you insist with the guards?" shouted another reporter, one Jim didn't know.

"That is what I intend to do," she said, approaching the other entrance, apparently less well-guarded than the previous one.

"And why don't you tell us your name first. So we can get it up there to the Count?" insisted Terry, sneakily, bending over her from his six-foot five-inch height, with his disheveled hair falling over his brow.

"The truth is that if I revealed my name it would be recognized, not only up there, by all the guests, but also by most Americans," she stated, suddenly stopping in mid tracks, with a triumphal air, looking one by one at all those expectant faces, hanging on her words, as if she were assessing the effect that they had produced on the reporters, before starting off again.

"So you are telling us that your name is so well known?" insisted Terry. "Who are you, madam? A princess, perhaps? But where have you come from?"

"From Chicago. I've come from Chicago. And now I am sorry, but I cannot say any more," she finished, finally coming to the entrance to Juniper Avenue, the guard for which had in the meantime been heavily reinforced by several policemen and detectives coming from inside the estate.

Whom might that mysterious woman really be? Jim Kelly found himself wondering again, while he witnessed the repetition of the scene that took place at the main gate, with the same heated requests by her, followed by the same peremptory denials by the guards and detectives. A bit on the side for the Count, over in Chicago? Who, when she saw she was being swapped for the rich and beautiful Stetson widow, had come there ready to cause a scandal, trying as hard as she could to stop the wedding being held? Perhaps even more than a little bit on the side, who knows? Since the lady said she met the Count some years ago, even before he had come to America, Jim found himself thinking, watching her going up Juniper Avenue alone, while his fellow reporters returned along the Old York Road on their way to the main entrance, apparently convinced they would not be able to get anything else out of her. Perhaps the count hat fooled her all these years with vague promises of marriage, while he was looking for a better match, like the one he had finally managed with the Stetson widow. And now that he didn't need her anymore he wanted to break off with her, except that she didn't accept the situation. Or worse even, perhaps the Count had seduced her and she was expecting a child of his, which he did not want to admit so as not to ruin his romance with the widow, Jim started imagining, as he watched her from afar, sitting down, looking defeated, on the edge of the little stone wall on the other side of the road. Yes, only something very serious could have brought a woman like her, who one could see was of good social status, perhaps even belonging to European high society, if what she said about her name was true, to come on her own, try to gatecrash a ceremony to which she had not been invited and was certainly not welcome. Subjecting herself to the supreme humiliation of being thrown out onto the street by a bunch of tough-looking police-men and detectives as if she were some kind of slut, and then left there prostrate and waiting for not even she knew what, Kelly concluded, as he himself sat down, there on the wall around the Stetsons' estate, tak-ing advantage of the shade of one of the trees to protect himself from the sun, which was increasingly torrid as the time passed.

The fact that Santa Eulália, even though he went to Mass every Sunday, was only a saint in name was shown on his face. One only had to see the dashing air, like a dandy, a *bon vivant*, that he put on in photographs. How could a man who looked like that, with such a figure, get to the age of fifty still single? How many broken hearts, like the one belonging to that poor woman, had he surely not left behind on the way before finally coming to this day that he would finally carry out that which was no doubt the dream of his lifetime, marrying a rich woman? wondered Kelly, before quickly glancing at his pocket watch, showing a quarter after ten, that is, fifteen minutes after the time set for the ceremony, without there being any sign of Monsignor Turner. Might they have decided to put everything off because of the reporters, or of the mysterious woman? Or was it just a natural delay? wondered Jim, only then noticing the presence of a shape that was half-hidden behind a tree, a few yards ahead of him, motioning to him to come over.

"Hello. What's the matter?" he asked when he came close to the figure, a tall, strong lad with his hat pulled down to his ears, wearing a dark cloth suit that did not appear to have been made for him.

"How much will you give me if I tell you a few things about what is going on up there?" he asked with a cheeky smile, after checking that there was no policeman or detective nearby.

"What type of things? And who are you anyway?" Jim wanted to know.

"My name is Joe and I'm one of the gardeners here on the estate. And I've just been up there in the kitchen, where I heard some things about the wedding that I thought might be of interest to you. But if you don't want to know, it's fine, I'll find another one of your colleagues. Fortunately, there's a lot of them around," he said, playing hard to get.

"Let's say that it depends on what you have to tell me, Joe. But I was thinking about a dollar bill, or maybe two. What do you think?"

"Can I see the bills first?" he asked, distrusting.

"Look, here you are: one, two," said Jim, taking two dollar bills from a roll he had in his trouser pocket. "Now, tell me, where is the breakfast going to be served, Joe?"

"On the library porch, up there, can you see?" he said, pointing to the south side of the house, where one could make out some moving shapes. "I was also there yesterday and this morning, helping to set it all up, the tables and the chairs. Before the women came, to do the decorating. And it looked very pretty, all covered in roses and orchids, which are Mrs. Stetson's favorite flowers."

"Interesting. And the wedding, where's that going to be?"

"It's going to be in the music room, there where there are three glass doors, under the balcony, do you see it? We were working there yesterday as well, along with the florists. They made an arch, all decorated with flowers. And behind the arch, we put an altar, like the ones they have in churches. Which is where the priest is going to celebrate the wedding. And now, do you think I deserve the two bills?"

"I think you've earned one. Here it is. Now, to deserve the other one you have to give me some more information. Like, for example, how many guests are up there for the wedding?"

"I heard one of the maids say there were about eighteen or twenty people."

"And do you know who they are?"

"Well, names, I only know the ones from the house. Young John and young G. Henry and the respective Miss Ruby and Miss Helen, which is what we call them. Then there's Mrs. Shindler, who is the boss lady's mother, and Mr. Harkness, who is her uncle. I also heard that there is an important lady from Chicago, but I can't remember her name. She came by train yesterday. It was Jim, one of the drivers, who went to pick her up."

"Mrs. Potter Palmer?" asked Kelly, suddenly recalling a buzz going round at the newspaper about the arrival of the Queen of Chicago the previous day.

"Yes, I think that's the name."

"And you don't remember anyone else?" Kelly insisted.

"Oh, yes. I was forgetting two people who arrived really early this morning in a car that entered the top gate, on the Sycamore Avenue side. They were wearing fine uniforms, full of medals on their chests, swords, and hats with feathers. I think they came from Chicago. So, do I deserve the other dollar bill now?" asked Joe, impatiently.

"You certainly do. Take it," replied Jim, handing him the bill. "And you've got another one coming if you can tell me the names of these guys in uniform, OK?"

"OK boss. In a minute I'll go up there and get their names written on a piece of paper and everything. I don't know how to write, but my Lucy does and she'll deal with it."

"I'll be waiting, Joe," replied Jim, not immediately noticing the vehicle that had just passed the main gate, on the Old York Road, where reporters and photographers had gathered again, along with some curious locals.

"About time too," Jim said to himself when he saw the car, a Ford Model T just like his, start to go up the track that led to the house covered in an enormous dust cloud, then passing only a few yards away from where he was and inclining to the right, which allowed him for a moment to reasonably clearly make out the austere features of Father Morrissey, Dean of Holy Angels Church at the wheel, and of Monsignor Turner, Chancellor of the Archdiocese of Philadelphia, on his right, both wearing cassock, and collar. It was only then that Jim noticed that the mysterious woman had suddenly left where she was sitting and run across the road, again going to the east entrance on Juniper Avenue.

"Let me in! I want to get in!" Jim heard her screaming desperately to the guards, who were holding her back by her arms.

"Poor thing," Jim said to himself, seeing her going away towards the Old York Road before he also took the same path to join his colleagues at the main gate.

"Hey Jim, so where've you been, buddy?" Terry inquired as soon as he saw Jim come over. "Did you see who just went in?"

"No. Who was it?" Jim feigned ignorance.

"Monsignor Turner, Chancellor of the Catholic Archdiocese of Philadelphia, in person, and accompanied by another priest."

"Meaning that this is really about to happen…"

"Of course it is. If there were any doubts about the wedding celebration they have been definitively cleared up, no matter how much they might want to give a different idea."

"So did you manage to speak to the man?" asked Jim.

"No. The most we could get was for the car to stop for a few seconds. When we were about to ask questions the police and Pinkerton's men started to push those who were at the front away and the car started off straight away without us being able to do anything else. But it doesn't matter. When they come out they'll have to talk, whether they like it or not, or my name isn't Terry."

"It won't be easy, with all these guards around," replied Jim, at the same time, noticing the mysterious lady, again approaching the main gate, with the same determination, but this time not going to the guards, just also standing there and waiting. How would things be going inside? Jim couldn't help wondering as he observed the movements of some shapes on the library porch, up there in the big mansion, until it progressively became empty, which might mean that the guests had now been called to take their places in the music room to attend the ceremony. A supposition that was indeed reinforced by the fact that the three glass doors to the room were now totally open onto the garden, unlike what happened previously. Unwillingly, Jim started imagining the arch in front of the altar, all covered in roses and orchids, while the guests took up their places in the chairs laid out in rows in the room, as if it were a real chapel, waiting slightly anxiously in silence for the entrance of the bride and groom. Once the two were together facing the altar, Monsignor Turner, assisted by Father Morrissey, would start the ceremony, which could both be celebrated during the Mass or in isolation. Although, with the Count probably being the only Catholic present, the most likely thing would be a celebration of the wedding without a Mass. Which would mean a short ceremony of about ten, fifteen minutes at the most, followed by the nuptial breakfast served outside, on the library porch. Only after this would there be any declarations about the wedding, Jim concluded, when he suddenly noticed that there was some movement of shapes by the garage again, from which he shortly after saw the little Ford Model T come out, quickly going along the main facade of the house and then taking up the path again towards the exit, where there was growing nervousness among the guards, but also among the reporters, the former wanting to stop the priests being bothered by the latter, and the latter ready to do anything to manage to get a statement confirming everything they already knew. But to everyone's surprise, the car stopped before the exit, just long enough for Monsignor Turner to be able to talk for a short while with Johnson, the head of the detectives, and then move a few yards forward and stop again outside the estate, without the guards doing anything to stop the reporters from approaching.

"Good morning, Monsignor Turner. Terry Thomas from the Philadelphia *Bulletin*. Can you confirm that you have just celebrated the wedding of Mrs. Stetson with Count Eulália?" asked Terry, as soon as the car stopped, bending over the Monsignor.

"What has just taken place up there is an absolutely extraordinary event. But, as you will understand, it is not up to me to say anything whatsoever about the matter," Monsignor Turner restricted himself to saying, with a forced smile, at the same time waving a hand.

"Monsignor Turner, Jim Kelly, from the Philadelphia *North American*. Is it true that the Count..." Jim started out but was unable even to finish the sentence, as the car had immediately started up, raising behind it the usual cloud of dust. So it was only a few seconds later that he noticed that the shape dressed in white that like a ghost went running after the car was no other than the mysterious woman, probably convinced that those in the car were not the priests but rather the bride and groom, as she had only managed to break through the barrier the reporters had formed around the car once it started off. And now there she was again, covered in dust, which she brushed off frenetically with her two hands, crying with rage and out of impotence, faced with the certainty of the consummation of the act that she had tried so hard to prevent. Independently of her reasons, which were certainly serious and weighty, judging by the behavior she had shown throughout the whole morning, the fact was that at the moment that Monsignor Turner spoke up there in the music room, transformed for a few hours into an Apostolic and Roman Catholic chapel, inviting the guests who knew of any reason for that wedding not to be held, to speak up or forever hold their peace, she had not been there and had not been able to say anything, whatever she might have had to say. And the wedding could be celebrated without further delay, with there now being nothing that she could do, thought Jim, seeing her open her handbag to take out a handkerchief, wipe her face and blow her nose, before crossing over the edge of the road and sitting down again on the little wall.

"Eleven twenty-five," Jim said to himself, after consulting his watch. It had all taken place in only half an hour, the time measured between the arrival and departure of the priests, he noted, looking again towards the house, just in time to see the shapes that were now starting to come out onto the library porch, where, once the wedding ceremony was over, the nuptial breakfast would certainly follow. It was only then that he noticed the figure of Joe, the gardener, back again, a little further down, hiding behind a tree and signaling for him to come closer.

"So do you have the names?" asked Jim when he got to him.

"They're here, boss," replied Joe, handing him a piece of paper folded in four, with two names on it—Miguel Alvarez e José Reyna—with the indication "Portuguese Consulate in Chicago" on the front.

"So what can you tell me about what happened inside, in the music room?"

"I know what my Lucy told me. She witnessed the ceremony with the rest of the house staff, due to a special deference by Mrs. Stetson."

"So tell me everything, man. I'm dying to know."

"The first one to enter was the Count, wearing an even more showy uniform than the other two, with a sword at his waist and his breast full of medals. Waiting for him at the entrance was young G. Henry, Mrs. Stetson's youngest son, who accompanied him to the altar. Then it was the lady's turn, entering on John's arm, the eldest son, with a beautiful bouquet of *American Beauty* roses that I picked early this morning, then followed in a cortège by Miss Helen and Miss Ruby, her daughters-in-law, as bridesmaids.

"Then?"

"Then it seems that it all went quickly. The priests asked those questions they usually ask and declared them married."

"Didn't they kiss or anything?" Jim asked, chuckling.

"It seems that in the end, when the wedding march started to play, the Count took the lady's hand and kissed it. And the wedding was over. Now, do I deserve another bill?"

"You certainly do. Good work, Joe. Take it," replied Kelly, putting the third and final bill in his hand and then going to the main gate, where all the other reporters had gathered again. Without it being possible to see the omnipresent Johnson, commanding his group of detectives and policemen, he noted when he joined his colleagues. It was necessary for some time to go by before he appeared again, coming from up top, from the big mansion, this time with a roll of sheets of paper, which he immediately began to distribute.

"What is that Mr. Johnson?" asked Kelly suspiciously, as he waited his turn. "It's an official statement about the wedding," he replied unwillingly.

"So, you mean that there was a wedding after all, right?" retorted Jim, after receiving his copy.

"They were my orders, Mr. Kelly. But now you have all the information you need to do your jobs, boys," he said, with finality.

It was a one-page statement, typed in blue, no doubt the color of the carbon paper that had been used to make the copies, and it contained an official declaration about the wedding, Jim noticed, for moments moving away from the gate. "Aleixo de Queiroz Ribeiro de Sotto-Maior d'Almeida e Vasconcellos..." he read, syllable by syllable, almost spelling out that long name written in a language that was totally unknown to him. The stuff of aristocrats, people who lived in a different world, not his, where no one had more than a name and a surname. And that was enough, he concluded to himself, for moments lifting up his eyes from the paper right in time to notice the mysterious lady sitting on the wall some yards farther ahead, also concentrating on reading a copy of the document, that someone, no doubt out of courtesy or by mistake, had given to her. Did she also have a name like that? Jim wondered, before continuing: "...Count of Santa Eulália, Portuguese Consul at Chicago, and Mrs. S. Elizabeth Stetson were quietly married today by the Rev. James P. Turner at the residence of the bride, on Old York Road, Ashbourne, Pa., the ceremony was witnessed only by the immediate members of the family."

There it was finally, in black and white, the confirmation that the wedding had taken place. But why the heck hadn't they done so earlier, sparing everyone time and trouble? What did they have to hide after all? This was a question to which he would now not get an answer, he thought before returning to the statement, to quickly notice that what followed was a textual reproduction of the previous statement, given out during the press conference held by Mrs. Stetson two days earlier. At the end was the following paragraph: "Upon their return from a European tour, the Count and Countess will make their permanent home at *Idro*, Ashbourne, Pa." Jim read before putting the statement away in his coat pocket, as he would definitely include it in the news item he would write for publication the following day, he thought. A news item that, due to its importance and interest, should appear in a prominent place on the front page, with photographs and everything. And he would fight Walker, the Editor-in-Chief, tooth and nail over this, he decided. Of course, the wedding was obviously the main event and would have to receive all emphasis, with a description of the ceremony that should be detailed as possible, which wouldn't even be very difficult to do after the data he had got from Joe. But it was also necessary to give the due importance to the police deployment around the property, as well as the case of the mysterious woman, as he had decided to call her, he thought, looking up again to see her leaving in distress towards the other side of the road and then getting into the carriage, which had remained there all morning waiting for her, then disappearing for good into the dust of the road.

"Hey, Jim, did you see that?" asked Terry, leaving his other colleagues and running over to Jim.

"She's finally gone."

"Well, if her aim was to stop the wedding the truth is that after this statement she didn't have anything to do here anymore."

"Well, for me she is the real big mystery of this day. Because as for the rest, for good or for bad, it's all explained. They are married, they are going to Europe on their honeymoon and after they come back they will live here, in *Idro*, and that's that. That's what the statement says," Kelly replied, looking pensive.

"Jim, Jim, look who's coming," Terry said suddenly, pointing to the figure of a chubby woman crossing the lawn towards the main gate. No one other than the famous Miss Beach, Mrs. Stetson's private secretary, or rather, secretary to the Countess of Santa Eulália, noted Jim Kelly, on seeing her come over to the guards to talk to Johnson before he introduced her, saying that she had a statement to make in the name of her boss. Miss Beach was quick to formally deny the rumors going around town about Mrs. Stetson's intention to abandon Protestantism and leave the Baptist Church, and then added in a measured voice:

"The Countess wishes to make it perfectly clear to public opinion that she has not embraced the Catholic faith in order to marry the Count, nor for any other reason, and is absolutely true to the faith in which she was received over twenty years ago along with her first husband, John B. Stetson."

"Miss Beach, Miss Beach…" several reporters shouted at the same time, "What time are the newlyweds leaving for their honeymoon?" asked Terry.

"Is it true that the bride and groom are leaving for Europe on Saturday on the *Carmania*?" Stevens asked in turn.

"Where are they going to stay until they leave?" Jim wanted to know.

"As I am sure you will understand, I am not going to answer any of your questions, given that, as you can imagine, the bride and groom do not wish to be disturbed until their departure for Europe," responded Miss Beach, with a complicit smirk.

"And what can you tell us about a woman who was here all morning, saying she was an old friend of Count Eulália and was prevented from entering the estate by the guards?" Jim suddenly fired at her.

"I don't know what woman you are talking about. I know nothing of this matter," she replied, after a few moments' hesitations. "And now I'm sorry, but other affairs require my attention. Good morning, gentlemen," she said sharply, and then set off back to the house, without giving the reporters any chance to ask any more questions.

"Well, we'll get no more out of her. I think I'll go to Juniper Avenue to see if I can find out what's going on up there. This calm and such prolonged silence looks suspicious to me," said Jim.

"OK. I'll stay here waiting. From one moment to the next they might come out, and I don't want to miss the opportunity for some more questions on top of the event," Terry replied, laughing, at the same time that Jim briskly went down the Old York Road, then turned right and started up Juniper Avenue, always looking at the house up there as it emerged in the gaps between the trees, hoping to hear some sound, some small movement indicating that something was about to happen.

"Hey, guys, this looks very calm over here," he shouted as soon as he reached the guards who were still there: two policemen from Cheltenham, boiling inside their heavy dark blue uniforms, two plain-clothed agents, almost certainly Pinkerton detectives, and two mounted policemen, looking distrusting from upon their horses.

Only then could he notice that the guests were no longer on the porch, which was now completely empty except for some servants who were clearing the tables.

"It is true, the wedding is over, so I'm surprised at how you guys are still here," replied one of the policemen, with his cap, pulled down to his ears, his face dripping with sweat, which he wiped away occasionally with a handkerchief he took out from his back pocket.

"We are waiting for the bride and groom to leave. To see if they will give us a statement on their way out," Jim explained.

"Is that right? Then I think you'll have to do a lot of waiting because as far as I know, they're only leaving tomorrow," replied the other policeman.

"Well, we'll see, won't we?" Jim retorted as he observed the arrival of a plain-clothed guy coming from the house, no other than the omnipresent Johnson.

"If I were in your place I wouldn't waste any more time and I'd go away," insisted the policeman, as Johnson spoke to the two mounted policemen.

"Right, that's why I'm a reporter and you are a policeman, isn't it?" Jim disdainfully replied, seeing Johnson, now the conversation was over, walking up the hill, followed at a distance by the mounted policemen. When they got to the house Johnson signaled to them to wait, and carried on towards the north end of the building, disappearing through one of the doors.

"Something is about to happen, but what?" Jim wondered, noticing the guards' badly disguised anxiousness about his presence. The bride and groom were surely preparing to leave, but which way out, and how? And why the mounted police? But he didn't have to wait very long for all of his doubts to be finally cleared up, as a car suddenly appeared from the back of the building, all covered up by a black oilskin so one could not see the inside, going around the house to the entrance into which Johnson had disappeared. For a fraction of a second Jim could see a tall man in a light brown suit and tie, whom he easily identified as the Count, followed by a lady in a light gray dress and with a parasol, who could be no one else other than the Countess, come out of the house and get into the car, after the oilskin had been partially removed. After a few more moments of waiting the vehicle, again covered completely by the oilskin, set off at a good speed along the side of the house and then drove around the lawn towards the exit gate, with the two mounted policemen galloping ahead of it as beaters, a maneuver that Jim watched at a distance from outside, as he went down Juniper Avenue, first walking and then breaking into a run as fast as he could as soon as he realized that instead of going to the main gate the car had turned right towards the side gate on the corner with the Old York Road. Once it reached the gate, instead of going out straight away, the car stopped for a short while on the inside, while the mounted policemen talked to the guards on duty, no doubt to check that the coast was clear. It suddenly started up again, going through the gate at the precise moment that Jim, soaked in sweat, was arriving on the outside, but not giving him time to do anything else except dive out of the way not to be run over, before being covered in an enormous cloud of dust.

"Hey, Kelly, I thought you'd gone. What was that?" asked Stevens, at the head of a platoon of reporters and photographers coming from the main gate.

"*That* was them, the bride and groom, in a car covered in an oilskin so no one could see them," replied Jim, panting, unable to contain his enormous irritation at not having managed to get to the gate in time.

"Are you sure?" asked Terry, distrusting, at the precise moment that a second car, bigger and heavier than the first, came into the Old York Road from Juniper Avenue.

"I saw them with my own eyes, up there, getting into the car; he was in a brown suit and she was wearing a light gray dress," Jim clarified.

"And who are they?" asked Stevens.

"They must be the servants with the bags, who else would it be?" replied Jim, as if it were blatantly obvious. "And now excuse me, I've got to go and get my car."

"Don't tell me you're going after them?" asks Terry again, following alongside Kelly.

"Of course, man. I want to know where they are going."

"But you'll never catch them at the speed they are going," retorted Terry.

"We'll see about that," said Jim, coming to his car.

"Well if you're going so am I. I'll just go and get my car and catch you up,"

replied Terry, carrying on up Ashbourne Avenue, while Jim took the starter and cranked the engine into starting, then driving off at full speed.

"Three-thirty," he noted, looking at his watch again, after passing the other reporters and photographers, most of them also in their cars ready to go after the bride and groom. At the worst he would be at the newspaper at about five, given that if the bride and groom had left at that time they were surely intending to catch the New York train that left Central Station at four, calling at Philadelphia North Station a quarter of an hour later. And once they were on the train there would be nothing left to do but to get back to the newspaper and write the news item, a task that, with everything he had already noted down and thought about on the subject, was made very easy, he said to himself as he left the Old York Road and entered North Broad Street. Indeed, his hopes of getting anything more than confirming what train they had departed on were very little. Yes, if they had made every effort to avoid any contact with the press, going to the lengths of hiding under an oilskin not to be seen by reporters and photographers, it wouldn't be now, in a public railway station, that they would change their attitude. Of course, the fact that a station is a public place, where anyone can enter, did not guarantee them the same protection they had in their own home, or in any other private place, with there always being the chance, albeit vague, of intercepting them as they walked to the train. In the end, everything depended on whether someone was protecting them, be this policemen, detectives, or servants, like, for example, those who were in the second car, not to mention anyone else. Which, if he wasn't greatly mistaken, was the car he was now beginning to see up ahead with increasing clarity as to the distance between the two gradually decreased. In any case, even if he only managed to confirm that they had left and on what train he wouldn't have wasted his time, given that as soon as he got back to the newspaper he could telephone the New York office in time for them to send a reporter to wait for them at Jersey City Station, if possible with a photographer. And there it might be possible to catch them unawares, without anyone protecting them, at least to take a photograph, that could then be included in his piece if they sent it from New York in time, he thought as he started to see up ahead, rising up on the horizon, the long station building on his right, between the buildings on the side of Broad Street. When he finally got there the two cars had already parked outside the building and left their passengers, which he managed to glimpse going in the main entrance, surrounded by the servants and a group of policemen. As soon as he parked, Jim ran to the station, bounding up the steps two by two, at the exact moment that Terry, Stevens, and the other reporters also arrived in their cars. Once inside the main hall, he glanced all-around among the many passengers who continually crossed the floor in all directions, or who were waiting there for the announcement about the next train, hoping to see the group in movement. "Bingo! There they are," he said to himself euphorically as he made out, further down near to one of the ticket sales counters, a numerous group of policemen surrounding the bride and groom.

"Hey, you! Where do you think you are going?" one of the policemen came out with, stepping in his way.

"Jim Kelly, from the Philadelphia *North American*. I just want to ask the Count and Countess one or two questions," he risked, taking out his notebook.

"What questions? Forget all about it. Make yourself scarce," the policeman replied threateningly, pulling out his nightstick.

"I'm just doing my job, officer," protested Jim.

"And I'm doing mine, which is to prevent guys like you from getting close," replied the policeman, at the same time, signaling to the others to increase the perimeter around the bride and groom. Only then did Jim notice his colleagues arriving in a bunch, pushing through the crowd that had in the meantime gathered, trying to find out what was happening.

"Hey, Jim, is that them over there?" asked Terry, seeing the little group made up of the Count and Countess and the servants, moving towards the train platform completely surrounded by the policemen.

"Of course it is. Can't you see how the police are protecting them? It looks like it's the State Governor or the President. I've never seen anything like it. And I came this close to getting hit by that big brute's nightstick, just because I said I wanted to ask the Count and Countess some questions," Jim complained, pointing to the policeman who had intercepted him. When the bride and groom reached the place where the Pullman carriage was stopped, more or less in the middle of the platform, the policemen again established a security cordon around them, making any attempt to approach the impossible.

"If I see any of you guys trying to take a photograph I'll rip his head off," bellowed out the brute again, with his nightstick in his hand, when he saw one of the photographers raising up his camera, then immediately putting it away lest the policeman carries out his threat, at the precise moment when, covered in an enormous cloud of smoke, the New York train was coming into the station.

"Four sixteen," noted Jim, looking at the station clock, after seeing the smoke from the train dissipating, and with it the Count and Countess disappeared, as if by enchantment, inside the Pullman carriage, not leaving any trace, no matter how much he and his fellow reporters tried hard to discover them from a distance through the steamed-up glass of the windows.

X

Lisbon, 15th of April 1898

THE TELEGRAM IS THERE, open on the bedside table where he left it
the previous night before falling asleep, and in which Rocha Paris,
Chairman of the Committee for Improvements to Monte de Santa
Luzia, requests his presence during the visit that His Excellence the
Very Reverend Papal Nuncio will be making today, at 4:00 p.m., to the
Church of São Vicente de Fora, to see his statue of the *Sacred Heart of
Jesus*, notes Aleixo, sitting on his bed after pushing aside the tray with
the remains of his breakfast. Now there is official, written confirmation
of the information given to him the previous evening by his brother
Gaspar about this visit and to the reception committee which is being
formed, including a handful of high-ranking figures from the political
and ecclesiastic fields, he recalls as he puts the breakfast tray down on
the Queen Maria-style commode at the foot of the bed.

"Prepare yourself because tomorrow is going to be one heck of a day,
kid," Gaspar had said to him as a goodbye when he left him there at
the door to the Braganza Hotel, where he was staying after challenging
him to have lunch together today in Chiado, after which they would
both go directly to the church.

"Don't forget, Aleixinho, half past midday at the Havaneza café,"
he shouted finally, just to make sure, before telling the coachman to go,
knowing as he does about his brother's distractions and forgetfulness,
being an artist. But how could he, Aleixo, forget an appointment with
his beloved and esteemed brother Gaspar, faithful and dedicated like
no other, particularly on a day with such a special, unique meaning as
today, in which the diplomatic representative of His Holiness the Pope,
accompanied by his acolytes, has deigned to come and visit his statue of
the *Sacred Heart of Jesus*? He wonders, as he puts on his *robe-de-chambre*
over his nightshirt to go to the window, where he remains for a while
looking at the cloud-laden sky, threatening rain, and the River Tagus,

the color of lead, which he can make out from the Mar de Palha until Belém, slowly flowing to the sea between the enormous distances of its banks.

Indeed, a visit that is the culmination of a month of formidable successes, like he could never have imagined it possible to happen, clearly showing that the ominous and pessimistic prediction by Mr. Eça de Queiroz, when he visited him two months ago at the consulate in Paris, has no reason to be true, at least in his case. "Be careful, Mr. Queiroz Ribeiro, very careful with the guardians of the temple, those who look upon us, those who come from the outside, the 'foreign-looking ones' as they call us, with distrust and envy. As if they were afraid that we might steal their place in the sun," the famous writer told him, with a raised finger. Well, it seems that this time "the guardians of the temple," if they really exist outside Mr. Eça de Queiroz's feverish imagination, had surrendered completely to him and his works, even though he was a "foreign-looking one," and thus the bearer of new and fresher artistic ideas, he tells himself with pride, looking at the impressive stack of newspapers piled up on the lid of the commode, with all the news items and articles published over the last month about him or his works. Which his always aware brother Gaspar had taken the trouble to have collected, put in chronological order, and underlined before handing them to him the previous evening. The articles began to come out even before he arrived in Lisbon, some relating to the conclusion and upcoming sending of the statue to Portugal, others dealing with his own arrival, he recalls as he brings the stack onto the bed, then leaning back on the pillows and slipping again into the warmth of the sheets. Like that one, published in the *Aurora do Lima* on the 23rd of February, the first in the stack, reporting that the statue had already been put aboard ship in Le Havre, destined for Portugal, on the steamship Corrientes. Or the next one, in the *Diário de Notícias* on the 15th of March, in which the Paris correspondent, Domingos Guimarães, in one of his "Letters from Paris," does not forget to mention the departure of "our dear friend and illustrious sculptor Queiroz Ribeiro" on that very day, by ship from Bordeaux. Also in the *Notícias* newspaper, but on the 17th, Domingos Guimarães devotes his entire column to him, except that on this occasion not to write about the state of the *Sacred Heart of Jesus*, but about his *Vasco da Gama*, the plaster model of which he brought with him from Paris for the sculpture competition for the Centenary. "It is a statue of the discoverer of the Indies, not of the sailor now tired of the efforts of conquest, with his face worn and pale, his gaze now dull and his hair graying, as we see him in the portraits, but of the young Vasco, little over thirty years old, robust and energetic, full of overwhelming faith and supreme ardor," says Domingos Guimarães, before going on to describe the statue itself a little further down: "An epic breath more than the wind and the froth of the ocean stirs and shakes his unruly hair. His eyes, which are empty in statues, seem to flash fire, resplendent with faith and hope. Saltwater runs down his scant beard. His physiognomy is granted extraordinary vigor. And his head, which emerges from a thick sailor's sweater, stirs in an agitated movement of unsurpassable virility of magnificent and powerful beauty."

This article is almost completely transcribed by the *Correio da Noite* and by the *Aurora do Lima*, coming ahead of further news and articles about the statue of the *Sacred Heart of Jesus*, among which there is one, published in the *Correio Nacional* on the 28th of March and entitled *A Work of Art*, in which it is stated that: "Queiroz Ribeiro's work is truly remarkable. The sweet Jesus with an expression of infinite tenderness and a pale, suffering face comes down to humanity and in an fervent impulse of love pulls aside his humble, poor tunic with his right hand in order to bare that burning heart cut through by a spear wound due to love for humanity, that humanity that He always loved and only in which He could find relief and remedy for his always great misery. The tunic, unprotected through the position of the right arm, which droops in the patient attitude of someone offering himself, naturally falls over the shoulder, and that disarrangement magnificently sets the whole absorption of that divine Martyr into relief."

Finishing off, the article states: "Those who know the many images of the *Sacred Heart of Jesus*, always in an erect and still position, that can be found in our temples, may well say whether there is something similar here, and acknowledge whether there is not a great originality in that work of art which at the same time is an eloquent document of a radiant talent."

This same article appears in its entirety in several other newspapers, such as the *Correio da Noite* and the *Aurora do Lima*, notes Aleixo, before picking up the *Popular* from the 30th of March, where there is another article, more apologetic than the previous one, entitled "Queiroz Ribeiro's Christ," in which there is the following description of his statue: "The image of the Christ is barefoot, serenely descending the mountain. On its way down, the body bends forward, in a movement full of naturalness, the tunic is dragged behind, revealing the breast. It is to the breast that it points, showing its heart. It comes down the mountain wrapped in the vague dream of someone who has let his eyes rest on the greatness of the sea and the infinity of the Heavens; it comes down in the abatement of someone walking in the abstraction of ecstasy; its forehead beating in fever, transfigured by the divine light of its eyes. An expression of bitterness floods its physiognomy, the immense sadness of tender sweetness, fused with an air of abnegation of an extreme anxiety of charity..."

Following this the writer makes a summary of his artistic career, with particular emphasis on his successes in Paris, at the *Salon*, ending with a curious reference to his figure, which he says vaguely reminds him of the "aesthetic type," "the Antero de Quental thin figure of a monk." This article is also published almost completely in the *Aurora do Lima* of the 4th of April, a newspaper that always keeps up with anything to do with him. Which Aleixo passes over, to then pay attention to the *Século* of the 3rd of April, with a much shorter and more concise article than the *Correio Nacional*, while nevertheless equally full of praise and eulogies, in which at one point it is stated about him, "that in each new work he presents he powerfully affirms the brilliant qualities of conception with which his original mind is gifted." The article ends with the following sentence: "This work of art which over recent days has been visited by many people is thus full of interest. Aleixo de Queiroz Ribeiro has a brilliant future ahead of him."

Further on, in the *Novidades* of the 5th of April, it is with a mixture of surprise and satisfaction that Aleixo reads the item in which it states that his statue, exhibited at the Geography Society, is receiving many visitors, with it having been seen on the previous Sunday by "over 1,800 people, among whom were the Duke and Duchess of Palmela, the countesses of Alcáçovas, Linhares, Costa, Bertiandos, Galveias...and many other ladies of our higher society." This same item is once again almost completely reproduced in the *Aurora do Lima* of the 11th of April, notes Aleixo before moving on to the final newspaper, the *Novi-*

dades of the 9th of April, in which there is an in-depth article signed by his dear friend Henrique de Vasconcelos, the poet and journalist. After expanding into long considerations of great theoretical value on the paths followed by Christian-inspired art over recent times, with a reference to the "prodigious fertility and originality of Michelangelo, de Vinci, Raphael, and Titian," Henrique concludes, referring to his Christ: "There is poetic and sculptural truth in that suffering face in which Sorrow has dug wrinkles and the whole general movement of the figure—the tunic torn at the angular knees, hardly holding to the breast that reveals the heart—is elegant and true, suffering, suggesting the idea of the greatly loving Father, who agreed to wear these dirty rags—the human shell—to purify and take it—to redeem it indeed!"

"11:25," he says to himself after again looking at his watch, leaping quickly out of bed with the stack of newspapers in his hand, putting them again on the lid of the commode, and only then noticing the issue of the Parisian newspaper *L'Evénement*, dated the 21st of March, which had been left there forgotten, the same one that Domingos Guimarães was kind enough to have sent to him a few days earlier there in the Braganza Hotel, as in the column "*La Vie Artistique*," written by George Eller, there is a short but quite eulogizing reference to his *Vasco da Gama*. "*Queiroz Ribeiro, un Portugais, mais un sculpteur de génie a formé le fac-similé de Vasco da Gama, une oeuvre qu'on admirera sincèrement*," he reads once again, enraptured, given that Eller is a renowned art critic, not only on the *L'Evenement* but also on the *Le Siècle*, and, as Gaspar says, to make his name as an artist in Lisbon it is better to have a good critique in a French newspaper than a thousand articles published in the Portuguese newspapers, he recalls as he looks through the window at the overcast sky threatening rain, then going to the basin placed near to the door and fills it with water from the pitcher. Then he takes off his robe and nightshirt, energetically washes his face, ears, armpits, and neck, and dries himself on a linen towel hanging on the towel rack running around the basin. Next to the commode, on the back of a chair, is the white shirt he had sent to be starched last night in the hotel, as well as his striped trousers, impeccably ironed he notices when he puts them on over his long Johns. Before buttoning up his shirt he splashes a little eau de cologne on his face and neck. Then he takes a white *papillon* from one of the drawers in the commode, which he ties over his collar, standing in front of the mirror, and a pair of black socks, which he puts on sitting on the edge of the bed, before putting on his boots, which he had left outside his bedroom door to be polished the night before. Standing in front of the dressing table mirror, he carefully combs his increasingly thinning hair, and his beard takes his flannel waistcoat and dark gray tail coat from the wardrobe and puts them on, looking at himself in the mirror with some discomfort, being little used as he is to this type of outfit, more suited to politicians and businessmen than to artists like him. But, *noblesse oblige*, that is, according to Gaspar, the correct dress for receiving a diplomatic representative of the highest standing, as is the case of the Nuncio of His Holiness the Pope, during which he, as the author of the work, will naturally be the center of attention, he tells himself as he puts his high hat on his head. Finally, he takes his Bengal cane and goes out into the long, narrow corridor with rooms on either side, but with no sign of any toilets or WCs for the guests to use. Which is somewhat extraordinary, given that it is one of the best hotels in Lisbon, visited by kings and queens, princesses and princes, actors and actresses, businessmen, politicians and goodness knows who else, when even his poor, modest Hotel Rauchès in Paris already has them, he thinks as he goes down the corridor on his way to the stairs connecting to the first floor, where the larger bedrooms and suites are. Perhaps this floor already had the comforts that are missing upstairs, he concludes before he begins to go down the long, curved stairway that connects the first floor to the hotel entrance hall on the ground floor. Which Aleixo crosses among a group of recently-arrived guests, with all their array of suitcases and trunks that two young porters are unloading from a carriage stopped outside the entrance, at the exact moment that an elegantly-dressed lady with a haughty look and wearing a wide hat over light brown wavy hair held back in a bun comes very stiffly down the great curved staircase followed by two maids.

"A thousand pardons, my dear lady," Aleixo is quick to say when the two almost bump into one another as they go to the reception desk further on, beneath the staircase.

"*Je vous en prie, Monsieur,*" she replies in French with a heavy accent, staring at him with her beautiful black eyes, then again moving towards the reception desk to leave the keys to her lodgings. Who might this unknown beauty be? wonders Aleixo, on his way out, after also having left the key to his room at the reception, just in time to see her get into a carriage stopped outside the hotel, along with her maids, then going off towards the Lisbon downtown area. Perhaps a foreign princess, or an opera singer, he thinks, walking up the road, heading to António Maria Cardoso street, when, as he passes by the Queen Amelia Theatre, he sees to his great amazement the face of the lady painted on the enormous canvas lining the whole width of the building's facade. None other than the extremely famous Italian actress Eleonora Duse, he reads the name written at the top of the canvas, the only actress to compete with the sublime Sarah Bernhardt, of whom she is considered to be the eternal rival. What a small world it is. He, passing through Lisbon, perfectly naturally coming across La Duse in the hall of the hotel where both of them, coincidence of coincidences, are staying, he says to himself as he is almost arriving at the Largo das Duas Igrejas square.

"Midday sharp," he tells himself as he hears the twelve chimes of the bells of Encarnação Church, which means that he still has a half hour to get to his meeting with Gaspar. Perhaps take advantage of this to pop into the Livraria Gomes bookstore, a little further down on the other side of the street, and a well-known place for chats among politicians and literary figures, with some artists and journalists in the mix, he decides when he's coming down the Rua Garrett, in front of the extremely new Eloy de Jesus jewelers, the shop window which he can't resist studying with some attention, hoping to find something he might take back as a present for his dear Nellie. But a gold necklace or a pair of earrings are not things to be chosen just like that, with a simple glance, one needs time to go into the shop and look at each item carefully until one discovers that which is most suitable, he thinks, before walking over to the bookstore, on the other side of the street.

"Mr. Queiroz Ribeiro, you cannot be a good person," he hears a metallic, commanding voice say behind him as soon as he enters the bookstore, none other than that belonging to the fiery infantry major and art critic Bartholomeu Sesinando Ribeiro Arthur, standing in the middle of the establishment with, next to him, a short, stocky figure with a long graying beard and a black beret pulled down to his ears.

"Me, Major, sir? Why do you say that?" asks Aleixo, surprised by this reception and at the same time walking straight to Aleixo with his hand out, his short hair, thick mustache upturned at the ends, very well turned out in his stylish overcoat, in flagrant contrast with the other chap's scruffy appearance, thick untreated wool trousers and shabby overcoat badly hiding his voluminous belly.

"Because we were just talking about you," replies Ribeiro Arthur with a knowing smile to his companion.

"Talking about me? To what do I owe such an honor?" Aleixo asks, puzzled.

"Well, Mr. Queiroz Ribeiro, you are the man of the moment. Not a day goes by in which there is not an article about you or your works in the newspapers. A good coverage, no doubt about it," says the Major, swiveling his heels from one side to the other as if he were about to salute, and then introducing his companion-in-conversation, who is none other than Fialho de Almeida, the well-known writer, and journalist.

"So, Major, have you had the chance to go to see my *Sacred Heart of Jesus?*" asks Aleixo, looking at the Major.

"Yes indeed. I saw it as soon as it was exhibited at the Geography Society," he promptly replies.

"I was also there last week, but there were so many dolts around that I couldn't see it properly," then says Fialho de Almeida.

"And may one know what you thought?" asks Aleixo.

"Well. Mr. Queiroz Ribeiro, if you must know the truth, the opinions are not very favorable. For someone who started so auspiciously, with those two works you exhibited precisely here at the Livraria Gomes some years ago. And whom, as you will certainly remember, I made it a point to hail enthusiastically in the pages of the *Revista Ocidente,* it is difficult to understand how you could fall this time into such a brutal simplification of lines and forms like that which you exhibit in your Christ. Besides clear disrespect for the most elementary notions of anatomy," replies Ribeiro Arthur, with a severity suited to an infantry officer used to admonishing his troops on parade, seconded by repeated head shaking by Fialho.

"But, Major, that simplification of lines precisely aims at stressing that which today is increasingly the essence of sculpture, that is, expression and movement. One only has to look at the works of that great and unquestionable genius who is Rodin," counterpoises Aleixo.

"Rodin, Rodin. There you go with Rodin. Rodin can't be imitated, Mr. Queiroz Ribeiro," replies Ribeiro Arthur, unable to disguise his growing irritation. "Artists like Rodin are isolated, untouchable eminences who in their eclectic fantasies cannot be followed."

"Far be it for me with my poor abilities to intend to do so, Major. But there is no doubt that his work, which is the work of a true genius, has inaugurated a new aesthetics for sculpture. After Rodin, nothing can be what it was before."

"Good Lord, Mr. Queiroz Ribeiro, don't bring me that rubbish about the new aesthetics. As I wrote in a recent article, 'Sculpture is the great art par excellence. It shows us the ideal of form in its highest purity. Showing us the beautiful, it takes us to the grandiose, and the grandiose nature of the form forces us to worship the grandiose nature of the idea.' Do you understand what I mean, Mr. Queiroz Ribeiro?" Ribeiro Arthur finally asks, thrilled by his own words.

"No. I confess I do not exactly see the connection," replies Aleixo, confused.

"It means that by being the art par excellence, sculpture cannot get lost in fancies, Mr. Queiroz Ribeiro. Its function is to clearly and palpably reproduce the form in its purest truth. And above all, it cannot be allowed to also suffer the contagion of the disorder that is extenuating literature and which, alas, has already struck other visual arts such as painting. Which is what the heralds of this new aesthetics want to do. Do you understand now?" the Major asks again, to a knowing smile from Fialho.

"If you allow me to be so bold, Major, I do not think that there is any fancy in my Christ, but precisely that constant search for the truth that you mention, in the expression and feeling of a redeeming Christ who lived and died for us," insists Aleixo, trying to remain calm.

"But that is exactly the problem: sculpture cannot, nor will ever be able to express abstract ideas through that form, such as expression, feeling. For the people, sculpture should be a clear book and not an enigma."

"Well, the numbers of the public who went to the Geography Society to see the statue, which on only one day reached, according to the *Novidades*, one thousand eight hundred people, does not exactly make it an enigma, don't you think Major?" Aleixo counter-attacks, exalted and unable to contain his irritation any longer.

"But the common people, as you know, go where they are told to go. They are a despicable anomalous and acephalous beast, incapable of knowing the difference between real art, the art capable of arousing emotions, and the most consummate trinket," pronounces Fialho de Almeida, coming to his friend's aid.

"Well, if you will allow me, I have to go. I'm already getting a little late," Aleixo suddenly takes his leave, outraged, holding out his hand to each of them before he hurriedly walks out of the bookstore.

"Good Lord, Mr. Queiroz Ribeiro, don't bring me that rubbish about the new aesthetics," Aleixo repeats to himself in indignation. The nerve of the man, giving him lessons, he who has seven years of studies in Paris at the best schools, with the best teachers. What does Mr. Bartolomeu Sezinando Ribeiro Arthur, a simple infantry major, a weekend watercolor artist, know about art or sculpture to be giving out opinions? What knowledge does he have, for example, about the works of Rodin, to be able to pass sentence on them? Has he ever seen one in real life? Surely not. All of his enormous knowledge is a result, at best, from brief glances at some photographic reproductions and from reading commentaries and opinions in newspapers and specialized magazines, from which he elaborates his own, definitive opinion as to if art could be appreciated in this manner, at a distance, through an intermediary. But, as they say, "all are not thieves that dogs bark at." What importance can Major Ribeiro Arthur's opinions have compared to his enormous critical and popular success? Aleixo concludes to himself as he goes past the door to the Turf Club, where a group of well-dressed young men is raising a row. As lunch hour approaches the movement of people and carriages up and down the street is more intense, he notes as he comes to the Casa Havaneza, at the door to which several men in overcoats and high hats, or felt hats, are chatting in a lively manner in small groups, or simply eyeing the ladies who go by on the sidewalk. After entering, Aleixo goes from one end of the establishment to the other, passing by the many customers, laughing and talking loudly, amid billows of smoke from their one-penny cigars, but no sight of his brother. This time, for a change, it is Gaspar who is late, Gaspar who never misses an opportunity to criticize his lack of punctuality, Aleixo thinks, amused, as he goes over to the counter, where Havas telegrams are displayed on the glass fronts of the cupboards, with the latest news, in this case about the imminent Spanish-American War. A sudden, intense rumble from the entrance forces him to shift his gaze, just in time to see Gaspar, being greeted from left and right, coming into the establishment surrounded by a numerous group of gentlemen, no doubt made up of other deputies and peers of the realm, who have just come, like him, from the Parliament.

"Aleixinho, how are you? A thousand pardons for my lateness, but today there was a plenary session and the works went on much longer than what was foreseen," explains Gaspar, energetically bounding towards him, stylish dark gray tailcoat, kid gloves, silk plastron, and high hat.

"Don't worry, lad. Strike it against all the times I have been late," replies Aleixo benevolently, arms open, greeting his brother.

"So? Reading the Havas telegrams? Any news?" asks Gaspar, avidly scanning the headlines with an intense gaze.

"It's all about the situation in Cuba. Things are ugly."

"A real mess. This means war, surely. And most probably *nuestros hermanos* will suffer a heavy defeat, with unforeseen consequences."

"You think so?"

"You can be sure of that. Spain today is a long way off from being the major power it used to be. While the United States of America is the opposite, increasingly a great nation, including from the military viewpoint. For them, this is the great opportunity they have long been waiting for to emerge into the concert of nations as a major world power, the great power of the new century. Stronger and better armed even than England herself, or Germany, mark my words. And after Cuba come the Philippines, Puerto Rico, and who knows what else. All of this under the cover of 'a sincere and disinterested desire for peace and prosperity', as the cunning McKinley hypocritically stated in an insidious message he sent a few days ago to Congress."

"Perhaps. Perhaps you're right. I'd never thought about it."

"Well, shall we have lunch?" proposes Gaspar, immediately walking towards the door.

"Where are we going? To the Grémio club?"

"No. This time I have reserved a table at the Tavares Rico. What do you think?" replies Gaspar, now outside the building.

"I don't know it, but I've heard good things about it," says Aleixo, as they are turning the small set of steps of the Loreto Church, with Largo de Camões square opening up in front of them, dominated by the monument to the poet Camões, which Aleixo studies from afar for a moment, before they enter the Rua de S. Roque, where the restaurant is located right at the beginning on the left side. After the glass door, which the suitably uniformed doorman opens for them with a low bow, they go directly to the dining room, walls lined all round with giant mirrors in giltwood frames, high ceilings with profusely worked stucco, with friezes and arabesques laid out in a geometrical manner spreading out from a large round fleuret, in the middle of which an enormous chandelier radiates out its soft, discreet light, completed by little appliqués set out on the walls between the mirrors. The tables, laid with linen tablecloths of impeccable whiteness, are set out along the walls and in the wide central aisle, many of them already occupied.

"Will the Doctor and company please be so kind," says the *maître d'hôtel,* tall, thin, black dress coat and white shirt with starched breast piece, coming over to them as soon as he sees them arrive.

"Hello, Manuel, how are things going, man?" replies Gaspar, with the relaxed ease of an *habitué.*

"Not so bad, Doctor, never worse," says the head waiter, with a constrained smile, after running his hand through his thinning hair.

"So where are you sitting us, Manuel?"

"What a question! Your usual table, Doctor" he replies, immediately going through the central aisle towards the corner table. As they cross the room Aleixo cannot help feeling a certain pride on noticing how a large number of the people sitting at the different tables turn to greet his brother, either with a discreet nod of the head or with a warmer greeting. His brother Gaspar is decidedly well set off in the public life of Lisbon, recognized and admired everywhere, whether passing through somewhere, like in the Havaneza, or right there, in one of the most select restaurants in the city, notes Aleixo as he follows him along the central aisle.

"So, what do you recommend for us today, Manuel?" asks Gaspar, when they are both finally sitting in their respective places.

"Well if you permit me, Doctor, I would be so bold as to suggest, to start, the *Consommé de Volaille aux Quenelles,* which is one of our chef's specialties. As a first course, I would recommend the *Turbot Sauce Homard*, which is extremely fresh, just in from the fish market. And for the second course a *Contre-filet de Boeuf aux tomates fraîches*. Or perhaps our *Pintades Bardées*, which are also a specialty," replies the man, at the same time as he hands Gaspar the menu, completely written in French.

"What do you say, Aleixinho?" Gaspar is quick to ask.

"I'll go for the *Consommé* and then the *Turbot*, if it is so fresh. And for the second course the *Pintades*," Aleixo replied without thinking very much.

"And the same for me, except instead of the *Pintades* I'd rather have the *Contre-filet*."

"Very good. And to drink, a Bucellas white, very chilled, to start, Doctor?"

"No need even to ask that, Manuel. And then, with the meat, the Collares Reserve, the one you know."

"Thank you very much, gentlemen," the man says, taking his leave after jotting down everything in his notebook.

"So have you had time to read the newspapers I gave you yesterday?" asks Gaspar, preparing to taste the Bucellas white wine.

"I spent the whole morning lying in bed reading them, imagine."

"A massive success, good grief. To be honest I can't remember ever having seen anything like this. Your colleagues here in Portugal must be green with envy," states Gaspar, before raising his glass to make a toast.

"Indeed. I never expected anything like this could happen. But now that no one can hear us, you must have had a hand in this, right?" Aleixo can't prevent himself from asking after he also has toasted his brother.

"No, Aleixinho, I just got the information to the right places, which is very different. The rest is your merit and of your works. Because you can be sure of one thing, if your works did not arouse real enthusiasm then newspaper articles would be of no use. And that is a fact. What happened was exactly the opposite: starting from one or two well-written and well-structured articles, showing a sincere and enthusiastic adhesion on the part of the person who wrote them for the way you conceived your Christ. Many people went to see it and the word spread. And then it was what you know: a veritable mass outing to the Geography Society. And now, in the São Vicente de Fora church, it looks like it is the same thing.

"Yes, but if you hadn't done what you did there probably wouldn't have been even a tenth of the articles that there were," Aleixo insists, before finishing his *Consommé*.

"Come on, don't be modest. Because all the merit is yours and no one else's," replies Gaspar, seeing a waiter has arrived with the first course.

"Mmm, this turbot is really very fresh. And the lobster sauce is sublime," says Aleixo, delighted, as soon as he tastes a bite of the fish, after dipping it well in the sauce.

"I'm glad you like it."

"What about the competition for the monument to Sousa Martins? How are things going?"

"Not bad. The problem is the lack of time. The deadline for handing in the maquette ends a month tomorrow. And instead of being in Paris working in my studio, I am here in Lisbon. All because of the intransigence of Rocha Paris, who insisted that I had to be here for the ceremony of the blessing of the statue by the Cardinal Patriarch," responds an apprehensive Aleixo.

"Well, well, but now with the blessing set for Sunday, you'll be able to go back with no problems. And then get cracking, so everything is ready on time. I'm sure you will manage it."

"May God hear you, lad. Anyway, I've already booked a seat on the *Sud-express* train for Monday the 18th."

"Isn't the 18th your birthday?"

"Yes. My 30th birthday."

"We've got to commemorate that, man. What time do you leave?"

"I'm going on the night train."

"In that case we'll have lunch together, that's that. Champagne and everything."

"Agreed. To be honest, I wasn't at all looking forward to spending my birthday alone. Above all with a long, tiring journey ahead," replies Aleixo, touched.

"You deserve it all, Aleixinho. But tell me something, is your maquette for Sousa Martins very far behind time?" asks Gaspar, after one of the waiters had served him a beautiful rump steak with cream and mustard sauce and fried tomato.

"Well, the broad strokes are already set out. And from what I've seen in the research I've done here it doesn't seem necessary to alter anything, at least not in the essential outline. Of course, there's still a lot to do before I can consider the maquette to be ready."

"Of course, but be careful with innovations, with modernisms. Above all in relation to the way you are going to represent the figure of Sousa Martins. His presence is still very alive in people's memories. After all, he died less than a year ago and his loss is greatly felt, both among the rich and powerful and the more humble folk. The way things are is that despite his being a positivist, a man of science, even sometimes using less orthodox means, there are those who want to make him a saint and put him on an altar."

"You don't have to worry about that. I'm taking many photographs of him with me, that I managed to get from friends of his I contacted. And I closely studied a portrait that is in the Society of Medical Sciences, done by Veloso Salgado. In which he curiously is seated, in a position rather close to the one I am thinking of representing him. Now, what is more important for me than a faithful reproduction of the model in all of his physical details, is to be able to give him life through the expression and movement I can impress upon the work. And that may be my greatest originality in relation to the other competitors," Aleixo points out, as he deals with carving up his *pintade.*"

"So, get to work, little brother. I'm sure the result will be a beautiful monument."

"May God hear you," replies Aleixo. When both of them finish, the diligent Manuel appears immediately, attentive and obliging, wishing to know what they would like for dessert. Aleixo chooses the *crème brûlée* while his brother goes for the *Diplomate* pudding, followed by two coffees.

"I hope that everything has been to your liking, gentlemen," says Manuel, accompanying them to the door. Once outside, the doorman immediately hails a company *coupé* that is coming down Rua de S. Roque.

"Do you know who I met this morning in the Livraria Gomes bookstore?" asks Aleixo, when they are now turning into the Largo das Duas Igrejas square.

"No idea," replies his brother.

"None other than our Major Ribeiro Arthur. Accompanied by his great friend Fialho de Almeida."

"Really? And what did that great man have to say?"

"You wouldn't believe it. As soon as we started talking he began to severely criticize my Christ, imagine. Which represents an exaggerated simplification of forms and lines. And does not respect anatomy. Which, as we all know, is punishable by death in Portugal, I felt like adding."

"What do you expect? Despite being a simple infantry major, today he is no more no less than the main and most respected art critic in Portugal, feared and flattered by anyone who is anyone in the art world."

"It really is extraordinary. And unthinkable in any civilized country," comments Aleixo as they are passing in front of the Queen Amelia Theater, where he cannot help again appreciating the picture of La Duse spread across the whole facade.

"An extraordinary actress, this Duse," comments Gaspar.

"You know, in an amazing coincidence I bumped into her this morning in the hall of the hotel, without having a clue who she was," says Aleixo at the precise moment they enter the Rua Victor Cordon, near to the door of the Braganza Hotel," only after I saw her face painted on that canvas did I realize it was her.

"You don't say! What's she like close up?" Gaspar is suddenly interested.

"She's a little worn, but even so she is an interesting woman. Not exactly pretty, but interesting."

"A woman of intense, tempestuous loves. Including with women, it appears. But her great passion was without a doubt D'Annunzio, the great Italian poet. And it still goes on, with massive rows followed by even greater reconciliations. At least that is what I am told by my friend Eugénio de Castro, who is a friend of theirs."

"Really? I had no idea," says Aleixo in surprise, when they are now going down the Calçada de São Francisco towards the downtown area.

"Do you know anything about your *Vasco da Gama*? When do the results of the competition come out?" Gaspar suddenly asks.

"From what they told me at the Geography Society, they are just waiting until the close of the deadline, at the end of this month, to show the several different maquettes at the Portugal *Salon*. And then the jury will decide."

"It is a real masterpiece. Hopefully, the jury will see this. Well, we are coming to the end and we haven't yet spoken about what's most important, which is the visit of the Nuncio," Gaspar reminds Aleixo, when they are passing in front of the Lisbon Cathedral, on their way to climb the cobbles of the Calçada do Limoeiro street.

"True. You are right. So what's it to be? Has the presence of the reception committee been confirmed?"

"Yes, unless there's some last-minute alteration they should all be there." "So what's the Nuncio like? Do you know him well?"

"I don't know him really well, of course, but I've met him a couple of times at Court meetings. He's a kind, pleasant man who seemed quite educated to me."

"And what language do I talk to him in?"

"He's Italian, but he speaks and understands Portuguese quite well."

"Just as well," exclaims Aleixo, at the precise moment that the hackney carriage comes into the Rua das Escolas Gerais, then going up the Calçada da Graça and finally coming to a stop in front of the steps to the São Vicente de Fora church.

"Look at our artist and his talented brother," they are immediately greeted by Councilor Rocha Paris, coming down the last steps to meet them as the church bells are ringing out four in the afternoon. "This is what we call punctuality," he adds, after greeting them with an energetic handshake. On the first landing of the staircase, a large group of personalities is awaiting the arrival of the Nuncio, among whom Aleixo only recognizes the Councilor Espregueira, an illustrious figure from Viana do Castelo and current President of the Chamber of Deputies.

"A colossus of expression, of feeling. My congratulations, Mr. Queiroz Ribeiro," he states, effusively greeting him.

"Thank you very much, Councilor," Aleixo replies, before beginning to greet the members of the numerous reception committee for the Nuncio, whom Espregueira successively introduces to him.

"There they are," he suddenly hears Councilor Rocha Páris exclaim at his side, pointing to two carriages that have just entered the courtyard with the arms of the Vatican painted on the side doors.

"The sculptor Queiroz Ribeiro, author of the statue of the *Sacred Heart of Jesus*, that Your Very Reverend will visit," Councilor Rocha Páris announces solemnly as he comes over next to Aleixo, after already having presented all of the reception committee to the Nuncio.

"Your Very Reverend's visit is a great honor for me and my work," says Aleixo, bending over to kiss the hand of the Nuncio of His Holiness the Pope.

"The honor is all mine, sir," replies the Nuncio, a tall, broad, dry man with bright blue eyes, his head covered in a skullcap, soberly dressed in black cape and gown, before going up the steps, followed by the whole entourage.

After going into the church, His Most Very Reverend Nuncio stops for a moment to contemplate the magnificent barrel vault of the central nave, quartered in marble sections, then continuing along the aisle paying attention to each of the side chapels until he comes to the transept, crowned by a domed vault, under which there is the statue of the *Sacred Heart of Jesus*, illuminated by the beams of sunlight coming in through the stained-glass windows of the main facade.

"*Bello, bellissimo,*" whispers the Nuncio in Italian, after spending a long time looking at the statue from different angles and perspectives, a verdict immediately corroborated by the other people present, through successive nods and low-voice murmurings. "There is the Christ who suffered, the Christ who died, the Christ who resurrected," he adds in his heavily-accented Portuguese, his eyes fixed on that face marked out by a feeling of deep bitterness, sadness, and suffering, in that thin, bent over body under the torn tunic. Then he kneels down, humbly kisses the feet of the statue, crosses himself, and ends the visit, swiftly going to the exit to the church.

"My warmest congratulations, sir. It is a beautiful and expressive statue, showing a very original concept, including in the way you represent the Sacred Heart of Jesus. Yet, I have one question that sticks in my layman's thought about these issues of art: Why is Jesus's body so bent forward?" the Nuncio makes a point of asking the sculptor as they come out of the church.

"My thanks to Your Most Very Reverend for your observations. In fact, this statue is to be placed at the top of a mountain, Monte Santa Luzia, overlooking the city of Viana do Castelo and the sea. It was thus designed to be in the pose of someone who is bending over in order to safely walk down a rather rough hillside," Aleixo explains, while the entourage spans out around him and the Nuncio, following their exchange of words with redoubled attention.

"Yes, I see. It makes perfect sense. And why did you decide to represent the Sacred Heart of Jesus not in the traditional manner, placed in the hands of the Lord, but inside his breast? " His Holiness's Nuncio insists with his curiosity.

"So that from on high, up on the mountain, Jesus could also bless the city that is at His feet, which could not happen if at the same time he was holding his Sacred Heart," adds Aleixo, to the silence of those present, awaiting the learned words of the Most Very Reverend.

"It is a greatly intelligent and sensitive justification. Which shows not only a genius of an artist but also a man of faith, who knows how to interpret the doctrine of the Church better than many theologians. For this, once more, my warmest congratulations and wishes for great future successes," the Nuncio states, holding out his hand to Aleixo, who immediately bends down to kiss it, thanking him for his kind words as the representative of the Pope.

XI

Ashbourne, outskirts of Philadelphia, 24th of July 1908

"FORTY-FIVE NEWSPAPERS! Forty-five newspapers with news about the wedding in a single day!" Miss Beach exclaimed to herself when she finished counting the stack she had piled up in front of her on the desk. To which she had added the thirty newspapers from the previous day, as well as the eleven from two days earlier, in a total of eighty-six, to which a few dozen more would no doubt be added over the following days. An absolutely surprising result, Miss Beach had to conclude, with satisfaction, knowing that, setting modesty aside, a good deal of that extraordinary success was due to her, in her capacity as private secretary to Mrs. Stetson, who had dealt with the press throughout the whole event. Starting with the meeting with the reporters right there, in the gardens of the house, two days before the wedding, to announce Mrs. Stetson's engagement to the Count, which she had organized and convoked, then including the two official communiqués that she had carefully drawn up under the direct instructions of the bride and groom, to be given out to the press, one before and one after the ceremony, and ending with the many telephone calls and personal contacts she had held with countless reporters over the previous days, in a permanent effort to guarantee the correctness and faithfulness of the information released, although never going beyond the limits of secrecy and confidentiality that had previously been established by Mrs. Stetson, as is obvious. Her satisfaction was great, but her worries were equally so, given that her long experience in the area told her that no matter how much effort she made, one could never really know what the journalists would end up valorizing in an event, what attitude or point of view they would adopt. Indeed, thanks to the harmful influence of Mr. Hearst and his methods of "fabricating" news rather than objectively informing, the newspapers seemed more interested in exploring only the sordid and scandalous aspects of the events they related, in an unbridled race to increase sales, Emma found herself thinking as she extended her gaze through the slightly open window over the vast lawn that stretched around the whole house, for a while feeling an enormous relief that she no longer had to worry about the presence of outsiders prowling around the house, or the untimely revealing of information and details about the wedding, as had been the case over the two previous days. No, now that the ceremony had taken place and that the bride and groom were in New York safely away from press curiosity, about to board the *Carmania* for their nuptial journey to Europe, everything had gradually returned to normality, and she had finally been able to isolate herself there, after lunch, in the quiet of her office, at her beautiful, robust mahogany desk, surrounded by shelves on which she kept the folders and files with the issues of the house and the property which was her responsibility to keep up to date, to freely get on with the idea she had that very morning when she saw such an avalanche of news items: to make a scrapbook with everything that was published about the event, before, during and after. Once it was complete she would have it bound in a beautiful leather cover to give to Mrs. Stetson on her return from her nuptial journey.

Ah, Mrs. Stetson! How happy she must be, now that she had finally realized her dream of being a countess, a true countess, even with a title from a small country like Portugal, which very few people in America knew where it was, despite in the past having been rich and powerful, "giving new worlds to the world," as the Count never forgot to say whenever he could, reminding them of the glorious period of the Portuguese discoveries. But what did it matter, if at the same time the bearer of this title was someone with the charm, the intelligence and the talent of the Count, elegant and better looking than most, someone who could make her really happy like she perhaps had never been before? Emma said to herself with a deep sigh before getting up from her chair and picking up the pile of the forty-five newspapers with two hands, then placing them on the low table she had beforehand placed at the right side of her desk. Then she took from the drawer her stainless steel pair of scissors with long, sharp points, cleared the desk of everything on it except for her magnifying glass, pen, and inkwell, sat down, opened the first newspaper, and avidly started cutting things out.

The sun began descending on the horizon when Miss Beach, with her right thumb and index finger aching so much that she could hardly bend them, finally finished the clippings from that first stack of newspapers from the 24th, which, after being duly identified, she placed in two little piles on the right side of the desk, one with the cuttings from the Philadelphia newspapers and another with the rest. For the following days she would leave the other two piles relating to the 22nd and 23rd, as well as the selecting and cutting out of the items that were still to be published, so that she would finally have an exact idea of the number of pages she would need to paste them in, given that without this it would be impossible to have an album of the right size bought, she concluded before putting what was left of the forty-five newspapers in the waste paper basket.

The quantity of data, elements, and information that the reporters had managed to gather in such a short time was truly impressive, ranging from the public announcing of the engagement to the consummation of the wedding. Whether or not one liked the way American reporters went about their business, there was no doubt that they carried out exhausting work, she couldn't help thinking, as she glanced over the cuttings she was placing, one by one, in horizontal rows on the top her desk so as to better analyze and compare them, first the Philadelphia newspapers, which quickly occupied the whole top half, then the rest in the lower half. And one would say that the secrecy that had surrounded the ceremony, instead of reducing press interest, had increased it, spurring on the reporters' curiosity and imagination beyond all limits.

Even without having been able to read all the news items inside out, Miss Beach had been able to get a feel of the articles as she cut them out, both through the photographs and the headlines and through reading one or two of the more significant excerpts, which she couldn't help reading. And as she was writing the date, the name of the newspaper and its state of origin on each cutting, she noticed the extraordinary interest that the wedding had provoked practically throughout the whole country, with news articles published in newspapers from such different and distant cities as San Diego, in the State of California, Indianapolis, in the State of Indiana, Milwaukee, in the State of Wisconsin, Boston, in the State of Massachusetts, Cripple Creek, in the State of Colorado, and Fort Madison, in the State of Iowa, just to quote a few. Also added to these were the main New York newspapers, like the *New York World*, the *New York Times*, the *New York Press*, or the *New York Herald*, and those from Washington, like the *Washington Post* and the *Herald* and the *Star*, and obviously from Philadelphia like the *Inquirer*, the *Bulletin*, the *Record*, the *Public Ledger*, the *Press* and the *North American*, besides those from other cities in the State of Pennsylvania, such as Trenton, Norristown, and Pittsburg.

It is obvious that the Philadelphia newspapers were a completely separate case in relation to all the others, both due to the depth and extent of the news items and the importance of the space they occupied, almost always on the front page, as well as the highlighting and size of their headlines and the profusion and quality of the accompanying photographs. Which, indeed, was not surprising, given the unique social and economic position that the Stetsons had occupied in the city for almost half a century, besides the privileged access to information that their reporters had benefited from over those days, not only the information she herself had provided for them but also that which they had obtained from other sources on their own account. Which did not mean that the newspapers from the other states and cities in the country had not also given due importance to the event, with most of them including at least one photograph, usually of the bride, and the use of suggestive headlines, such as "Mrs. Stetson marries Count," or "Mrs. Stetson is now a Countess," or also "Mrs. Stetson gains a Portuguese Title." But the articles themselves had a certain monotony and lack of imagination, generally, besides the names of the bride and groom, and some forebears, only referring to the time and place of the wedding, who celebrated it, the name of some more well-known guests, such as the inevitable Mrs. Potter Palmer, the departure for New York on the afternoon train and the foreseen embarkation on Saturday on the *Carmania* to Europe. As well as these general facts, some newspapers also added details on the room where the ceremony was held and what the bride and groom were wearing, about the police deployment that had surrounded it, and also about the inheritance that Mr. Stetson had left his widow.

"Excuse me, Miss Beach?" she heard Millie's shrill voice suddenly ask from outside.

"Come in," she replied, without looking up from her desk.

"It's your tea, Miss Beach. With some freshly-made scones."

"Thank you, Millie. Set it down here," replied Miss Beach, pointing to the low table to the right of the desk.

"So many newspapers, Miss Beach. Is it all about the wedding?" the girl asks out of curiosity, after setting down the tray.

"It's true, Millie. Almost a hundred newspapers altogether. Just yesterday there were forty-five."

"It was such a beautiful ceremony, wasn't it Miss Beach? I think I'll never forget it no matter how long I live."

"Indeed, it was a lovely ceremony. And so simple after all," added Miss Beach, after raising her cup of tea to her lips.

"Often beauty lies in the simplest things."

"Often beauty lies in the simplest things!" Emma repeated word for word, looking at Millie over her spectacle, surprised at the aptness of the statement, coming from whom it did, a poor country girl with no education. "That's absolutely true, Millie," she had to comment before she enjoyed a piece of buttered scone.

"Well, I'll leave you with your newspapers, Miss Beach. Begging your pardon, until later," Millie said, trying to disguise her sudden awkwardness, before closing the door.

Having finished her tea and scones, Emma finally got down to the task of analyzing and comparing all the news items, starting with the photographs illustrating them, particularly those published by the Philadelphia newspapers, which were by far the best and greater in number. Like that one there, right in the first row from the top, from the *Inquirer*, to which she quickly stretched out her right hand. Where one could see Mrs. Stetson, in full-body, considerably stouter and heavier than she was now, thus from before the strict diet she had imposed upon herself immediately after Mr. Stetson's death, with a plain skirt and blouse with lace frills and high neckband, long white kidskin gloves up to the elbow and broad-brimmed hat in silk tulle, and underneath it the caption "*Countess of Santa Eulália*," as if written by hand. Where did they get that from? perhaps from the newspaper's own archives, given that the photograph was at least three years old, if not more. And the other one next to it, where one could see the Count in white jacket and tie, with his mustache upturned at the ends in the style of Kaiser Wilhelm, in profile but with his head turned to look at the camera, pretending to apply the final touches to a life-size bust. Which was no more or no less than the bust of Marshall Field, the famous and extremely wealthy Chicago magnate, owner and founder of the well-known Marshall Field & Company department stores, Emma immediately recognized, recalling the photographs published in the newspapers after his death, in early 1906, indeed a short time before the death of Mr. Stetson, of whom he was a friend and business partner. And the least one could say was that the bust reproduced him totally faithfully, in the stern expression of his face and the harshness of his gaze, which is what she most remembered of the pictures she had seen of him, she concluded, putting down the photograph and picking up the two other ones also published by the *Inquirer*. These were not archive pictures, but taken the day before, she realized, one showing a policeman on horseback near to one of the entrance gates, where one could also see one of the detectives, hand on hip, straw hat, looking at the camera, and who was none other than Mr. Johnson, the head of the Philadelphia Pinkerton Agency, and another, round photograph with a uniformed policeman standing next to a tree alongside another man, in shirt sleeves and with his hat pushed back over his neck, who was none other than the reporter from the *North American*, that Kelly, the same man she had caught the day before the wedding peeking in at the entrance door, Miss Beach immediately noted before she put the photograph down next to the others. To then immediately pick up the cutting that was next to it, with a photograph of Mrs. Stetson, sitting down, with a very frilled dress and hat, and the Count, just as he had appeared at the wedding, with his beautiful uniform as a Gentleman Knight of the Royal Household, two-pointed hat with ostrich feathers on the top and his chest brimming with medals. On the row beneath it were the cuttings from the *Press*, including two beautiful photographs of the bride and groom, side by side, he in civilian clothes, overcoat, hair, and mustache well-groomed and shiny, and in front of him, as if holding it in his two hands, a photograph of that bust of a woman sculpted in marble with which he had won the Grand Prix at the Paris Salon, above a capitalized headline: "COUNT Eulália AND HIS 'SALOME'." And her, with her hair tied up and with an ermine coat on her back, drawn on the photograph, inside an oval medallion, beneath a caption, also in headlines, where one could read: "*PHILADELPHIA'S NEWEST COUNTESS.*" The *Bulletin* only published a photograph that she herself, Emma, had provided for them, in which one could see the Count posing next to his statue of Queen Amelia of Portugal, but on the other hand, they had given it a prominent position, occupying a good part of the front page. Next to the item in the *Bulletin* was that of the *North American*, also with a single large-scale photo, but of Mrs. Stetson, showing only the bust, framed by a hand drawing with a crown in the upper right corner.

As for the headlines and size of the news items, that of the *Inquirer* occupied two top-to-bottom columns on the front page, right below the photographs of Mrs. Stetson and the Count, continuing onto page two, and above it was a curious headline: "*Many Prominent Guests Attend Ceremony by Which the Millionaire's Widow Becomes Bride of Portuguese Nobleman.*" The *Record* had in a capital-letter headline, "*MRS. STETSON IS NOW A REAL COUNTESS,*" while the item also occupied two columns from top to bottom on the front page. As for the *Press*, it had a two and a half column item on the front page, with a headline that was almost the same as that of the *Record*, while the *North American* didn't do things by halves, and under the photograph of Mrs. Stetson a huge headline said, in total dissonance to the others: "*COPS GUARD ESTATE WHILE COUNT WEDS MRS. J. B. STETSON.*"

Although that police deployment set up around the estate while the wedding was taking place might have seemed over the top, leaving a somewhat negative impression on the reporters present, it made no sense at all to bring this matter into the main headlines for the item, but, after all, coming from where it came from it wasn't surprising, thought Miss Beach, recalling the brash and cheeky tone with which Mr. Kelly, the same man whose photograph she had just seen in the *Inquirer*, had addressed her when she had gone outside after the ceremony to the main gates and denied the rumors about Mrs. Stetson's alleged abandoning of the Protestant faith, asking her what she had to say to them about that woman who had spent the whole morning trying to get into the estate and who said she was a friend of the Count's, recalled Emma, at once starting to look for some reference to the matter in the item in the *North American*. Which she obviously very soon found, right there sticking out on the front page, under the sub-heading "*Mysterious Woman Appears.*" The article stated that in the early morning a woman with a foreign appearance and accent, dressed in white and with a parasol of the same color, had appeared at the gates to *Idro* trying to force her way into the estate, and was prevented from doing so by the guards.

Had the other newspapers also dealt with this subject? Wondered Miss Beach, worriedly, as she quickly picked up the cuttings from the *Inquirer* in search of them, yet not finding any headline alluding to the matter, nor in the *Record*. But unfortunately the same could not be said of the *Public Ledger*, in the cutting from which she soon discovered a reference completely identical to that of the *North American*. Also, the *Press*, the cuttings from which she picked up next, had two sub-headings, "*Mysterious Woman at the Gate*" and "*The Uninvited Guest*," relative to the issue, but while under the former there was nothing new in relation to what appeared in the other newspapers, under the second sub-heading there was some information that seemed to her, Emma, to be at the least strange, not to say disturbing:

"When the woman was questioned as to who she was, she replied that she was a personal friend of the Count and that she had known him before he came to the United States, and if she could get her name to him, he would gladly see her. When asked for her name or title she said that it would make trouble for her family if she gave it out, but she boasted that if the name were disclosed it would be known to all the guests and, 'in fact, to the majority of the people of the United States.'"

Was there any foundation in what this woman said, or was she just a paranoid lunatic wanting to be noticed? But in that case, how would she have known about the ceremony, when there had been such secrecy surrounding it? Because even if she had been able to read the first news items about the announcement of the engagement on the 22nd, nothing in this would have given her the slightest indication about the holding of the wedding the next day and much less about the time and place. And if she had come from Chicago all the worse, given that the newspapers that had published news about the matter of the previous day were almost all from Philadelphia or neighboring cities. Might she have found it out through the Portuguese consulate, where someone might inadvertently revealed what was going to happen, where and when? No. That was very unlikely, as the consular staff were under the orders of the Count, and he was certainly the last person to be interested in the woman turning up. Might Mrs. Palmer have told her? No. That was impossible, as the mere possibility of a woman like that getting to speak to someone of the status and social standing of the Queen of Chicago was simply ridiculous, concluded Miss Beach, yet still unable to forget the expression on the Count's face as he sat on one of the sofas in the Gothic hall next to Mrs. Stetson, as they waited for the arrival of Monsignor Turner and Father Morrissey when he heard Mr. Johnson tell them of the presence of the woman at the main gate to the estate when he went suddenly very pale and nervous like she had never seen him before. And the strange exchange of glances he had with Mrs. Stetson, before she asked Mr. Johnson some routine questions about the woman. As if her appearance were not really a surprise for them, but merely the confirmation of something they probably expected to happen and for which they had prepared the adequate response. Which indeed was not long in coming, not from the Count's mouth, but from Mrs. Stetson, who, with unshakeable coolness and presence of mind, gave strict instructions to Mr. Johnson to prevent the woman from entering under any circumstance, but with the greatest possible discretion so the reporters did not understand anything, she hastened to add. And then a somber idea flashed through Miss Beach's mind like a lightning bolt: did the rushed manner in which the wedding had been decided have anything to do with that woman or with something she knew about the Count's past that could possibly prevent the ceremony or make things difficult? And could there be, or have been, some relationship between the presence of that woman and Mrs. Stetson's orders to have the estate guarded as it was all day long? "I do not want reporters, curious observers, or anyone else here inside, Emma," she had told her peremptorily, two days before the wedding, immediately after the press conference in the garden. Might that "anyone else" have been specifically intended for the mysterious woman? No. It couldn't be, decided Miss Beach, thrusting the idea away from her thoughts, as it seemed to be so frightening and contrary to everything she thought and felt for her employer and for the Count.

Although she was forced to acknowledge the strangeness she had always felt by the fact that someone with the Count's figure, charm, intelligence, and education had remained single until his forties. Why had he not married before, precisely now when he could be considered an inveterate bachelor? Because he had not met a suitable woman for him until then? Why, being an artist and wishing to carry on so, had he not managed to gather the personal fortune necessary to keep a wife and constitute a family, in keeping with the economic and financial standard in which he had been brought up? Might that woman have been an affair of the Count's in Chicago, or even still back in Europe, given that, according to the *Press*, he met her before he came to the United States? Might the Count even have been married to that woman, who had come there legitimately to claim her rights and duties, preventing the wedding of her husband, or ex-husband, to another woman? Emma found herself wondering again, before deciding to definitively put an end to those upsetting reflections, replacing them with more joyful and festive issues, such as, for example, the way that the Philadelphia newspapers described the ceremony itself. Yes, that was, or ought to be, the subject par excellence of the news items and the center of her own concerns, she told herself, determinedly picking up the part of the cuttings from the *Inquirer* alluding to the ceremony, where it stated that the wedding had taken place in the mansion's visitors' room, located in the north wing of the house: "The room was very well decorated for the occasion, with the magnificent hothouses, which were the pride of the late Mr. Stetson, having been stripped of their beautiful flowers in order to add to the beauty of the room. Precisely at fifteen minutes to eleven in the morning, Monsignor Turner and Father Morrissey entered the room and walked to the altar, followed by the small but brilliant procession of guests." Further on it said that after the guests had taken their seats Mendelssohn's wedding march was heard, played on the organ acquired for the house by the late Mr. Stetson. But it was said that initially, Mrs. Stetson had wanted the wedding march from *Lohengrin* to be played, but that "her fiancé's visceral aversion for German music had forced a sudden change in the program." Who could have given the reporters all that information about an episode that, once again, only she and she alone had witnessed? Yes, her…and the organist. Of course, it could only have been him, Miss Beach concluded, without being able to imagine what could lead a musician, someone whose main activity was to perform beautiful melodies on the organ, to stoop so low as to go running to tell reporters such a thing, as if they were a maid or gardener? His irritation at suddenly being prevented from playing the aria he had previously rehearsed, by Wagner, no doubt his favorite, given that Wagner was clearly in vogue in the United States, replaced at the last minute by another one, by Mendelssohn, which he probably considered to be less interesting and original, all of this because of a whim or tantrum by another man, and a foreigner to boot? Or only because of a few more dollar bills in his pocket? It was a matter she would try to get to the bottom of next time she saw him, she decided before returning to reading her cuttings, this time those from the *Public Ledger*, where, under the sub-heading "*Flowers for the Wedding*," there was another description of the ceremony, in almost identical terms to those of the *Inquirer*, surprisingly finishing off in the following manner: "Miss Annabelle Beach, the Countess' Secretary, and a few of the servants also witnessed the ceremony." Where did that name come from again, "Annabelle," Miss "Annabelle" Beach? Why did the newspapers insist on calling her this if she had always said her name clearly and audibly, Emma, Emma Virginia Beach? Anyway, it was always pleasant to see herself mentioned in the newspaper: "Miss Annabelle Beach, the Countess's secretary." Yes, Mrs. Stetson was now a countess, and she had to get used to addressing her as one. And also get used to seeing herself as the private secretary to a countess, Countess de Santa Eulália, she thought with a touch of pride as she returned to the *North American*, anxious to see how the daring Mr. Kelly had described the ceremony: "The guests were already gathered in the drawing-room. The broad windows, open to the breeze, let in long shafts of yellow sunshine, which fired an arch of white roses erected before an altar against the eastern wall and contrasted strongly with the flickering candles."

How pretty, how poetic, there was no doubt that despite being insolent and forward, Mr. Kelly was not totally without talent, Miss Beach commented to herself before continuing reading the article, in which it mentioned the names of the people present at the ceremony, not just the members of the family, but also the other guests: "…a Representative of the Portuguese Embassy in Washington; Miguel Alvarez and José Reyna, from the Portuguese Consulate in Chicago; Mrs. Potter Palmer, from Chicago; John S. Stevens from Philadelphia and Mr. and Mrs. Theodore B. Van Steuyphen, from New York." Here indeed was the full list, provided by the guards according to Mr. Kelly. But what guards, if their instructions had been clear and definite about not providing any information to the reporters? One of the estate workers, wishing to earn a few dollars? Yes, it could only be that, given that she didn't believe that the Pinkerton detectives, or even the policemen from the Cheltenham station, would be involved in that sort of thing. But anyway, now that it was all over, what did it matter? Emma said to herself resigned, returning to her reading, surprised by the detailed way that Mr. Kelly described the Count's outfit: "The Count's black suit, which we Americans would call evening dress, was perfectly fitted to his figure. His black velvet collar was adorned with gold galloons and lace, also decorating his shoulders and reappearing at his wrists. On his breast the Count had a row of a dozen decorations from European orders and, finally, in his hands, he held a two-pointed hat, a real "*chapeau diplomatique.*"

A beautiful description, no doubt about it, doing justice to the Count's presence and figure. With only one off point: the suit wasn't black but dark blue, Emma noted, preparing to get into the best aspects of the article: "For fully a minute perfect stillness reigned in the drawing-room. Then were heard footsteps on the stairs beyond, the rustle of gowns and a stirring among the servants gathered at the doorway. The eyes of all present were turned in the direction of this sound as, from the Gothic hall, there entered Mrs. Stetson, her hand resting upon the arm of her son, John Stetson Jr., and, following her, as matrons-of-honor, her two daughters-in-law, Mrs. John B. Stetson Jr., and Mrs. G. Henry Stetson.

"Attired in a simple gown of white silk, almost severely cut, the bride, who carried a large bouquet of American Beauty roses, proceeded, in absolute silence, to the altar. There she was given in marriage by John B. Stetson Jr., and then, immediately at the conclusion of the ceremony, as the big organ in the hall outside pealed into the opening notes of Mendelssohn's "Wedding March," the count lifted to his lips and kissed the countess' hand," Emma read in one breath, captured by the description that Kelly made of the ceremony, so realistic, so well-written. Here indeed Mr. Kelly definitively displayed his talent, narrating the event as if he had really witnessed it in person, when the best he could have managed to obtain were descriptions made by third parties. But who? One of the guests? Very unlikely, given who they were. Yes, no one could imagine Mrs. Palmer, or Mr. Stevens, or even Mr. Van Steuyphen giving out information of that kind to reporters. Perhaps one of the maids, whom Mrs. Stetson, indeed against her, Emma's, opinion, had generously allowed to attend the ceremony from the Gothic hall.

Yes, that was the most natural thing. And the rest, one had to admit it, was the imagination and talent of the reporter at work, nothing else, she thought, herself unable to resist recalling Mrs. Stetson's entrance, that she could witness personally from inside the music room, where the ceremony took place, unlike the rest of the staff, through special deference on the part of the bride and groom, walking on John's arm, serene and proud, down the aisle, between the guests who from either side turned to greet her, to the altar, where Monsignor Turner, assisted by Father Morrissey, awaited the moment to begin the ceremony, impressive in the rich canonical vestments. Ah! The refined manner in which the Count, at the altar, received her from John, gently taking her hand to help her take her place at the genuflection stool under the arc, wonderfully decorated with roses and orchids. After a brief exchange of impressions with the bride and groom, Monsignor Turner had started reading an excerpt from the Gospels in Latin, had blessed the bride and groom and then addressed the congregation, asking whether if there was anyone in the room who knew any reason why that wedding could not be celebrated then they should speak then or forever hold their peace. Then, as no one spoke, as at least inside the music room there didn't seem to be anyone in a condition to do so—unlike what would probably happen at the entrance to the estate with that mysterious woman—Monsignor Turner turned again to the bride and groom, addressing them by their given names and asking the sacramental questions, before finally stating: "Elizabeth and Aleixo, I declare you husband and wife," which was followed by that memorable kiss, not on her face, or even on her mouth, as was already boldly done in certain places, but on her hand, so elegant, so refined. And indeed to which the reporter, even though he had not witnessed it, made a point of alluding, recalled Emma, moved, unable to hold back a treacherous tear in the corner of her eye, which she hurriedly wiped away with the tip of her lavender perfumed handkerchief before reading the final paragraph of that part of the text, which mentioned the newlyweds' departure by car for the station on their way to New York: "The couple covered their car up with an oilskin so as to fool the photographers, but even so it was possible to notice that the husband had changed from his official dress to a simple brown suit and that his wife was wearing a gray dress."

But how did the reporter manage to see what the Count and the

Countess were wearing from the place he was? During the brief moment when they got into the car? Or later on, at the station, before they caught the train? Wondered Emma as she moved on to the cuttings from the *Press* looking for references about the same subject. But this newspaper, despite there being a chapter with the sub-heading "Off to Europe," only mentioned that the newlyweds had left the house for New York by car in the first paragraph, with no further details. On the other hand, the *Inquirer* dedicated the whole end of its report to the subject, stating: "The manner of the escape of the Count and Countess to their New York train late in the afternoon, without anyone even catching a glimpse of them, was remarkable. The Secret Service bureau was ordered to redouble its efforts to keep strangers away from the road which winds near the rear of the Stetson home."

The way that they had left for the station and then from there to New York had indeed been extraordinary, with them managing to avoid the curiosity of the reporters, who were unable to see them close up or photograph them, Miss Beach was pleased to recall, given that she was responsible for organizing that "flight" along with Mr. Johnson, from the Pinkerton agency. This was despite some exaggerated attitudes by the police, leading the reporters to focus too much on the police presence set up around the estate during the wedding. As was the case, for example, with the *North American*, right there in front of her devoting to this not only the main headline of the article, but also a sub-heading, "*Special Guard of Cops,*" above a text with three paragraphs: "Not even at the station was the guard about them relaxed. Not only were they followed by four men-servants from the estate, but to these were added as many policemen from the Twenty-second District, who threatened to "punch the head off" of any photographer who presumed to take a picture."

"What an exaggeration, what violence, good gracious," Emma said to herself. Even if the threat to 'tear their heads off' was not intended to be taken seriously by the photographers, it wasn't the sort of thing one said to anyone, much less to reporters, she concluded before moving on to the cutting from the *Press*, where a curious sub-heading was above the last part of the article: "*Where Romance Began.*" Which she felt compelled to read: "It is whispered that Cupid lurked behind a colossal bronze bas-relief of H.L. Deland of Fairport, N.Y., which was executed by the Count and which stood in the reception hall at *Idro*. Many friends believe that this piece of sculpture is responsible for the marriage. The work was done many years ago, during the life of Mr. Stetson. Mr. Deland was the founder of Deland, Fl., where Mr. Stetson afterward founded Stetson University. Mr. Deland posed for the work while visiting the Stetsons, and it was at this time that the Count and Mrs. Stetson became acquainted. The Count is now engaged in modeling a similar bas-relief to show the head and shoulders of the late Mr. Stetson."

Who gave the information to the reporter this time? Information that although they start from a real situation—the fact that the Count had been at *Idro* working on the bas-relief in homage to Mr. Deland contracted by Mr. Stetson himself to do so—permitted all sorts of errors in almost suggesting, in the way it was written, that the romance could have started while Mr. Stetson was still alive. Not, certainly, a gardener or maid. It had to be someone closer to the family, a friend who knew what had really happened. Perhaps Mr. Stevens, the only guest who resided in Philadelphia. Who might even have given the reporter the information with the greatest objectivity, but which the reporter twisted so as to suggest what he was suggesting. Yet what the item wished to do was to give an answer to the question that deep down everyone was asking: how did a rich American widow from Philadelphia become acquainted with a European Count, sculptor, and consul, resident in Chicago, in the center of the country, over a thousand miles from the East coast and end up getting married?

Finally, finishing off the item in the *Press*, two paragraphs under the sub-heading "*Count is Not Wealthy*," which Miss Beach had to read, suddenly concerned about what they might insinuate on such a delicate issue as the Count's finances: "The embarrassing fact that the Count is not wealthy has called from Mrs. Stetson and her friends' indignant denials that he is a mere fortune hunter. He is a friend of the former King, his family is one of the noblest of Portugal, and his estates have been in the family's possession back to the Crusades. The statue of the present Dowager Queen Amelia was completed in the Count's studio in Chicago, while the Count was acting as Consul of the Portuguese Government. It will be placed in the royal palace. Despite connecting ties which hold him to his fatherland, the Count has become so attached to America, he says, that he will make his abode here permanently, residing at Mrs. Stetson's palatial home, 'Idro'."

What would the other newspapers say about the matter? Wondered Miss Beach, once again picking up the cuttings from the *North American*, looking for some reference, yet without success, with the same happening in the *Inquirer*. Only in the *Public Ledger* did she find, at the end of the item, a reference not to the Count's incomes but to the financial benefits he might obtain from his marriage to Mrs. Stetson, whose annual income was stated to be around $150,000, given that, according to them, Mr. Stetson's will clearly stated that "the income was to be respectively attributed to his wife and children for their individual and exclusive use and benefit, and could in no manner be disposed of or parted with by anticipation, nor be subject to execution, attachment or sequestration, for any debts or liabilities whatsoever."

Why were the reporters unable to understand that there was more to life beyond money? That there were still people who were capable of loving and having feelings, far beyond what they might benefit materially by this? Wondered Emma, throwing the cuttings from the *Public Ledger* onto the desk, then glancing quickly at the clock: a quarter after eight. What had happened to those people downstairs, George, Millie, and the rest of the staff? Just because Mrs. Stetson was not home were there no timetables to respect? What time did they expect to serve dinner? She said to herself, standing up to turn on the desk lamp as she realized that she was almost in the dark now that the sun had definitively set on the horizon, at the precise moment that she started to hear quick footsteps in the corridor, followed by three knocks on the door and George's exalted voice calling:

"Miss Beach, Miss Beach!"

"Come in!" she replied, preparing to upbraid him.

"Miss Beach, Mrs. Stetson, begging pardon, the Countess is on the telephone and wishes to speak to you."

"The Countess, on the telephone? I'll be there right away, George," replied Miss Beach, suddenly very excited, running after the butler down the corridor to the Gothic hall:

"Yes, Mrs. Stetson, pardon, Countess? How are you? And the Count?" she said, panting, with the earpiece to her ear and mouth against the base.

"We are fine, Emma."

"Did everything go well on the journey?"

"Everything went perfectly. The idea of us getting off the train at Newark and making the rest of the journey by car to New York was indeed a genius idea. Apparently, at the exit from the train in Jersey City, there was a battalion of New York reporters waiting for us—who must have been very disappointed, I imagine."

"If you knew how many articles there are in today's newspapers, Countess…"

"Don't they have anything else to report? Why all this interest in our wedding, what importance does it have for people after all, for public opinion?"

"Apparently it's what sells newspapers, Countess."

"Well, but let's change the subject. How are things there?"

"Everything is calm, Countess. Too calm even, after all the agitation of the last days."

"I imagine, Emma, I imagine. And any news about John and G. Henry?" "I didn't see them today. I suppose they stayed at home, resting."

"Yes, that's natural. I must phone them."

"And in New York. Has your stay been good?"

"It couldn't be better, Emma, it couldn't be better."

"I'm glad to hear it, Countess…"

"Well, Emma, I'll have to hang up. Tomorrow the departure is in the morning, very early. Then I will be in touch when I get to Liverpool."

"I'll be waiting, Countess. I wish you an excellent journey and my congratulations. For the Count also, obviously."

"Thank you, Emma. And thank you for all your effort. And for your support and friendship."

"It was a pleasure and an honor, Countess," replied Miss Beach, then hanging up the earpiece and going to the kitchen, where dinner was waiting for her.

XII

Lisbon, 19th of May 1898

"A MONTH AND A DAY. Exactly a month and a day, since my departure for Paris. And here I am again in Lisbon," Aleixo says to himself, sitting in one of the stands adjoining the royal pavilion, set up in the middle of the Avenida da Liberdade, waiting to see the emergence of the head of the civic cortège on the horizon, the high point of the Program of the Commemorations of the Fourth Centenary of the Discovery of the Sea Route to India, which for the last week has livened up the city of Lisbon, capital of the Empire, albeit in vain, as almost half an hour after the time stated in the program for the cortège to go past, the central lane of the avenue is still completely deserted. On the other hand, the sidewalks are bursting with thousands and thousands of people, among them Lisbon residents and visitors who have come from all over the country on the cut-price trains placed at their disposal by the government, and who are crushed behind the rows of chairs lined up along the curbsides, going from the Restauradores square to the stand, almost exclusively occupied by ladies, whose dresses, seen from where he is, add a beautiful touch of color to the proceedings.

"A month of so much work, so much expense, and what for in the end?" he asks himself in disgust, at the same time as he quickly glances at the royal pavilion, up there in the middle of the stand, under a great red platform with gold fringes, which is completely empty except for the archers with their halberds, posted in the four corners of the stands, a sign that their Majesties King Carlos and Queen Amelia had not yet arrived, nor any member of the royal family, no doubt forewarned by the officials of the delay with which the cortège left the Terreiro do Paço square. Just as empty as the place next to him, reserved for his brother Gaspar, the prince of English punctuality, but who is once again irremediably late, given that on the note he sent to him that morning at the hotel, accompanying his free pass to the rows on the royal stand reserved for the members of the Chamber of Deputies and their respective families, it stated that he would be there at one o'clock in the afternoon at the latest. Well, now it is a quarter to two and Gaspar is nowhere to be seen, he concludes after consulting his watch.

"Yes, don't get your hopes up. After what happened yesterday it will be difficult for the initial classification to be upheld," he thinks, at the same time noticing the rows set aside for the diplomatic corps, which, contrarily, are almost totally filled by the ministers from the several different countries and members of the respective Embassies, all of whom are no doubt still unfamiliar with the proverbial Portuguese lack of punctuality, the men sitting there in their showy and rich court outfits, with bright colors, trimmed in gold, the ladies in their elegant silk or satin dresses, adorned with gems, sitting behind the gaudy Indian cloth mantles that drape the whole balcony area.

"A dream. A dream that—Alas!—disappeared all too quickly. Proving right the warning by Eça de Queiroz, and the care one should take as to what he calls the guardians of the temple," he recalls, looking blindly at the side stands, like the one in which he is sitting, also being filled up little by little with the successive arrival of the members of the Court, the civil household and the king's military household, of the members of the ministry, of the honorary ministers, of the high officials of state, of the deputies and peers of the realm, of the higher officials of the navy and of the army, all in their sparkling ceremonial outfits or in their well-styled black dress coats, accompanied by their respective wives, whose outfits, seen from a distance, are in no manner beneath those worn by the ladies from the diplomatic corps in terms of elegance and distinction.

"And there goes the dream of the prodigal son's return to his homeland," he concludes to himself with deep bitterness, before plunging into reading the program for the Centenary, which he takes out of his coat pocket, with nothing better to distract him. The commemorations officially started on the 11th, the day of his arrival in Lisbon on the *Sud Express* train, and go on for eleven days, only ending on the 22nd. But in fact, the main manifestations and festive events are practically concentrated over the four days of the National Gala, starting on the 17th, the date which is exactly four hundred years after the arrival of Vasco da Gama and his companions in Calcutta and ending on the 20th. On the other days there are events of a more cultural, scientific, or sporting nature, which will only interest some sectors of the population, such as the National Congress of Medicine and Hygiene, inaugurated on the 11th in the Portugal Hall of the Geography Society; or the National Fine Arts Exhibition, promoted by the Artists' Guild, inaugurated on the 12th; or events with a clearly popular inclination, such as the Open Fair, on the roundabout of the Liberdade Avenue, or the two international yachting regattas to be held in Cascais and Paço de Arcos. Out of all of these events he had only been present, as a matter of duty, at the inauguration of the Exhibition of the Artists' Guild, where some of his works were on display, given that for the following days he was too busy with the customs release, transportation, and delivery of the models for the competition for the monument to Sousa Martins at the Royal Academy of Fine Arts, the deadline for which was the 15th. Indeed, that was the main reason for his coming to Lisbon, but not the only one, as at the same time the sculpture competition promoted by the Executive Committee of the Centenary was taking place, the only two models in competition for which had in fact been on exhibit since a few days ago at the Portugal Hall of the Geography Society: his much-praised and celebrated *Vasco da Gama* and a sculpture group by Tomás Costa, an artist also resident in Paris, with the emblem *Ganges*, he recalls, not noticing the increasing signs of impatience coming from his companions in the stands, who are gesticulating and standing up, fed up with that interminable waiting, while, contrarily, the representatives of the diplomatic corps resisted, impassive, in their places.

As for the days of the National Gala, his participation had been considerably greater, in some cases due to his own wishes, and in other cases because he had no choice, such as at the "Daybreak Feast," as it is pompously called in the Program for the Commemorations, which took place on the 17th. Yes, it will be hard to forget those rounds of rifle fire that, two days earlier, had made him jump out of bed startled at half-past five in the morning, he finds himself thinking. Followed by countless *girandoles* of rockets fired from the highest points in the city, accompanied by the pealing of the bells in many churches, activities that he could witness from the balcony of his bedroom before going back to bed, but now unable to get back to sleep again. And which, to his chagrin, has been repeated invariably since then at the same time, for the same length of time and with the same intensity, he recalls before he sees a reference to the international rowing regatta in the program, promoted by the Executive Central Committee of the Centenary, with the cooperation of the Portuguese nautical recreation associations, from between the quays of Alcântara and Belém. Which he inadvertently watched from the balcony of the imperial salon of the hotel Braganza, along with many other guests at the hotel, as he was there awaiting the imminent arrival of the final classifications for the Sousa Martins monument competition, which had been promised for that day by the executive committee, he recalls. But which after all only arrived in the evening, when he was already preparing to watch, from the same hotel balcony, the "grandiose" firework display announced in the Program, brought to him by Gaspar, who had received the classifications from one of the members of the committee with whom he was friendly. "You can start moving your studio to Lisbon, lad," Gaspar greeted him euphorically as soon as he saw him leaning on the balcony, then immediately suggesting they send for a bottle of the best French champagne to celebrate.

"What? What are you talking about?" he asked, incredulous, turning to his brother.

"Your project, Aleixinho. It is in first place among the seven competitors," insisted Gaspar, embracing him.

"It can't be true. You're joking," he replied, not wishing to believe what he was hearing. He, classified in first place? No, it's not possible, he thought, leaning on Gaspar's arms so as not to fall over.

"It's true, absolutely true, lad. The decision wasn't made public today because before doing so the committee decided to listen to some trustworthy people, more versed in the arts than they are, because, as you know, they are almost all doctors and men of science. Which, when one thinks about it, seems to be a good idea," replied Gaspar.

"Who are these people? Don't you think there is a risk that they might question the committee's decision?" he asked, somewhat worried.

"The member of the committee I spoke to didn't tell me who they were, but told me that the idea was to invite people who would corroborate the committee's decision and not the contrary, so that this would appear in the form of a technical opinion, and thus avoid future complaints," explained Gaspar, calling a butler to have the champagne brought.

"Not champagne, Gasparinho, don't overdo it. After the decision has been confirmed you can order all the champagne you want, but not before, it's bad luck. Don't count your chickens before they've hatched," he said prudently, at the precise moment when, as if on cue, an enormous salvo of mortar fire went up in the air, finally starting the long-awaited firework display, except not at ten o'clock, as stated in the program, but at eleven o'clock, for whatever reason. After the salvo of mortar fire, there was a long and drawn-out stationary firework display, reproducing, as was to be expected, figures related to the discoveries, such as the facade of the Hieronymite Monastery, a fifteenth-century galleon, and the portrait of Vasco da Gama with his name written in fire, among many others, lit up intensely for a moment and then burning out to give way to the next figure. Indeed, nothing that had been greatly surprising or amazing, particularly when in the background one could witness a much more brilliant and spectacular "stationary fireworks" performed on foreign ships anchored in the River Tagus, all lit up with electric lights around their hulls, on their masts and around their cannon, and at the same time as, from the more distant battleships electric light beams shone on several different points in the city, recalls Aleixo, without noticing the agitation that suddenly ran across the whole stand, followed immediately by the noises of horses' hoofs trotting down the avenue: this is the cavalry squadron that precedes the gala coach that transports Their Majesties, moving down the avenue until it stops in front of the royal pavilion in order to let out its illustrious passengers: first Queen Amelia, extremely elegant in a light blue dress with white lace trimmings and a feathered hat, also blue, immediately followed by King Carlos, impressive in his admiral's uniform, with the Great Cross of the Ordem da Espada, then Prince Luiz Filipe, in the uniform of the honorary commander of the Military College, and Prince Manuel, in a sailor's outfit. At the first sounds of the Hymn of the Charter, played by the band of the Second Lancers, which secures the Guard of Honor, the royal couple walks to the front of the royal pavilion and the whole audience stands up. At the end, the royal party greets the applauding crowd before going up the steps of the central aisle laid out with a long red carpet, until they come to their pavilion, followed by the princes and a large entourage.

It is exactly two o'clock, but no sign of the cortège. The central lane of the avenue is still deserted, Aleixo notices once again, looking at his watch, before returning to his reading of the program, which, for the previous day, had announced the holding of a further "Daybreak Feast" at five in the morning, and at one in the afternoon a "Solemn *Te-Deum*" at the Church of Santa Maria de Belém, near the Hieronymite Monastery. And at four in the afternoon, a parade by the land and sea forces and military schools in the Liberdade Avenue.

Yes, the previous morning he again awoke startled by the infernal row of the cannon fire, followed by the unbearable fireworks display, but this time he didn't even bother getting up to see what was going on, and when it was all over he turned to the other side and fell asleep, waking again close to ten o'clock. Before leaving the hotel he went to the Imperial Hall, where he was flicking through the newspapers looking for news about the competition. Which he only found in the *Diário de Notícias* newspaper, fully confirming what Gaspar had told him; that is, the "adjudication"—that was the term used—of the first prize for his project, with the title *Light,* the second place for the project by Alberto Nunes, with the title *Glória Victis,* and third for the project by Costa Motta, with the title *Serra da Estrela.* So it was in a state of great euphoria and enthusiasm that he took a carriage to the Hieronymite Monastery to attend the *Te-Deum* that was held there at one o'clock in the afternoon in the presence of the King and the whole royal family, followed by another visit to the same spot, in the Liberdade Avenue, to watch the parade by the military forces and the military schools, a laborious procession that lasted for several hours, but which had the great virtue of keeping him distracted while he waited with natural anxiety for further news about the competition, brought to him once again by his tireless brother Gaspar, now after eight in the evening. Yet unlike the previous day, they could not have been worse, nor—Alas!—more disappointing: after a meeting lasting several hours, the group of people that the committee decided to hear proposed nothing more nothing less than switching his proposal to third place, promoting that of Costa Motta from third to first place, but had not come to a definitive conclusion, which it had adjourned until today, recalls Aleixo dejectedly, once again buried into his reading of the program, which for that day only has a single offering, precisely that cortège, "of homage and civic commemoration," probably the most important and eagerly-awaited event of the Centenary commemorations. To which, in all truth, he was ready to avoid going, such was his indignation and revolt over the news about the competition that he read, early in the morning, in the *Diário de Notícias*, which, besides confirming everything that Gaspar had told him about the decision by the executive committee to hear the opinion of a group of people that is considered to be more competent in technical terms before releasing their final vote on the works in competition, also carried the news about the alterations to the final classification proposed by this group and the list of names who had accepted to be members of the same group. Officiating among these were António José Nunes Junior and José Simões d'Almeida, both sculptors and teachers at the School of Fine Arts for ages, and as such were the main figures responsible for the imposition of the most backward and conservative classicism and naturalism on their pupils, in total ignorance of the new tendencies in the field of sculpture. But also the painters Ernesto Condeixa and Carlos Reis, who, from the works of theirs he could see a few days earlier at the Artists' Guild Salon, seemed to continue to ignore the existence of impressionism and of everything which, along with its appearance, had changed in painting over the last thirty years, recalls Aleixo, not immediately aware of the hubbub rising in the stands. A new entourage comes down from up the avenue, this time bringing Queen Maria Pia, accompanied by Prince Dom Afonso, the king's brother, nicknamed *Out-o'-the-way!*, due to the speed with which he likes to drive his team of horses; her, elegant as ever, in a black silk dress with lace of the same color, as befits a widow such as her; he in his fine uniform as an artillery officer.

So, what will be the committee's decision in the end? Will those illustrious doctors and men of science accept the dictates of the two teachers, who are only trying to promote their student and follower Costa Motta, whose model is an example of banality and lack of imagination, as he himself could witness when he went to see it at the Academy? Or will they have the courage to go against all and sundry and accept their own initial decision to grant him the first prize, backing his work, a more innovating and original conception in relation to everything that was being done there? The decisive meeting is being held at that very moment in an office in the Royal Academy of Fine Arts, in the Biblioteca Pública square, and it won't be very long before the result is known, Aleixo tells himself, with a glimmer of hope, but without fostering great illusions, before delving once more into the program for the following days. For tomorrow, and fortunately for the last time, the "Daybreak Feast" will wake Lisbon up with its gunfire and fireworks at five in the morning, followed by the inauguration of the *Vasco da Gama* Aquarium, which is all that will remain for posterity from these commemorations, but which, so it seems, is still not entirely finished. In the afternoon there will be a Portuguese bullfight and in the evening the local councils' ball, thus ending the program of the days of the National Gala. Which will be followed by two further days of festivities during which there will be two shooting contests and one cycling race, Aleixo finally notes, before putting the Program away in his pocket, with an enormous feeling of emptiness filling his heart, his heart as a Portuguese man and patriot, seeing the pettiness of these commemorations, particularly when compared with those that Spain held about the fourth centenary of the discovery of America by Christopher Columbus, not to mention the famous Chicago Colombian Exposition, held by the Americans over the same event. Which Nellie, his dear Nellie, described to him in the tiniest detail, with its monumental pavilions covered in works of art, lit up by electricity, its wide avenues, its beautiful ponds, indeed, a massive area set aside on purpose to house the commemorations. But in the end, Portugal is Portugal, eternally steeped in an economic and financial crisis that no one knows how to get out of, so that this "dull and vile sadness" is the best one could come up with in order to commemorate the feats of the great Vasco da Gama, concludes Aleixo, again looking at his watch, showing half-past two, with the whole royal tribune steaming with impatience, waiting for a cortège that does not seem to want to appear. Not even Gaspar, the extremely punctual Gaspar. What could have happened to him? Where might he be at this time of day? He worries to himself. Perhaps he met up with a friend on the way, with whom he became lost in conversation, he thinks. Or he may have had a last-minute meeting in the Party offices. Or might he be held up in the traffic that since the morning had filled the main thoroughfares of the city because of the cortège. He had clearly seen what was happening in the Chiado and São Roque street areas when he passed through there in the morning. Coaches, open carriages, hackney carriages, carts, all stopped on the way up and down, and the municipal police unable to sort out the problem. Fortunately he had the good idea to go from the hotel on foot and at his own pace, enjoying that splendid day of sun and warm temperature, he concludes, at the precise moment when there is the dull sound—*Eureka!*—coming from the bottom of the avenue, gradually increasing in intensity, until one can finally see the head of the cortège, formed by a police force in ceremonial outfits, immediately followed by the representatives of the students of the several different degrees of study, with the Shelter for Abandoned Children at the front, clearly identified by a strip of painted cloth stretched across the whole front of the cortège, the several different shelters, the official primary schools, the academic schools of Lisbon, in a large number, including the technical schools, the grammar schools, the industrial institute and the higher colleges, and finally the representatives of the Oporto and Coimbra academies and the provincial high schools, all also clearly identified with their respective badges and standards, he realizes as the cortège goes by in front of the stand. Most of the academics are wearing their traditional gowns, with colored ribbons on the shoulders indicating their courses. When they reach the corner where the diplomatic corps is sitting they suddenly start hailing Spain and throwing flowers, and even their own capes, to the Minister from Spain, in a lively demonstration of support and solidarity concerning the war that Spain has been fighting for over a month against the invasion of Cuba, the Philippines and Puerto Rico by the Americans. For which the Minister thanks them, feeling moved, and kissing one of the roses that the enthusiastic students threw to him.

"Well, lad? Have you been here for long?" He suddenly hears his brother Gaspar stating, panting after having crossed through the whole stalls, which is full of people.

"Since one, waiting for you. So what happened?" he asks, surprised by his brother's cheerful expression, turning up with a red carnation in the lapel of his black jacket, which was a little wrinkled after being crushed among the crowds.

"You can't imagine. I've just come from the Havanesa..." replies Gaspar, still standing, opposite the place reserved for him, next to his.

"The Havanesa? Doing what might one know?" Aleixo insists, increasingly intrigued.

"Well, waiting for news about your competition," replies Gaspar.

"Really? And what are they? I'm sure they succumb to the opinion given by the technical committee and gave first place to Costa Motta, isn't that right?" Aleixo cannot help saying with some foreboding.

"You think so? Well, you are very wrong, lad. The winner of the competition is you, now you know," states Gaspar, hanging on to hear his brother's response.

"It's not true. You're joking. And one shouldn't joke over serious issues," Aleixo replies, incredulously.

"You don't believe me? Well by now telegrams must have come to the newspapers communicating the good news. And to your hotel, of course," Gaspar insists.

"Me? Did I win the monument to Sousa Martins? Are you sure? What happened really?" he asks, still not trusting the news.

"I'll explain everything later, lad. Now get down here because you deserve this award," Gaspar replies, embracing his brother at the precise moment when the Embassy from Guinea passes in front of the stand, making the whole cortège stop. Shortly after one of them peels off from the rest of the troupe, takes a few steps forward with a cutlass in his hand, and starts to perform a series of leaps and pirouettes, makes grimaces and swishes with the cutlass, now putting it under his arms, then brandishing it as if to wound someone, then holding it up in the air for a moment, then suddenly banging it on the ground. As soon as this extravagant character ends his number, out of the group there comes an old man, then another, and then even another, and they all start to perform the same dance with the same gestures and looks. In the meantime, some women stand out from the troupe, squat, and start to drum with sticks, but also with their fingers, on the little drums they are carrying under their left arms, and humming along, thus accompanying the dance carried out by the dancers. Once this performance is over it is the turn of the delegation from Inhambane. Like the others, this group stops in front of the royal box and, on the orders of an African army officer, the men separate from the women, who form a line, and begin to perform their warlike sounds and chants. The sounds are made with enormous wooden marimbas and antelope horns. As soon as the chants begin about twenty members of the troupe stand apart, wearing red caps on their heads, truncheons in their right hands, and a shield on their left arms, with which they begin to threaten the sky and the ground, repeatedly banging the ground with their shields, producing a noise similar to infantry rifle fire. Having repeated the ritual half a dozen times, two more members of the troupe separate from the group, one wearing a Portuguese army officer's kepi and with paper and a pencil in his hand, and the other with an enormous tube made out of leaves and string, standing in front of the others, who, armed only with their shields and truncheons, immediately back away, increasing their threats and cries. The one carrying the tube starts to fill it up with flour, then "firing" the flour at the others, as if the tube were a piece of artillery, an act that is repeated several times. At each "shot" some of the others fall to the ground until no one is left standing. As this is happening the one in the kepi pretends to be taking notes on the successive casualties. In the end, they all return to the troupe, a sign that the performance has ended.

"What a strange performance. What was it? A battle?" asks Aleixo, truly surprised by what he has just seen.

"From what I read in a newspaper, it must be a representation of the famous battle at Macontene, where our army achieved an overwhelming victory," explains Gaspar, at the moment when, after the more sober and westernized performance from Cape Verde, the cortège moves on again.

"So those with the "cannon" and the kepi are the Portuguese. Smaller in number but armed with artillery equipment, while the others only have shields and assagais. A little unfair fight, don't you think?"

"That's true, lad, but what can you expect? They are the advantages of civilization. Which it appears they have already assimilated."

"So, tell me: what was this *volte-face* in the result of the competition?" Aleixo can't resist asking, now calmer, but not yet fully back to his senses, as the Geography Society allegorical cart passes in front of the stand, pulled by six horses ridden by artillery soldiers, pulling the poop deck of a fifteenth-century galleon on a cart covered in canvas and framed by a border of golden cords. Inside it one can see five seated sphinxes, supporting an enormous gilt armillary sphere on their heads, with the Portuguese flag above it. The sphinxes are holding shields in their hands, with the names of the five parts of the world written on them.

"Deep down, when we really look at it, there was no major turn-around. The executive committee took notice of the decision by the so-called technical committee but decided to ignore it, maintaining the initial classification," replies Gaspar, as he nods from afar to one of the members of the Geography Society accompanying the exhibition car.

"Well, considering the importance of some of the names on the technical committee it mustn't have been so easy. Anyway, I applaud their courage. Besides being very happy about the decision, obviously."

"According to my friend, the debate was in fact somewhat heated, but the vote of the technical committee was not taken at full value when someone did an analysis, concluding that out of the eight people invited only five turned up and that among these five two were teachers of sculpture and two others were painters. As there were two votes in favor of your project and two in favor of Costa Motta, it was not difficult to discover that the former were teachers and the second group was painters, with the fifth element being there to decide in case of a tie, albeit without great conviction, as he himself confessed later on. Being it public knowledge that Costa Motta is a student and protégé of Simões d'Almeida and of Nunes Junior, the Committee thought it best to consider that their vote would not be unbiased, and the project that he presented was seen by many to be limited and ungracious, with no original factors," Gaspar explains, while the representatives of associations of education and leisure walk by the stand bearing their standards.

"Just as well. Just as well that good sense and objectivity prevailed," Aleixo states euphorically.

"Another aspect that, according to my friend, the committee took into consideration was the fact that the two painters present, Condeixa and Carlos Reis, who had no protegés, both voted for your project. But, so it appears, what definitively swayed them was the above-suspicion opinion of Fialho de Almeida..."

"Which was totally against my project, I can imagine..." Aleixo abruptly interrupts.

"That's the point. To everyone's surprise, he, who is always against everything, was in this case in favor, not of Costa Motta's project, but of yours, considering it to be by far and away that which was of best interest to the aims of the competition, the most harmonious and well-planned project."

"Well, after the chat I had with him and with Ribeiro Arthur in the Livraria Gomes bookstore, just over a month ago, he would be the last person I would expect to take a position like that."

"You and many members of the executive committee, you can bet, but it was what happened. Now you have to think about moving here to Portugal soon so you can start working on the monument. Because, according to my friend, they want to sign the contract as soon as possible."

"Yes, but it's not so simple for me. The truth is that for a while I've been thinking about whether it is worth keeping a studio in Paris when my main source of commissions is here and not in France. And there's no better time than now to make this change, as I have won the competition, I have guaranteed work, at least for the next two years. And also, after this triumph, more work will come along, even against the will of the so-called 'guardians of the temple'."

"You can be absolutely sure of that. Right now you are the artist who is the talk of Lisbon, Aleixinho."

"But at the same time, Paris is Paris, the capital of the world. An extraordinary city, bustling with people, with events, with new ideas. And where, without realizing it, I have lived for seven years, where I have put down roots, built friendships and relationships…" Aleixo goes on, with a sudden expression of enormous melancholy filling his eyes.

"What relationships? Don't tell me you've got yourself a little fancy girl…" ventures Gaspar, who appears to have captured his brother's expression.

"No. Let's just say that it is more of a friendship. But a very special friendship. For some time I had hoped that it might become something else, but now I am more and more convinced that it won't."

"And all this time you kept this to yourself, you rascal. You never said a single word about the subject," replies Gaspar, pretending to be annoyed.

"Don't take it badly, Gasparinho. It's just that I don't like talking about what I feel in my heart."

"So who is she, anyway? Or don't you want to say that either?" Gaspar insists.

"She's American. Nellie. Who was a colleague at the Académie Julian. A greatly talented sculptor, at the moment the assistant to Saint-Gaudens, who is considered to be the greatest American sculptor of the century. With whom I had the chance to socialize a few times, in Paris. Where he also has set up a studio."

"An American woman? That's complicated. Different habits, a different upbringing, a different culture. And an artist to boot. A sculptor."

"That's true. But at the same time, there is sensitivity, intelligence, a shared passion for beauty, for the arts, for sculpture, and all of this brings us together."

"So it's a sort of Platonic love," Gaspar interrupts, looking like a specialist in the subject.

"Call it what you like. What I know is that, whatever happens, Nellie is a person for whom I nurture great, enormous esteem. And I shall miss her greatly. But besides her, there are other friends, former colleagues at the Académie, at the Fine Arts School. While here, apart from your illustrious person, I practically have no one. On the contrary, what I feel is an attitude of some hostility and coldness with me on the part of several of my colleagues. Indeed, this was obvious a few days ago during the pre-opening of the Artists' Guild Salon. Some of them avoided me, others were constrained in the way they spoke to me. The good thing was the warm greeting I received from the King and Queen when they saw my works," Aleixo points out at the moment when three bullfighters on horseback appear, wearing their glimmering suits, sitting on beautiful horses with ornamented harnesses, followed by a group of banderilleros in their best suits of light, preceded by the barb-carrying mule, dressed up just like in the bullfights at the Campo Pequeno bullring. Behind them, there is a group of bull catchers, preceded by three combat horses with their respective grooms, and six mounted herdsmen armed with long prods.

"What did you expect, tell me? You arrive here and in a couple of months you achieve public recognition that none of them have ever dreamed of having, first with the *Sacred Heart of Jesus*, now with *Vasco da Gama*, and then you win the most hotly disputed sculpture competition of recent times. It is all summarized in three words: *Veni, vidi, vici!*... By the way, have you read the review that appeared in the *Século* about your *Vasco da Gama*?"

"No, I haven't. When did it come out?"

"Three or four days ago, in the section dedicated to the Centenary. Look, I've got it here," replies Gaspar, taking a folded page from a newspaper out of his inside pocket and passing it to his brother, "Read what it says and then tell me whether your colleagues aren't right to all be green with envy," he adds. Aleixo takes the clipping and rapidly runs his eyes over the long article, stopping at one or two paragraphs that seem more significant to him, such as the one in which the article writer imagines his *Vasco da Gama* emerging on the deck of his caravel when his fleet rounds the Cape of Storms. Or further down, when he starts saying that 'all or almost all of the works of this kind that we can see here and there give us the impassive, petrified, dead form, as if they intended to reproduce sleepy, lifeless and cold nature instead of perpetuating the struggling movement, the life that is expanded, the spirit that radiates the human being, driving things on. We know those busts well: mutilated forms, extinct physiognomies, freezing in the rigidness of the marble, cold blocks, inexpressive stones, something of dumb paralysis like death,' goes the article, then describing his work as:

'That robust, manly body bows, his robes ripple, the terrific musculature of his arms are contracted, his long, shapeless beard hangs, waving in the wind, his head is raised in an impetuous contraction, his fixed, leonine pupils have reverberations of stupefaction and temerity; the wheel of the helm creaks in a herculean effort and so that for us everything stands out and lives as those four palms of sculpture speak as loudly as a group in a tragedy, and one feels that what is taking place there is the surging of an enormous combat as if they rose up and were extended from that figure, singing long verses of sea battles in epics resembling the warlike pages of the poem '*The Lusiads*'."

"What do you think?" asks Gaspar, observing his brother.

"A beautiful article, no doubt at all," he replies, momentarily raising his eyes from the newspaper cutting, then continuing to read the following paragraph: '…the bust of Vasco da Gama has all the marks of an artistic renewal. This is a new art, art in agitation, full of vigor, of exuberance, of life; art that beats, gesticulates, has warm, colored pulp, red blood in its veins, waving hair, human phrases, gaze on fire as if the artist's soul, full of passions, sparkling with triumphs, had illuminated the plaster or gone in crackling flames into the forms of the marble. When a statue or bust thus takes on life, it talks to us and it tells us and impresses us so much that art rushes to its zenith and achieves its supreme triumph. The path to a wider and more powerful aesthetics is this one'."

"A truly remarkable article, with great intelligence and sensitivity for the things of art. And which denotes a deep understanding of the ultimate sense I wish to impress upon my work," Aleixo finally says, moved.

"So now imagine how your colleagues feel when they read texts like that about your works. When theirs are almost totally ignored. So make sure you take advantage of the luck and success you have had and are having. Settle in, even if it is only for you to make the monument, and then you will see what is best for you: to stay in Lisbon or go back to your Paris. As for the others, your colleagues, they'll have no choice but to accept you: 'all are not thieves that dogs bark at', isn't that so?"

"I'll think about it," Aleixo replies, somewhat enigmatically, at the moment when the Embassies from the several different municipal councils finally finish going past, then followed by a group of fishermen from Aveiro, with their white cloth outfits contrasting with their black caps, barefoot, trousers rolled up, carrying their nets, followed by the cart from the naval Club, pulled by six mules, driven by three rowers from the royal galleys with their traditional uniforms, flanked by eight sailors.

"For the love of God, another fifteenth-century galleon! What a lack of imagination," protests Aleixo, looking bored at the galleon mounted on the Naval Club cart, equipped with several different artillery items at the front and back, along with navigation instruments, such as helm wheels, horns, and canvas buckets.

"I see that you are not very enthusiastic about the cortège, Aleixinho," replies Gaspar.

"To be honest, not about the cortège or about the rest of the com-memorations. A short while ago, while I was waiting, I took the trouble to read the program from end to end, and I think it is startlingly weak. Unworthy of the great feats one wishes to commemorate."

"Well, even so, a lot of people spoke out against holding these com-memorations because of our chronic foreign debt. Which, according to them, would be increased by the commemorations."

"One only has to think of what the commemorations of the discov-ery of America by Columbus were like in Spain. Or the ones held in the United States, in Chicago."

"True, but what do you expect? There's a lack of enthusiasm, a lack of ambition. And more than that, a lack of money. Perhaps only a hundred years from now, in 1998. Perhaps by then the crisis will have passed and the country will pick up, and whoever is here then will be able to organize good quality commemorations," replies Gaspar, visionary like, as the members of the Centenary Executive Committee go past the stand, to a standing round of applause from everyone present and cheers ring out in the name of Portugal and of the event. Finishing off the cortège is the *Artillery 4 band*, with its standard raised high, playing the national anthem, followed by a group of several dozen ranking officers from the municipal guard.

"Look, the King is getting up. What if we go and say hello?" suggests Gaspar, standing up.

"No. If you want to you go, you who are a member of the Parliament. I'll wait for you here," replies Aleixo, ill at ease.

"No, sir. That wouldn't do at all. Come on, don't be shy, and follow me. I'm sure the King will be pleased to see you," insists Gaspar.

"You and your power of persuasion, Gaspar. Let's go, then," Aleixo finally accepts, going up the steps behind his brother towards the royal pavilion, where he joins the line of illustrious personalities which has in the meantime formed, including high-ranking military officers, members of the diplomatic corps, high officials of state, ministers, etc.

"Look what two artists we have here: Queiroz Ribeiro the poet and Queiroz Ribeiro the sculptor," His Majesty King Carlos greets them as soon as he sees them approach, one behind the other.

"My warmest greetings, Your Majesty," replies Gaspar, bending forward to kiss the King's hand, followed by Aleixo.

"Congratulations, man. I've just heard that you won the competition for the monument to Sousa Martins," King Carlos states, stroking his thick blond beard.

"My humble thanks, Sire," replies Aleixo, surprised, before kissing the Queen's hand.

"My felicitations on this further triumph, Mr. Queiroz Ribeiro," says Queen Amélia, rolling her Rs a little, "I am sure that you will make a work befitting the great personality who was our late lamented Dr. Sousa Martins."

"Thank you for your wishes and for the confidence shown by Your

Majesty," replied Aleixo, touched, before stepping aside and giving way to the next person in the line.

"So, was it worth it or not?" asks Gaspar, euphoric, as soon as they come to the central aisle of the stand.

"Of course it was. But I never expected His Majesty to already know the result of the competition."

"He looks like he doesn't care, but he is always aware of everything," adds Gaspar when they come to the end of the aisle, where they pass through the gate and come out into the avenue itself. "Well lad, shall we go for that champagne?"

"Let's go. But this time I'm paying," Aleixo replies when they are coming to the Rua Barata Salgueiro, where dozens of carriages are waiting in a line for the end of the *cortège*.

ALEIXO DE QUEIROZ RIBEIRO (Paris 1898)

PORTRAIT OF ALEIXO DE QUEIROZ RIBEIRO
(1895), by Veloso Salgado, private collection

ALEIXO DE QUEIROZ RIBEIRO & ELIZABETH STETSON WEDDING
(1908) author's family private collection photo

STETSON FAMILY AT ALEIXO AND ELIZABETH WEDDING
(1908) author's family private collection photo

COUNT OF SANTA EULALIA
(Lisbon 1910) wearing his Gentleman
Knight of the Royal Household suit

SPECIAL PRESENTATION DAY NUMBER.

STETSON WEEKLY COLLEGIATE

Students' Publication of Stetson University

VOL. XXI.   DeLAND, FLA., THURSDAY, FEBRUARY 25, 1909.   NO. 17.

THE COUNT OF SANTA EULALIA.

THE COUNTESS OF SANTA EULALIA.

The Guests of Honor of Stetson University.

The great social feature of the University year at Stetson has been the visit of the Count and Countess of Santa Eulalia on February 19 to attend the Presentation Day exercises. They found a warm welcome awaiting them both in DeLand and at the University.

The Countess is well known here for her many good works, for her interest in Stetson University, for her large gifts in money and endowment to education. She is wealthy and gifted, and abounds in good works.

The Count is very popular in the highest circles of society in Portugal, and in the foreign diplomatic service in his country. He is one of the few who combine the artistic and practical. In art circles he has the reputation of being one of the foremost in the ranks of sculptors, and in the diplomatic world he is respected and esteemed as one of the representatives of Portugal in the United States.

The Count is a remarkable person. He comes of one of the most distinguished families of Portugal.

One of the marked elements of his personality is his modesty. Another is his sincerity, and still another his simplicity.

Early in life he developed a taste for the fine arts, especially for sculpture. His father being of an artistic temperament, indulged his son's tastes. He was sent to Paris. He there studied under some of the best artists for fourteen years. He has since exhibited a number of times in the Paris Salon.

He designed and built the Statue of Liberty in Sofia, the capital of Bulgaria. For this statue he was decorated by the King of Bulgaria, receiving the title of "Officer of Civil Merit of Bulgaria."

The Count has been decorated a number of times in Portugal. On his last visit his numerous titles were still further augmented, in recognition of the beautiful piece of statuary representing the present queen which he recently placed in Lisbon, the capital of Portugal.

Last summer he was appointed "High Commissioner to the United States of America and to Mexico."

Distinguished as the Count's family connections are, and eminent as he is among the nobility of Portugal, and efficient as he is in the capacity of a diplomat, his chief interests are in his art. He loves art for art's sake. He has a passion for beauty. He is full of poetry.

IDRO'S MAIN FACADE: in forefront, Count of Santa Eulalia riding his
Lusitano horse (circa 1912), author's private collection photo

Another view of **IDRO,** photo generously offered by Lewis Stetson Allen

PAÇO DA GLÓRIA, Arcos de Valdevez (circa 1912), author's private collection photo

PAÇO DA GLÓRIA MAIN FACADE: at forefront, Count of Santa Eulália
driving his own carriage (circa 1912), author's private collection photo

REFOIOS MONASTERY, Ponte de Lima (circa 1912)

ALEIXO AND HIS BROTHER GASPAR (Lisbon 1898)

SACRED HEART OF JESUS (Paris 1898), Santa Luzia, Viana do Castelo

VASCO DA GAMA
(Paris 1898),
sculpture in white stone,
Refóios Monastery

SOUSA MARTINS MONUMENT (Lisbon 1898-1900), front view

SOUSA MARTINS MONUMENT, back view

FROM TOP LEFT, CLOCKWISE:
SCIENCE, plaster (Lisbon 1899) with the sculptor seated on the left;
MONUMENT TO TZAR ALEXANDER II, model in plaster (Bulgaria 1900);
EXTASE RELIGIEUSE/SALOME, marble (Paris 1896)
ROMAIN BUST, bronze (Paris 1893), owned by the author

**HENRY A. DELAND
BAS RELIEF**
(Chicago 1906-1908),
Stetson University,
Deland, Florida

HENRY A. DELAND BAS RELIEF, detail

FREDERICK WARD PUTNAM BUST
bronze, (New York 1913),
Peabody Museum of Archaeology
and Ethnology, Harvard University
Copyright Presidents and Fellows,
Harvard University, 2004.1.139

STATUE OF DR. F.A. COOK, Discover of the North Pole
(New York 1909), plaster owned by the Arctic Club of America

QUEEN AMELIA OF PORTUGAL, statue in plaster (Chicago 1908),
with the sculptor standing on the right. Photo from *The Chicago Daily News.*

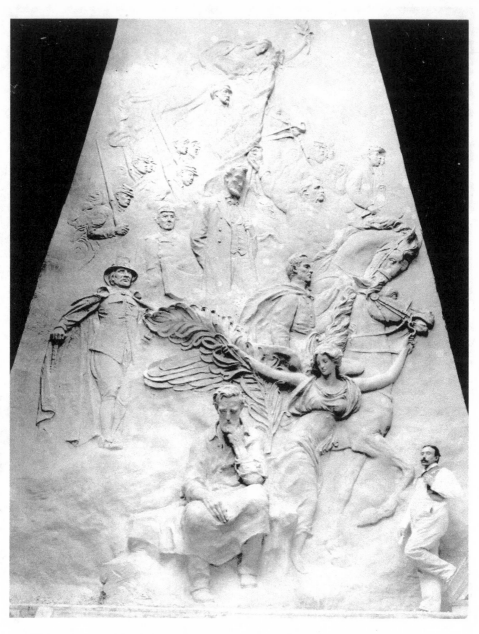

The sculptor and his bas relief for a **MONUMENT TO SAINT GAUDENS**
(New York 1909-1912), plaster (photo by Dewitt Clinton Ward,
owned by Saint-Gaudens National Historic Site)

XIII

"*MAIS OÙ DONC M'EMMENEZ vous cette fois-ci, mon cher Alexis?*" asked Elizabeth, Countess of Santa Eulália, elegant cream silk dress with lace applications, V-neck with bib, hair up under a wide hat profusely decorated with feathers and plumes, increasingly more uncomfortable over the jolting carriage ride, the dust clouds and the bends in that road on which they have surely been traveling for about an hour in a carriage pulled by two horses, she who in the USA would only travel in speedy, comfortable motor cars on wide, tarmacked and clearly-marked roads like those around Ashbourne and Philadelphia.

"*Ne vous inquiétez pas, chère Isabel.* We are almost there," was the Count's reply, with a mysterious smile, in his shiny high-hat, gray overcoat and striped trousers, beige waistcoat and dark blue silk plastron with white dots, fastened on with a pearl pin, at the precise moment when they enter the Roman bridge, which is so narrow that two carriages can only cross with difficulty, with the Church of St. Anthony of the Old Tower on the left, and, a little further in the background, the small, unique Chapel of the Guardian Angel which they had visited on the previous day, and after they carry on over the wider and more solidly constructed Gothic bridge towards the town of Ponte do Lima, on the other side of the river, with its beautiful and striking array of houses stretching off to the right along the river bank.

"Ponte do Lima, again? For the love of God, Alexis, we were here almost all yesterday afternoon," protested the Countess, imagining herself once again hurriedly wandering around streets and alleys looking for some mansions and chapels in ruins, and on the way visiting some ceremonious and haughty relatives, looking her up and down as if she were some rare species from another planet.

"No, my darling. This time we are not going to Ponte do Lima, but to another place, a little further off," replied the Count enigmatically, when they came to the end of the bridge, immediately turning to the left to the Vasco da Gama Street, directly to the main road to the town of Ponte da Barca without going through the Camões square, the reception hall for that which had always been considered as the oldest town in Portugal.

"Well, I have given up trying to convince you of the advantages of motor vehicles in relation to horse-drawn carriages, but what do you think of the idea of us having one sent from France or Germany so we can have one here for us to use whenever we are here?" the Countess suddenly asked, unable to stop thinking about her comfortable outings by car with Alexis around the outskirts of Ashbourne and Philadelphia during the whole month before their wedding, as a contrast to the end-less day-long excursions that he had made a point of organizing since they had arrived, with the no doubt praiseworthy, albeit a little exces-sive, intention of showing her all the fantastic wonders of his native region one by one.

"Motor vehicles, that plague..." hissed the Count as they were going past the House of Nossa Senhora da Aurora, an impressive Baroque facade punctuated by a long succession of balconied windows headed by stone pediments and beautiful masonry work on the angles and cornices, followed a little further on by the House of Garridas, another magnificent example of the best Baroque architecture of the Minho region.

"I know, I know: 'They make a horrible noise and smell terribly of petrol' as your dear José Maria Eça de Queiroz used to say," the Count-ess hurriedly replies. "But one has to admit that they go faster and are much more comfortable than a *charrette* like this one."

"On that matter, you'll have to forgive me, my dear Isabel, but I still have my doubts. Besides the fact that these roads, with their endless bends, were not made for motor vehicles, but horses, so that they would not fall asleep on the way. On the other hand, motor cars need flat, wide and straight roads, like those around your house in Ashbourne," the Count definitively replied when, coming to the end of the Vasco da Gama street, they were entering the main highway to the town of Ponte da Barca, with a whole new succession of bends, bumps, and clouds of dust.

"It is true that these roads have many bends and the pavement is somewhat irregular, but I do not think that this makes it so difficult for motor vehicle movement, as long as it takes place with due care. Besides, soon the Portuguese government should undertake a program of building new roads more suited to motor vehicle travel, as most of the governments in other civilized countries have been doing, don't you think? Or at least widen and straighten those that already exist, because, whether we like it or not, motor vehicles are an unavoidable reality, one which is completely revolutionizing the means of transportation throughout the world," insisted the Countess, somewhat triumphantly, while the Count finally discovered, down among the trees and the lattices, a very blue stretch of river, immediately lost to sight after the next bend.

"I'm afraid that will not be during my time, dear Isabel. No matter how good the intentions of our current government may be, with the chronic lack of means in Portugal I doubt that they can do anything much in this field in the coming years," he replied coyly, after for a good while appreciating the House of Barreiros, located halfway up the hillside on the upper side of the road, another beautiful house, although of an architecture that is more modest than the previous ones.

"Well, I have realized that you are really not interested in having a motor car here. And that you prefer to carry on traveling by horse-drawn carriages at full throttle along these roads," the Countess thrust at him dryly and incisively.

"I have never hidden what I think about this issue, dear Isabel. And as long as the roads do not get better and the motorcars are not more silent and smell less of petrol I cannot see the advantage of us having one here for our use. But a much more comfortable *charrette* than this one, pulled by one more or two pairs of thoroughbred horses, would be another matter entirely," replied the Count, at the moment when, as they entered São Martinho da Gândara village, they turned left, then going down a beaten track, much narrower than the main highway.

"Whatever. Let your will be done, my lord and master," replies Elizabeth, resigned and ready to put a stop to that useless argument, almost not noticing the rare beauty of the landscape now opening up to her, made up of green pastures and fields of corn, divided up by rows of trees and lattices, allowing one to see, further down among the thick forest, the tame waters of the River Lima.

"What…? What is all this? What are all these people doing here?" she asked, astonished, as they finally came to rest at the Carregadouro landing stage, and she noted the small crowd of ladies and gentlemen in full ceremonial attire parading along the riverbank promenade, the ladies in afternoon dress and the gentlemen in overcoats and high hats.

"These people are the cream of Minho high society. And they have come here, to this jetty, to welcome you and pay homage, Madame Countess de Santa Eulália," replied the Count, waving to the guests from afar, with obvious satisfaction, after telling the coachman to stop the carriage.

"But why here, of all places? Why not in Boavista, or somewhere else?" insisted the Countess, extremely ruffled by all this, at the same time as she took hurriedly out a small mirror and box of face powder from her bag.

"You'll soon see why," he replied, with the same enigmatic smile, looking at the two barges moored on the jetty, decorated with flags, now joined by a third one, crossing the river with a numerous and merry group of girls onboard. "I should have guessed. I should have guessed that something like this was being prepared," she complained in a whisper, as she powdered her cheeks, nose, and forehead, and arranged her hair with the tips of her fingers.

"Well prepare yourself, because there is more to come," he warned, as soon as he saw her put away the mirror and the box of face powder, finally moving to the carriage door, which the coachman had just opened, while the first notes of the national anthem were ringing out, played by the São Martinho da Gândara musical band, one of the best and most well-known bands in the whole River Lima area, and which was set up only a few yards from them. Everyone was standing, listening in absolute silence, while Elizabeth took the opportunity to look around, wondering what would be the surprise that was about to come next: were they going to sail down the river in those wretched, old barges moored on the banks in front of her, crafts more suited to transporting cattle or goods than people? And in that case, where would Alexis' fantasy lead them? Or the fantasy of the person who had planned this original event with him, one about which it appeared she was the only one who didn't know the details? Ponte do Lima, which they had just passed through? Or even further down? And once they reached this mysterious and unsuspected place, what would happen next? A common reception followed by a lunch or a banquet, or something else? And what would that enormous group of young girls next to the jetty do? Dressed up in joyful, gaudy outfits, some of whom were blond with blue eyes, like one would expect to see in Scotland or Ireland, but never in Portugal? And how had all those elegant, well-dressed ladies and gentlemen gotten to that far-flung place if one could not see a single carriage nearby?

"Shall we go, Isabel?" the Count asked in his soft, delicate voice as soon as the band finished the anthem, suddenly putting an end to that whirlwind of questions with no answer, giving her his arm before walking off towards the guests, who, at a convenient distance, were impatiently awaiting the moment to be introduced to the new Countess de Santa Eulália, whose fortune and personality, as well as the details of the wedding, had been the favorite subject of conversation among the most well-known families in the region for some days.

"My dear Gonçalo, how are you?" Aleixo greeted the first guest in the line, a tall, thin gentleman, his white hair thinning at the temples, and gray beard and mustache. "Dear Isabel, allow me to introduce the Count de Bertiandos, worthy Peer of the Realm and one of the greatest landowners in our region," added Aleixo ceremoniously.

"*Enchanté de faire votre connaissance, ma chère Comtesse,*" replied the Lord of Bertiandos Palace in reasonable French but with a strong north Portuguese accent, seconded by his wife.

"*C'est pour moi un grand plaisir, cher Comte,*" Elizabeth replied in turn, distinguished and proud at her husband's side, making an effort not to show the enormous emotion she was feeling seeing herself like this, acknowledged and accepted in her new quality as a Countess by such an illustrious representative of the best and oldest nobility in Portugal. Then it was the turn of another gentleman, shorter and stockier, but of a similar age to the first one, whom Aleixo introduced to her as the Count de Paço de Vitorino, the Lord of the Palace of Vitorino das Donas, accompanied by his wife, the Countess. Further on were the cousins Francisco Queiroz de Lacerda, a lawyer, and João Teixeira de Queiroz, an engineer, both accompanied by their respective wives, and his brother Francisco, a graduate in law, journalist and writer.

"Well, Aleixinho? I thought you had gotten lost along the way," stated his brother Gaspar, shaking his head in a sign of reproach for their enormous lateness, as soon as his turn came.

"It might not seem it, but it is almost twenty kilometers from Boavista to here," Aleixo said in his defense, giving him a tight embrace before moving on to his youngest brother, António, his accomplice in the preparation and organization of the party that was thereupon about to begin.

"All of that just to travel only a few kilometers downriver. A lot of trouble," commented Gaspar, surprised by this further fantasy of his brother's.

"What do you expect, lad? We have to move heaven and earth to show the best of our region to our illustrious visitor and my dearest wife," said Aleixo, then adding to Elizabeth, standing two paces away, "*N'est-ce pas, ma chérie?*"

"What are my dear husband and his esteemed brothers preparing? Another surprise?" she asked, drawing out a half-smile.

"Nothing, nothing. We were just chatting, the three of us," replied Aleixo, almost without time to finish his sentence, as the first *girandole* of fireworks had just been set off into the air, frightening Elizabeth, who looked from side to side in astonishment, as if it were not simple fireworks but shell-fire.

"It's only fireworks, my dear, nothing else," he explained, noting his wife's frightened expression, suddenly very pale, eyes bulging, as the explosions continued on loudly above their heads.

"Is it habitual to set off fireworks in Portugal just like that?" Elizabeth asked, still shaking from the shock, after the last round exploded, a sign that, at least for now, the firework show had ended.

"It is a way of marking an important situation or event. And of alerting the local villagers to what is happening. Soon the riversides will start to be filled with people, you will see," explained Aleixo, noting his wife's badly disguised expression of strangeness and amazement, as she could not understand how explosions like those, which were identical to heavy artillery fire, could be used to denote situations or events such as what was taking place there.

"Well, all's set for us to embark," said António, joining his brothers, after a brief exchange with the boatmen, who were waiting impatiently next to their barges.

"And now, my dearly beloved husband, what is going to happen?" asked Elizabeth in her mother tongue, no doubt convinced that no one else other than herself and her husband could understand her.

"We are all going down the river on these barges: guests, band and singers," he explained, also in English.

"I'd already realized that. But where to, exactly?"

"Wait and see," he replied, once again determined to keep the program of the events a secret.

"Aleixo, the men are waiting," António reminded them again, pointing to the barges, of which the second and third were already filled, one with the musicians from the band and another with the singers.

"My dear friends, it is time for us to honor our brilliant past as a navigating nation, taking place on this ship, towards the storm," shouted Aleixo loud and clear to the remaining guests, who were hesitatingly starting to get onto the barge reserved for them, aided by the firm hand of the boatman. When everyone had finally taken their places, the boatman stuck his pole in the sand and started to slowly push the barge into the middle of the river, where, helped by the current, it started to gather speed.

"So, Elizabeth? What do you think of this landscape, this view?" Gaspar enthusiastically asked his sister-in-law, sitting in the front next to her husband, when they had traveled a few dozen meters downriver.

"*Marvelous! Beautiful!* A truly sublime landscape," she replied, genuinely surprised by the extraordinary variety of the trees and bushes that were stooping down on either side of the river, with its clear, transparent waters here and there illuminated by the few rays of sun that managed to pierce the dense foliage, while on the two banks one began to hear the echoes of the songs of the young girls, following in the last barge.

"Have you noticed that house painted yellow, up there on the hillside?" asked Aleixo suddenly, pointing to the right bank of the river.

"Yes. It looks a lot like Boavista. What's it called?" she replied squeezing his hand in hers.

"It doesn't look like it. That house is Boavista."

"Boavista? How is that possible?" she asked, puzzled, unable to believe that after having traveled over an hour and a half in a *charrette*, across hills and vales, she was now again only a few hundred yards away from the place she had set off.

"You probably didn't notice, my dear, but what we did earlier was to go down the right bank of the river to Ponte do Lima, and then go up the left bank to a little further up from where we set off," explained Aleixo, as if it were the most natural thing in the world when one could start to see, on the right bank, the enormous, dense woodland of the Friaça Woods, near to which, on a recess over the riverbed, there was now a little stone pier jutting a few meters into the water.

"Yes, now that you tell me, I'm starting to understand," she agreed, yet still amazed by such an idea, that only someone with the soul of an artist could think of, forcing her and a good number of those people, at least those who lived on the right bank of the river, to take such a path, just so they could come down the river and enjoy the landscape for a few hundred yards.

"Now we are coming to our destination, the world-famous Friaça Quay, from which generations and generations of Malheiros, Botelhos, and Queirozes set off to navigate the deep, grand waters of the River Lima," Aleixo stated emphatically, turning to the guests, at the moment when the barge was docking at the small stone jetty, on which they were awaited by his sister-in-law Ernestina, the wife of his brother António and, to his great surprise and satisfaction, his sister Cláudia and her husband, Alfredo Vaz Pinto, besides some other guests who, for one reason and another, had preferred to go directly to the locale.

"Dear Claudinha, dear Alfredo. I'm glad you could come. I was afraid that you might not have received my telegram in time, shouted Aleixo, quickly running across the little jetty that separated them to affectionately kiss his sister and embrace his brother-in-law.

"Indeed, but you've no idea what an adventure it was to get here, Aleixo. We had to leave Arouca before daylight to get the train to Espinho, then to Oporto. And then another train from Oporto to Viana. And finally, from Viana to here, as well as two hours in a rented carriage" explained Cláudia.

"The little ones, José Augusto, Gaspar, and Luiz. How are they?"

"They are fine, thanks be to God. They are still in Arouca, being looked after by their wet-nurses," his sister replied, at the same time as he noted out of the corner of his eye that tall, slender woman, extremely elegant in her cream silk dress and who stood there smiling at her husband's side waiting to be introduced.

"Chère Isabel, permettez-moi que je vous présente ma petite soeur Cláudia, dont je vous ai tellement parlé…" said Aleixo, fianlly turning to Elizabeth.

"Enchantée de faire votre connaissance, ma chère belle soeur" was Elizabeth's greeting, moving towards her.

"Je suis également très heureuse de faire votre conaissance, chère Isabel," replied Cláudia with a warm smile, giving Elizabeth a kiss on the cheek instead of simply shaking her hand, to Elizabeth's great surprise, and leaving her a little taken aback.

"Now, my dear Alexis, what is the next stage in this original and curious welcoming session?" Elizabeth asked with some curiosity, turning to her husband as soon as she saw that all the guests had disembarked, as well as the band and the singers.

"Let us now take the trip up to the top, to the very noble and ancient House of Boavista, where a banquet will be served in honor of Her Excellency, the Countess of Santa Eulália, and of this her humble servant," he replied, jokingly, before giving her his arm to lead her to the first carriage, which would also carry Cláudia and Alfredo, António and Ernestina, as soon as it was assured that the remaining carriages were enough to transport all the guests. While they were taking the slow and difficult path up from the quay to the main highway Elizabeth could not help feeling some surprise as she noted the narrowness of the beaten earth path they walked along, on which a simple carriage like theirs would find it difficult to travel, but which, so it seemed, was the only connection between the private jetty of the property, at which they had just disembarked, and the Boavista House, to which they were going now. How was it possible for a family with such honors and traditions like those of her husband to not have gotten round to do the work of widening and paving this path? Because there was no money to do it? Out of a simple lack of interest and initiative? Or because they didn't care about the state of their estates, as long as, in the medieval style, the housekeepers kept on meeting the annual payments of the rents? How could a country like Portugal progress and be modernized if the members of its nobility, the most educated and enlightened members, were the first to give a bad example in the way they looked after their properties? Elizabeth wondered, yet unable to feel she could say this out loud, in order not to embarrass her husband in front of his family, now that they had crossed the high road to Arcos de Valdevez and the gates to the estate, and were going up the drive to the house, which was wider and better laid out than the previous one, going up among the grapevines that covered the whole hillside, set out in staggered terraces that had just been harvested a few days ago.

"Here we are," exclaimed Aleixo, with some relief, when the carriage, followed by the others, finally passed the second gate bearing the stone carving of the family coat of arms, then continuing across the large yard to the house with its broad stone staircase in the middle, which then opened to the sides in a spacious balcony running along the whole facade. Standing on the first step to receive the guests was Ernestina da Rocha Passos, or simply Tina, as she was known to friends and family, the widow of Luiz, the eldest member of the family, and thus the owner of the house. As the guests went up the staircase they immediately noted an enormous table placed in the middle of the balcony, covered by countless plates and trays with slices of ham and smoked sausages, different types of cheese, fish cakes, and recently-fried meat rissoles among other delicacies, besides homemade bread to go with it, while two uniformed servants poured the house *vinho verde* or a refreshing lemonade. Yet many of the ladies preferred to take the suggestion made by the lady of the house and go first to the bathroom to freshen up and recover after the outing before returning to enjoy all those delicacies, which for the moment were left almost exclusively to the gentlemen.

"The view from up here is truly superb," exclaimed the Count of Calheiros from the top of the staircase, impressed by the stunning panorama that opened up before him, now that the sun was beginning to disappear behind the house, gradually casting a shadow over the whole hillside that softly slipped down to the river, with its intensely blue waters visible between the trees bordering it on both banks, and beyond which stretched thick pine forests, green meadows and grapevines all the way to the Soajo mountains, punctuated here and there by little white houses.

"Whoever called this house Boavista, could not have found a better name," then commented João Gomes Abreu e Lima, preparing to enjoy an appetizing fish cake.

"So, Francisco, what do you think of our new Countess of Santa

Eulália?" the Count of Bertiandos asked his friend the Count of Paço de Vitorino, in a low voice, at the other end of the balcony, both enjoying a good slice of ham on a piece of cornbread, which they accompanied with little sips of wine.

"A real, proper woman, just between us here where no one can hear. Elegant, pretty, and well turned out. And with class. A lot of class," answered the other count, looking like someone who knew the subject.

"And besides this, filthy rich, so it seems. One of the biggest fortunes in America," Bertiandos pointed out.

"That's what I was told as well. Millions and millions of dollars," replied Vitorino, his eyes sparkling.

"So who are our two illustrious counts plotting against this time?" asked João Gomes Abreu e Lima slyly, approaching the couple in the company of Calheiros.

"Against no one, João. Against no one. We were just here exchanging impressions about the Lady Countess of Santa Eulália, to whom we have come to welcome and pay our respects," Paço de Vitorino replied with a mischievous smile.

"For someone who is a mother of two children and a grandmother she isn't bad at all," declared João Gomes solemnly.

"Mother and grandmother, with that figure? It isn't possible," Bertiandos stated in surprise.

"It's true. That was what I was told the other day by António, Aleixo's brother. And he should know what he's talking about," the other replied.

"You know, I wouldn't say she was more than thirty-eight or forty, if that old," said Bertiandos.

"Well, that's how old he is. She must easily be ten years older. You only have to do the sums," stressed João Gomes, before biting into another fish cake.

"I'd rather add up the millions of dollars she's said to be worth," Paço de Vitorino came out with, unable to ignore the lively conversation taking place on the other side of the table near to the entrance door, in a group in which Aleixo's brother Gaspar was holding court, having recently been elected deputy by the new Dissident Progressive Party led by José Maria d'Alpoim. Some ladies had in the meantime returned from the inside of the house, forming a third group on the other end of the balcony.

"But where did she get such a huge fortune after all? Does anyone know?" asked Calheiros, motioning to one of the servants to fill up his wine glass.

"It's from her first husband, owner of one of the largest hat factories in the world, the famous Stetson hats. Which indeed earned him the title of the King of Hats, as he was known in America, apparently," João Gomes explained again, sarcastically.

"So that means that he, Santa Eulália, is the Prince Consort to the Queen of Hats," concluded Calheiros, immediately provoking guffaws all around.

"Prince Consort to the Queen of Hats. That's a good one. A very good one," exclaimed Paço de Vitorino when he finally managed to stop laughing.

"The turns life takes. He, who only a few years ago was the laughing stock of the Lisbon satirical newspapers because of his famous Sousa Martins fountain…" recalled Abreu e Lima.

"But he shouldn't have been treated the way he was. He did the best he could. And if those who made the commission had objections to raise about his work, they should have done so before and not after the inauguration, as they did," Bertiandos immediately came out fighting in defense of Aleixo the sculptor.

"At the time he really went through a bad phase. I remember seeing him going round crestfallen, shabby hair and beard, scruffy clothes. Until he suddenly had that wild idea to go and try his luck in America…" João Gomes came back with.

"…to where it is said that he left penniless. Forced to ask his brother to lend him the money for the journey," added Calheiros.

"And now, half a dozen years later, there he is again, with his beautiful and attractive Queen of Hats, looking like a dandy, a fop, coat, and trousers in the finest style, high, shiny top hat. And that toupee, that ridiculous toupee, parted in the middle and plastered down with grease, with which he disguises his enormous bald spot. As if now, instead of art, all he was interested in is high society life, triumph in the salons," João Gomes stated with some disdain.

"If that's a toupee, it's very well made, because at first sight, one can't notice anything. It looks like real hair," Bertiandos replied in surprise, at the same time as he unwittingly passed a hand over his bald head.

"And after that extraordinary nomination to a consulate in Chicago that didn't even exist before, and was created deliberately for him, tailor-made. And no doubt this was helped by his brother's requests and influences," Paço de Vitorino reminded, with a nod towards Gaspar, who was still the center of attention on the other side of the table.

"Yes, I recall seeing him at the time at a reception at the Palace, very elegant in his uniform as Gentleman Knight of the Royal Household, laden down with decorations. But if I'm not mistaken, still without the wig," said the Count de Bertiandos with an ironic smile.

"Apparently he had the uniform made specifically for him to go to the wedding of King Alfonso XIII in Madrid, even though he wasn't invited," Abreu e Lima came out with.

"You don't say. I had never heard that. One needs to have a lot of nerve," Paço de Vitorino commented, amazed by such boldness.

"And after the consulate came the title of Count, on the pretext that in the United States of America a European diplomat is nothing without a noble title, particularly coming from a small country like Portugal. At least that was the pretext I heard being said in the Palace at the time," stated Bertiandos.

"But the curious thing is that at the last minute, now with João Franco's ministry in office, for some reason the decree granting the title was not signed, which didn't stop him from using it from then on. Only now, a little over a month ago, was the issue finally regularized, by the express order of Ferreira do Amaral, Prime Minister and Minister of the Realm," Paço de Vitorino clarified.

"That's a good one. I knew that the title was recent, but not so recent," said Bertiandos, surprised.

"And what about his sculpting. What has he done with sculpture in the middle of all this?" Calheiros wished to know.

"According to what his brother told me it appears that even so, he has carried on working, although not with the same commitment as before," replied João Gomes.

"But what exactly is he doing? Does anyone know?" insisted Calheiros.

"Busts of some local rich people, it seems," João Gomes clarified, yet again.

"Well, his art should reach that far. What about the lady? How did he meet her, anyway?" asked a curious Paço de Vitorino.

"It appears it was in a hotel in Chicago, where he was exhibiting some works. The lady was staying there with her husband and was bowled over by the works exhibited, then asked to be introduced to the artist. Shortly afterward her husband dies, and, two years later, Aleixo and she unite their destinies," replies João Gomes.

"It's like a fairy tale, dash it!" stated Paço de Vitorino.

"A European Count and a rich American widow. It's a classic story. One only has to read the mundane newspapers of Paris and London," Bertiandos reminded them very fittingly, unaware that Santa Eulália himself had also just come out onto the balcony, and was now walking towards the group surrounded by smiles on all sides.

"My dear friends, I hope you are totally recovered now after the forced outing along the waters of the River Lima," said Santa Eulália pleasantly as he reached them, no doubt with his ears burning after everything that had been said there earlier.

"A beautiful outing, indeed. Which reminded me of my childhood days, when I would come here to Carregadouro with my father to watch the embarking of our barrels of wine for Viana do Castelo, from where they would go off in cargo ships to England," recalled Bertiandos, not giving anything away.

"The lady of the house has asked me to inform you that dinner is served. And to request you to accompany me to the dining room," added Aleixo, with a broad gesture towards the entrance on the other side of the balcony, giving on directly to the living room, with its plaster ceiling with the family arms painted in the middle and several oil paintings on the walls. Between the two terraced windows, which opened onto the garden, there was a great fireplace with a long settee and several arm-chairs in front of it. Next was the dining room, occupied from one end to the other by a long table covered in an embroidered linen tablecloth, on which were set out the plates of the Portuguese Company of the Indies China, which was reserved for special occasions, the cutlery in old silver and the crystal glasses, sparkling under the flickering light of the dozens of candles on the two candelabras hanging over the table. It was Tina, the lady of the house, who had personally taken charge of the distribution of the places, starting with Aleixo, whom, the one being paid homage, she sat at her right, followed by the Count of Bertiandos, the oldest and most illustrious of the guests, whom she sat on her left. At the opposite end of the table was Gaspar, a widower like her, to his right Elizabeth and to his left the Countess of Bertiandos. On Elizabeth's right were the Count and Countess of Paço de Vitorino, with the rest of the guests being distributed without ceremony in the remaining places.

"So, Countess, what impression has our country, our region left on you?" asked Count of Bertiandos, speaking in his creaking French to the Countess de Santa Eulália, at the other end of the table, as soon as the guests were seated.

"The best possible, Count. Lisbon, one of the few European capitals I had not had the opportunity to know, left me truly stunned. It is a unique city, due to its layout, its light, its climate, the soft way the hills slip down to the river. And it has absolutely magnificent monuments, like those pearls of Manueline architecture the Hieronymite Monastery, and the Belém Tower, which Alexis kindly took me to visit. Or the Terreiro do Paço square, no doubt one of the prettiest squares in Europe, only comparable in beauty and grandeur to St. Mark's Square in Venice. That is not to mention Cascais or the Estoril Coast, which owe nothing to the Côte d'Azur or Biarritz. Or Sintra, which is a veritable wonder of nature," replied the Countess in her immaculate French and soft, pausing voice.

"As to monuments and landscapes, our region also has its share," the Count de Calheiros made a point of stating, before the approving silence of the other guests.

"Yes, Alexis has also already shown me some of these wonders, as soon as we arrived here. Such as the Refojos Tower, with all of those ancient stones so full of history; or that little but extremely beautiful monument the Chapel of the Guardian Angel; and also the Mother Church of Ponte de Lima, which is beautiful. Not to mention all the magnificent mansions that one comes across every step of the way along the roads," the Countess pointed out with a courteous smile, after politely refusing the wine with which the servant wished to fill her glass.

"With such a positive appreciation of our country and of our region as you have, all we can hope is that you and your illustrious husband might come and settle here in this beautiful and hospitable country," Paço de Vitorino then said, sitting in front of her on the other side of the table, while one of the servants appeared behind him with a terrine of steaming cabbage broth to serve.

"Well, that will be a little difficult, my dear Count, at least in the near future, as my whole life is centered on the United States. Where I have my house, my mother, and my two sons, both married and with descendants. Besides the fact that, as you know, Alexis also has serious responsibilities as the Portuguese consul in Chicago and as a sculptor," the Countess promptly replied, while the lady of the house waited for all the guests to be served with cabbage broth to begin the meal.

"And is the place where you live close to Chicago?" João Gomes Abreu e Lima was curious to know, after finally taking two or three spoonfuls.

"Not at all, Mr. Lima. My house is in Philadelphia, on the East Coast, over one thousand and two hundred kilometers from Chicago," Elizabeth immediately explained, with a constrained smile, almost offended that someone could imagine that she, the Countess de Santa Eulália, could live in such a provincial and inhospitable city as Chicago, and not in cosmopolitan and aristocratic Philadelphia.

"So where do you intend to reside when you return to the United States? In Philadelphia or Chicago?" then asked Francisco Teixeira de Queiroz, a little confused by the explanation.

"In Philadelphia, my dear Francisco. Which will certainly oblige me, to my great regret, to leave my position as consul in Chicago, so great is the distance between the two cities. Indeed the matter was brought up with Minister Venceslau de Lima and with the King himself during the audience His Majesty granted me a few days ago, me and Isabel," replied Santa Eulália.

"But as the Countess has just reminded us, besides the consulate you still have your work as a sculptor in Chicago, isn't that so Aleixo?" Calheiros questioned with some curiosity.

"Indeed, but that is very easy to solve. It's just a matter of transferring my studio from Chicago to somewhere nearer Philadelphia. Perhaps even New York, which is only two hours away from Philadelphia by train," Aleixo clarified.

"Well, we can only hope that you can at least come here and spend some time now and again. After all, crossing the Atlantic doesn't take more than a week nowadays. And from here to Paris it is only forty-eight hours by train," said Paço de Vitorino, after wiping his lips and mustache on his napkin. The servants then began to take away the soup bowls and take them to the kitchen.

"Certainly we will come, my dear Count. More often than you can imagine, given that we were considering buying a house here, isn't that right Alexis?" she replied, raising her eyes to her husband.

"Yes. It is a possibility we have been mulling over recently, although nothing has been finally decided," said Santa Eulália evasively.

"Well, my dear Aleixo, if you are interested, I know of an estate that is for sale, not very far from here. Good arable land, plentiful water supply, many fruit trees, and vines. It is a beautiful eighteenth-century manor house, although it needs a good deal of work," his cousin Francisco Queiroz de Lacerda informed him on the matter.

"Really? What's the name of the estate?" asked Aleixo, interested, before his wife's inquisitive glance, given that this time the dialogue took place in Portuguese.

"It is the Glória Estate," the other replied.

"The Glória Estate? the one that belonged to the Pereira de Castro family, right here in Jolda? With that house with two turrets and an Italian style loggia?" asked Aleixo.

"The very one."

"So we will have to arrange to go to see it as soon as we can, my dear Francisco. It might be exactly what Isabel and I are looking for," Aleixo finally said, after obtaining his wife's agreement.

"Whenever you like. I am entirely at your disposal," the other replied, just as the servants began to serve the famous dish of *bacalhau com troços*, one of Aleixo's favorite dishes, which Tina had ordered to be made especially in his honor, as she pointed out in French so that her American sister-in-law could understand.

"You will excuse my asking, Countess, but how is it that with you being American you speak such perfect French, without any accent?" the Count of Bertiandos could not risk asking, taking advantage of the sudden silence that had fallen upon the room as soon as, following the lady of the house's example, everyone began to eat the first course.

"I know that Americans are renowned for not speaking languages and having little knowledge of geography, Count. But I am perhaps the exception that confirms the rule, as on my mother's side I descend from an old French family, the Rognion, who went to America to flee the Revolution. So in our house, French was always the second language. And on the issue of geography, I must confess to you that I did not have to meet my husband to know that Portugal has been independent from Spain for many centuries," Elizabeth made a point of stating before, somewhat distrustingly, also trying a small slice of cod, which she immediately drowned in a good gulp of water.

"Whether an exception to the rule or not, the fact is that you speak excellent French, Countess. And what you know in geography and history is in no way lacking either," Bertiandos concluded.

"Hum! This cod is a specialty," the Count of Calheiros couldn't resist exclaiming as soon as he tasted the first forkfuls of that wise mixture of cod with slices of cabbage and potatoes, well soaked in olive oil, to the general agreement of all those present.

"But, my dear Aleixo, after all, what sculptures are those you have been doing in America which we know nothing about over here?" Calheiros suddenly asked.

"Some busts, some bas-reliefs, nothing very special," answered Aleixo laconically.

"Why don't you bring some of those works here and exhibit them in Lisbon, in one of the salons of the National Fine Arts Society, or even here, in Viana do Castelo?" Calheiros insisted. "After all, we've seen nothing more of your work since…since…since you left for the United States."

"My dear Francisco, when one day you wish to pay my wife and me the honor of a visit in America I will be extremely pleased to show you some of my most recent works," replied Aleixo, measuring his words, after a few seconds' hesitation.

"Indeed, but surely I am not the only person interested in seeing them. Thus my suggestion," replied Calheiros, not to be outdone.

"Yes, but as you know sculpture works are usually done in stone or bronze, and therefore are heavy and difficult to transport. Added to that is the fact that most of those I have done over these last years in America are in private collections. So to get some of them to Lisbon it would be necessary to get their owners' consent, which does not seem easy to achieve."

"Yes, but with a little good will it might be possible, don't you think?" insisted Calheiros.

"Perhaps. But to be honest, for someone like me, who participated so many times in the Salon in Paris, and has works in such different countries as Bulgaria and Abyssinia, not to mention Chicago and other cities in the United States, I fail to see what might be the interest in participating in such a parochial and minor salon as the one you mention, by the Fine Arts Society. It would be, as the folk expression goes, 'swapping a horse for a donkey', don't you think, Francisco?" Aleixo replied coldly and incisively, to the astonished gaze of Elizabeth, unable to understand whatever it was that her husband had just said, given that the conversation was once more in Portuguese.

"For God's sake, don't get me wrong, Aleixo. Far be it from me to question your track record as a sculptor of acknowledged international prestige," Calheiros replied with a certain sarcasm. "What I think is that it is enough for an artist of your talent to be forced to go and try his luck far from his homeland, but then to be deprived of showing his compatriots the result of his work."

"But don't despair, dear Francisco, because perhaps sooner than you think you will be able to have the chance to see one of the works that Aleixo has carried out in America, finally placed on the streets of Lisbon. Or at least in one of the royal palaces," Gaspar cut in, defending his brother, beneath the attentive gaze of Elizabeth, increasingly curious about the subject of that heated exchange of words, the meaning of which completely escaped her. In the meantime, with the cod finished, the servants began to take away the plates and cutlery.

"Really? That's good news. And may one know what this work is?" asked an interested João Gomes.

"It is a statue of Queen Amelia that I finished recently in Chicago. It is a unique but heartfelt homage to the determination and courage with which our Queen was able to deal with the tragic events that robbed her of her husband and son, may God keep their souls," Aleixo explained, touched.

"And the Queen well deserves this homage, poor thing, after all, she suffered," commented Bertiandos in turn, as the servants were serving the second course around the table, an appetizing and steaming roast Barrosã veal course, accompanied with roast potatoes and finely chopped greens.

"If I may say a word about this new work by my husband, I should say that in the United States it has been the object of great praise in the newspapers by the specialized critics. And during the audience granted to us by King Manuel, after carefully observing the photographs we showed him, he was also full of praise," the Countess de Santa Eulália suddenly cut in, having been informed of the subject of the conversation by her neighbor at the table, Paço de Vitorino.

"And is there any idea where the statue will be placed?" asked Abreu e Lima, after enjoying a good chunk of veal.

"His Majesty told us he would like it to be placed in a prominent place in one of the Lisbon squares, and that he would discuss the matter with the government. But Ferreira do Amaral was not so receptive, arguing that placing a statue of the Queen in a public square in Lisbon at this precise moment could serve as a pretext for possible attacks by the republicans against the Crown and the Monarchy. Which might jeopardize the aims of calmness and national agreement established by his Government. As an alternative, he suggested the possibility of the statue being placed in the garden of Necessidades Palace or another of the royal palaces," Aleixo clarified.

"Well let's see whether with so much calmness the government is not really kneeling to the republicans," noted the Count de Bertiandos, somewhat irritated. "Because the Portuguese are still essentially profoundly monarchical, there's no doubt at all about that. And in my opinion, the inauguration of a statue of the Queen in a public square in Lisbon would be, to the contrary, an excellent opportunity to affirm the superiority of the monarchical ideals and values in relation to the anarchy and chaos that the republic will definitely lead to."

"You are totally correct, Count. It is not by giving in to the republicans that one can stand up to them," cut in Alfredo Vaz Pinto, after also savoring a good chunk of veal, which although not being bad, was not up to the standard of the famous *Arouquesa* veal, from the region of Arouca, his place of birth. In the meantime, the servants had begun to serve the champagne.

"Well, it seems the time has come for us to toast my dear brother Aleixo, Count de Santa Eulália. Who, in circumstances known to everyone, felt it necessary to leave his country and go far across the Atlantic to try to find the glory and notoriety that were denied him here," said Gaspar, standing up after banging on his glass repeatedly with a knife to call everyone's attention, as soon as they all finished their second course. "Now, after several years have gone by, here he is again, in triumph, to introduce us to his gracious and genteel wife Elizabeth, or Isabel, as he very Portuguesely calls her. To the health of Isabel and Aleixo, Count and Countess de Santa Eulália!" he finished, raising his glass high.

"To the health of Isabel and Aleixo," all the other guests replied in unison, glasses raised.

"I also want to propose a toast to the Countess of Santa Eulália, for her kindness and warmth, and to our friend Aleixo, for his talent as an artist and diplomat: to the health of the Count and Countess of Santa Eulália!" the Count of Bertiandos toasted in turn, after which several of the other guests did the same, among whom were Calheiros and Paço de Vitorino.

"My dear brothers, relatives, and friends: first I wish to thank you, in my name and in that of my wife, for the kindness and warmth of your words, and to show you my deep recognition for having accepted to join this reception to welcome my wife Isabel. I also wish to thank our hostess and my dear sister-in-law, Tina, for the way she showed such availability to receive us here in her House of Boavista, where I was born and grew up, and of which I have such grateful memories. Thanks which obviously extend to my dear brother and sister António and Ernestina, for the inestimable help they gave us in the preparation and organization of this event. To the health of all of us! To all of you!" the Count de Santa Eulália finally replied, to great applause.

"And now, because the party is not over, I suggest we go on to the balcony, where coffee and spirits will be served," said the lady of the house with a mysterious smile, before getting up, then followed by the rest of the guests.

Outside, the temperature was pleasant, although a cool breeze was blowing up from the river. As they came out from inside the house, the guests distributed themselves into groups along the balcony, where the large table on which aperitifs had been served to them had been replaced by chairs, laid out in a row along the wall. In front of the house, the yard was now all lit up with balloons hanging from the trees.

"So Gaspar, what news do you have for us from Lisbon, about

the government: will it last or not?" Alfredo asked his brother-in-law, standing at the end of the balcony, side by side with the Counts de Bertiandos and Paço de Vitorino.

"Well, a few days ago when Ferreira do Amaral finally decided to call administrative elections, unbeknown to José Luciano and Vilhena, I was convinced that he was signing his death warrant as Prime Minister," Gaspar replied, referring to the attempts made by the leaders of the Progressive and Regenerating parties, José Luciano de Castro and Júlio Vilhena, to delay the elections.

"But even so he held on," observed Alfredo, accepting his cup of steaming coffee offered by the servants.

"True. José Luciano invited Vilhena for a lunch event on his estate in Anadia, and they came to the conclusion that for now, it was better for them, progressives and regenerators, to maintain their support for the government.

"But why were they so obstinate about delaying the elections, to the point of jeopardizing the survival of a government which, even being headed by an independent, is made up only of members of their parties?" asked a confused Francisco Teixeira de Queiroz, joining the group, with a shrewd gaze behind his glasses.

"Because they are afraid that the republicans might get a good result, why else?" replied Gaspar, taking a cigar from the box that one of the servants held out to him. In the meantime, the party was restarting, with the musical band entering the yard to the sound of Bizet's *Carmen*, one of the most well-known works in their repertoire, and stopping walking facing the balcony.

"A good performance, no doubt about it," commented Calheiros when the musicians finished that first aria in their repertoire to great applause.

"But don't you think that the risk really exists, particularly in the cities, where they seem to have more support, Gaspar?" asked Bertiandos, while the musicians were preparing to begin their second piece.

"Of course it does. Just that for me such a risk can't be fought by indefinitely delaying elections through juridical skills or dilatory processes, as José Luciano and Vilhena tried to do. But rather through concrete measures of governing, promoting the effective progress of the country and the social well-being of the populations. That is the only way possible to save the monarchy, no other," replied Gaspar, lighted cigar in his mouth and lowering his voice so as not to disturb the attention with which the other guests were listening to the band, this time performing Strauss's popular *Blue Danube*.

"Yes, but in the short term that isn't what will stop them winning. At least in some of our cities and towns. Particularly with the strong support they have been getting, even from people with a monarchist background, such as Anselmo Braamcamp Freire and Bernardino Machado," Bertiandos countered apprehensively as soon as the applause for the second piece died down.

"And the inestimable support of the Free Masons and the Carbonari Society, one shouldn't forget. First they assassinated the King and the Prince Royal, and now they are gradually preparing to seize power," added Paço de Vitorino acrimoniously, as the band finished its performance and orderly walked out of the yard.

"Slow down, it's not exactly like that," replied Gaspar, cigar in his mouth, after taking a good gulp of cognac.

"Well, you must know, as your party gets on with them like a house on fire. Ever since you got together to conspire against the King," insisted Paço de Vitorino.

"Not against the King, Francisco, against João Franco and his dictatorship, which is very different," Gaspar vehemently defended himself, at the moment that a lively folk dancing group was entering the yard, made up of an equal number of boys and girls, the boys wearing black trousers with a stripe and waistcoats of the same color over open white shirts, and the girls in their beautiful colored traditional outfits. Accompanying them, a well-tuned musical group that included a concertina, two drums, triangles, large guitar, and Portuguese ukulele.

"Yes, but three days later after the plot you and the Republicans had set up to overthrow João Franco had been discovered, the King is assassinated along with the heir to the crown. Don't you think it is too much of a coincidence?" Paço de Vitorino again attacked exaltedly, as the folk dancing group was now launching into a typical *vira* dance from Minho.

"My dear Francisco, as you must know, in the investigations carried out after the assassination of the King, there was nothing to prove any relationship between those two events. Besides which, on the day of the assassination the main republican and progressive dissident leaders were either in jail in the stinking calabooses of the dictatorship or they had left the country so as not to be arrested," replied Gaspar, trying to stay calm, as soon as the first dance ended.

"Which means that you believe that Costa and Buiça acted alone, with no one behind them," insisted Vitorino.

"Unfortunately they are both dead, so it isn't possible to make them speak. But as far as I know, nothing was concluded about the existence of possible accomplices in the crime. Anyway, with or without accomplices, for me the main person responsible for the crime was João Franco and the fierce dictatorship he imposed upon the country, with the consent of the King himself," replied Gaspar definitively, with the group now taking their first steps in a new dance.

"Do you believe that, Gaspar? Don't you think you are being a bit naïve?" asked Bertiandos.

"Look, my dear Gonçalo. As I said some time ago in the Chamber of Deputies, we are living through the last monarchical experience. If the monarchists themselves carry on with the old processes of government inherited from rotativism, the days of the regime are numbered. But if they decide to govern correctly, putting the higher interests of the country and the people before anything else and not their own interests, there will be no lack of support or future for the monarchy," said Gaspar, prophetically, from a distance observing the effort that his brother Aleixo, Count de Santa Eulália, was making, in the middle of the group, to teach the Countess how to dance a typical Chula from the Upper Minho.

"Indeed, but the parties of rotativism are what they are, and no one can change them. They are increasingly alike; almost nothing distinguishes them. While the republicans are gaining support and strength, waiting for the right moment to deal the final blow to the monarchy and set up a republic," the old Count de Bertiandos said in an outburst of lucidity, at the moment when, with the folk dancing exhibition, a bright firework display was rising in the sky, set off from behind the house.

The bells of the Church of Santa Maria de Refojos were sounding eleven at night when it was the end of the firework display and with it, the end of the party, and the guests began to return to their houses.

XIV

Paris, 9th of September 1898

IT IS A VERY SMALL, rectangular package wrapped in blue silk paper, tied with a gold satin bow, that Aleixo suddenly takes out of the right pocket of his beige linen jacket, then places in front of him on the outdoor café table, next to his Panama hat and his empty coffee cup, and then spinning it round between his thumb and forefinger.

"Almost a half-hour late," he notes with a certain impatience, looking once again at his pocket watch, at four twenty-five. "Maybe the telegram arrived after she left the house. Or she received it, but for whatever reason, couldn't come," he thinks, restarting, reflexively, the rotating movement of the small package. And in the end, why such a hurry, such urgency in setting up a rendezvous on the very day of his arrival, when it would have been more natural and sensible to leave it for the following day, after a good night's sleep, completely recovered from the exhaustion of the trip? Yes, why all that rush as soon as he had disembarked from the train, a little after five-thirty in the morning, running to the telegraph office in Gare d'Austerlitz, with a sore, tired body after a forty-eight hour trip from Lisbon to Paris in one of the uncomfortable third-class compartments of the *Sud-Express*? Aleixo asks himself, while again stopping the rotating movement of the small package as suddenly as he had restarted it.

"*Arrivé Paris stop Rendez-vous 4 heures Deux Magots stop,*" he dictated, lips glued to the glass partition of the small booth, while the sleepy clerk scribbled the text on a piece of paper, which he gave back to him to verify before sending, he remembers, while observing the foot traffic next to the table, in the hope of seeing her emerge at any moment among the hurried forms that incessantly crisscross the sidewalk of the Boulevard Saint Germain, some coming from the direction of the church, some from the opposite side, and some from the Rue de Rennes, right in front of him.

A desire, an imperious need, that had obsessively pursued him during the entire trip, to see her, to hold her longingly in his arms, to kiss her hands and face, to stroke her hair, to look into her beautiful deep, dark eyes. And to tell her how much he missed her, of the solitude and emptiness he felt for not having been able to have her with him during those four long months spent in Portugal, unable to return until all the formalities relating to the Sousa Martins monument were concluded, from the signing of the contract to the ceremonial laying of the first stone to the desperate search for a studio large enough to make a life-size version of the different pieces that would form it. Which he was able to find only a few days earlier, in Campolide de Baixo, a little suburb just outside Lisbon. Yes, never before, throughout all of his other stays in Portugal, had he felt such a powerful, intense longing as this time, despite all the attention he received from so many of the people that surrounded him since he had won the competition, not to mention the care and admiration with which he was treated by those close to him, friends and family, principally his tireless brother Gaspar, as was always the case. But no, none of this replaced or made him forget, for even one moment, his Nellie, quite the opposite: as the inevitability of his lock, stock and barrel move to Lisbon became clearer to him, at least until he finished the monument, the greater was his desire to have her there, with him, at his side. He had told her all of this in the letters he had sent her, in which he also recounted his successes, his glories in the lands of Lusitania, even sending her clippings from Portuguese newspapers about him and his works, although he knew that she wouldn't be able to read them, he recalls, as he continues to search the passing crowds, still hoping to see her materialize at any moment.

Yet her replies had been scarce and brief, reduced to half a dozen postcards and two or three letters. Because the work at Saint-Gaudens' studio and the classes at the Académie left her little free time to write, on top of it all in French, a language she continued to find difficult? Or because, as the old proverb says, "out of sight out of mind"? And if that's the way it was during these four months, how was it going to be over the next two years, during which, because of the contract he signed with the executive committee for the monument, he will have to definitively remain in Lisbon? And once it is finished and unveiled, who will say whether the new professional commitments he will take on, as he hoped, thanks to his success in Lisbon, will allow him to once again move his studio to Paris? And what sense would it make to open his studio here, so far away, since the majority, if not all, of his commissions will come from Portugal? All of this, based on the assumption that she will also remain in Paris for a few more years, while the opposite is possibly most likely, the fact that she will return to the United States as soon as she finishes her studies so that she can pursue her artistic career there. Especially since Saint-Gaudens, her patron and protector, will also not be staying in Paris for much longer, at the latest until the *Universal Exposition* in a year and a half's time, as he, himself, has already hinted. Indeed, too many doubts and uncertainties tormenting his spirit and embittering his heart, for which he needs the urgent answers that can finally let him know what to be sure of, at the beginning of this new and so important stage of his life, when, after seven long years of tough training in Paris, he is for the first time about to fully exercise his chosen profession in his own country. Answers that only she can give him, which in itself is more than enough justification for the haste with which he had set up this meeting, although apparently, without great success, since at forty minutes past the appointed time, she has not yet appeared, and probably won't in the end, he concludes after consulting his watch one more time. So the best thing is to wait for tomorrow and see what happens then. Yes, if she went out in the morning before the telegram arrived, she will receive it upon her return home this evening, and she will surely try to contact him tomorrow morning by sending him a note or a telegram to set up a new rendezvous, he decides, signaling over to the *garçon* to bring him the check. Yes, the best thing to do is to leave and take advantage of the rest of the afternoon by stopping at the studio so that he can program his work for the next few days, which is, in fact, the main reason for his trip to Paris: to pack and box his various works, sketches, statuettes, drawings, tools, and utensils of all kinds. And to decide what destiny to give to the different pieces of furniture he had accumulated throughout the years, such as easels, plinths, frames, tables, stools, and chairs, not to forget the old chinaware cupboard, selecting those that are really worth taking and deciding what to do with the others. In short: to completely dismantle the studio and transport it to Lisbon, so that he can resurrect it again in Campolide de Baixo, in the large, new space he had just rented.

So a lot of work to get through before everything is duly ready to be dispatched by boat to Portugal, the same boat, he, himself, will board for his return, thus avoiding the tiring and exhausting train trip on the *Sud-Express*, he thinks to himself, as he deposits a few coins on the table after the *garçon* had brought him the check. Only then does he notice the little package, there on the table, next to the Panama hat and the empty coffee cup, which he puts back in his jacket pocket, before standing up to leave.

"*Ah, heureusement que vous êtes encore là, mon cher Alexis,*" he suddenly hears Nellie's voice, with its unmistakable American accent, screaming from a distance.

"*Nellie, ma chérie, vous voilà enfin arrivée,*" he answers, hardly recovered from the surprise, as he finally turns to see her arrive, almost running, from the Rue de Bonaparte.

"A thousand pardons for my lateness. But you won't believe what just happened to me," she says, breathlessly, red-faced, holding out her hands, which he kisses emotionally and with longing, one after the other.

"I must confess that, given the time, I wasn't counting on you coming, darling Nellie, you just caught me," he answers, with a slight tone of reproach in his voice. "But let's sit down, my friend, let's sit."

"Ah, yes, that's exactly what I need, after all that running," she says, accepting the chair that he offers her.

"What would you like?" Aleixo asks her after he too takes a seat, while again signaling for the *garçon* to come over.

"A tea. Yes, a very hot tea, please," she replies while carefully removing her broad-brimmed hat, decorated with pheasant's feathers, which she places on one of the chairs, thus showing her light brown hair, tied back and slightly wavy over her high forehead.

"So, Nellie, *ma chérie*, tell me what happened to you to make you so tired?" asks Aleixo, noticing with delight the emerald pendants that adorn her ears, the exact ones he brought her the last time from Lisbon, purchased at Eloy de Jesus, happily matching her natural-colored silk blouse, tightly fitting into the beige linen skirt, with almost the same shade as his jacket.

"My God, it's too much. I'm still not myself," she replies, speaking in English, as she always does when excited while removing a small fan from her purse, which she then starts to wave firmly in front of her flushed face.

"But what is this all about? Is there a problem?" asks Aleixo, intrigued.

"No, not at all. Just the opposite. It's some news I just received, news so extraordinary I can hardly believe it," she answers, greatly agitated.

"News? What news? Tell me what it's about, Nellie, for God's sake," he says, becoming impatient with so many vagaries.

"Today I got a letter from the State of Illinois, commissioning me to create a statue of a great American woman who recently passed away, Frances E. Willard. One of the first women to become a professor at an American university. She eventually became the chancellor of it for several years. Besides having been an intrepid fighter for the rights of women: suffrage, equal pay for equal work, and the eight-hour workday."

"And how did they think of you, in such a distant place as Illinois?" says Aleixo with surprise.

"I don't know. Since it's to honor a unique person in the women's rights movement, they probably thought it was a good idea to award the work to a young female sculptor from a neighboring state, who has already proven herself somewhat. And I'm obviously thankful," answers a boastful Nellie, before picking up her teacup again.

"Is there a deadline for completing the work?"

"Not exactly a deadline. That doesn't exist yet. But they want me to go there by the end of the year, at the latest, to sign the contract and gather all the necessary information: photographs, documents, articles about Frances, and everything else necessary for me to complete the statue."

"And where do you intend to create the statue, there or here?" he asks her again, suddenly uneasy.

"How do you expect me to know something like that already, darling Alexis?" she replies in a soft but firm tone, at the same time taking his hand and squeezing it tightly between hers. "First, I have to go there to see what conditions they give me to create the work, talk to them about how to develop it, and only then will I know how to organize everything. But the most likely thing is for me to do it there, I'm not hiding that. All things considered, it doesn't make much sense to make such a piece here, and afterward have to take it by boat to the other side of the Atlantic, with all the extra costs and labor implied. That's fine for a Saint-Gaudens who has other means and priorities, but not for me.

Anyway, the same will probably happen to you, with your monument, right?"

"Well, at first I thought about doing it here, at least until I finished the various plaster statues. But they, the promoting committee, want all the work to be done in Lisbon so that they can follow it closely. It's in the contract itself."

"See? So we're in exactly the same position, darling Alexis," she points out, caressing his cheek with her hand.

"Yes, but I thought that even working in Lisbon, I could still come to Paris somewhat frequently. And that nothing would stop you from going there to visit me from time to time. And when the work was finished, then we would see. Now—alas!—even that isn't going to be possible," he says somberly.

"But, darling Alexis, these are the realities of the life we both chose, let's not forget. Which isn't, and can never be, a life like that of others, a stable, bourgeois, family life with all its comforts and commodities," she says trying to console him. "For us, art is above everything, no matter how much that costs us, how great the solitude and the suffering it makes us feel, isn't that so?"

"You can't imagine how much I missed you during these last four months I spent in Lisbon, darling Nellie. And to think that in a few days I will return to Portugal and that after...most likely...we'll never see each other again..." he insists, with a look of infinite sadness.

"Never, is too strong a word. It's hard to know what the future holds for us. Perhaps a few years from now we'll meet again, here in Paris. Or even in Lisbon. Or in the United States, you never know..."

"There's no point avoiding the issue, Nellie: we both know that the probabilities of that happening are tiny," he suddenly says, in an outburst of lucidity.

"But we will always have Paris and the memory of the good times we spent here. And we still have the days left before you leave. By the way, when are you thinking of going?"

"Two weeks from now, three at the most. Just enough to dismantle the studio and send everything off to Lisbon, as the committee wants me to start as soon as I can."

"Well, it's after five-thirty. I have to go to Saint-Gaudens' studio today to give him the news. And it's getting late," says Nellie, after looking at her watch.

"In that case, I'll get back to my hotel. I'm still a little tired after the journey and I want to get to bed earlier to recover," he says, after a long yawn.

"No, please don't go yet, Alexis. Why don't you come with me? You could take the opportunity to see the plaster for the monument to Sherman I've been working on. And the works that were in the *Salon* this year," she proposes persuasively, insisting until she manages to convince him to accompany her.

"It is an extraordinary coincidence," he says after a long silence, the two of them walking side by side along the sidewalk of the Rue de Rennes, which is very busy at that time of day, with people packing the sidewalks and lines of carriages, carts and buses slowly moving forward towards the Gare de Montparnasse.

"An extraordinary coincidence? What do you mean?" she asks, giving him her arm.

"I've won the competition for a monument in homage to a man of great generosity, who devoted his whole life to treating and helping the poorest and most underprivileged. And you have been invited to make the statue of a woman who was also a noble, generous spirit, a great fighter for the rights of women in your country."

"You're right. I hadn't thought about that," she replies, surprised, as they come to the crossroads with the wide, busy Boulevard Raspail. Through the compact and chaotic mass of vehicles that bump into each other along the way, one can now start to see the long and symmetrical stone facade of the Gare de Montparnasse at the end of the street, with its two pediments in the middle over the great half-moon windows that illuminate the inside of the hall.

"When I come here and see the station down at the end I always remember our trip to Meudon, to Rodin's studio, remember?" Aleixo risks saying, looking nostalgic and turning towards her.

"I remember it like it was today. No train journey ever went so fast as that one. We were so absorbed in our conversation that we didn't notice the time go by, did we?" she replies, staring at him for moments, as they enter the Rue de Vaugirard on the right.

"True," he replies, before once again diving into a heavy silence on the way to the first crossing, where they again turn right.

"Ah, here it is, the Rue de Bagneux. It must be almost a year since that day we came here to see Saint-Gaudens. He had just rented the studio, remember? I had also just come back from Portugal, like now, after the holidays," exclaims Aleixo after reading the name of the street engraved in the stone of the corner building.

"Yes, and it was a beautiful day, like today, although a little cooler," she recalls as they come to the iron gate. Nellie pausingly pulls at the bell one, two, three times, until finally, someone shouts in bad French from the inside, "*Un moment, j'arrive!*"

"Hi, Jim! How are you?" says Nellie to the thin, tall young man with a long lock of hair over his forehead, who comes to open the gate for them.

"Hi, Nellie. I didn't expect to see you here today. Is something the matter?" the young man asks in English with a strong American accent, as he wipes his plaster-dirty hands on his apron.

"I really need to speak to the Master. Is he still here?" she asks, now on the patio.

"No. He's just left," the man answers, somewhat intrigued as he observes Aleixo coming through the gate.

"*Dommage.* Don't you know where he went?"

"No. I just know he's going to dine at the *Procope* at around about 7:00 p.m."

"Yeah? So I have to go to see him. By the way, I don't know whether you know my Portuguese colleague, Alexis?"

"James. James Fraser. *Enchanté!*" says the man, holding out his hand to Aleixo. "*Enchanté aussi, Monsieur,*" he replies.

"Well, if you don't mind, now we are here, I'll take the opportunity to show Alexis the studio and the works that were in the *Salon,*" she says, before walking to the door to the pavilion.

"Yes, but don't be long, because there isn't much light now and soon we'll be going," replies the man, motioning to Aleixo to go ahead of him. Inside, instead of the three rooms that Aleixo could see a year earlier, now there is one single enormous space, with headroom of over six meters, full of works in clay and plaster, some large-sized ones, the shapes of which Aleixo discovers better as his eyes get used to the faint light that enters through the *verrière* that runs along the whole north facade of the pavilion.

"This is the plaster of the *Shaw Memorial*, the one that Saint-

Gaudens decided to alter after it had been inaugurated in Boston. Mainly because of that angel up there, which has since undergone several alterations. This is after the thirteen years he spent working on the piece," explains Nellie, while Aleixo closely observes the composition, dominated by the figure of an army officer on horseback in the foreground, juxtaposed to a numerous regiment of soldiers equipped with rifles, backpacks, and canteens, marching to the front. Above the officer's head, as if protecting the whole regiment, the figure of the angel, reclining, tunic flying, one arm stretched forward while the other arm held back, holds an olive branch.

"Very interesting, particularly in the movement, he grants to several different figures. And in the way that the plane of the horseman stands out from that of the soldiers, of whom one can only see the heads and the rifles, there on the other side. Creating an interesting effect of perspective," exclaims Aleixo enthusiastically. "Now the angel; I would risk suggesting that it isn't really necessary."

"Perhaps you are right, but that certainly isn't Saint-Gaudens's opinion, believe me. For him the mixture of the real and the allegorical is very important," she replies. Further on, on a frame, is another statue, representing an energetic man marching, with a broad-brimmed hat, his cape fluttering, with an enormous book under his left arm and a Bengal cane in his right hand.

"This is the original plaster for *Puritan*, a statue that is over ten years old, the bronze version of which is in a park in Springfield, Massachusetts. But which, even so, Saint-Gaudens also decided to bring from New York to show at the *Salon*. It is a homage to the Puritans, those who watched and watch over good customs and Christian faith. So he has the famous Puritan hat on his head and a heavy Bible under his arm.

"Although the representation is naturalist, it still has soul, expression, and energy," says Aleixo, remaining to contemplate the works for a few moments before carrying on to an enormous equestrian statue on a great wooden frame in the middle of the studio, on which Fraser and two other colleagues, upon high scaffolding and ladders, are working almost in the darkness, aided by some petrol lamps.

"And here, finally, is the monument to General Sherman, one of the great victors of the War of Secession. This is what we have been working on for the last few months, as Saint-Gaudens wants to present it at the *Salon* next year," she says, at the precise moment when Fraser and the other two colleagues start to come down from their scaffolds and ladders, ending their day's work. Aleixo looks at the work from afar, impressed by its over six-meter height and eight-meter length, with its central figure of the soldier on horseback, led by a beautiful Victory, who points the way forward in front of him with her raised left arm.

"Indeed a magnificent work," says Aleixo, impressed, after a long silence. "It is an entirely different, almost opposite, path and search to that of Rodin, with whom I obviously identify much more. But it is remarkable how he brings together an extreme realism of detail with such great elegance of movements. That horse is not trotting but levitating. And the general is superb in his proud demeanor."

"And what do you think about Victory?"

"Victory is also remarkable, in the way she leads the horseman, how she projects him forward and points out the way for him to follow."

"You can't imagine the hours we have spent recently working on this statue, me, Fraser, and the other colleagues. Every day there are more and more corrections to make. And to think that Saint-Gaudens began this statue ten years ago, without one knowing when he will stop if he ever will stop," she laments, as Fraser and the others wait for them at the entrance to lock the door.

"Well, Nellie, now I am feeling really very tired. So don't be upset with me, but I am going back to my hotel," says Aleixo, as soon as they come through the gate and say goodbye to the others.

"No, Alexis, please, come with me to the *Procope* restaurant. I really have to speak to Saint-Gaudens today, and Jim said he would be there from 7:00 on. What time is it?" she asks.

"A quarter to seven," he answers, after looking at his watch, when they are almost coming to the Rue de Vaugirard again.

"You see? Just time for us to catch a hackney. And then we could even have dinner there, like in the old days, what do you think?" she insists, giving him her arm again. "Like in the old days," Aleixo repeats to himself, without being able to understand how she could so easily invoke the dinners they shared in the old restaurant on the Rue de l'Ancienne Comédie now that it is all over, precisely now that nothing can be "like in the old days." But when they again come to the Rue de Rennes he inadvertently hails a cab and gives an order to the coachman to drive to the *Procope*.

"*Merci, mon chéri*," she thanks him as soon as they sit down inside the cab, to which he does not respond, remaining silent throughout the journey, but lacking the courage to say no to her, to refuse to carry on that farce, in front of Saint-Gaudens or anyone. Yes, now nothing will ever be like it was before, he thinks. In a few days, when everything is ready for his departure, Paris, Nellie, and Saint-Gaudens will be a part of a past that will never return, that will slowly fade away in his mind until they become nothing more than a far-off memory...

"We're here Alexis," she says, shaking his arm after noticing that he has fallen into a deep sleep, rocked by the jolts of the carriage.

"We've arrived? Ah, yes, sorry," he babbles, looking out of the window at the large glass windows of the *Procope* on either side of the door, then alighting and giving his hand to Nellie for her to step down. Having passed through the door and the windbreak, they enter the long, narrow restaurant dining room, which runs parallel to the facade, its walls lined in pink and *grenat* satin and decorated with the portraits of the many celebrities who have passed through here, tables with extremely white linen tablecloths set out on either side of the aisle, at this time of day almost totally occupied by a noisy crowd of *habitués*, made up of businessmen, theater people, the literati and artists from the Quartier Latin, among whom they finally discover Saint-Gaudens, alone, at a table next to the back wall.

"Nellie! What a surprise," he exclaims radiantly, as he notices the presence of the two of them. "Alexis, *comment allez-vous?*" he adds, now standing, greeting them with an effusive handshake.

"I'm sorry about disturbing you, Augustus, but we went by the studio and Jim told us you were coming here for dinner," she explains.

"You're not disturbing me," replied the American Master, pointing to the two empty chairs in front of him before sitting down again. "But is something the matter?"

"No, but something fantastic has happened. I have just received a letter from the State of Illinois inviting me to make a statue of Frances E. Willard," she says, straight to the point.

"A statue of Frances E. Willard? Congratulations, my dear Nellie. That's great news," he replies enthusiastically, but without showing great surprise.

"There's more: the statue is to be given to the Capitol, where it will be placed in Statuary Hall," she adds proudly.

"It's a great honor for you, my child. But also a great responsibility."

"I know, I know. Just thinking about it frightens me," she replies.

"There's no need for that. I am sure that you will be up to such a great challenge. And now we have to celebrate," he says, motioning to the *garçon* to bring him a bottle of champagne.

"Thank you, Augustus. Thank you for your words of encouragement," says Nellie, moved by this, as the *garçon* fills her glass.

"Let us drink to the success of our dear Nellie, for this commission to be a decisive step in her already auspicious career!" exclaims Saint-Gaudens, raising his glass high, then for moments joined by both Nellie's and Aleixo's glasses. Then he calls the *garçon* to set two more places at the table.

"But we don't want to disturb you, Augustus. We just came here to give you the news," protests Nellie.

"It is a great pleasure to have you dine with me," Saint-Gaudens replies definitively, as the *garçon* is already setting the plates, glasses, and heavy alpaca cutlery in front of them. "What would you like to eat? I've already ordered a *pâté de Canard aux Morilles* for starters, and a *Coq au Vin*, which is one of the specialties of the house. And to go with it a carafe of Bordeaux red.

"Well, faced with such kindness, all we can do is thank you, Master," replies a touched Aleixo.

"So how will it be? What is the deadline for the work?" asks Saint-Gaudens, after the two of them had made their orders: *Escargots de Bourgogne* for starters and *Coq au Vin* as the main course.

"I don't know yet exactly, but they want me to go there by the end of the year at the latest," she hesitatingly puts forward.

"In that case, there's still three months left, which I hope will be enough for us to finish the *Sherman*. And if there's anything else left to do Jim can handle it. So, for now, I don't see any problems with that date. And even if there were I wouldn't be the one to stop you going ahead with a commission like this.

"Thank you, Augustus. I am eternally grateful for your understanding," she replies, visibly moved, as the *garçon* arrives with the starters and the red wine.

"There's no need to thank me, my dear. It's the least I can do for someone whose devotion has been so great. No matter how sorry I am about not being able to continue to count on your collaboration. Don't you think, Alexis?"

"It is indeed a unique opportunity for Nellie's career, which would be a crime not to seize," replies Aleixo circumspectly, after tasting the *escargots*.

"What about you, Alexis? How did those competitions in Portugal go? Do you have any results?" asks Saint-Gaudens suddenly, also tasting a sliver of *pâté* on a slice of bread.

"Haven't I told you, Augustus? Alexis has just brilliantly won one of those competitions, the most important one. For a monument to a doctor who is very famous in his country," Nellie jumps in.

"No. You hadn't told me anything. Congratulations, Alexis. It is an entirely well-deserved award, judging by the works I could appreciate when I was in your studio."

"Thank you very much, Master."

"I particularly remember a statue of Vasco da Gama. Which despite appearing to me to be rather influenced by Rodin's latest works, impressed me greatly," recalls Saint-Gaudens, when, with the starters finished, the *garçon* starts to serve the *Coq au Vin*.

"Alexis is a great admirer of Rodin, as you know, Augustus."

"Yes, but there are those who simply copy what he does, without any trace of imagination of their own. While Alexis, although basing himself on the principles put forward by Rodin, reinterprets them, making a work of his own, with imagination and authenticity," Saint-Gaudens makes a point of saying.

"That is very generous of you, Master. I just followed my convictions as best I could," replies Aleixo.

"How do you intend to organize your life now in order to carry out the making of your monument? Are you keeping your studio here or returning to Lisbon?" asks Saint-Gaudens after silently savoring his *Coq au Vin* for a few moments.

"Unfortunately I will have to return, as the promoting committee for the monument demands it. And what about you? Are you still prepared to stay here until the *Universal Exposition*?"

"Yes. Without any doubt. This French adventure of mine is proving to be excellent, for me and for my sculpture. I now feel much more confident about what I am doing and the path I want to follow. Even if this means I have to review and alter some works I had considered finished. Call me a perfectionist or whatever, but I cannot do otherwise," he says, after ordering desserts and coffees. Which the three of them enjoy as they chat pleasantly on the most wide-ranging subjects, from the Cuban war, which ended up being a humiliating defeat for the Spanish by the growing military might of the United States, who then also moved in on Puerto Rico and the Philippines, to the controversial work of Rodin, particularly the statue of Balzac, which Saint-Gaudens says reminds him of an enormous candle melting.

"Well, my dear Master, my thanks once again for the dinner, and I expect to see you again before I return to Portugal," says Aleixo, now on the sidewalk after having left the restaurant.

"I thank you for your company, you and Nellie. And if I can ever be of use, or if for any reason you come to the United States, don't hesitate to contact me. Despite all of its excesses, America is the land of opportunities. It is a great country, where almost everything remains to be done. And where there is always room for a talented young man with a will to work, as seems to be your case," says Saint-Gaudens, saying goodbye with an energetic handshake, before going to one of the Hansom carriages parked outside the restaurant, while Nellie remains behind with Aleixo.

"I hope you don't feel bad about what I said, Alexis. I'm going to miss you a lot also. But it is the life we chose," she finally says, squeezing his arm and trying hard to hold back her tears.

"I know, dearest Nellie. I know. We will surely have more chances to see each other and talk about all this before I go away for good," he replies, movingly kissing her hands. "*Au revoir, ma chérie.*"

"*Au revoir,* Alexis," she replies, before going to the carriage where Saint-Gaudens waits for her, while Aleixo walks towards the Boulevard de St. Germain. It is only when he reaches the Boulevard de St. Michel that he remembers the little rectangular blue silk paper package tied with a gold satin ribbon in the right pocket of his jacket: a silver and precious stone brooch inside a box lined with *grenat* velvet, that he had once again brought from Eloy de Jesus, in Lisbon, to give to his darling Nellie.

XV

"MAY I, COUNTESS?" asked Miss Beach after lightly knocking on the bedroom door with her knuckles.

"Ah, Emma. Come in, come in. I was just expecting you," replied Elizabeth from the other side of the spacious bedroom, sitting on one of the wing chairs near to the bow window, satin robe over her cambric nightshirt, loose, straight hair falling to the middle of her back.

"Good morning, Countess. Here are today's papers, which Vinny has just brought from Philadelphia," informed Emma, walking into the room with a sizable pile under her arm, which she unloaded onto the open top of the bureau, next to the bow window.

"Well? Is there any news?" asked Elizabeth, looking at her with some anxiousness, after putting her teacup down on the breakfast tray in front of her on the low table.

"Well, at first glance, with the Philadelphia and Chicago newspapers everything appears calm, just one or two sporadic references, but nothing new. With the New York and Washington newspapers the issue is a little more delicate, given that through reports from their correspondents in Chicago and Philadelphia, they start developing the issue further, with reports, interviews, and commentaries of all kinds. Yesterday it was the *New York Times*, today it is the turn of the *Washington Post*, with an extremely developed item right on the second page," replied Miss Beach, standing, leaning on the bureau with one hand, opposite the Countess.

"Yes, but I was on the telephone to them for over an hour yesterday. I hope that they have at least taken the care to correctly transcribe my statements," Elizabeth pointed out, glancing sideways at the pile of newspapers laid out on the top of the bureau.

"There are no complaints about that. The transcription is quite faithful, and in some places is even a direct quote. The worst thing is the new statements by Mrs. Ernest. Even though there are also several people who deny her allegations, in particular one Father O'Callahan, from the Paulist Church, who says he is very close to the Count," clarified Miss Beach as she opened the newspaper looking for the item that she had previously highlighted with a red pencil circle around it.

"Ah, yes, Father O'Callaghan, a wonderful person. And in fact a good friend of the Count's. But what does that woman, Mrs. Ernest, in fact, say that is new?" asked Elizabeth, unable to disguise the deep aversion she felt just by pronouncing that name.

"Perhaps you should see with your own eyes, Countess," replied Miss Beach, walking towards her employer with the newspaper open and folded on the second page.

"No, no. I prefer you to read it, Emma. I'm fed up with reading newspapers, ever since this all began. Just a while ago I was reading the article in yesterday's *New York Times* again. Which isn't among the worst," said Elizabeth, pointing to the newspaper on the low table.

"As you wish."

"But sit down, woman. Sit here, next to me," ordered Elizabeth, with a nod to the other wing chair.

"Thank you, Countess," replied Miss Beach, touched as she accepted her employer's invitation, then opening the newspaper on her lap:

"The headline is completely ridiculous, as usual, 'WOOING FOR COUNT'. Followed by three sub-headings and a summary of the news item: "Chicago Woman declares She Fitted Out Portuguese Nobleman With Good Clothes and Arranged for Him to Meet Rich Philadelphia Widow—Asserts She Wrote His Love Letters and Prompted All His Courtship for Two Years."

"What? What nonsense is that? As if the Count needed anyone to teach him how to dress. Or how to write love letters," immediately stated Elizabeth indignantly.

"Well, if you would rather I stopped, Countess…. This is nothing compared to what follows," warned Beach.

"No, no. Carry on. It was just an outburst, don't worry," replied Elizabeth, her forehead resting on her right hand, her elbow on the arm of the chair, preparing herself for the worst.

"Well, right at the beginning of the second paragraph there is another sentence that reveals that woman's unconfessable designs:

"According to Mrs. Ernest's allegations, she picked up Santa Eulália in Chicago the same as any other raw material and turned him out a polished, finished product."

"What nerve! She must have no shame at all!" exclaimed Elizabeth, unable to restrain herself in the light of such cheek: her husband treated like a piece of simple raw material, transformed by that Ernest woman's torture into a polished, finished product…for consumption. By her, obviously, she concluded to herself.

"Further on there are direct speech accounts of several other declarations made by the woman, the content of which I think should have your special attention, Countess: 'I feel sorry for Mrs. Stetson, and for her sake must refrain from stating the details of my claim, but I can assure you that the story will make exceedingly interesting reading when the case is heard in court,'" Miss Beach continued reading.

"This means that she is threatening to reveal more in court. But what, good grief? Does she indeed know something else about the Count, or is she just bluffing?" asked Elizabeth, worried, and again with her head resting on her right hand.

"Well, she says she has twenty to forty witnesses to help to prove her allegations. But curiously not one of these witnesses appears to corroborate her statements in the whole news piece. On the contrary, everyone who was contacted denies them, starting from a certain Mrs. Bishop, who she says helped in her work of "preparing" the Count for marriage. And by many of the residents of the Chicago Beach Hotel, where they say that the Count is well-known. Ending in Father O'Callaghan, who, according to the reporter, was indignant on hearing of the threat of a court case, stating: 'I have been perhaps more intimately associated with Count Santa Eulália than any man in Chicago. He is a gentleman, and no such contract as is alleged could possibly have been entered into by him.'"

"Ah, finally someone says something sensible in the middle of all this pack of nonsense," commented Elizabeth a little more cheerfully.

"And it doesn't end here. I quote: 'I may say that I have always believed I knew who introduced Mrs. Stetson to Count Eulália. The person I have in mind was not Mrs. Ernest, but a woman prominently known in the society of Chicago, and the rest of the world, for that matter.'"

"Bertha. Bertha Potter Palmer. He knows she was the one who introduced me to the Count. And the same is true of the people who truly matter in that city. And now this little woman appears, whom I do not know from Adam, saying it was her?" asked Elizabeth disdainfully.

"But she pays no attention to that. And further on she attacks again, this time much more insultingly, saying that the Count spoke to her as a child speaks to its mother and that he told her that his family wanted him to marry a rich woman. That she dressed him in fine clothes, that she taught him how to behave and that later on, she and Mrs. Bishop managed to get the Countess to telephone the latter at the Chicago Beach Hotel. And that this was eight months after the death of Mr. Stetson."

"That is completely ridiculous, good Lord, it has no consistency whatsoever. It would totally fall flat in court. Who in their right mind would believe that the Count, a renowned sculptor, and diplomat, Consul of Portugal in Chicago, could have addressed this woman in those terms when he hardly knew her and only vaguely crossed her path in a language school in the city, confessing to her that his family wanted him to marry a rich woman? And why on Earth would he, who has such a refined upbringing, belonging to one of the oldest families in his country, one with great tradition, need help from some little woman from Kankakee, Illinois, to teach him how a man of his standing should dress and behave? It is inconceivable. Purely and simply inconceivable. What I cannot understand is how there are newspapers that waste so much time, paper, and ink on people who make such declarations," exclaimed Elizabeth in a crescendo of irritation.

"And she doesn't stop there. She goes even further, suggesting that at the beginning the Count did not progress very quickly due to his personal defects, although he advanced well in the area of correspondence. As, according to Mrs. Ernest, she herself wrote all the love letters that the Count sent, as well as drawing up the proposal of marriage and presenting arguments concerning all the objections raised by the Countess before she accepted it. And she ends by saying that 'these were two tough years of work, but in the end they were successful.'"

"What letters? What proposal of marriage?" Elizabeth again interrupted in astonishment, her breast panting. "If the letters I received from the Count were always written in French, a language in which he is fluent? And if the marriage was arranged here in *Idro*, without any written document, over the four weeks he spent with me immediately prior? One really must have no shame to go to the newspapers and say such nonsense."

"Fortunately your statements come next, Countess, completely rubbishing everything that was said by that woman," points out Miss Beach with relief.

"Really? So read what they wrote," Elizabeth asked, now a little calmer.

"Right at the beginning they transcribe some words directly, and I quote: 'I did not know such a woman as Mrs. Josephine P. Ernest,' said the countess, "and a statement that she brought about the meeting between myself and my husband is simply preposterous. I cannot imagine her purpose in circulating such reports or threatening a suit.... I shall pay no further attention to the matter; and I'm sure that the count will follow the same course. He is a quiet gentleman, an artist, who enjoys his work. He bothers no one. Why should he be annoyed?"

"Not bad, don't you think? asked Elizabeth, visibly more relieved.

"Absolutely. Serene but firm replies, as is required. Worthy of a true countess," replied Miss Beach venerably and thankfully, at the moment when Millie, the chambermaid, knocked on the door to come to collect the breakfast tray.

"Of course, after everything you have just read to me, I no longer have great doubts about the intentions of this woman. Everything comes down to one word: blackmail," concluded Elizabeth, after Millie had left, as silently as she entered.

"Yes, but to go to court for an indemnity of ten thousand dollars, to which she claims she has a right, she would have to present something more solid, more consistent. With what she has presented up to now she does not have the slightest chance of achieving her aims," Miss Beach commented pensively.

"Go to court? Are you so naïve as to think that she ever seriously intended to take this to court? Because if that were the case she would not go to the newspapers and make threats: she would take out the action first and only speak later, don't you think?" the Countess replied harshly.

"Yes, that's true. But if it isn't through the courts how does she intend to get what she wants?" insisted Miss Beach, not giving up.

"That's what we shall see later. By the way, what time is the Count arriving?" Elizabeth suddenly asked.

"Arrival time at North Station is now, at eleven," replied Beach after checking her watch, with the hands on ten fifty-five. "So if there is no delay he will be here in half an hour. Vinny went there a while ago."

"So we have to hurry. Finish reading the news piece," ordered Elizabeth.

"Well, the rest doesn't have a lot to do with the matter. It's all about the woman who appeared here on the day of the wedding without being invited," replied Emma hesitatingly, after glancing over the end of the item.

"Ah, yes. I remember the question that the reporter asked me, at the end of the interview: whether I thought there was any connection between Mrs. Ernest and that woman. Without thinking much about the matter I said that I didn't see what connection there could be between the two," recalled Elizabeth.

"And they transcribed that answer completely. But the fact is that, according to what is written further down at the beginning of the last paragraph, the person who established that connection wasn't the reporter but Mrs. Ernest herself," Miss Beach pointed out.

"But what for, for heaven's sake? Do you think that connection could in fact have existed?" asked Elizabeth, suddenly apprehensive.

"Everything is possible, Countess. After all, didn't that woman who turned up on the day of the wedding also come from Chicago?"

"That was what the Count told me at the time. But that fact alone is no guarantee of anything," replied Elizabeth, as if thinking aloud.

"Well, but coming back to the item, the next to last paragraph is totally devoted to new declarations by you," insisted Miss Beach, somewhat impatient over those constant interruptions.

"Really? Then read it."

"'I wish to deny the impression that at the time of my marriage I had detectives and mounted officers with clubs guarding my estate. I had only my own employees and they had positive orders not to permit any strangers to trespass. That was my right'," Miss Beach read in one breath, before raising her head to look at her employer, her eyes wide open behind her round glasses with thick tortoise shell frames.

"For heaven's sake, Emma, don't look at me like that. It wasn't really too much. After all, if there were police officers and detectives, there were also a lot of domestic staff. Besides, I have every right to prevent the entry of undesirable people onto my property, by whatever means, and it was particularly this that I wished to make clear in my answer to the reporter," Elizabeth said, doing her best to justify herself.

"Far be it from me to criticize you, Countess. I fully understand how it is sometimes difficult to deal with tricky reporters," replied Miss Beach, lowering her eyes.

"You're telling me."

"That's all for the *Washington Post.* Would you like me to read some items from the other newspapers?" Miss Beach wished to know.

"No, it's not worth it, Emma. You can take them away. Just leave me the *Washington Post* to show the Count, if he hasn't read it already."

"Certainly, Countess," replied Miss Beach, standing up after carefully folding the newspaper and putting it on the low table.

"I feel so tired today, you can't imagine. And I don't feel like going out at all. I tossed and turned all night, unable to stop thinking about all this. The result: I slept badly and little," Elizabeth stated with a sigh, sitting back in the armchair with her eyes closed for a moment.

"Indeed you don't look very well, Countess. The Count should be arriving at any moment. Do you want me to call Millie to help you get dressed?"

"No. It's not worth it. Don't bother, I'll get dressed later. And when the Count arrives tell him to come up, that I'm here in the bedroom expecting him."

"Very good, Countess. In that case, with your permission I'll be going," Miss Beach finally said on her way to the door with the pile of newspapers under her arm.

"Everything is possible, Countess. After all, didn't that woman who turned up on the day of the wedding also come from Chicago?" Elizabeth repeated the words she had just heard from her secretary to herself. Why hadn't she thought of this before? Yes, Alexis himself had clearly stated this when he decided a few days before the wedding to inform her of the existence of that woman, warning her about the possibility of her appearing during the ceremony, ready to do anything to stop it taking place.

"She is an unfortunate and crazy woman, with whom I had a relationship for some time in Europe before I came to the United States," he had explained, and then constrainedly telling her about the systematic and obsessive way she had begun to pursue him wherever he went, with insistent declarations of love and threats of suicide if he didn't marry her. When he came to the United States he was convinced he had finally managed to end the nightmare, but three years after he arrived, he was beginning his activity as the Portuguese consul in Chicago and she appeared again, now settled in the city, where her father, in the meantime nominated minister of her country in Washington, had enrolled her at the Art Institute of Chicago, on Michigan Avenue, coincidentally only a few yards away from the consulate. And the persecutions and hysterical scenes had started again, now more insistently than ever, without him having found a way of putting a definitive stop to them, he had finally said, downcast. So it had been decided then and there to contract police officers and detectives to reinforce the security around the property on the day of the wedding. And just as well, as, just as he foresaw, and despite all the secrecy around the ceremony, the "unfortunate and crazy" woman had appeared early in the morning at the gates to the property, ready to do anything to get in and do goodness knows what, to the glee of the many reporters present, who immediately used her presence and her statements to grant a sensationalist and scandalous character to the news that they wrote about the wedding.

Since then and until that interview she gave over the telephone to the *Washington Post*, two days earlier, she had heard nothing more of her, neither through the newspapers nor from him, Alexis, so it was with great surprise that she suddenly heard the reporter trying to relate her to this other woman, Ernest, and then she immediately, without thinking, denied that there was any connection between one woman and the other. But now, faced with this simple statement from her secretary, that they both came from Chicago, the city where Alexis lived until his wedding, and to which throughout this first year of wedlock he continued to go with some regularity given his functions as a consul that he still carried out, it was clear that she could not completely cast out the idea that such a relationship might exist. Had Alexis told her the whole truth about this "unfortunate and crazy" woman, as he liked to call her? What sort of relationship had, in fact, existed between the two for her to feel she had the right to pursue him for so long, "with insistent declarations of love and threats of suicide if he didn't marry her," as he alleged had happened? And how was it possible for a woman who, according to Alexis, was the daughter of a minister of her country in the United States, therefore someone of good social standing, a student of sculpture in such a prestigious art school as the Art Institute of Chicago, to have such little pride and dignity to pursue a man for so many years, as he accused her of doing, to the point of trying to force her way into a house whose owners she did not know, no doubt with the aim of preventing the wedding ceremony taking place inside? Did Mrs. Ernest know another version of the events, different from the one that Alexis had told her, with details that were perhaps more sordid and which he, out of shame or modesty, or simply out of being afraid of her reaction, had hidden from her? Were they in fact lovers in Europe, before he came to the United States? Or later on, in Chicago, where she sought him out years later when he settled there? Might a child have been born out of that relationship, which she had used to force him to marry her and thus regularize the situation? Wondered Elizabeth, her heart suddenly beating rapidly. Might this after all be the trump card on which Mrs. Ernest counted in order to blackmail her and receive money from her, preparing to threaten her and tell everything in court and thus provoke a scandal of unimaginable proportions, which someone of her status and social position obviously could not tolerate? But in that case, what type of man would he, Alexis, be if after over a year of marriage he had not yet had the courage to tell her about everything, instead of allowing that insignificant little woman to come and threaten her with such revelations in court? And what in turn might be the degree of intimacy that he had with her, to the point of frequenting her home and consulting her husband, as he had confessed to her on the telephone? That which one has with a simple English teacher, with whom one shares the doubts that arise during her classes or more than that? What could he, Alexis, have revealed about his life to that woman, about his forebears, about his future projects, during the period they had known each other, including referring to her, Elizabeth, that might have led her to be convinced that she could take monetary advantage from this to the point of feeling encouraged to hurl herself into a campaign of such great proportions? Might there, after all, be some reason in the doubts raised before the wedding both by her sons and by some close friends about her husband's personality and character, doubts, to which until then she had never wished to attach any importance, convinced as she was of her proverbial intuition and good sense about people and who, in the case of Alexis, led her to trust him unreservedly against everything and everyone? A trust which, the truth be known, until then, now married to him for over a year, not only had never been questioned but had rather been reinforced, to the point that the whole family had adopted him unreservedly after the wedding, going on to unanimously call him by the tender diminutive form of Uncle Lexy, a term which he had been baptized on a day of inspiration by her eldest granddaughter Lizzy, she recalled as she looked at the blue sky through the bow-window.

When three days earlier she had confronted him for the first time on the telephone, in his studio in New York, with the news that had just been published in several Chicago newspapers, his surprise appeared sincere and total, first by stating that he indeed knew a Josephine Ernest, who had been his English teacher at the Chicago Alliance Française, and that he met her when he went there to learn English about four years ago, but that she couldn't be the person behind the wretched accusations that were made about him in the newspapers, as she had been a serious and well-educated person, and thus incapable of such acts. "My English teacher? It isn't possible. Yes, I even consulted her husband, Dr. Ernest, in Chicago. And I went for dinner several times at their house, in Kankakee," he had said, incredulous, on the other end of the line. And only after great insistence on her part, showing him irrefutable proof provided by the reporters that this was one and the same person did he accept the facts, but even so immediately vehemently denying that he had ever promised money or anything else to this woman, for whatever reason, and also stated he was prepared to go to court to refute all the accusations against him, given that they intolerably stained his honor and dignity and the noble traditions of his family, she recalled as she began to hear the growing noise of a motor car engine outside, getting up and immediately going to the window in time to see that it was her red Buick coming up the hill from the Old York Road, and then parking next to the *porte-cochère*.

"Isabel, *ma chérie!* What's the matter? Emma has just told me that you are not feeling well," he exclaimed with a concerned face as soon as he entered the room in his light brown cheviot suit, shirt with a starched front and collar under an ivory-colored waistcoat, dark blue silk plastron with a pearl brooch.

"Nothing, in particular, Alexis. I just slept badly, thinking about everything that has been happening," she replied in a bad mood, without moving from where she was, standing near to the bow window.

"To tell you the truth I also didn't sleep a wink last night. Who could imagine that something like this could befall us from one moment to the next?" he asked, before taking the hand she held out to him to kiss.

"Have you read the item today in the *Washington Post?*" she came out with as soon as she sat down in her chair again.

"I read it and read it over and over again on the train for the whole journey. That woman's declarations are absolutely scandalous and insulting. A list of improper lies, with no sense at all. Who could imagine such a thing? People in whom I trusted, for whom I even had some respect and consideration. And in the end, they come out with something like this. But in court they won't have the slightest chance, I can guarantee," he said, raising his voice, after also sitting down on the other wing chair, where Miss Beach had been until a short while earlier.

"How naïve, Alexis. Don't you understand? This has nothing to do with court or justice. When people like her threaten a lawsuit it is only to make the accusations they put forward more credible to the newspapers. To guarantee that they receive adequate coverage," she explains harshly but without raising her voice.

"So what do they wish to get from this? Can you explain?"

"Money. Because they know that someone in our position, of our status, cannot bear to see our name slandered and defamed by the newspapers for very long, do you understand?" she said, looking at him sternly.

"Well, then I hope that you are not thinking of giving in to this blackmail. Because if you do so it will take away my chance of defending my honor in court," he replied with conviction.

"My dear Alexis, I understand that for a European, from a country with over seven centuries of history, and brought up in the best principles and values, as is your case, it is difficult to understand and accept the mechanisms and contradictions of a society that is as young and open as ours, where everything can be bought and sold. And in which the rich and powerful like us, no matter how many actions of philanthropy are taken to help the poor and underprivileged, are always subject to envy and threats of extortion which may come at any time and from where one least expects it, for which we are obliged to be prepared, under risk of being irredeemably stained, or even destroyed, by such events," she said implacably but never altering her tone of voice.

"Yes, all of that is very well, but the person being accused here is me. It was my honor and my dignity they have put in doubt in the most infamous and vile manner it is possible to imagine, not yours," Aleixo exaltedly countered.

"But you can be sure that none of this would have happened if the circumstances of marrying me had not taken place. Because it is my millions that they wish to obtain, Alexis, not your honor and dignity, believe me.

"Even so, Isabel, even so. I want an opportunity to respond point by point to the accusations against me and I see no other place to do so other than in court. No matter how difficult this might be for you. As we say in Portugal, "the truth is like olive oil; it always comes to the surface," insisted the Count, refusing to give in.

"We shall see. There are several different ways to solve the matter…"

"No, Isabel. I'm sorry, but for me, there is only one way: the one I have just stated. Come to an agreement with these people? After their accusations against me? Not at all. I absolutely refuse to accept even to discuss the matter."

"Well, if that is the way it is, if your intention is to let this go to court, with all the consequences arising from that, then there are some aspects that have to be very well clarified first, otherwise we risk an unpleasant surprise," she put forward determinedly.

"I don't understand. What are you referring to more precisely?"

"I'm referring to a veiled insinuation that that woman, Ernest, makes in the item published today in the *Washington Post*. Which you certainly noticed if you read it carefully," Elizabeth clarified enigmatically.

"Veiled insinuation? I can't exactly see what you are referring to."

"At one point she says she feels very sorry for me and because of this she has avoided giving further details about her complaint. But she guarantees that the story will become much more interesting; that is, with further revelations when the case comes to court. So the question I am asking you is the following: Do you know what she might be referring to when she says this?" Elizabeth pressed him, again staring at him sternly.

"But how can I know something like that, Isabel? I confess I do not really understand the meaning of your question," replied the Count, astonished.

"The meaning of my question is very clear, Alexis. Everything she has said or insinuated up to now is no more than a pile of lies and nonsense. Even because we both know better than anyone that it was Bertha, Bertha Potter Palmer, who introduced us to each other and not that Ernest woman. And that the letters you wrote to me during our engagement were always in French and not in English, so, being fluent in the language as you are, you would never need your former English teacher to write them for you. And that someone with your upbringing and social background does not need anyone who lives in Kankakee, Illinois, to explain to you how to dress and behave…"

"I'm glad to hear you say that. All of a sudden it seemed you were granting credit to the accusations she made against me…" the Count interrupted with a sigh of relief.

"…So precisely because nothing she says makes any sense at all, nor stands up to the slightest criticism, is it hard to believe that she has set out on such a campaign without having anything else to present in her favor? Anything, any trump card hidden, ready to be played at the right moment. As indeed she suggests in her statements…"

"But what, for God's sake? Explain yourself, Isabel, please. Tell me what type of thing you are referring to," asked the Count despairingly.

"Something about your life, about your past, that you told her in confidence, I don't know. And that she can now use against you. After all, you told me on the telephone that you cultivated a relationship of some intimacy with that woman. That you even went for dinner at her house several times and that you were treated in her husband's surgery in Chicago," Elizabeth insisted bitterly.

"No. What an idea. My relationship with the Ernests was cordial and friendly, but without that degree of intimacy, she suggests. It is true that at the beginning when I still had difficulties with English, I used her services to translate some letters for me and to write to others. Mainly business work for the Consulate, and on occasion personal letters also. After all, she was my English teacher," the Count promptly clarified.

"And how did things go with her husband?"

"Nothing special. One time when I was ill I went to see him at his surgery in Chicago, that's all."

"Are you sure that during your contacts with those people you could not have unwittingly told them something about yourself, about your life, about your past? For example, about your relationship with that woman who turned up here on the day of our wedding?" Elizabeth inquired again.

"Good Lord, Isabel. Why on Earth would I entrust things about my past and, therefore, about what happened between myself and that woman, to people I hardly knew and with whom I had no intimate relationship?" asked the Count, increasingly exalted, contrasting with his wife's imperturbable impassiveness.

"I don't know. What I do know is that the reporter from the *Washington Post* who interviewed me over the telephone yesterday asked me whether I thought there was any connection between that woman and the Ernest woman. Then, to my amazement, in the item, they published they stated, black on white, that it was precisely the Ernest woman herself who established that connection.

"Where is that? Can you show me?" requested the Count, looking somewhat nervous.

"Look here at the beginning of the last paragraph," said Elizabeth, picking up the newspaper from the table and handing it to her husband, open at the page with the news item on it.

"'*Mrs. Ernest's allegations recall the presence of a mysterious woman at the Stetson residence on the day of the wedding...*' But that doesn't make any sense. What does one thing have to do with the other?"

"That's what I would like to know. Did Earnest meet that woman in the meantime? Did they exchange confidences?" insisted Elizabeth.

"I've no idea. Although now I think about it, it isn't impossible for Maria, when she got to Chicago to have gone to learn English at the Alliance Française like me. And become Ernest's student," he said as if thinking out loud.

"Do you think she might have told that woman, Ernest, something that she could now use against you?" Elizabeth put forward.

"What a question, Isabel. How can I guess what might have been said by an 'unfortunate and crazy woman' who is capable of doing what she did here outside the house in the presence of dozens of policemen and reporters on the day of our wedding?" he replied, irritated.

"What exactly happened between you and that "unfortunate and crazy" woman, as you like to call her? And why has she pursued you all these years, to the point of leaving Europe and coming after you to Chicago?" she inquired, staring at him harshly, straight in the eyes.

"I met that woman, Maria, when she was still a young student of Fine Arts in Bulgaria, where she was my assistant in making the model for the competition in homage to Czar Alexander II. Two years later I met her by mere chance—I repeat, mere chance—on a street in Paris, shortly before my departure for the United States, and for about a month she helped me make the model for the bust of Napoleon that I brought with me to St. Louis," he replied dryly, his right elbow resting on the arm of the chair, nervously twisting the tip of his mustache over and over again.

"Do you mean that, unlike what you told me before, there were no pursuits or declarations of love in Europe, only the honest and dedicated work of a poor, humble assistant? Who, years later, to your great surprise, turns up in Chicago, enrolls in the Art Institute and, without anything foreseeing this, starts to pursue you everywhere, with blackmail and threats that if you do not marry her she will throw herself into Lake Michigan. Or off a bridge," Elizabeth uttered sarcastically.

"Unfortunately things were not that simple, Isabel. And, *mea culpa*, perhaps I should have confessed everything to you from the beginning so no doubts were hanging over your mind on the matter. But it was such an uncomfortable and difficult subject for me...that, to be honest, I didn't have the courage..." he replied, lowering his gaze and at the same time again nervously twisting the tip of his mustache over and over.

"But you're going to have it now. Because I want to know everything about you and that woman. Once and for all, do you hear?" she said, waving a finger, for the first time raising her voice, which was usually soft and low.

"The truth...the truth is that there was some involvement between the two of us...after she arrived in Chicago..." stammered Aleixo, after a long, heavy silence.

"Some involvement. What type of involvement?" insisted Elizabeth, not prepared to let up.

"Let's say it was an amorous involvement. And things happened… that shouldn't have ever happened…"

"Did you at least love this woman? Did you have serious intentions about her? To get married and have a family?"

"No. That never entered my mind. You see, she was at least fifteen or sixteen years younger than me. And even if I wanted to I would never have the means to support her, and much less a family."

"You have only answered the second part of my question," Elizabeth pointed out implacably.

"Did I love her? No. At least not in the way she said she loved me. And that's where the problems started," he replied, fidgeting ceaselessly in his chair.

"You wanted to end it and she wouldn't accept it," she deduced.

"Yes. Let's say that…after what happened…she started to think she had rights over me…and insisting, increasingly stubbornly, that I had to marry her…that there was no other solution…"

"And from what happened between the two of you, could there have been, let's say…consequences?" asked Elizabeth, again staring at him sternly.

"No. Heaven forbid. At least as far as I know…"

"And so after your rejection the pursuits and threats began…" deduced Elizabeth, now more relieved.

"Yes. When I stopped receiving her, first at home, then in my studio, and finally at the Consulate, she started waiting for me out in the street. Or in places where she knew I would be, such as receptions in other consulates, or even public ceremonies. And then she would accost me with accusations and threats, several times causing me serious embarrassment."

"And do you have any idea what has happened to her now?" inquired Elizabeth.

"I was told that she left Chicago right after our wedding and never returned. I imagine she is with her father, in Washington. Or that he, knowing about what happened here on our doorstep on the day of our wedding, had her sent back to Bulgaria."

"You mean that even if she told Ernest something, without her being here to back up her statement the whole thing collapses."

"Yes. That seems obvious," he replied, his eyes set on the tops of the tall, leafy trees in the garden.

"So, it only remains to be seen what other trump Ernest might have to present in court. That is if we ever get there, of course," stated Elizabeth, sighing with relief.

"Well, there is in fact one other thing that I haven't told you about," he said, turning to her and then immediately turning his gaze away. "But it was so long ago…that I doubt it could have any influence on the case…"

"My dear Alexis, to get a good fistful of dollars these people are capable of anything, believe me…" she replied, expecting the worst.

"As you can surely imagine, my first times in Chicago were not exactly a sea of roses. The money I had earned during the St. Louis Exposition only lasted for a few months and I had to struggle with some difficulties…. After a certain time, still, without permanent work, I found myself forced to borrow money from some people…"

"…Let me guess: one of them was Mrs. Ernest…" she interrupted incisively.

"Yes. But she was the one who offered to help me, believe me. And I always paid her promptly and with interest," he hurriedly clarified.

"Do you have proof of this?"

"Proof? What type of proof do you mean?" asked an astonished Aleixo. "Receipts signed by her, giving you a settlement, or the debt papers that she surely asked you to sign for each amount she lent you," clarified Elizabeth, as if it were the most obvious thing on earth.

"No. To be honest I never thought it necessary to ask her for the loan papers back. For me, they were honest people and their word was enough."

"This is America, my dear Alexis. You can't trust anyone here, least of all those who lend money. And by the way, just to have an idea, what amounts are we talking about?"

"In the main small amounts, except in one or two cases."

"What cases, can you explain?" Elizabeth inquired again, being meticulous.

"The one I remember best was that for my trip to Madrid, to the wedding of His Majesty King Alfonso XIII, in 1905. I had just returned from Portugal shortly before. And although I had been Portuguese chargé d'affaires in Chicago I didn't have enough money for the trip. And as she knew about this she immediately offered to lend me the thousand dollars I needed," he recalled uneasily.

"A thousand dollars. That's money."

"And then there was another thousand. To pay for the suit I wore to the wedding."

"What suit was that, to cost a thousand dollars?" asked Elizabeth, surprised.

"It was my uniform as a Gentleman Knight of the Royal Household. The one I also wore at our wedding. That I had made at the tailors to the Royal Household in Lisbon.

"So, one thing is certain: with those papers in her possession, she can always say that the loans were never paid, and thus give some substance, at least partially, to her request for indemnity," Elizabeth pointed out.

"Oh, Good Lord, what a world, what people," complained Aleixo, shaking his head.

"Unfortunately it is the world we live in, my dear Alexis. At least here, on this side of the Atlantic," she countered, like someone who knew what she was talking about.

"And it had to be now, right now, when I am finally managing to get some recognition as a sculptor in New York—with the statue of Dr. Cook being so well received...and several commissions on the way..." he complained, hand on his chin, elbow on the arm of the chair.

"Well, as to that I don't think you have much to complain about. At least concerning the news item in yesterday's *New York Times*," she said, ready to definitively change the subject.

"That's only due to the fact that the journalist is an educated and well-informed person in the matter of art, which is rare. And that he was very touched because when he finally caught me coming back from Dr. Cook's conference at Carnegie Hall I invited him to come into my studio and showed him some of the works I have there."

"Really? And how did things go with the statue of Cook during the dinner at the Waldorf Astoria?" she inquired, more and more interested.

"It was an enormous success, you can't imagine. When at the end of the dinner they announce the author of the work lots of people stood up to congratulate me. Starting with Cook himself, who was very moved by the way that I, here in America, in my studio, had 'managed to so expressively reproduce that unique moment of his arrival at the Pole.' His words. And at the end he concluded, before going back to his seat among the people who were acclaiming him: 'My dear Alexis, sometimes fantasy goes beyond reality'," recalled the Count with a touch of pride.

"And what about his conference at Carnegie Hall? How did it go?" Elizabeth couldn't resist asking, becoming engaged by her husband's enthusiasm.

"Rather well. Cook was very convincing in his description of the expedition and the arguments he presented to defend his discovery, one by one dismantling the arguments of Peary, who maintains that he never really reached the North Pole. But, if you ask me, what was much more impressive than the conference was the reception he received on his arrival in New York, with a crowd of over three hundred thousand people acclaiming him in the streets as his cortège went by."

"Ah yes. I saw the articles in the newspapers. And the photographs. It must have been truly impressive."

"And he deserved it. An event like that only has a parallel, due to its importance and the risks involved, in the discovery of the sea route to India by Vasco da Gama," Aleixo pointed out.

"And the discovery of America by Columbus as well," added Elizabeth.

"Not so fast, my dear Isabel. Don't forget that when Columbus discovered America he thought he had discovered India, which is exactly the opposite direction of Europe. The result being the natives of America came to be called Indians," Aleixo observed sarcastically.

"But he discovered it, that no one can deny," Elizabeth made a point of saying.

"True, and that is why, and for his courage and abnegation that this year I decided to pay homage to him with the statue I exhibited in Philadelphia, *Columbus Discovering America*. Just like I did ten years ago with one of Vasco da Gama. And now I've just made this one, of Dr. Cook."

"Well, Alexis, the conversation is no doubt very interesting, but it is almost lunchtime and I am still here in this pretty state," she said, suddenly getting up after glancing at the clock on the stone mantelpiece, with its hands displaying 12:15 p.m.

"You're right, time flies. And in relation to this mess of the Ernest lawsuit, what shall we do?" asked Aleixo, also standing up.

"Nothing. The best thing is for us not to pay any more attention to the issue, to see what happens. According to Emma, today's Chicago and Philadelphia newspapers hardly mention it, probably because they have realized that her accusations make no sense. Let us hope that the same thing happens with those in New York and Washington. If in the meantime she goes ahead with any initiative, then we will be here, with our lawyers, to stand up to her and give her the response she deserves," she retorted.

"Well, as you know, I was thinking of going to Portugal soon. And I would very much like you to accompany me," he reminded her, combing his mustache again.

"Yes, but nothing stops us going. Indeed, it might be the best thing we could do at the moment, as we wait for the issue to die down. And if there are any new developments our lawyers will defend us. When is it best for you to go?"

"Two or three weeks from now. I still need some more time in New York, to see what I can do with the Cook statue, now that the possibility of it being placed in a square or garden has been raised."

"Ah, really? That's extraordinary, Alexis. Why didn't you tell me before?" she asked, suddenly enthused.

"Because I don't like counting my chickens before they've hatched, Isabel. It's bad luck. And I, with statues in public places, have been sorely burnt," he replied prudently.

"Ah, no. You'll see that everything goes well this time. Not for nothing are we in America, the land of opportunities," she said, slowly passing her hand across his face, now reconciled. And he takes her hand in his, and then kisses her fingers one by one, before taking his wife in his arms.

"Ah, Alexis, how I've missed you these last few days," she finally said in a whisper, with her face leaning against his and her hand stroking his neck.

"I know, I know, my dear," he replied, almost whispering, before pulling her towards him again and kissing her long on the mouth.

"It's very late, darling. I need to get ready," she said softly, delicately releasing herself from his arms and then straightening her robe and her ruffled hair.

"Well…then…in that case I'll be going down to the library," he replied, before turning around, somewhat disappointed.

"Do me a favor, Alexis. If you see Millie tell her to come up here immediately to help me get dressed," she asked, already on her way to her dressing booth.

"Certainly, my dear, certainly," he replied, before closing the bedroom door after him and going out into the corridor.

XVI

Lisbon, 7th of March 1900

"AGAINST WINDS AND TIDES, the monument to Doctor Sousa Martins is finally completed and ready to be inaugurated," Aleixo says to himself with satisfaction, going up the Rua de São Roque in a company carriage towards the Campo de Sant'Ana, yet unable to stop thinking about the many contretemps and tribulations he had to put up with in order to reach this point. Starting right away with the meticulous and endless inspections made by the fiscal committee for each of the different phases of making the monument, during which it was not uncommon for him to be confronted with the less than cordial opinion of one of its learned members, Mr. Casimiro José de Lima, worthy keeper of the gold and silver of the National Mint, considering that the statue of Sousa Martins had an affected pose, "lacking the simplicity and human warmth of his dear José Tomaz," and that in his serious "almost sullen" face, one would not see the shine of the "brilliance of his incomparable expression, his communicative capacity, his openness, and readiness to help his fellow man." And Simões d'Almeida, professor of Fine Arts and one of the "experts" who voted against his proposal during the competition for the monument, in favor of his protégé Costa Motta, but who even so did not refuse to accept being one of the technical delegates nominated by the committee to accompany the works, insisted that there were anatomical errors in the statue of the doctor, and pointed out examples such as the left arm, which, according to him, appeared not to have a shoulder; and the right leg, which with its knee raised too high would be clearly false; and also the angle formed by the foot, which in his opinion would be too much, as it was impossible for anyone to place their foot like that except a cripple. And that there was also a lack of correctness in the outfit, clearly visible in the trimming of the gown or the shape of the shoes. This was not to mention the physiognomy of the model himself, or his hair, which seemed false, or his mustache. Aleixo patiently countered all this throughout the several inspection sessions, stating the point of view that much more important than a strict correction in the clothing or certain details of the physiognomy was the capacity to translate into plastic effects the truth, the soul, the life, and the inner strength contained in a determined figure through its expression and movement, within the spirit of the new tendencies of the art of which an example was that great name in French sculpture who was Auguste Rodin. And that besides this one should not forget that the statue of the deceased doctor would not stand alone, isolated, as was the case with other monuments, but set within a harmonious group made up of several pieces and decorative elements in a permanent dialogue in which each of them had their own place and meaning, as parts of a whole. And little by little the majority of the members of the committee became convinced by the goodness of his aesthetic and artistic options, against the strictly naturalist point of view of Mr. Casimiro José de Lima, ending up by almost unanimously approving the final plasters of the statues and the decorative elements of the pedestal, he recalls as they are reaching the bottom of the Rua das Taipas, heading to the Praça da Alegria square.

Then, now in the phase of construction and assembly *in situ* of the pedestal, there were difficulties in installing running water into the two fountains that were a part of the monument by the Municipal Council services, forcing the works to be suspended for some time until it was finally sorted out. In the meantime, the setting of the several statues into bronze was taking place in the Cannon Foundry, which was also not problem-free due to the inexperience and lack of skill of the technicians in place, who were obviously more prepared to make cannons than works of art. Finally, as they became ready, it was necessary to transport each piece one by one on ox-carts from the Campo de Santa Clara, where the foundry is, to the Campo de Sant'Ana, where the monument was being erected, meaning a long and labyrinthine journey through the streets of the Baixa and Martim Moniz square. All of these activities were accompanied by him personally in their different phases so that everything worked out the best way possible, he recalls as they go round the Alegria square, towards the Liberdade avenue.

With the statues finally set in the places reserved for them, the last of which, *Modern Science*, less than a month ago, it was now the turn of the final touches he had decided to make to the monument: a *patine vert de gris* on the statues, to accentuate the chiaroscuro contrast between the most luminous and the most concave parts, a coat of ochre on the obelisk to further highlight the green of the statues, and another of cerulean blue on the cloud on which the feet of the figure in *Modern Science* is standing. But here he was faced with opposition from the committee and its technical delegates, who only accepted, and even so after some reluctance, the *patine* on the statues, and who had the other paintwork cleaned off, indifferent to his arguments and protests for some reason, he recalls with some hurt as they crossed the wide, tree-lined Liberdade Avenue, then on the other side entering the Pretas street.

All this was done and carried out in a year and five months, without him having time for any delays, any pause for reflection, between the model presented to the competition, with all the inherent contingencies of deadlines and scale, and the definitive version of the monument, with the risk of jeopardizing the date foreseen from the outset for its inauguration. This at a time when any of the great masters of sculpture, such as Rodin, Falguière, Mercier, or Saint-Gaudens himself, took and take years on end to carry out the works that made them famous, with advances and setbacks, sudden changes of direction, versions upon versions, until they finally come to the definitive work, as he had pointed out many times to the worthy members of the committee, but to no avail, he recalls once again when they are crossing the São José street, then immediately starting to climb the Telhal street.

In the meantime, he had also received plenty of criticism from his usual detractors, like Mr. José de Figueiredo, who only a few months earlier, in an article he wrote in the publication *Novidades*, called him an "ignorant and incapable artist," stating that it had been a "deplorable error" to have entrusted him with the making of the monument to Sousa Martins, which he, Aleixo, "absolutely or relatively considered, in no way deserved, given the worthless quality of his merits exhibited until today." This, of course, was without the gentleman in question ever having even set his eyes on the monument, or on any of the statues that form it, which were still being completed at the time. Or Major Ribeiro Arthur, illustrious art critic and weekend watercolorist, for whom all pretexts are valid for attacking his work, as he did two years ago with the *Vasco da Gama* and the *Sacred Heart of Jesus*, or less than a year ago with his *Sketch for a Monument to Mouzinho de Albuquerque* that he presented at the *Salon of the Artistic Guild*. Or also Fialho de Almeida, who, although having been favorable to the choice of his model during the competition, now also never wastes an opportunity to attack him, for whatever reason. But anyway, as the folk saying goes, and as his brother Gaspar tirelessly reminds him when he sees him run down because of attacks from his detractors, "all are not thieves that dogs bark at," he concludes when they are entering the narrow Rua de Santo António dos Capuchos, forced to almost stop to let pass a cab which is coming down in the opposite direction.

In the middle of all this he also had to bear the irreparable loss of his dear mother, may God keep her, on the 17th of September of the previous year, when the statue of Sousa Martins had been cast and the plaster form of *Gratitude* had been made, but more behind schedule was *Modern Science*, which did not allow him more than a brief trip to the Minho region to attend the funeral, without even being able to spend some days at Boavista with his brothers and sister Luiz, Claudinha and António, those who accompanied her until the end. Fortunately, he will be able to see them again shortly today, as they had all decided to accept his invitation and come down to Lisbon to attend the inauguration, he recalls as the carriage finally reaches the top of the Rua de Santo António dos Capuchos, then turns right and begins to go round the Campo dos Mártires da Pátria following an enormous line of vehicles of all kinds, sizes, and styles which was advancing slowly towards the south of the square where the monument has been set. Through the carriage window, Aleixo observes the crowd that follows them along the sidewalks on either side of the street, groups of young students, modest employees, whole families with their packed lunch baskets, humble people who have come to pay homage to the deceased doctor. Among the trees on the left there suddenly appears the elegant royal pavilion, all lined in crimson cloth, followed a little further on by the monument, impressive in its height of almost eight meters, with the statue of the doctor covered by the blue and white flag, both surrounded by a wire fence marking off the area reserved for the guests, and around which an enormous crowd of onlookers is already accumulating.

"A quarter past one in the afternoon," notes Aleixo, looking at his

watch after paying the coachman his fare. The windows of the buildings all around are packed with ladies in colored, showy outfits, and
on the scaffoldings of the new Medical School building, behind the
monument, one can see dozens of workmen hanging off them, forming
veritable human bunches of grapes, all anxiously awaiting the arrival
of the royal family and, with it, the beginning of the ceremony. Before
going into the fenced-off area, Aleixo cannot resist looking at it from
afar for a brief moment, with the strange sensation, which he also had
felt during the inauguration of the *Sacred Heart of Jesus* on Santa Luzia
hill, that this work, now definitively placed where he had thought and
planned for it, is no longer his, does not belong to him anymore; it had
won its total autonomy and independence from him and gone on to
belong to the public, who are going to see it and appreciate it. But after
all, is that not the destiny of all works of art after they are ready and
finished? he wonders, before finally going to the entrance to the closed-
off area, being immediately recognized by the guards, who stand aside
to let him by.

"Look who is here! Our great artist!" his brother Luiz greets him
from afar as soon as he sees him, as he sits there very upright and solemn in his tailcoat inside the royal pavilion that is still almost empty,
with his wife, Tina, at his side, as well as his brother and sister Cláudia
and António, all equally dressed impeccably.

"So, you're already here? I thought you were coming later, with Gaspar!" exclaims Aleixo radiantly as soon as he reaches them.

"Gaspar had to go to the parliament early in the morning, so we
decided to come here slowly on our own, after a walk around the Baixa,"
explains Luiz, before embracing him.

"So what do you think of all this?" asks Aleixo, smiling, after the
greetings are over.

"It's going to be a smashing party. And seen from here the monument is impressive, a masterpiece. Congratulations, Aleixinho," replies
Luiz, patting him on the back.

"Let's wait and see. Let's see what the critics say," counters Aleixo,
at the precise moment when the Philharmonic Orchestra of Alhandra,
the late professor's native town, stopped at the left of the royal pavilion,
launches into its vast repertoire. As he nods from afar to some of those
present, among whom are several members of the great committee of

homage to Sousa Martins, Aleixo pauses for a moment and observes the octagonal royal pavilion, with, on a dais at the back, a sort of throne with four high-backed chairs, headed by a small canopy, certainly intended for the royal family, and with two impressive ebony sideboards next to it. Above this, in the middle of the ceiling, a beautiful Arras cloth, and, hanging from the sides, wide damask pelmets and extremely rich Indian quilts.

"So what do you think of the Avenida Palace Hotel?" asks Aleixo, as soon as the band stops playing.

"The best there is. Real luxury. Rooms with private bathrooms, excellent views over the avenue. And those great halls are marvelous. Nothing like the Braganza," replies Luiz.

"Good, I'm glad you liked it. Lisbon is modernizing, and it's about time," comments Aleixo, turning to his side as he is warmly greeted by two gentlemen, elegant in their well-cut tailcoats, lapels lined with showy decorations, when one can hear the band of the municipal fire brigade crossing the square ahead of a numerous unit of firemen in their ceremonial outfits, with their typical helmets and axes, going over to take up a position in front of the royal pavilion. In the meantime, there are several professional and amateur photographers who, armed with their lenses, use this opportunity to take photos of the monument and the multitude of guests from the most varied angles and viewpoints.

"Twenty-to-two sharp," notes Aleixo, nervously looking at his watch again, and then noticing the Duke of Palmela, chairman of the great committee of homage, who had just arrived at the pavilion alongside Dr. Serrano, vice-chair of the executive committee, and who waves for him to come over.

"Mr. Queiroz Ribeiro? How are you? A good thing I've seen you. I was going over the reception ceremony for the King and Queen with Dr. Serrano. And we would like to count on your help to give Their Majesties all the explanations they require," the Duke says to him cordially, after shaking his hand effusively.

"After all, you are the father of the child, aren't you?" says Dr. Serrano, with some irony in his voice.

"It is not just a duty, but a great honor for me, my dear Duke. As soon as Their Majesties arrive I will join you here," replies Aleixo, retiring with a bow to go to meet his brother Gaspar, who has just arrived in the company of some Deputies, upon which some gentlemen approached him to greet him, while others, farther away, whisper to each other and point in his direction.

"Ah, Gasparinho, about time. Good to see you here," he says to his brother, engaged in a lively exchange of greetings with Luciano Cordeiro, secretary of the Geography Society, as soon as he comes over to him.

"Congratulations in advance, Mr. Queiroz Ribeiro. From what one can see it is a beautiful work," the latter says to him effusively before moving away.

"I'm sorry, but, just my luck, there was an early session in the Chamber all morning and a bill proposed by me was being debated. So I could only get here now. But let me look at you: how *chic*, what elegance. And the decoration from the *Negus* of Abyssinia is overwhelming, worth ten of ours," Gaspar tells him, for moments staring at that strange gold, five-pointed star encrusted with precious stones, that Aleixo is wearing on his lapel, then embracing him tightly, at the exact moment that a contingent from the Fighter Regiment No 1, with its respective band, stops at the entrance to the closed-off area to provide a guard of honor to the King and Queen.

"It's no problem. You got here in good time," he replies, leading him through the crowd that now almost fills the square to the place where their other siblings are sitting, inside the pavilion.

"Here he is, our distinguished lawyer. He was hard to find, but I got him," says Aleixo, disguising his growing anxiousness about the coming event with a guffaw.

"Look, there is Zé d'Alpoim, who is here to represent the government. Come on, let's go and say 'hello'," Gaspar tells him, pulling at his arm as soon as he sees the Minister of Justice of José Luciano de Castro's government, his cousin and fellow member of the Progressive Party, surrounded by a large entourage, on his way to the steps up to the royal pavilion, now almost full with the members of the great committee and the executive committee, as well as with all the other civil and military dignitaries present.

"This is packed with important people. I just find it strange not to see any high-ranking members of the Church here: not the Cardinal, nor the Papal Nuncio, nor even a simple priest to bless the monument," says Aleixo to his brother in a low voice, taking advantage of the moment when José d'Alpoim turns to greet the Duke of Palmela and Dr. Serrano.

"What did you expect, little brother? The man was a heretic and it is even said that he committed suicide," replies Gaspar, also in a low voice.

"What? You're ribbing me. Didn't he die of tuberculosis?" asks Aleixo, stupefied.

"Yes. But they say that being an atheist and non-believer in eternal life, he decided not to wait any longer and brought forward the time of his death, administering a lethal dose of morphine to himself."

"Well, I never! I couldn't have imagined such a thing. Good Lord! And there is me, over two years I've been doing nothing else other than devoting myself to perpetuating his image as a saintly and generous man," replies Aleixo, stupefied at such a revelation, as the bands of the municipal fire brigade and the Fighter Regiment 1 start to play the National Anthem in unison, signaling the arrival, in a *grand carriage à la daumont*, of Queen Maria Pia, accompanied by her youngest son, Prince Afonso, Duke of Oporto, to great applause from the multitude of guests, who make way for them to cross the area, she in an extremely elegant black velvet dress, he in the uniform of an artillery Lieutenant Colonel, until they reach the steps to the pavilion, where they are greeted by a group of high-ranking dignitaries of note, among whom are again José d'Alpoim, the Duke of Palmela and Dr. Serrano, as well as The Civil Governor of Lisbon and President of Lisbon Council. After leading the Queen Mother and the Prince to the royal tribune, the group returns to the entrance to the pavilion, where a few minutes later they receive King Carlos and Queen Amélia, she wearing an elegant burnt-yellow leisure walk outfit, and he the great uniform of a major general with the stripe of the three orders. After some minutes of socialization and mutual greetings, the King and Queen go to the center of the pavilion, accompanied only by José d'Alpoim, the Duke of Palmela and Dr. Serrano, to be informed by them of the details of the ceremony to follow.

"Your Majesty certainly will know Mr. Queiroz Ribeiro, the renowned author of the monument that will be inaugurated today," says Dr. Serrano, as soon as the whole ceremonial is settled, noting the presence of Aleixo only a few meters away, alongside his brother Gaspar.

"Of course I do. Both I and the Queen greatly appreciate his work," replies King Carlos, his bright blue eyes lighting up his wide, round face behind his thick mustache twisted in the style of his cousin Kaiser Wilhelm of Germany.

"Your Majesty is very kind," says Aleixo, having taken two steps forward to kiss the King's and Queen's hands.

"The bust he made of the Queen is a little masterpiece," recalls King Carlos.

"It is my *favorrrite* bust," says Queen Amélia, grating her Rs *à la française.* "How long ago was it, Queiroz Ribeiro? Three or four years ago, wasn't it?" insists King Carlos making an effort of memory.

"The first sittings were done in '96, Sir. And the bust was ready the following year, in Paris. I am very sorry that I have not yet had the opportunity to also make a bust of Your Majesty to complete my patriotic composition *The Aphoteosis,* through which I intend to celebrate the victories of our army in Africa," laments Aleixo, suddenly recalling his old unfinished project, the model for which was awaiting better days in his studio.

"Let's see if one day I can find some time for that. But you have already very well celebrated our victories in Africa, man, with that study for a monument in homage to Mouzinho that was in the Artistic Guild Salon last year. Did you see it, Luís? An absolutely remarkable piece," says King Carlos, turning to the Duke of Palmela.

"No, Majesty. Unfortunately, I didn't get the chance. But I clearly remember the very favorable comments by Helena, who is a specialist on the subject," replies Palmela, referring to the Duchess, a leisure-time painter.

"That dying horse, making one last effort to resist death and run to the enemy, is a prodigy of expression," the King continues, not seeming to be slightly concerned about starting the ceremony, to the great nervousness and anxiety of Dr. Serrano, who occasionally discreetly looks at his watch.

"And the *figurre* of Mouzinho, our *dearr* Mouzinho, proudly on his horse, *indiferrent* to the *dangerr* that threatens him, is *trruly extrraordinarry,*" says the Queen.

"Let's see how you've done now with this monument to Sousa Martins. No doubt a difficult work, with great responsibility. Shall we start, Serrano?" says the King finally, immediately walking out of the pavilion on his way to the monument without waiting for the reply, followed by the two queens, the prince, and by the large committee of dignitaries, among whom is Aleixo, next to the Duke of Palmela and Dr. Serrano. When they reach the monument, the latter, in his quality as Vice-Chairman of the Executive Committee, takes hold of the edges of the national flag that covers the statue of Sousa Martins and hands them to the Duke of Palmela, who, as Chairman of the Great Committee, in turn, passes them to His Majesty King Carlos, Head of State. There is an enormous silence. The King takes off his impressive bicorn hat with ostrich feathers, and all those present remove their hats following his example, as a sign of respect for the memory of the person being paid homage. Then, in one quick, dry movement, King Carlos pulls at the edge and lets the flag drop at his feet, finally unveiling, to prolonged applause, the bronze statue of José Thomaz de Sousa Martins. The monument is inaugurated. Immediately, the Alhandra Philharmonic Orchestra starts to play a triumphal march specially composed in homage to the deceased doctor, while the King and Queen take advantage of the moment to make a complete tour of the monument, followed by a numerous entourage, stopping here and there to observe the different statues and the other components, at the same time listening to the explanations given by its author. Following this, again to the sound of the National Anthem, played by the two other bands, the King and Queen return to the royal pavilion, then occupying the chairs reserved for them on the tribune, while the numerous entourage of high-ranking dignitaries and guests are distributed orderly in lines from one side of the pavilion to the other. It is the turn of the Duke of Palmela, standing behind one of the ebony sideboards flanking the tribune, to give way to Dr. Serrano, who, at his right, paper in hand, glasses on the end of his nose, thus begins his speech: "Sir! Majesties and Highness! Here is raised, as was foreseen, and here will last in memory to those to come, facing the Medical-Surgical School, the unique, gracious and expressive monument to the great Portuguese Doctor Sousa Martins—uniqueness like his life and condition, the graciousness of lines like that of his spirit, expression and a mark of gravity as was his character."

Following this Dr. Serrano recalls the way that, as soon as the country knew of the death of the prestigious doctor there arose the idea of perpetuating his name through the most varied plans and suggestions:

a tuberculosis hospital, a sanatorium in the Serra da Estrela mountains, a free teaching school, until coming to the much more modest decision of building a monument and publishing a book in his memory.

"Brilliant speech, don't you think? The man is inspired, there is no doubt," comments Gaspar quietly at his side, but Aleixo, enraptured, almost doesn't hear him, looking around him at the harsh faces, concentrating on the eloquence of Dr. Serrano's words, of all those illustrious personalities who have come in the representation of the most varied institutions and sectors of Portuguese life to participate in the official act of inaugurating his work, which is now totally uncovered, offering itself to the gaze of the crowd who flock to it to see it more closely in the complexity of its several statues and decorative elements. For him that is definitively a moment of supreme glory, like he will perhaps never live again, he thinks as he vaguely hears Dr. Serrano's words, as he now discourses about the evolution of medicine and the role of the doctor throughout time, from antiquity to the modern age.

Once the speech is over there is a tremendous round of applause from the select audience. Then the orator removes his glasses, puts the paper with the speech on it in his tailcoat pocket, and hands the Duke of Palmela the cases containing the three silver medals commemorating the ceremony that had been expressly minted at the National Mint, which offered them with thanks to the King and the two Queens. Then there is the reading by Dr. Hygino de Sousa, secretary of the Executive Committee, of the act of inauguration, after which it is first given to the King and Queen and the Prince to sign, followed by the Minister of Justice, the Civil Governor, the President of Lisbon Council, holders of civic positions, doctors, etc.

"Come on, lad. You also have a right. After all, you are the author of the monument," says Gaspar, pushing his brother into the line formed in front of the sideboard to sign the document.

"Only if you come too. If I am the author, you are a Deputy and private secretary to the Treasury Minister," Aleixo replies before the two go to the end of the line.

"Mr. Queiroz Ribeiro, my sincerest congratulations. It is a beautiful work," says Dom Thomaz de Mello Breyner, doctor to the Court, as he passes him after signing the acts, followed by many more words of praise from other gentlemen and well-known figures. The Duke of

Palmela is the last one to sign the document, as is correct, after which he goes to the royal family. It is exactly three o'clock when the National Anthem is heard again, now played in unison by the three bands, signaling the departure of Their Majesties and His Highness, whom the Minister of Justice, the Duke of Palmela, and Dr. Serrano accompany to their carriages to the applause of the crowd.

"Aleixinho, if you don't mind, I'll take the opportunity to go also, as I have some important business to deal with at the ministry," says Gaspar when they join the rest of their siblings.

"And we'll perhaps take advantage of the ride, as Claudinha had almost nothing to eat before we came and she's feeling weak," Tina says, holding her sister-in-law's arm.

"Yes, of course. Quite right too. The important thing was the inauguration, and that's over. The rest is mere formalities," replies Aleixo, understandingly.

"It was a beautiful ceremony, Aleixinho. I'm so sorry that Mum was not able to have witnessed this. How she would have liked to see her beloved artist son being consecrated like this, in the presence of the King and Queen and all the important people who are here," his sister Cláudia tells him, unable to hold back a tear, which runs down her cheek betraying her feelings.

"That's true. I also thought a lot about her during the ceremony," says Aleixo, moved.

"Look, the ceremony must be about to start again. I can see them all standing up, Palmela, Serrano, and Zé d'Alpoim," warns Gaspar, attentive to the maneuvers inside the pavilion.

"What if you two, after your business affairs, came to us at the Avenida Palace Hotel to take tea? That way we can be together for a while before our train," suggests Tina.

"Good idea. I'll be there as soon as this finishes," agrees Aleixo.

"Me too. As soon as I finish business at the ministry," Gaspar promises, as Aleixo has turned on his way to the inside of the pavilion to hear Dr. Serrano speak once again, this time to the Count of Restelo, the President of the Lisbon Municipal Council, to whom he gives the formal delivery of the monument. Then the President replies, accepting the duty of conserving it.

Having read the acts of delivery by the secretary of the Executive

Committee, Dr. Hygino de Sousa, there is a further session of signatures by all of the public figures present. When this is over it is the turn of the Duke of Palmela to subscribe to the document, after which he announces the end of the session. Slowly, among smiles and greetings, the guests begin to disperse, while down below the guards remove the wire fencing that until now had enclosed the pavilion and the monument, finally allowing the common folk, who had witnessed the ceremony from outside the cordoned-off area, to come over and see the work more closely.

XVII

Ashbourne, outskirts of Philadelphia, 5th of September 1910

ONLY A FEW DOZEN separated the two houses, his, facing Sycamore Avenue, close to the edge of the property, and *Idro*, the main family mansion, in the center, dominating the hill that stretched softly to the south to the Old York Road, a distance that he briskly walked, as he did every morning, along the wide and well-worn path that connected them, only slowing down opposite the stables, where one of the stable boys was busy brushing the shining black hair of two short, stocky and upright horses that he had never seen before and the breed of which he was completely unable to identify.

"A handsome pair you've got there, Walt. Where did you get them from?" he asked, stopping on his way after a knowing glance at the steeds.

"That's right. Two beautiful horses. It's hard to find ones as agile and tame as this. But I didn't get them, Master John: It was Count Eulália," explained Walt, stroking the neck of one of the horses.

"Count Eulália?" asked John, taken aback, again looking at the pair and the groom.

"Yes sir, Master John. The Count arrived last night from Europe, and brought these horses with him on the ship, along with that carriage over there. We had to go and collect them really early this morning from the freight from New York," replied Walt, nodding towards the shed adjoining the stables, where, next to the several motor cars belonging to the household, there was now a luxurious Victoria carriage, wheels with chrome rims and tires like those on cars, shining black bodywork, canvas hood in the same color and bright red leather upholstery.

"Well, take good care of them, Walt. After such a long journey they must need it," John ended before continuing on his way, not wishing to believe in that wild idea of his stepfather's to bring a pair of horses and a carriage expressly from Portugal, when horses and carriages were no use to them and were all over the property, while totally obsolete with the advent of that extraordinary means of individual transportation that was the automobile. Not to mention the suffering of the poor animals, crammed into a closed compartment on a train or hanging in the air inside the hold of a ship, not seeing sunlight for days on end. Not to mention the cost that such transportation implied, from the north of Portugal by train or ship to Le Havre, and then again by ship from Le Havre to New York, and finally by train again to Philadelphia. Indeed, artist's business, as his mother might say, always ready to make excuses for him over his excesses and eccentricities, John reminded himself as he walked around the end of the building where the kitchen was, then carrying on to the door to the Gothic hall.

"Good morning, Emma. Do you know where my mother is?" he asked, now inside the vast hall and coming face to face with Miss Beach as she came out of the music room.

"Good morning, John. The Countess is in the greenhouse," she replied as she stopped.

"Is the Count up yet?"

"The Count is in the library reading the newspapers."

"He is? Then I'll go to see him," John announced, crossing the hall towards the corridor that led to the library, while Miss Beach went back on her way to the stairs leading to the first floor.

"Uncle Lexy, how are you? Welcome home," he says jovially from the doorway as soon as he sees his stepfather sitting in one of the arm-chairs next to the fireplace, his head buried in the newspaper open in front of him on his knees.

"Thank you, my dear John. Good to see you again too," the Count replied, in his beige linen suit, white shirt, and brown tie, immediately getting up to meet his stepson with a warm handshake.

"How was the journey?" asked John, following his stepfather with his gaze, as he sat down again, before himself sitting down on the large settee on the other side of the fireplace.

"Pretty good. The *Lusitania* is indeed a very comfortable and fast ship," replied the Count as he folded the newspaper and put it on the low table in front of the armchairs.

"So, this time you decided to bring a pair of horses with you from Portugal? And a Victoria carriage," John couldn't resist commenting.

"Indeed. Have you seen them?"

"Just now. A beautiful pair. What breed is that?"

"The Lusitano. A breed that originated in Portugal. These are from the Alter Stud Farm, created in the eighteenth century by the Marquis of Pombal in a town in the south of Portugal, called Alter do Chão. To maintain the purity and characteristics of the breed," the Count explained.

"Walt is enchanted by them. He says they are very agile and tame."

"It's true. I became so attached to the damn animals that I can't get by without them."

"So, you still prefer horse-drawn carriages to cars?" asked John, even though he knew the answer beforehand.

"When I am with your mother I have no option but to go by car, as she utterly refuses to go in horse-drawn carriages. But when I am alone no one can convince me to swap a good, comfortable *charrette*, pulled by two thoroughbred Lusitanos like those you have just seen in the garage, for an automobile. Except in Portugal, I add two more to these, which greatly increases their performance. And to make them go even faster I sometimes couple up two beautiful English mares that I have just bought. And then no one can catch me, not even automobiles," replied the Count, his eyes shining with enthusiasm.

"Isn't that dangerous?" asked John, somewhat concerned.

"No, because most of the time I'm the one driving," explained the Count.

"Even so…"

"In any case, it's best not to say anything to your mother about this, lest she get worried."

"But didn't she see you ride like this when you were there in the spring?"

"No, because I only ride like this when I'm alone," the Count confessed with a sneaky smile.

"How are things over there?" asked John, deciding to change the direction of the conversation.

"The country is doing badly, very badly. The governments follow on from one another at a dizzying speed. Since King Carlos was assassinated, two years ago, we have now had six governments. Unrest on the streets, in the barracks, and in the press is growing. And instead of uniting around the King and the monarchy, as would be expected, the monarchists prefer to wear each other down in a fratricidal struggle between parties and factions, fatuous powers and personal hatreds, of which the only ones to benefit are obviously the Republican party," explained the Count.

"What about the King? What's his role in the middle of all this?" John wished to know.

"The King, poor thing, is a weak man who lets himself be influenced by everyone, starting with the Church and ending with his own mother, including some skillful politicians, who take advantage of his naïveté and lack of experience to manipulate him. Unfortunately, he doesn't seem to have inherited anything much from his father, who was a true king, a real statesman."

"You mean that in Portugal the prospects for the monarchy are not brilliant."

"Worse than that. They are catastrophic. That is despite the current Government trying to open up new paths, implementing a program of reform, which is in fact very similar to that proposed by the Republicans. But I fear it is already too late," replied the Count pessimistically.

"What about your brother, the one who's a representative, what's his position about all this?"

"Until a short time ago he was a very active member of the Dissident Progressive Party, which is a small but fierce party headed by a relative of ours, Zé d'Alpoim, a brilliant man with great talent, but a little bit excessive and radical. And if it were not for the tragedy that recently befell him he would certainly be in the parliament helping the current Government in its attempt to breathe new life into the monarchy.

"Yes, my mother told me. A terrible tragedy, which must have destroyed him."

"He doesn't seem to be the same person anymore. And he immediately decided to completely abandon all political activity. He didn't even run for the recent elections."

"How old was the boy after all?"

"Seventeen, imagine. A young man with a future ahead of him," said the Count sorrowfully.

"Does anyone know what led him to commit such a desperate act?"

"Some people talk about disappointment in love. But his father, poor man, insists that he's all to blame. That's because on the night before he shouted at him really strongly and nastily because of his studies."

"Why? Was he a bad student?"

"Yes. The boy was studying in Lisbon in his final year at high school, but it appears he was not very dedicated. And his father used to get angry with him and hit him with a riding crop."

"But that alone doesn't seem to be enough of a reason to make a seventeen year-old boy shoot himself in the head with a revolver."

"I find it hard to believe as well, but my poor brother can't be convinced of that."

"Unfortunately, these situations are more common than it appears at first sight. Only a short while ago I read in the newspaper an item about a very similar case that happened with a boy from an old Southern family called Quentin Compson, a first-year student at Harvard. Curiously he went to the same college as me. And one fine day, for no apparent reason, bam! He throws himself into the river with two irons tied to his body and drowns."

"Didn't he leave a goodbye letter, or a note, explaining the reasons that led him to commit such a lunatic act?"

"No, nothing. According to the report he was the eldest of four brothers, and to put him through Harvard his parents had been forced to sell a part of the land they possessed down in Mississippi, to build a golf course or something like that," John explained.

"Indeed, who can guess what is going on in the mind of a boy like that, or like my poor nephew, to decide to put an end to their own lives?" the Count wondered gravely.

"True. That's the great problem. Speaking of more cheerful subjects: how is the work on the house going? Is it finished yet?"

"Yes. Everything's finally ready. But I had to be standing there watching them all these months, otherwise, they would never have finished. The worst thing was what I left to be done in my studio. Yesterday I didn't have the courage to go there before I came here."

"Are you at least satisfied with the results?"

"Yes, I think it is rather good. I happen to have some photographs there that I had taken after the work was completed. Do you want to see them?" asked the Count.

"Of course," replied John, getting up from the settee to follow his stepfather to the other side of the room.

"This is an overall view, taken from up a very tall tree in front of the house," explained the Count, standing up and leaning over the top of the long mahogany desk and pointing at the first of the photographs, in which one can see a fortified house on the slope of a mountain, with two symmetrical turrets in the corners separated by a balcony made up of a succession of full arches.

"It looks like a fortress with all these ramparts. Was it like that before?"

"The turrets were there before, but without ramparts, which I built from the stone from a demolished monastery."

"From a monastery?" John said, finding this strange.

"Yes. The Monastery of Nossa Senhora dos Remédios, in Braga. An old construction from the eighteenth century, that the local council decided to demolish to widen some streets, imagine. And when I found out about it I went there and bought everything: the stones from the demolition, the Church carvings, and even the bells."

"And this loggia in the middle, with all these arches, did that exist?"

"Yes, but it was considerably improved. Not only with the ramparts now on top of it, on the platband, but also with an iron railing, which then runs up the two flights of steps."

"Congratulations, Uncle Lexy, the result is admirable. It reminds me of one of those strange and beautiful castles built by Ludwig II of Bavaria," said John, looking once again, attentively, at the photograph before giving it back to his stepfather.

"You think so? Perhaps you are right. I'd never thought about it," replied the Count, proud about the comparison.

"Did you make many changes to the inside?"

"Some. A little elevator was put in between the kitchen and the dining room, to make it easy to transport the plates and trays. And a bathroom was put in, with a tub and sink with running water...."

"...Just one? Do you think that is enough? We've got seven or eight here..." interrupted John.

"...Yes, but don't forget that the number of bedrooms is much lower. Besides, this house was built from scratch by your father about twenty-five years ago, if that, while *Glória* is from the eighteenth century when no one thought about a WC or bathrooms. The one we have now was made in a storage space, which was next to the pantry. To make any other one we would have to take away space from one of the living rooms, all with painted plaster ceilings, which would be sacrilege, or to sacrifice one of the bedrooms, and there aren't very many."

"Yes, well, it's a shame. What about heating?"

"We made two beautiful fireplaces, one in the dining room and another in the library. Besides the stables being underneath the living room, which, although one might not think so, helps considerably to maintain the temperature..."

"Yes, but it also brings some bad smells, according to my mother," commented John, half laughing. "What about the bedrooms?"

"When it's cold we put braziers in the bedrooms. And hot water bottles in the beds, as they help to warm up and take the dampness off the sheets. But you mustn't forget that Portugal has a very temperate climate, nothing like what happens here. We rarely have temperatures below zero."

"Yes but my mother says that she has never felt such cold as last winter when she was there. So much so that she felt forced to come back earlier than foreseen," retorted John.

"But she certainly didn't feel the same when she went back in the spring. That's a good time to be in Portugal: not too cold and not too hot," stated the Count definitively, just as one of the uniformed servants came into the room carrying a tray with a silver coffee pot, a small cup, and a little plate of *petits fours*.

"Will you join me, John?" asked the Count politely from his armchair, waiting for the servant to fill his cup of aromatic, steaming coffee, brought expressly from Portugal.

"No thank you. That coffee of yours is gunpowder. The last time I tried it I didn't sleep a wink all night."

"That's because you are used to that insipid water, that chestnut water you drink all the time. But one day you'll discover what real coffee is and then you won't want anything else," joked the Count, before tasting his first sip after the servant had beaten a retreat.

"I have serious doubts about that. But you never know," replied John, not very convinced.

"And what's new over here?" asks the Count, filling his cup again.

"Everything has been a lot calmer here, thank God. Which doesn't mean that there isn't an article in the newspapers now and then."

"Articles about what?" the Count inquires, unable to disguise his sudden ill-at-ease.

"Well, the last one I can remember speculated on rumors about an impending divorce. All because of Mother coming back alone last year before Christmas, imagine."

"But what did the article say exactly?" the Count insisted anxiously, putting down his cup after drinking the last sip of his coffee.

"As far as I recall they insinuated that your long stay in Portugal would be expedient to allow Mother to request a divorce, alleging abandonment."

"That's absolutely extraordinary. Where do these people get such ideas?"

"This is America, Uncle Lexy. Here anything goes, as long as it sells newspapers. And at the end, they came back to the story of Mrs. Ernest and the ten thousand dollars you supposedly still owe her. As well as the issue of the Portuguese medals, that you are supposed to have sold for large sums to some people in Chicago."

"Good grief! That's all been more than made clear by our Ministry for Foreign Affairs, after the strict investigation I asked about my acts as Consul of Portugal in Chicago," protested the Count in a crescendo of irritation.

"I know, but what do you want? Since Mr. Hearst discovered that articles like this would send newspaper sales through the roof everyone has wanted to copy him."

"But why me, for God's sake? Why me, who's never done any harm to anyone, and all I want from life is to be with my family and make my sculptures in peace and quiet?" questioned the Count in despair.

"Never mind. Don't get so worried about so little, Uncle Lexy. As far as we know this is the only news item to come out since my mother went to Chicago. And the references to the medals are very slight, particularly when compared to what was being published just a few months ago."

"Since your mother went to Chicago? When was she there?" the Count cut in, surprised as if hearing only the first part of the sentence.

"In early February. When she went there with Emma to try to come to an agreement with that hag Ernest…and with Courrège…"

"To try to come to an agreement? What agreement?"

"Don't tell me that.… Heck, I can see I've said too much…" finished John, realizing his gaffe.

"No, you haven't said too much at all.… You know very well that your mother and I don't have any secrets.… What I didn't know is which of her trips to Chicago you meant…that one or an earlier one," the Count hurriedly said.

"I sure hope so," replied John, not seeming very convinced.

"Anyway, I think you are right: I can't let this get me down. I have to move on and face the future with confidence."

"Now you're talking. By the way, what are your plans for the near future?" asked John, seizing this chance to change the subject again.

"Well, as you can imagine, after so long away I'm dying to get back to work, with all I have on my hands in the studio. Starting with the bas-relief of your father that is almost ready to be cast. And the haut-relief of Saint-Gaudens, which is considerably more behind schedule, but is a work for which I have great expectations. After all, it is a homage to one of my great masters, perhaps the one who most influenced me after Rodin. And who is, without a doubt, the greatest living American sculptor."

"That means that you intend to be here in the coming future," concluded John.

"Yes. With the works on *Glória* finally ready I can't see any reason to return to Portugal anytime soon."

"Well, my question isn't totally innocent. The truth is I have a commission for you. But I need to know whether you have the time to take it on," added John.

"Really? And what is it exactly?"

"It's a bust of a former teacher of mine at Harvard who has just retired. Something simple but dignified, to put in the University in his memory. And I obviously immediately thought of you to make it."

"I'm very honored, my dear John."

"Not at all. I'm the one who should thank you. You know how much I appreciate your work, Uncle Lexy," John made a point of saying.

"I know and I'm grateful to you for that. And what's the gentleman's name?"

"His name is Putnam. Frederick Ward Putnam. He is a renowned anthropologist, member of the National Academy of Sciences. And perhaps the greatest specialist in the country on American archaeology and ethnography, subjects in which he was the leading Professor at Harvard for many years.

"Excellent. A man of science. Which suits me fine after Marshall Field and the other millionaires from Chicago whose busts I made," Santa Eulália said with satisfaction.

"Well, Dr. Cook is also a man of science, even if in the meantime he fell into disgrace," John reminded him on the subject.

"That's true, who would have thought it? After such great success, with hundreds of thousands of people on the streets of New York applauding him. It was enough for a few scientists to consider that the proof he had reached the North Pole was insufficient for him to be almost unanimously considered a charlatan. While Peary, who did everything to discredit him, received all the praise."

"What about the statue you made of him? Where is it now?"

"It stayed with the *Arctic Club of America*, who commissioned it from me, along with the decorative metal on the discovery of the North Pole. But as since then they expelled Dr. Cook from the club, I have no idea what happened to it."

"You have to see if you can get it back. Because whoever was the first to reach the North pole, the fact is that it is a beautiful statue, that deserved to be put into stone or cast in bronze," John made a point of stating.

"And it was made without a single sitting, only from photographs, when the man was still on his return journey from the Pole. But what do you expect? It's my fate. I don't have any luck with statues of public figures. In Lisbon, with another man of science, Sousa Martins, what happened happened. And here, so it seems, things are following the same path," replied the Count somewhat downheartedly.

"Maybe not. Now, when you go to New York you must go there, to the Arctic Club, and find out what's going on."

"Indeed. But I confess I don't have high hopes. I'd rather think about my latest commission: by the way, how do you want to do it?"

"Well, first we will have to go to Boston and pay a visit to Professor Putnam for you to get to know each other and arrange some sittings, if need be."

"Great idea," replied the Count, suddenly more cheerful.

"Look, it seems as though my mother is coming," John suddenly announced as he saw two shapes of women and a child through the glass of one of the bow windows as they came to the covered balcony running round the whole of the library from the back of the house.

"Ah, so what Emma just said is true. That you have both been here in the library chatting pleasantly for over an hour," stated the Countess, cheerful and in a good mood, as soon as she entered the door giving on to the balcony, followed closely by the tireless Miss Beach and Lizzie, a four-year-old girl with a round face and bright eyes, the daughter of G. Henry.

"And we have been fine here, haven't we John? After all, we haven't seen each other for almost a year. And a lot has happened in the meantime," replied the Count, standing up, followed by his stepson.

"Carry on, you're doing very well, and I don't wish to interrupt," said the Countess, her face flushed by the sun under her wide straw hat, cool and scented in her very full beige linen skirt, perfectly matching the tone of her embroidered natural silk blouse, held in by a leather belt with a large silver rosette.

"Those flowers you are carrying are beautiful, my dear," says the Count, pointing to the basket full of roses and orchids that his wife is holding on her arm.

"I'm glad you like them, Alexis. We've just been in the greenhouse picking them, Lizzie and I," the Countess replied, passing the basket to Miss Beach and then turning round in search of her granddaughter, hidden in the fullness of her skirt.

"Lizzie? Where has that mischievous little girl got to now? I can't see her anywhere?" asked the Count, pretending to look for her from the other side of the skirt.

"Have you bought a present for me, Uncle Lexy?" she suddenly asked, putting her head out from the skirt and then immediately hiding again.

"Lizzie! You mustn't ask questions like that," the Countess scolded her somewhat severely. "Uncle Lexy has more to do than to go around buying presents for badly behaved little girls."

"Oh, she's disappeared again. What a shame! And I had such a nice thing to give her," replied the Count, pretending to be disappointed.

"Hello!" she shouted, then leaping out of her hiding place and running to his outstretched arms.

"How big and heavy my little Lizzie is!" he exclaimed, picking her up and then throwing her up into the air once, twice and three times, to the astonished air of her grandmother, uncle, and Miss Beach, who were not at all familiarized with such excesses typical of the Southern European peoples.

"Alexis, please!" begged the Countess, in a crescendo of anxiety at her granddaughter's squeals and laughter, no doubt concerned about the bad example that these games may provide, coming from where they did.

"What about my present Uncle Lexy? Where is it?" little Lizzie insisted, opening her eyes wide as soon as he put her down on the floor.

"Present? Now I remember...I brought a present...but where did I put it?" he replied, shifting his eyes from one side to the other as if trying to remember.

"Hot and cold! Hot and cold!" requested the little girl, jumping up and down in enormous excitement.

"Alexis, *voyons*...It's late...She's going to have a piano lesson now..." the Countess reminded him, at the end of her tether, while her son John looked impatiently at the clock, with the hands about to reach eleven.

"Calm down, my dear Isabel, it's just a moment," he requested, ready to take the game to its end, as Lizzie was going to the settee where he and John had been sitting.

"Is it here?" asked the girl.

"Cold! Very cold! Freezing!" he exclaimed loudly, seeming to enjoy the game as much as her.

"Here?" asked Lizzie, now going to the fireplace at the other end of the room. "Cold! Very cold!"

"Then here?" she insisted, going to the end of the room.

"A little hotter. Warm. You're getting warmer," he said as she went along the bookcase towards the desk. "Now?"

"Hotter and hotter, almost boiling," he added, seeing her come to an old wooden chest covered in magazines and books.

"Found it. It's here," she shouted, beaming with joy on discovering a yellow satin paper package with a gold ribbon hidden behind the chest.

"Let's see if you like it," he said, coming closer as she tore at the paper and pulled off the ribbon in a fit of excitement that only ended when she opened the box and took out a beautiful blond doll with blue eyes.

"It's beautiful, Uncle Lexy. Thank you!" the girl thanked him, at the same time staring intensely at the doll.

"Right, Lizzie. Now go with Miss B. to the music room; your teacher is waiting for you, do you hear?" said the Countess, relieved that the game had come to an end.

"Well, Uncle Lexy, I'll be going as well. I still have to go to the factory before lunch," John then said, holding out his hand to his step-father.

"It was a pleasure chatting with you, John. See you later," the Count said in farewell, accompanying his stepson to the door, closely watched by his wife.

"You can't imagine the joy and satisfaction I feel when I see you both like that, suddenly, so close, Alexis," the Countess said, enraptured, having in the meantime gone to sit on the large settee by the fireside. "Who would have thought so? He who at the beginning was so opposed to our marriage. Perhaps even more so than G. Henry."

"A perfectly understandable opposition, given the circumstances. But the fact is that with time, that initial distrust has faded and given way to increasing mutual esteem and respect. Of which I have today once again received confirmation," said the Count, also sitting down on the settee next to his wife.

"Well?"

"Your son John has just commissioned me a bust of an old professor of his at Harvard. Someone called Putnam."

"Really? He hasn't mentioned anything to me," replied the Countess, surprised.

"It's true. Besides anything else, it is proof of his trust in my talents, which I am very pleased to see."

"So are you going to accept the task?"

"Of course. Of course, I am. We just have to arrange a day for us to go together to Boston and talk to this professor. Changing the subject: How do you feel today, this morning, Madam Countess of Santa Eulália?" he asked with a devilish look, softly taking her hand to kiss it.

"Like I haven't felt for quite some time," she confessed with a giggle, holding his hand between hers.

"Just as well, just as well. I'm glad to hear it," the Count said happily, looking her in the eyes intensely, then holding her and kissing her on the lips.

"And my dear husband, how do you feel this morning, now that you mention it?" she asked as soon as he freed her from his arms.

"Still a little confused about the time. Besides that, I woke up with a nightmare."

"A nightmare?"

"Yes, a terrible nightmare, you can't imagine. I dreamt about Ernest… and Courrège…chasing me along Michigan Avenue…and then in Lisbon, near my monument…"

"Well, in relation to Ernest and Courrège you can rest at ease because they won't bother us again," the Countess was quick to state.

"You seem very sure of what you are saying," noted the Count, his expression suddenly heavy.

"I've got my reasons," she insisted enigmatically.

"Is there something I should know that you haven't told me yet?"

"Why do you ask that?" she asked, suddenly looking restless.

"No reason. Let us say that your son John alluded, unwittingly, to a trip of yours to Chicago. No doubt convinced that, as would be expected, I was aware of it. Only, unfortunately, I wasn't. And my surprise was so great that he must have understood everything…"

"My dear Alexis. I do not have, nor have ever had any doubts whatsoever about your innocence concerning the accusations that both Ernest and Courrège made about you. Those who have my financial means soon get used to recognizing processes of extortion and blackmail, and detecting them from miles off. Now what I could no longer tolerate any more was seeing my name and yours constantly dragged through the mud in the newspapers. And so I had no other choice but to cut this off at the roots," she said, looking at him harshly.

"But you could have let me know at least, so I might not make such a sorry figure in front of your children, who, it appears, seem to be much better informed about matters that directly concern me than I do," he complained, feeling offended.

"I only didn't do so to avoid you having more bother and trouble.

Because more than attacking you, what these people wanted was to get at my pocketbook."

"And apparently they did."

"Not as much as they would have liked, believe me."

"Are you telling me that you agreed to negotiate with them?"

"In this country everything is negotiable, Alexis," she replied coldly.

"So when did these negotiations take place?"

"In early February, shortly after my return from Portugal. When here all the newspapers were rejoicing in the story of the sale of your medals, spread by Courrège, and they were insisting on the lawsuit that Ernest was threatening to bring in court. Mixed in with insinuations that a divorce between us was imminent because I had come back alone before Christmas. And then I couldn't take it anymore. I got a train to Chicago, settled in the Congress Hotel under a false name, to avoid the newspapers finding out, and sent for them," the Countess explained bluntly.

"Did you go just like that, alone, with no one else?"

"No. I took Beach with me."

"And how did things go?"

"First I spoke to Ernest, who turned up with her husband, and after a lot of discussing we came to a first agreement: I would pay her three thousand dollars and she would definitely drop the lawsuit and would never again talk to the newspapers about the matter."

"Three thousand dollars? That's robbery, good Lord," the Count said, indignant.

"Yes, but wait, because the matter didn't stop there. As soon as I get back to Philadelphia news starts appearing in the newspapers, mentioning my presence in Chicago under a false name, and denying that there had been any agreement reached between us and that the case was going to court. Then a bill is published with the ten thousand dollars distributed over several different items, such as love letters, five dollars each, totaling five hundred; introducing the Count to the Stetson widow, one thousand dollars; amount advanced to the Count to go to the wedding of King Alfonso XIII, one thousand dollars, etc."

"What a nerve! They must have no shame. This is after unduly receiving three thousand dollars. And what happened then?"

"Then I decided to get our lawyer to contact theirs and ended up paying another two thousand dollars. But this time with an agreement signed at a notary public, with direct recourse to the courts if it were not complied with. It was the only way."

"What about Courrège?"

"He was a lot easier; I didn't even need money. It was enough to show him the letter I wrote to Viscount d'Alte, in which I held him personally responsible along with Ernest for the campaign of discredit that was being held against you in the American newspapers and he was terrified. Probably out of fear of the measures that the Viscount, as Minister of Portugal in the United States, might take against him."

"Wait a minute, what letter is that to the Viscount d'Alte?" the Count asked, stupefied.

"A letter that I, in my despair, decided to write to him, when Courrège's denunciations about the sale of your medals were added to the lawsuit by Ernest."

"But why on Earth didn't you keep me informed?"

"Because I didn't want to upset or embarrass you, more than I imagine you already were when you wrote to me and said that the Portuguese newspapers had also mentioned the subject. So I thought it was my strict duty to support my husband at such a difficult moment when he was facing such grave accusations about his honor and dignity, as a man and as a diplomat."

"I am very grateful to you about that, but…I would have preferred you to have informed me beforehand."

"If I had done so you surely would have prohibited me from sending the letter, am I right?"

"Yes, but…"

"So you can see I did the right thing."

"But how do you explain that after all this there are still items in the newspapers about the subject? Like one that John was telling me about just now, about rumors of an imminent divorce…"

"As far as I recall that was the last one and it came out two months ago. Yet at that time there were articles every day. And with a profusion of details that left me apoplectic."

"That means that the worst is over. That we can finally rest a little more easily," he said, suddenly changing tone.

"Let us hope so."

"I just don't know how to thank you once again for your support and friendship, my dear Isabel. Without you, I don't know what would become of me," the Count finally said after a long silence.

"Without me probably none of this would have happened."

"Perhaps, but even so…"

"Well, it's getting late and I still have some things to do before lunch," she said after looking at her wristwatch.

"Then I'll take the opportunity for a stroll outside. I'm dying to see how my Lusitano horses are doing," he said in turn.

"They're beautiful after Walt brushed and groomed them. I saw them just a while ago."

"Then promise me that after lunch you'll come for a drive with me in the carriage, Isabel. Even if it is only here on the property," he asked her, again taking her hand and kissing it.

"Only if you accept to come for a ride by automobile with me afterward," she replied with a playful smile.

"Fair enough," he agreed, standing up.

XVIII

THE IDEA WASN'T even his, but once again that of his tireless brother Gaspar, his guardian angel, his protecting saint for better or for worse, and who was also concerned about the effects of the ignoble campaign launched in the newspapers against his monument to Sousa Martins straight after the inauguration and which since then has never ceased to spread and increase in volume, Aleixo recalls, his face buried in his hands, sitting in his armchair in front of his work desk in the Campolide de Baixo studio, a long, narrow room with double headroom prolonging to the roof recess and lit by a wide window all along the back wall.

"Why don't you send your masters in Paris some photographs of the monument and ask them for a few words of appreciation, or even praise, for your work? And if their responses are favorable you can rub them in the faces of your detractors by publishing them in the main Lisbon newspapers," Gaspar suggested to him the last time they had lunch together, at the Literary Guild a little over a week ago, when a further caricature had appeared in the *Illustrated Supplement* of the newspaper *O Século* abjectly and absolutely ridiculing the monument, referring to it as the "Sousa Martins Fountain."

"Yes, it's certainly an interesting idea. The problem is knowing who I can ask such a thing from, with some certainty of receiving the answer that is most favorable to me," he replied, immediately starting to conjecture: Alexis Corbel, his teacher at the School of Decorative Arts, which he attended for a while after he arrived in Paris? Most probably he would not even remember him, besides which he had some doubts about whether the old professor would be able to favorably appreciate his work. Denys Puech, his teacher at the Académie Julian for some years, one of the greatest exponents of French naturalism, whose classes he had stopped taking precisely because he disagreed with his obsession for minuteness of detail as opposed to expression and movement, which for him were then increasingly becoming the essence of sculpture? No. Indeed not. If there was a reply there would be the risk of it being even more destructive of his work than the articles by José de Figueiredo and Ribeiro Arthur together. Louis-Ernest Barrias, whose studio at the Paris School of Fine Arts he attended for a couple of years?

The risk would probably be similar, given that in relation to naturalism and the new tendencies in sculpture, Barrias was largely in tune with Puech.

"So why don't you try Rodin? After all, isn't he the great inspirer of your work, the person you most identify with today?" his brother Gaspar came up with pragmatically, faced with that apparent deadend street.

"Yes, Rodin is probably the only great master of sculpture capable of appreciating the scope of my work. And also of understanding what I am going through," agreed Aleixo, recalling the situation very similar to his that Rodin had had to face a little over two years ago when he saw his *Balzac* being rejected by the institution that had commissioned him to make it. And the response he had decided to give to this rejection, exhibiting the work at the Champ de Mars *Salon*, scandalizing the press and the artistic circles of Paris, with the overwhelming majority of opinions condemning the work, considering it to be a simple offensive *ébauche* of the memory of *Balzac*, a criticism that was curiously similar to that now being made of his *Sousa Martins*. "This work which is being laughed at, which has been the subject of scorn by some because they cannot destroy it, is the result of my whole life. The axis of my aesthetic," the great master had declared at the height of the controversy, a declaration that he himself, Aleixo, could apply *ipsa verbissima* to his monument, obviously maintaining the due distance between the *Balzac* and his *Sousa Martins*, as he confessed contritely to his brother. But how could he make such a request from so great a name in sculpture if he had never worked nor studied with him, nor knew him personally?

"You wouldn't be the first nor the last, believe me. Besides, what really matters here is not you, my dear, but your work, and he can get to know that through the photographs you are going to send him. And from them he can express his opinion if he wishes," replied Gaspar in his unbeatable logic as a brilliant lawyer, he recalls as he looks forlornly around his practically empty studio, without a single new commission having come in, against all his expectations, since the plaster statues of the monument came out. Then he takes the envelope with the photographs, which he picked up that morning at the studio of José Artur Leitão Bárcia, one of the best and most renowned photographers in Lisbon, taken from angles and viewpoints that he chose himself in order to make sure that the pictures thus obtained would most favorably reproduce his work. And they are beautiful, he thinks, a little more cheerfully, after spreading them out in front of him on the table: the first, taken from a distance, shows the monument from the front, with the statue of Sousa Martins in the foreground and the facade under construction of the School of Medical Sciences in the background; then a closer view, with the statue of *Gratitude* below, on the *socle*, hand outstretched to Sousa Martins sitting on his professorship chair, with a serious air and a pose of deep reflection; followed by another one, focusing on the statue of *Modern Science*, superb, with that extremely light mantle which, in a spiral movement, uncovers the naked body from head to toe; then others, with views of the side parts, highlighting the deliberately sinister faces of the *mascarrons*, from whose open mouths comes a jet of water into the stone shells set against the base of the obelisk, decorated with the leaves of stylized marine plants, very much in the *art nouveau* style.

How can a monument like that, to which he devoted the best of the two last years of his life with such commitment and enthusiasm, in which he sought to express his personal view of the figure and personality of Sousa Martins in all of his vast complexity in the most original manner possible and in accordance with his own aesthetic and artistic principles, and which was inaugurated by the King and Queen in the presence of the highest dignitaries of the country—how could this monument be thus disdained and dishonored as if it were an aberration, a veritable monster? And how is it that he—who for the two years before the inauguration of the monument was adulated and flattered in the newspapers as one of the most promising figures in Portuguese sculpture—can now be witnessing his name dragged through the mud as an "ignorant and inept artist"? wonders Aleixo, once again burying his head in his hand, distraught, before without great conviction picking up a sheet of writing paper, dipping his nib in the inkwell and starting to write on the top of the first sheet: "*Mon cher* Maître." Then immediately putting the pen down again, not knowing what to write next. Perhaps starting by saying how much he has admired his work since the visit he made to his studio in Meudon with his colleagues from the Académie Julian, over three years ago, or even by mentioning his ill-fated meeting at the entrance to the Fonderie des Frères Thiébaut, he thinks as he looks over the photographs, then putting them back in order on the table. No, too banal and ordinary. Perhaps starting simply by stating who he is and what he requests, mentioning that he studied in Paris and is sending him photographs of a monument that has just been completed in Lisbon, he decides, allowing the first sentence to take shape in his mind as he again dips the nib in the inkwell, then moving on to the sheet of paper and setting down in his best handwriting: *"Permettez à un jeune artiste, ayant fait ses études à Paris, de vous offrir les photographies d'un monument qu'il vient de conclure à Lisbonne et qu'il soumet à votre illustre appréciation."* ("Allow a young artist, who studied in Paris, to offer you the photographs of a monument he has just completed in Lisbon and which he submits for your illustrious appreciation.")

Yes, to start off, the facts, just the facts, he thinks, pen in hand, rereading what he wrote, but without any idea how to start the most difficult part. Indeed, how can he in a few words explain his inconfessible reasons and aims? he wonders, unwittingly looking at the pile of newspapers there on the left of the table, where there are all the articles and caricatures that had come out until now about his monument, with the newspaper *Novidades*, which carries the execrable article written by Mr. José de Figueiredo, on top. In it, Figueiredo defends that he, Aleixo, had "fooled" the jury for the competition with his model, and which, having been seduced by it, had attributed the commission to him even without knowing whether he was capable of carrying it out, instead of opting for someone "whose competence and special value had been proven in previous works." Which, when it came down to it, meant Alberto Nunes or Costa Motta, respectively classified in second and third places in the competition, and who had indeed repeated the same naturalist formulas that Messrs. Figueiredo, Ribeiro Arthur, Simões d'Almeida and others so liked, these being the "guardians of the temple," as Eça de Queiroz called this type of person: "those who look upon us, we who come from the outside, the 'foreign-looking ones' as they call us, with distrust and envy. As if they were afraid that we might steal their place in the sun," Aleixo recalls the warning words of the great writer on the occasion of his visit to him in the Consulate in Paris. Then, in the arrogant and professorial tone used by someone who considers himself to be a great authority on the matter, Mr. Figueiredo pulls his monument apart from top to bottom in one stroke of his pen, literally not leaving any stone unturned, without even taking the trouble to justify a single one of his statements in the long argument that follows, in which he simply develops his theories and conceptions about art as if anyone were particularly interested in knowing them. Like when at a certain moment he says, referring to him, Aleixo: "This gentleman has made a mistake, like some time ago with Christ which he said was in the style of Rodin. Using a simple style does not mean one doesn't know how to do it well, nor is the broad style of an artist something that, besides temperament, does not demand as much if not more art and application than that which is demanded by the more meticulous and detailed manner involved in the other."

And what does Mr. José de Figueiredo think he, Aleixo, was doing for seven years in Paris other than studying and deepening his artistic and technical knowledge, so that he could go on from that long period of learning and be able to follow his own path, simplifying that which could be simplified so as to highlight what is really important, expression and movement? wonders Aleixo, suddenly recalling a sentence he wrote in an article in response to Mr. Figueiredo, also published in the *Novidades*, some days later, which he looks for among the other newspapers next to him on the table: "I could reply to my censor that my artistic feeling matches the process of finishing the luminous parts, leaving the chiaroscuro aspects indecisive in their making, but well-defined by the overall lines." Indeed, this is a clear summary of his aesthetic and artistic option, to which he only came after a lot of work and study at the best schools and with the best masters in Paris. Just as in the sentences that follow this one, in which he utterly rebuts Mr. Figueiredo's clumsy accusations, at the same time boldly stating his own personality and identity as a sculptor. But what is the use of arguing and counter-arguing, if for Mr. Figueiredo and the like, everything that is outside the immutable norm that they have established as being the only path existing for the arts in Portugal, the one that leads to the most trivial and banal naturalism, can only be seen as a result of

the artist's ignorance and incapability, and not as a clearly and unequivocally assumed option of his? They are the lords and masters of the
Portuguese art field; they are the ones who dictate the rules and impose
them. And when anyone dares to think and do things differently they
fall upon him like a ton of bricks, he laments, then wearily pushing
the pile of newspapers aside and returning to his letter to Rodin and
to the photographs, now that a further sentence has suddenly come to
his mind: "*Ce travail dans lequel j'ai cherché à mettre un peu d'originalité
de mon âme d'artiste, me vaut une campagne acharnée de la Presse Portu-
gaise, m'apportant le découragement en récompense de mes efforts et de mon
travail,*" ("This work in which I have sought to put a little originality of
my artistic soul has earned me a relentless campaign by the Portuguese
Press, bringing me discouragement as a reward for my efforts and my
work"), he writes in one go, then suspending the point of the nib over
the sheet of paper, as he recalls the reply he received a few days after his
letter was published by Mr. Figueiredo, in an article he had published
in the *Novidades*, this time on the front page. The great trump card of
which was a letter sent to him with a request for publication by his
friend Simões d'Almeida, setting aside his responsibilities as a technical
delegate on the committee in relation to the making of the monument
to Sousa Martins. However, in the letter Simões d'Almeida in no way
contradicts the essence of what he himself, Aleixo, stated in his article:
"None of the figures was made in plaster without prior examination
and approval. The same formalities occurred before the works were cast
in bronze. After I had sculpted the works they were examined further
to be approved. And the same was the case with the other component
parts. If there are doubts, the committee is there to confirm this. Always
making myself available to the meticulous inspections that were made
of my work, I merely carried out the contract to which I was committed
by public subscription…"

    "…How is it, then, Mr. José de Figueiredo, that you consider that
the illustrious members of the committee and their technical delegates,
despite so many and such legitimate precautions, were fooled by me
during the making of the work? On purpose? Only by doubting their
honor. Out of ignorance? That would be attributing them a very lowly
status." Yet it is significant that there is almost total agreement of opinions between Mr. Figueiredo and another of the main "critics" of the art

field in Lisbon, the Infantry Major and water-color painter Bartolomeu Sezinando Ribeiro Arthur, in the two articles he also wrote and published during the days after the inauguration of the monument, Aleixo suddenly recalls, beginning his search among the mess of open newspapers he has on the table. In the first one, after using terms very similar to those used by Figueiredo to recall the way the competition for the monument was run, going so far as to even criticize the "action of doctors in matters of art" as "somewhat incongruous", and "the idea of inviting a jury of experts to absolutely revoke its decisions" as "absurd", the Major writes: "Unfortunately our fears were more than founded, and the monument to Sousa Martins is in no way an improvement on the *Christ* in Viana do Castelo. It is carried out with the same artistic lack of awareness; no anatomical study was performed before the modeling of the figures; no model posed for them; they are made by heart by a man who daydreams his sculpture, attempting to imitate the colossal Rodin, but only in his fancies. There is no lack of harmony nor elegance in the general lines of the monument; the idea and the conception are not unworthy of an artist; Mr. Queiroz Ribeiro has no lack of imagination: what he doesn't have is the ability to be a sculptor."

Besides the reference to the *Christ* in Viana, which for him, Aleixo, is not a cause for concern, but rather pride, given that it clearly shows the formal and aesthetic coherence that his works increasingly possess, and the false and irresponsible accusations about the modeling of his statues, the theory is more or less the same as Figueiredo's: the idea and conception are not bad, but what was lacking was his capability to carry out the monument according to these plans. Also, in his criticism of the unfinished nature of the statues, there is absolute agreement with Ribeiro Arthur, saying that "all three of the figures are entirely without any study and are unfinished; it is a *pochade*, not a monument."

All things considered, there is only one small difference of opinions between the two, in relation to the veil on the head of Science: while Figueiredo considers that it is too "loosely removed from the architecture" of the monument, Ribeiro Arthur states that "the clothing on Science, which, even made of bronze, should float gently, is extremely heavy." So where do we stand then, gentlemen? Aleixo wonders, before taking up the second article by Ribeiro Arthur, which is very similar to the first in its references to the course of the competition and the way he models his statues: "Mr. Queiroz Ribeiro makes sculpture by heart the way he, probably, plays any instrument by ear. It is a sitting-room gift, is pretty, brings light to his aristocratic name, and brings beauty to his hours of solitude."

Ah, finally the clear and explicit reference to his aristocratic name, in the absence of any other argument, as if someone who belonged to the nobility was prohibited from the serious, devoted and responsible exercise of an art like sculpture, which was only reserved for common folk who had to struggle hard to work their way up to where he is and now does not wish to let go. Like himself, Ribeiro Arthur, and a good number of his friends? But further on: "Working in an unaware dilettantish-style without concern for the seriousness of his art, by chance making figures whose anatomy he should have studied in his models, covering over apparent faults with inadmissible tricks, Mr. Queiroz Ribeiro makes that monument, which could be a handsome work, and is no more than a lamentable thing."

How can the Major make such accusations knowing him as he has since his youth, and having accompanied, as he did, the studies he followed during his long stay in Paris? Indeed wasn't he the first person to write an article about him and his artistic qualities in the magazine *Ocidente*, back in '94, at the time of the solo exhibition he held at the Livraria Gomes bookshop, saying of him that a fine future awaited him, "full of applause and of the noble satisfaction that should be felt by all those who through their work honor the name of their homeland"?

But the worst thing of all is the sinister suggestion he makes in the sentence with which he ends his article, notes Aleixo, feeling a certain chill down his spine as he reads it: "Demolishing the monument and melting down the bronze would be the only possible solution for such a disaster."

No, Mr. Ribeiro Arthur cannot be serious when he suggests such a thing: demolishing a monument built by public subscription, inaugurated in a solemn ceremony by the King and Queen of Portugal, and formally donated to Lisbon City Council? No, it isn't possible for anyone in their right mind to even imagine such an attack on art, unless it is as a mere figure of speech to finish off the article, Aleixo concludes. Envy, yes. Envy and jealousy are what is behind this orchestrated campaign against him and his work, there can be no doubt about that. Envy and jealousy over his success achieved in the recent past with his other works, over the recognition he obtained in the French and Portuguese press and with the public itself, he who came from abroad, without ever going to any of the fine arts schools in the country. And because against all expectations he won the competition for this monument, challenging the consecrated artists, those who considered themselves to be lords and masters of everything that was done in the field of art in Portugal, he concludes before he again takes up his pen to write: *"Croyant avoir deviné derrière mes détracteurs des envieux et des jaloux je sens le besoin d'un réconfort pour continuer envers et contre tous la lutte, qui hélas! Commence à peine pour moi..."* ("Believing that I have guessed what's behind my detractors, envy and jealousy, I feel the need for comfort to continue the fight, which alas! is just starting for me...")

Yes, ask him for a word of encouragement, of comfort, in order to be able to carry on, against all and sundry, with the fight for the affirming of his art, of his own ideas and convictions, as Rodin had done his whole life. Yes, following the example of the Master, thinks Aleixo, before he continues, now inspired: *"...et c'est dans le but de trouver une consolation (dont je serai fier si je la mérite), que je m'adresse à vous, cher Maître pour que vous appréciez mon travail avec l'indépendance que vous donne votre grande autorité artistique."* ("... and it is with the aim of finding a consolation (of which I will be proud if I deserve it), that I address you, dear Master so that you appreciate my work with the independence of your great artistic authority.")

What an extraordinarily polite rebuke he would give his detractors if in a few days' time he could publish a letter in all the newspapers from the genius Rodin unequivocally praising his monument, he finds himself thinking, only then noticing the *Diário de Notícias* newspaper from the 12th of March, right next to him, in which there was, also on the front page and in the space normally reserved for the serialized stories, another article with the title "The New Statue," by Luiz Moraes de Carvalho, in which the latter states at a given moment: "On the day of the inauguration of his work, if Mr. Queiroz Ribeiro had heard what everyone was saying about it he would have understood that kings and queens, friends and acquaintances are very often forced to disguise what they feel in homage to the practice of courtesy."

Kings and queens? What does Mr. Moraes de Carvalho know

about what the King and Queen think about his work? thinks Aleixo, insulted, recalling the glowing praise that King Carlos gave him after inaugurating the monument: "A brilliant concept, of great originality." Then adding somewhat enigmatically: "Let's hope the people of Lisbon know how to appreciate it also." What might he mean by that comment? Might he already be foreseeing, with his special artistic sensitivity and deep knowledge of the sad realities of the country, difficulty that the public at large would have in understanding the work he had just inaugurated? And in relation to his friends and acquaintances, what opinions had Mr. Moraes de Carvalho heard so that he could say what he did, given that he, Aleixo, didn't even recall seeing him during the ceremony? Was everyone "disguising what they felt in homage to the practice of courtesy" when they congratulated him and poured great praise upon him? Of course not. If some of them didn't like the work, and they had every right to do so, others certainly enjoyed it enthusiastically, as indeed always happens with every work of art when it is exhibited to the public gaze. But why don't these people make their voices heard in defense of the artistic merit of the work in the streets and cafés and in the press, just like they had done over the last few years in relation to each of his creations, from *Religious Ecstasy* to *Vasco da Gama*, including the *Viana do Castelo Christ* and his *Mousinho de Albuquerque*? And what are the distinguished members of the executive committee waiting for to issue a statement, a clear official position in defense of the monument they commissioned and the creation of which they carefully watched over and approved? wonders Aleixo, before going on to the part of Moraes de Carvalho's article devoted to the detailed analysis of the work, in which he speaks of the "burlesque nature of the accessories", with which he, Aleixo, had intended to "grant a breath of imagination" to the monument. But which after all, according to the writer, had totally erased "the striking brilliance that ought to radiate from it," and through which the result was, "instead of an ordinary, banal work, a bad one."

"Good Lord! How is it possible to write so much nonsense in so few lines!" Aleixo exclaims to himself about this indignant and impoverished reasoning, as he ends his reading. Hilarious if it were not pathetic and revealing of the author's lack of preparation, all the more obvious when he is indignant about the fact that the statue of Sousa Martins has its back turned to the Medical School, not understanding that what was important was for it to be there, where it is, facing the city, the country, where he justly earned the fame he possesses, as a doctor who sacrificed himself and devoted himself like no other to saving lives and relieving the suffering of his patients. Not forgetting, of course, his connection to the Academy, which is there, well symbolized in the figure of Modern Science, which is indeed facing the facade of the school, Aleixo recalls, suddenly taking up his pen again to add another sentence to the text of the letter: *"Si je puis mériter non pas un éloge, mais quelques mots d'appréciation seulement, à la pensée que j'ai voulu rendre, je serai mille fois dédommagé de mes ennuis passagers et je me sentirai plus fort pour continuer à travailler sans souci, des obstacles que l'Envie et la Jalousie sèment sur mon chemin…"* ("If I can deserve not a praise, but only a few words of appreciation, as my wish in return, I will be compensated a thousand times for my temporary troubles and I will feel stronger to continue working without worry, obstacles that Envy and Jealousy sow in my path…")

Yes, praise, a few words of appreciation would suffice to compensate for all the shame and humiliation he is going through, he says to himself as he lifts up his pen from the paper, recalling the abject caricatures of the monument by Mr. Jorge Colaço that came out in the *illustrated supplement* of the *Século*, and which are also there on the table among the confusion of the other newspapers, one published on the 15th of March, only a week after the inauguration, under the title, "The Monument to Sousa Martins," and another one on the 29th, with the title, "True Picture of the Sousa Martins Fountain." Which he cannot resist opening to look at once again, starting with the first one, which shows him, Aleixo, as if he were the statue of *Modern Science*, long hair and beard, right hand raised as the left hand holds the mantle that covers his naked body, and on his head, as if it were a high hat, an obelisk. As for the other one, it shows the monument from the side, with a Sousa Martins with a shapeless head, sitting down as if on the toilet, and a figure with a pose similar to that of *Gratitude*, at his feet, holding out a sheet of paper to him, while on the other side is a figure similar to *Modern Science*. In the middle, between the two figures, a cylindrical obelisk with a pear on the top. At the base, a giant *mascarron*, water flowing from its mouth, while a group of rough peasants elbow each other to get to the water first, under the watchful gaze of two local people. As for the text accompanying the caricature, it is as lacking in wit and sense of humor as the first one.

So, what to do faced with such meanness, such narrowness of mind, other than hope that Master Rodin may dedicate a little of his attention to looking at the photographs he will send him of his work, and send him some words he can use against his detractors as quickly as possible, thus reducing them to their true insignificance. Yes, it is never too much to insist, to beg for a reply, he thinks before he again dips the point of his nib in the inkwell and writes: *"Vous excuserez, l'artiste découragé, qui s'adresse à Vous et qui, espère de votre bienveillance une réponse contenant un arrêt quel qu'il soit."* (You will excuse, the discouraged artist, who speaks to You and who, hopes from your kindness for a response containing any stop whatever.")

Then he takes the letter, reads it from top to bottom once, then twice, before adding:

Votre respectueux et tout dévoué admirateur Queiroz Ribeiro
(Your respectful and devoted admirer Queiroz Ribeiro)
Lisbonne Campolide de Baixo
9—Avril, 1900

Then he runs the blotting paper over it, folds the letter down the middle, puts it inside the envelope along with the photographs, and finally writes Rodin's name and address on the outside.

"Four o'clock," he notices after looking at his pocket watch. "With luck, I can get it posted today," he says to himself as he closes and glues the envelope, writing his name and address on the back, and gets up on his way to the vestibule and the door to the street.

XIX

New York, 3rd of January 1913

SIX YEARS, ONLY SIX years had passed since he had been there for the first time, and what a difference, what progress, Good Lord, he thought, standing on the rear platform of the tram and stretching his head above those of the other passengers. As the vehicle went northwards towards Central Park, he could look through the half steamed-up windows and appreciate the new, modern buildings that were sprouting up here and there on each side of Fifth Avenue, instead of the modest houses and warehouses of the past. And the same thing was happening in many other areas of the city, in an unstoppable urban growth that was taking place particularly vertically, through the famous skyscrapers that were growing up everywhere like mushrooms, in a permanent challenge to the limits of imagination and technique, as he himself had been able to see the previous evening during the drive through the city given to him by his new friend, Mrs. Adelaide Heaton, in whose house he was lodging, he recalled when the tram was passing in front of the famous Waldorf-Astoria Hotel, occupying the whole block between 33rd and 34th streets. Thus guided by his informed hostess, he was able to visit, among others, that which was currently considered to be the tallest building in the world, the giant Metropolitan Life Insurance Company skyscraper, opposite Madison Square Park, on the crossing between Broadway and Fifth Avenue, and on top of the ten stories that the building already had, a tower had been built with over thirty more. Over the main facade, the building had a giant four-sided clock, the hands of which each weighed no more, and no less, than almost half a ton, Mrs. Heaton had told him with undisguised pride, as they went up in one of the building's luxurious elevators to the terrace on the top floor, where one could enjoy an extraordinary view of the whole of Manhattan Island and its surroundings. Following this, they had gone to visit the no less famous and surprising Singer Building, the head offices of the well-known sewing machine manufacturers, which was located further down on the crossing between Liberty Street and Broadway, and the outside of which was coated from top to bottom, on alternate levels, with red brick and bluestone, in a curious and original contrast of materials and textures, and which was now the second tallest building in the world, a position to which it had been relegated in 1909 by the Metropolitan Life Building, he recalled as the tram slowed down until coming to a complete halt at the stop between 41st and 42nd streets, giving him time enough to observe on his left the facade of the new New York Public Library in some detail, which had been inaugurated the previous year and which they had visited after the Singer Building. The building was also magnificent, with its vast, impressive Main Reading Room occupying no more and no less than two city blocks, and its 140 kilometers of shelves with over two million books that, according to Mrs. Heaton, were kept in the giant deposits in the basement, but which on the outside followed the pompous neo-Classical style of the French Second Empire, just like the very new Central Station, about to be opened next door, and which was clearly the dominant style in most of the public buildings in the major American cities, as he could see in the visits he had made during his previous stay in the United States. One might say that the authorities in the country found it difficult to assimilate and accept the new architectural styles connected to the development of new building techniques based on materials like iron, glass, and concrete, as well as the proliferation of elevators working with electric power, preferring to take refuge in the models of the European revivalist architecture of the second half of the previous century, he concluded as the tram approached the next stop—his, between 49th and 50th streets, right next to St. Patrick's Cathedral. He then started excusing his way through the great number of passengers who filled up the tram at that time of day, the ladies with their profusely decorated wide-brimmed hats, protected from the rain and cold by fur-lined coats, the gentlemen with their high hats of bowlers and heavy overcoats almost down to their feet. And which were totally necessary for this weather, he thought as he turned up his overcoat collar and tightened his black woolen scarf around his neck before he alighted onto the pavement. The monumental Cathedral was now in front of him, with its two beautiful white marble Gothic towers, over a hundred meters high, which he knew well on the inside and out. In its monumental nature and size, the central nave owed nothing to most important European Gothic cathedrals, with its two-capital ogival arches, surrounded by an enormous succession of side chapels, which extended along the apse and transept. With luck he might finish his visit to Count of Santa Eulália in time to find the cathedral still open, he thought as he crossed the avenue opposite the opulent Vanderbilt mansion on the corner of 51st Street, also built in the pretentious style of the French Second Empire, with a total of six floors, set in hierarchies of types of windows separated by salient friezes and colonnades with capitals. From here up until Central Park, where six years ago there was little more than some warehouses and factories, new three-or four-story mansions now rose up on both sides of the avenue, built in the much more sober and austere Victorian style, salient entrance portico, strictly symmetrical facade, and all-round platband. The avenue itself, which in this area was little more than a narrow road on the outskirts, had also been widened and the sidewalks and roadway were paved, he noted before he turned to West 52nd Street, where further down, at number 119, the illustrious sculptor's studio was to be found, according to the address given to him over the telephone by a Miss Beach, who had introduced herself as the Countess's private secretary when he had telephoned the house in Philadelphia this morning hoping to find the Count.

Although they had both been born in the year of Our Lord 1868, at only a few kilometers distance from each other, he in a modest house in the village of Cendufe, in the borough of Arcos de Valdevez, and Mr. Queiroz Ribeiro, later the Count of Santa Eulália, in the old House of Boavista, in the parish of Santa Madalena da Jolda in the same borough, one could not say that they were intimate or even friends, as everything else separated them, starting from their condition of birth and ending in the direction that each one of them had taken in life with the help of Our good Lord. He, from a humble family of farming folk, after primary school in his village, had gone directly on to the seminary, the only opportunity for a young man of his condition to reach higher studies, while Mr. Queiroz Ribeiro, coming from one of the noblest and wealthy families from Minho, had gone directly to Paris after his secondary studies at the High School in Viana do Castelo, remaining in Paris for six or seven years, where, at his own expense, he attended the best schools and art academies, developing and deepening his talent for sculpture, he recalled as he passed number 21, a residential building with three floors, with a much more modest facade than those he had just left behind on Fifth Avenue.

He was in Oporto as a teacher of Physics and Chemistry at a private school, when he first heard of Mr. Queiroz Ribeiro in relation to the controversy surrounding the Lisbon presentation of his statue of the *Sacred Heart of Jesus*, which was considered to be out of proportion, ugly and without any anatomical precision, according to his detractors, but which to him seemed simply astonishing when, a year later, on the eve of his departure to Paris, he went to see it for the first time up there on the Santa Luzia Hill. That Christ with a soft, suffering face, an expression of infinite tenderness, was a prodigy of originality, both in relation to Christian iconography, given that it rejected the traditional representation, in which the Heart of Jesus appeared in flames in the hands of the Lord, removed from his Divine Body, and also in relation to the art of sculpture itself, in departing from a naturalistic approach, with all of its realism and profusion of details, in favor of expression and movement, which were the apanage of the most modern and innovating currents, centering around that great master of sculpture, Rodin, of whom Queiroz Ribeiro considered himself to be a disciple, he recalled again, precisely when a strong downpour of rain started to sweep down the street, forcing him to hurriedly take cover in the entrance to a building, more or less in the middle of the block.

The following summer he was in Sorède, in the South of France, doing experiments with his solar machine, carried out under his direct supervision in Paris, when he read in the Portuguese newspapers about yet another heated controversy involving his sculptor compatriot, this time about a monument in homage to the famous positivist doctor Sousa Martins, inaugurated by King Carlos that same year in Lisbon. Having finished his experiments in Sorède with relative success, he had returned to Paris at the beginning of the autumn, in time to finally visit the *Universal Exposition*, which had been inaugurated in April that same year of 1900 and was about to close its doors when he had the opportunity to get to know, not only in name but in person, Mr. Queiroz Ribeiro, as he had also just arrived in Paris, from Bulgaria, where he had achieved yet another remarkable triumph in second place in a hotly disputed international competition for the construction of a monument in homage to Czar Alexander II of Russia, he recalled as he sheltered in the doorway waiting for the rain to pass over.

Four years later he was in St. Louis, Missouri, presenting a new and greatly improved version of his solar machine, called the *Pyrheliophero*, at the 1904 World Exposition when to his great surprise he again encountered Mr. Queiroz Ribeiro, who, after the unfortunate outcome of his monument in Lisbon, had decided to leave Portugal again and came there to work on the decoration and embellishment of one of the many pavilions built in the exhibition grounds, along with other sculptors and artists. Two years later, when passing through Chicago on another of his many trips to the interior of the United States before his definitive return to Portugal, he had again encountered Mr. Queiroz Ribeiro, who had taken on the functions of Consul of the city. Two more years later, in 1908, he was residing in Lisbon, where he was developing a project for the making of a new quality of explosives, when he received a letter from his good friend Adelaide Marion Fielde, sent from New York, where she was living, asking him about a certain Count de Santa Eulália, sculptor and Consul of Portugal in Chicago, whose marriage to a lady from Philadelphia, the widow of the multimillionaire hat magnate John Stetson, was at the time the major story in the American newspapers from North to South and East to West, deserving of front page items and full-body photographs in most of them. A year later he found out through his brother Gaspar—yes, because he also had a brother Gaspar, except he was neither an illustrious member of parliament, nor a talented poet, nor a brilliant lawyer like the brother of the Count, but a simple, modest village priest—that the illustrious Count had just bought an extensive property in the borough of Arcos de Valdevez, known as the Glória Estate, with an eighteenth-century house on it which was somewhat dilapidated but which he had soon restored and embellished using the stones and the carvings from the demolished Monastery of Nossa Senhora dos Remédios in Braga.

More recently, in the previous year, the Count's name again appeared in several newspapers, but this time deserving of unanimous applause because of his purchasing of the impressive Refojos Convent in the Borough of Ponte de Lima, and of the vast agricultural properties that were a part of it, along with a publicly announced intention of setting up a model agricultural school, with the introduction of the most advanced methods of intensive farming used in America, as well as proposing to carry out major works of conservation on the convent building. Which, at least at the time, did not stop there being rumors that he was using huge amounts of money to finance the purchasing of weapons and munitions for Paiva Couceiro's monarchist forces with a view to a further attack in the North, which ended up taking place in July, albeit with no success, as it was completely crushed by the forces loyal to the Republic. Might there be any foundation to these rumors? It wasn't very likely, as the Count, despite his monarchist convictions, was an artist, a man of broad ideas, who had lived for a long time in America, which had had a Republican regime since its independence.

Whatever the case, nowadays the Count of Santa Eulália was a prominent figure in America, both due to the direct or indirect access he had to his wife's colossal fortune and to the high-ranking contacts he had been establishing in the country through his diplomatic and artistic career and was thus particularly well-placed to help him in his actions in America, and perhaps able to help him financially in his new projects and scientific research, for which reason it was extremely fitting to make this visit to his illustrious compatriot in his New York studio, he found himself thinking when he finally came to the door to number 119, a three-story building which from the outside was almost no different from the other buildings on the street. Small factories, shops, and workshops stood on either side of the building, he noted after he knocked on the door for the first time, apparently to no reaction, sound, or sign of movement inside. Had the Count changed his mind and decided to go somewhere else instead of working in his studio, going against the information he had been given over the telephone from Philadelphia? he wondered as he knocked on the door again, now more insistently, until he finally heard a voice inside, which he immediately recognized as that of his illustrious compatriot, shouting, "Coming! Coming."

"Father Himalaya… What is Your Reverence doing here?" the Count exclaimed, stupefied, when he finally opened the door, white dungarees over a starched-collar shirt, as he sees in front of him, in the flesh and on a cold and rainy winter morning at the beginning of the new year, there in his New York studio, none other than the famous inventor-priest Manuel António Gomes, better known as Father

Himalaya, due to his impressive six foot four inches in height. "Come in, Father, come on in, it's freezing out there," he added, stepping aside to let his visitor in, after which he slammed the door shut.

"First of all, allow me to apologize for this sudden appearance without any notice. But, unfortunately, the circumstances of my short stay in New York did not permit me to proceed in any other manner," Father Himalaya finally said in his high, sibylline voice, shaking with cold under his black overcoat, as he allowed himself to be led by the Count across the entrance hall with the staircase to the upper floors towards the studio proper, made up of two spaces connected by a wide arched passage, one with normal depth and headroom and the other one much higher and longer, stretching into the yard of the building. In the first space, on the wall opposite the entrance door, a large iron salamander heated the room, flanked by two comfortable leather armchairs, and followed by a sideboard full of plaster models and statuettes of several different sizes, while standing out in the middle of the room there was a wide table covered in drawings, books, and glasses with charcoal pencils.

"And you were quite right to do so, Father. It is a great honor for me to be able to receive you here in my New York studio, you being a figure of such reputation and great prestige in the international scientific circles, although not having yet received due recognition in your own country. But that is something to which, unfortunately, we are both accustomed, are we not?" said the count, after inviting his unexpected guest to sit down on one of the armchairs next to the heater, as he himself occupied the other.

"Well, lately I can't complain too much. Thanks to the support of the Portuguese Society of Sciences, I have achieved much greater recognition for my work from the authorities and from public opinion.

"Really? I'm glad to hear it. I can't say the same for myself, but nor am I very worried about it. My sculpture is reserved for America. In Portugal, I prefer to be a farmer, to busy myself with the cornfields, grapevines, and horses," replied the count sarcastically. "But you said that this visit to New York would be short. So when did you arrive?"

"Two days ago, on the *Oceanic*. Curiously the same steamer on which I made my first trip to America, eight years ago, when I came to the St. Louis World's Fair."

"But that's a steamer on the White Star Line, the same company as the *Titanic,* the ship that sank last April on its maiden voyage, taking over one thousand five hundred souls with it," the Count observed with concern.

"Yes, I read it in the newspapers. A terrible tragedy. It's hard to believe how such a modern ship, with such advanced machinery and navigation methods, could crash into an iceberg like that without being able to divert its route in time…"

"Yes, and that's the point. According to what was found out later, despite it being so modern and so full of commodities, the ship wasn't carrying any binoculars. And the number of lifeboats was only enough for a third of the passengers."

"You don't say, Count. How could they make such an oversight?"

"I don't know. What I do know is that from now on I only go on Cunard liners. Such as the *Carmania,* on which I made my honeymoon journey, and the *Lusitania,* on which I came back to Portugal a little over two weeks ago.

"Very good for you. And if I hadn't already bought my return ticket I would do the same."

"Until when are you intending to stay here in the United States?"

"Just about another month. But tomorrow I am off again, to Seattle, on the Pacific coast," the priest pointed out.

"Seattle? I know it well. I've been there several times. An area of great industry, great development. But note that on the serious side, from New York to there, it is three or four days by train. You will have to cross the whole country from one end to the other," the Count pointed out.

"Yes, I know. But fortunately, I am not going alone. I am taking with me an American lady who was in Portugal recently to witness some of my experiments with explosives."

"I see.… In that case, what are you going to be doing in Seattle, if you don't mind me asking?"

"Well, it's a study visit, to assess the possibility to use an explosive invented by me, *himalayte,* in the construction works for the new port. This lady, Mrs. Adelaide Heaton, who lives here in New York, was recently in Portugal at the request of her son, an influential Seattle lawyer, to see the results and the possibilities for the use of *himalayte;* she accompanied me on several experiments I carried out in some quarries in the north.

"And she was very impressed apparently."

"Yes. The information she gave to her son was so positive that he immediately invited me to make this journey to his city to try out the new explosive in the new port."

"You mean that if the experiments in Seattle go well they will need to import a large quantity of *himalayte* from Portugal."

"Yes. Or even set up a factory which in the first phase would produce the explosives necessary for the works in the port, but which later on could start to supply the rest of the country," Himalaya clarified.

"Even better. As a patriotic Portuguese man I am very pleased about such a project if it goes ahead," the Count made a point of stating.

"Indeed. And it's exactly on this issue that I wished to hear your good counsel, as someone who is experienced and knowledgeable in relation to the Americans' mentality and manner of proceeding. And also to inquire as to your own personal interest in associating yourself with this initiative. It goes without saying that it would give me great pleasure and even greater security in order to carry this out. Even because business negotiations are not my strong point," the priest acknowledged with humility.

"Well, Father Himalaya, to be honest with you, nor are they mine. After all, we are both people who are devoted to creating, to invention, albeit each in his own area, and thus we are very little versed in the unfathomable mysteries of the vile metal. But I do not mind talking to the Countess and her sons in order to find out how far they are interested in investing in this project, as they, indeed, are capitalists, people from the world of business, of industry, capable of seeing what is worth investing in. And at the same time, I could also try to obtain information about this lawyer Heaton, from Seattle," promised Santa Eulália.

"I would be eternally grateful to you, Sir. Because after all, I do not know them very well, I have no information about them other than those coming from my personal contact with the lady I mentioned during her short stay in Portugal. And now, since I arrived in New York, as I am staying at her house. She is a very pleasant and kind lady, but I well know, from my own experience, how these high finance people can sometimes be false and self-seeking, only concerned about achieving their own profits and not caring about anything else."

"After Seattle, are you going straight back to Portugal?" the Count wished to know.

"No. From Seattle, I go directly to Texas. For some years now I have been studying the possibility of producing artificial rain through the use of explosives. And I know that a certain C.W. Post, who is a great magnate in the food industry, has carried out several experiments in the same field in a sort of utopian city founded by him in Texas, called Post City. So I am very curious about going there, getting to know his experiments, and witnessing the results he has obtained."

"Now that's something I would never have thought of, producing artificial rain. Which, if it worked, could bring enormous benefits to the planet, extraordinarily improving conditions for farming production, which is so often affected by drought. Like what happens in our Alentejo, for example, and even in the Algarve."

"That's my intention. Let's see how things work out."

"It is certainly a very interesting project, but I must be honest with you, Father Himalaya, out of all the projects I know of, the one that has always fascinated me was that of the *Pyrhe...Pyrhelio...*"

"*Pyrheliophero!*" the inventor priest immediately corrected.

"Indeed, *Pyrheliophero.* What an extraordinary machine. And at the same time what a beautiful, abstract, extremely modern sculpture, with that giant hood in the shape of a trapezium, covered in thousands of tiny mirrors capturing the sunlight and then reflecting it onto a single point, then reaching extremely high temperatures. Capable of reducing a wooden log into ash in a few seconds, as I saw happen several times in St. Louis, to the joy of the crowds that gathered there every day gaping around the device," recalled the Count.

"It's true. It was certainly an extraordinary success. It's a shame that it wasn't possible to continue the experiment, following it up by developing all of its potential, which was a great deal. But unfortunately, no one was interested, neither here nor there in Portugal," said Father Himalaya with sadness.

"What happened to the device?"

"It was left there to rust, vandalized by the local population after the exhibition ended. Not one of the 6,170 mirrors was left as a sample. I even tried to get the local authorities to build a pavilion where it could be kept, but that wasn't possible either," lamented the priest.

"It's a pity because it was indeed a magnificent device."

"Perhaps one day I'll get the financial support needed to take the project up again. And even perhaps—Who knows?—manage to produce electrical energy from solar energy, which is an inexhaustible source. Yes, because one should not have any illusions: coal and petrol are limited resources, which will end in one or two centuries from now. And then how will one produce the electric energy necessary for industry and daily life?" asked the visionary priest.

"It's something to think about, no doubt. You never stop, Father Himalaya, always bubbling over with new ideas and projects," commented the Count.

"Neither do you, Count, so it seems, judging by the number and size of the works you have there," replied Himalaya, nodding towards the other room, where one could see several different statues on plinths or easels, and in the middle what looked like a giant bas-relief, almost reaching up to the extremely high ceiling.

"Yes, now that I don't need sculpture to survive, I can have the luxury of just doing what I like, not having to put up with the whims and bizarre requests of those who give me the commissions. Which, one might say, is the ambition and dream of any artist.

"And would it be great trouble for you to show me the works that you have here? Even though I am a man of science I am fascinated by matters of art, and of sculpture in particular. I will never forget the effect produced on me by the statue of the *Sacred Heart of Jesus* that you made for the Santa Luzia hill when I saw it for the first time up there, in front of the little hermitage that existed there then. Stunning, a revelation, a prodigy of inspiration and originality," Father Himalaya recalled with emotion.

"Thank you very much, Father. It was also a very significant work for me, even though it was done in my youth, with all the inherent qualities and defects. I did it when I was still in Paris, right after finishing my studies, my training as a sculptor," replied the Count, rapidly standing up on his way to the other room, closely followed by Himalaya.

"Even so, it is a fascinating work," insisted the priest, as the Count turned a porcelain switch near the passage connecting the two rooms and illuminated the several electric light bulbs hanging from the extremely high ceiling of the room, until then plunged into almost pitch darkness as outside the day had ended and very little or no light entered through the window that ran all along the back wall.

"The works that you see here are almost all recent works, and obviously possess greater maturity. We can start right here with the haut-relief in homage to the great American sculptor Saint-Gaudens, my master and my friend, whom I met in Paris shortly before the *Universal Exposition*," suggested the Count, stopping in front of the gigantic trapezoid work with over seven meters in height and another seven meters on its base, with a figure at the bottom in the middle totally standing out from the background, showing a bearded man sitting down, deep in thought and with his left arm resting on his knee and his hand on his chin, with his right arm resting on the other knee. Above it there were several superimposed figures, among which Himalaya could only identify that of the unfortunate President Lincoln, standing up at the center of the composition.

"This figure here at the bottom… I presume is the sculptor himself, is it not?" he asked, turning to the Count.

"Yes. That is him, just as I recall him when I went to visit him the last time in his studio in Cornish, in New Hampshire. Where he worked and lived over the last years, along with his wife, his brother, and a vast team of sculptors."

"The artist at a moment of reflection and doubt, before returning to his work. Very interesting."

"Yes. But after all, is that not what all sculpture comes down to? Capturing the moment, between the before and the after?" the Count asked, pensive.

"What do those other figures up above represent?"

"Those figures are taken from Saint-Gaudens's most famous and well-known works, but reinterpreted and worked so as to form a single composition, obviously centered on the figure of their creator.

"For example, you mean that the image of President Lincoln there in the middle is taken from one of his works…"

"Yes. It's one of his most famous statues. It is in Lincoln Park in Chicago. The President is standing in front of his chair, the back of which you can also see depicted here. And that gentleman there on the right is the famous General Sherman, a great hero of the American Civil War, just as Saint-Gaudens represented him in the statue that is today at the entrance to Central Park on the Fifth Avenue side. Except for that Victory, who in the original statue is at the front, guiding the horse and rider, is here side-on, tenderly turning to Saint-Gaudens, as if protecting him with her angel's wing," Santa Eulália explained.

"Very interesting. And what are the other figures?"

"The one on the left, after Victory's wing, is the *Puritan*, also a very famous statue, which is in Springfield, Massachusetts. Higher up, to the left of Lincoln, is Admiral Farragut, another of the great heroes of the War of Secession, just as it is in the monument in Madison Square Park, here in New York, made in collaboration with the famous architect Stanford White, the first of several done together by the two. To the right of Lincoln, also on horseback, is General Logan, holding the American flag, another great hero of the Civil War and whose original monument is in Grand Park in Chicago.

"And what is that battalion of soldiers up there?" asked Himalaya, curious to know about the upper part of the work.

"It is the first regiment of the American army wholly made up of Negroes, and which was commanded by Colonel Robert Gould Shaw, also during the Civil War. The colonel is there on horseback in the middle of the composition, with that horizontal angel flying over his head, protecting him. Behind and in front are the soldiers from the regiment, marching to the final assault on Fort Wagner in South Carolina, during which Shaw and a great many soldiers died. The original monument is in Boston, Shaw's home town, and is considered by many people to be Saint-Gaudens's masterpiece.

"Remarkable. This haut-relief really is an extraordinary, superior composition. I imagine the work you must have had to make it, Count," commented Himalaya, unable to take his eyes off the work.

"I started it in 1909, almost six years ago. But before I started it I went to see all of these works one by one in the places they stand. I collected as much information as possible about them, through drawings and written notes, and in some cases photographs. Only then did I really start to work on it piece by piece before I finally connected everything in a single composition. First still in the model stage, after successive versions in increasingly large sizes until I came to the haut-relief and the statue you see before you, now in plaster. And to which I am now applying the final touches before casting it in bronze," the Count explained.

"What do you intend to do with this afterwards? Is there some public site to place them so they can be appreciated and admired?"

"Well, for now, I intend to take them to Paris, to have them cast before I present them at the Salon. And then we'll see. Perhaps the New York City Council might want to place them in a square or in one of the city parks, given that Saint-Gaudens lived and worked here for most of his life," the Count replied, motioning to the priest to follow him to another piece on an easel next to the haut-relief.

"This here is a statue of my friend Dr. Cook, the discoverer of the North Pole, but who, as you probably know, has in the meantime fallen into disgrace. The result is that what was supposed to be a statue in homage to him, promoted by the Arctic Club of America, is nothing more than this little statuette," explained the Count, while Himalaya admired the figure of that contemporary discoverer, with his feet firmly standing on a base that suggested the frozen peak of a mountain, his shapeless body, covered in snow, left arm raised in greeting, while the right arm held the mast of an enormous flag which, in a spiral movement, wrapped his shoulders and head, also covered in snow, only leaving his face showing, which was clearly marked and shaped, in contrast with the ill-defined lines and outlines of the other elements of the piece. On the base of the piece, one could read, written on the plaster, the date of arrival at the Pole—April 21st, 1908—and the discoverer's name.

"It indeed is a pity, because the work would definitely make a beautiful monument, all in white marble, from Carrara or from our Alentejo region."

"That was my idea, but unfortunately it got left by the wayside, like so many other ones. And here is the plaster bust of Professor Putnam, of Harvard, a man of science, an anthropologist by training, but who devoted himself to a great many other areas, such as zoology, archaeology, and ethnography," explained the Count, pointing to a small piece on a box turned on its side, and looking little more than a head, surprisingly only joined by a hand and the right fist.

"Why did you represent him with his right hand in his ear?" the priest asked out of curiosity.

"Well, perhaps because it was a gesture I saw him make often when he was sitting for me. Perhaps due to some hearing difficulty, or simply to better capture the sounds around him during his activities of observation and gathering of elements for his scientific research."

"Very interesting, without a doubt," commented Himalaya.

"And over here we have the statue of Queen Amelia, which I finished in Chicago, in 1908, right after the assassination of King Carlos and the Royal Prince, God keep them in eternal rest. I made it with the intention of paying homage to that great figure of a courageous and self-sacrificing woman and mother that she is. Then I tried everything possible to have it sent to Portugal so it could be set in marble and placed in one of the public gardens in Lisbon or in one of the royal palaces, as was the wish of King Manuel and of the Prime Minister of the time, Admiral Ferreira do Amaral. But there were so many difficulties and hesitations that the monarchy ended up falling first. Result: yet another work that did not fulfill its destiny.

"And what a piece! Impressive, beautiful. Curiously with a much more realistic approach in its details. Something which I haven't seen in the other works," Himalaya pointed out after noting the manner in which that three-meter high statue had the details of not only the Queen's clothing, ranging from her dress, with an open neckline, to the cape she had over her shoulders, and including the necklace and hairstyle, to the bouquet of roses she was holding in her left hand and the royal insignia on the throne.

"Yes, but none of the others represents the Queen of Portugal," the Count replied definitively.

"It's really a pity that in Portugal the extraordinary artistic work you are carrying out here in America is completely unknown. And yet it would not be so difficult to organize an exhibition of all these works in Lisbon or Oporto. Or even in Viana," suggested Himalaya.

"I thank you for your suggestion, Father, and I know it is sincere and out of friendship, but frankly I am not interested. It is like I said before: in Portugal, I want to be known as a farmer and horse breeder, nothing else. I have undergone enough unpleasantness from those people and am not going back to subject myself to their criticisms and nonsense," the Count declared peremptorily.

"Times have changed, Count. Many of those behind the attacks of which you were the unjust victim either are no longer with us, as is the case of Fialho de Almeida and of Ribeiro Arthur, or they have retired. And the new people seem to be much more open to the new tendencies in art," Himalaya insisted.

"Perhaps you are right, Father, but frankly I don't think it is worth the effort. And with such upheaval, so many conflicts underway in the country, I doubt that anyone might be really interested in my work. Unfortunately, things do not seem to have improved much with the change of regime, instead, to the contrary. And if the people have changed, the methods and the intrigues seem to be the same, if not worse," replied the Count pessimistically.

"Well, please do not take offense, Count, but it is getting late. And now that I am here I would like to visit St. Patrick's Cathedral and say my prayers," said the priest after a quick glance at his pocket watch.

"Certainly, Father Himalaya. In that case, all that remains to me is to wish that your trip to Seattle is a success. In the meantime, I will speak to the Countess and her children to find out about their interest in supporting your project. And if I find out any information about this Heaton fellow I will write to you at the general delivery office in Seattle," said the Count as he accompanied the priest to the door.

"I am eternally grateful to you for what you can do, Sir. And, once again, my thanks for receiving me," replied the priest, taking his leave with a warm handshake before plunging into the cold and rainy New York evening.

XX

"THE ONLY THING he cannot conquer is the *Baixa,* our *Baixa,* the critics of the monument to Sousa Martins. They are the implacable ones, the intransigent, those who never let up—like bulldogs..." Aleixo, sitting at the window in one of the compartments of the first-class carriage of the *Sud-Express* train, once again reads the precise words with which Xavier de Carvalho, a correspondent for the *Século* newspaper in Paris, finishes the excellent article which he has just published in the magazine *Brasil-Portugal,* devoted to the enormous success he achieved in Bulgaria with the model he presented at the international competition for the monument to Czar Alexander II of Russia, to be erected in the Parliament Square in Sofia. He received the copy he has in front of him when he was still in Paris, on the day of his departure for Lisbon, sent personally by Xavier himself, no doubt thinking about the great joy he would derive from reading it after all the criticisms and attacks he had suffered in the Portuguese press about the monument to Sousa Martins. Dominating the page on which the article is published is a beautiful photograph of the model, which he himself gave to Xavier, highlighting the superb figure of Czar Alexander II on horseback on the pedestal, above which is the Angel of victory, crowning him with a halo. Addorsed to the two side faces of the pedestal are the figures of the four generals who commanded the Russian army during the war against Turkey, also on horseback, and below this, leaning against the front face, two soldiers, a Russian and a Bulgarian, side by side, wearing their respective uniforms in combat position. On the side faces of the base of the monument, there are also four bas-reliefs portraying the most important moments from the Turco-Russian war, but which are unfortunately almost imperceptible in the photograph, he notes before closing the magazine and placing it on the empty seat next to his, on top of the pile of newspapers he brought with him to read on the journey, then casting his gaze for a moment over the slow, gray waters of the River Tagus, running side by side with the train line along this last stretch of the journey, between Santarém and Lisbon.

It was at the beginning of May that, having become fed up with waiting almost a month for the much-desired letter from Rodin in response to his and being unable to put up with the scandalous campaign launched in the Lisbon newspapers against him and his monument, he decided to drop everything and go to Bulgaria, at the other end of Europe, to participate in that important international competition he had seen advertised some considerable time previously in the *Gazette des Beaux-Arts*. The first part of the journey was taken by ship across the Mediterranean to Genoa, and then by train to Rome, with an obligatory stopover in Florence to see the famous *David* by Michelangelo, to wonder at its Renaissance palaces and churches and to get lost in the corridors of the Uffizi Gallery, one of the richest and most extraordinary museums in the world. In the capital he had spent several days wandering around among the ruins of the Roman temples, but also through its Baroque squares and buildings, its magnificent museums and monuments, not forgetting to visit the Vatican to see the *Pietà*, the ceiling of the Sistine Chapel and the dome of the Basilica of St. Peter, all works from the genius of Michelangelo. Then he carried on by train to Naples, where he caught a ship that took him to the north of Greece and then he finally went, again by train, to Sofia, the capital of Bulgaria.

When he arrived, the organization team for the competition immediately granted him a studio to use in the Fine Arts School so he could carry out his work, alongside many other competitors from the most varied European cities and capitals, such as Paris, from which had come the consecrated artists Mercier, Nöel and Soulez, among others, but also Florence, Prague, St. Petersburg, Berlin, Berne, Vienna, Budapest, Copenhagen, The Hague, Hanover, Turin, and many others. And there, determined not to be put off by adversity, to prove what he was capable of doing and what his talent as an artist was, more to himself than to his detractors, that he set out and got down to work hard for the five months left before the deadline to enter the competition, producing something far superior to what he had ever done until then. Indeed, if the monument to Sousa Martins was a work of considerable complexity in the set of statues and other elements which made it up, his model for the monument to Czar Alexander II ended up by being much more so, with its five equestrian statues, the figures of the two soldiers and the four bas-reliefs, all worked in a detailed manner never previously tried out by him. The statue of the Czar is particularly elaborate, in relation to anatomy and the movements of the horse as well as in relation to the two figures, that of Alexander II himself and that of the Angel. In modeling it in its final version, Aleixo clearly had in mind not only his *Mousinho de Albuquerque,* in which Albuquerque, the hero of the Battle of Chaimite, rises up calmly on the flanks of a dying horse but also the *Monument to Sherman,* that remarkable equestrian statue by Saint-Gaudens, which he saw for the first time, not yet finished, when it was still unfinished on the visit he made with Nellie to the studio at Rue de Bagneux in Paris, just over two years ago before his definitive return to Lisbon. And he just saw it again less than a week ago in pride of place in the sculpture section of the World Exposition at the Grand Palais. Yes, there is doubtlessly a relationship, an analogy, between his statue of the Czar, up there on the pedestal of his model, and Saint-Gaudens's *Sherman,* even though it is only now, looking at the latter work again, that he has realized this, he finds himself thinking, at the moment that the train begins to slow down as it comes to Braço de Prata station, then coming to a complete stop along the platform with some jolts and a great screeching of brakes. Which even so does not seem to affect the sleep of his travel companions, a couple from Setúbal, returning after their first trip to Paris because of the World Exposition, she sitting opposite him with her head against the window, he next to her, his head on her shoulder.

And the analogy begins right there in the posture of the rider and of the horse itself, in the serenity and confidence with which the two of them go to the battlefield, then stretching to the allegorical figures, in his monument with the Angel, protecting the Czar, and the crown with a halo, in Saint-Gaudens's work a Victory, going ahead and opening up the path for the rider. At the same time, one cannot deny that in this work there is a far greater concern for the definition of the forms, for detail and the finishing touches of the several statues than was the case, for example, in the Sousa Martins work. Was it because it was a monument almost completely made up of equestrian statues, thus demanding much greater care in the movements of the horses and riders? Or because this time he did not want to be subjected to further criticisms and lack of understanding, instead preferring to play it safe? Perhaps a little of both, who knows? But the truth is that the result was far beyond all expectations, as when the competing models were exhibited in one of the salons of the Sofia School of Fine Arts his work immediately became the object of articles and references praising it in the main newspapers in Bulgaria, often accompanied by photographic reproductions, and was considered to be the clear favorite in relation to the other competitors, he recalls with satisfaction, feeling the train start moving again, this time not along the river towards the Santa Apolónia Station, as was the case a little over ten years ago, but along the new branch line that went directly to Rossio Station, skirting the whole of the city of Lisbon.

However, in no small way associated with this success was the enthusiasm and precious help he received from Maria, a young student of sculpture, the daughter of a Bulgarian count who was currently in the service of the court as a diplomatic representative in the Baltic countries. Ah, Maria, Maria, what energy, what vigor, what desire to learn, always ready to collaborate in whatever way necessary, from kneading the clay to preparing the plaster, including carrying and shifting the easels and the works themselves. And what youth, what beauty, what perfection and opulence of forms, forcing him into a constant effort not to become lost in the charms of the young lady and throw everything away, he recalls, unable to avoid briefly and emotionally seeing again the last image he has of her in his mind, in Sofia railway station on the day of his departure, her standing in front of him, not managing to utter a word, two full tears suddenly welling up in her big, beautiful, blue eyes while he delicately kissed her two hands and thanked her from the bottom of his heart for her efforts and generosity throughout those months.

"Excuse me for being so bold, sir, but could you tell me what time it is?" suddenly asks his traveling companion, waking up startled opposite him.

"A quarter past seven, my dear sir. We are running a little late, but whatever, twenty minutes or half an hour or so and we will arrive in Rossio," Aleixo replies, after taking out his pocket watch, observed attentively by the lady opposite him, a lock of hair falling over her forehead and her dress slightly disheveled. Had the two of them slept in one of the bunks in the *Wagon-Lit* carriage they would not now be overcome by that overwhelming sleepiness that made them drowse for almost the whole journey, he thinks.

"Thank you most kindly, sir," replies the man, now sitting down in his seat again, calmer, while she takes a little mirror out of her bag and applies some touches to her hair, before adjusting her wide hat, decorated with plumes and dried flowers.

Not only does the excellent Xavier de Carvalho talk about all of these triumphs of his in his article in the magazine *Brasil-Portugal*, but also Silva Lisboa, correspondent of the *Diário de Notícias* newspaper in Paris, whom he also visited on his return from Sofia to show him the photographs and articles about him and his model that were published there. Indeed, Xavier himself did not stop at his article in the magazine *Brasil-Portugal*, but also published a long and thoughtful reference to his triumph in Bulgaria in his column in the *Século* newspaper, although obviously without referring to the "bulldogs," as it is in this newspaper that many of them find their shelter. It was the *Século* that first brought out an explicit appeal to demolish the monument, in an article published at the end of July; that is, less than five months after its inauguration, after which there had been constant news reports about the initiatives of a supposed "group of friends and admirers of Sousa Martins" aiming at building a new monument to replace his. And it is the *Illustrated Supplement* of the *Século* that has, in almost every issue for several months, published abject caricatures accompanied by anecdotes and bad taste jokes about him and his work, he recalls, unable to feel rising up in his stomach the same mixture of revolt and sadness with which he received them all far away in Bulgaria, where he made the mistake of redirecting his subscription to the newspaper, seeing himself so badly treated in his own country, in complete contrast to the enthusiasm with which his work was received there in a country totally unknown to him. But if the issues of the *Illustrated Supplement* invariably ended up in the waste paper basket as soon as he opened them, being the only destination compatible with the low tone of the jokes and caricatures directed against him, the same could not happen with the issues of the *Século* in which there were items referring to the new monument, which were carefully put away, just in case, as they arrived. In one of which there was a picture of the model of the supposed new monument to Sousa Martins by Costa Motta, who was classified in third place in the competition and with whom, according to the accompanying news item, a contract had already been signed, and this was without the committee having ever taken any official position on the subject or having said a single word to him.

There is an attempt to give the impression that everything has been defined and settled in relation to the demolition, when things are not so simple, given that the Lisbon Council will not simply authorize the destruction of a work that had been formally given to it by the executive committee on the day of its inauguration in an official act signed by all the dignitaries present, with the legal consequences that might arise. On the other hand, it was necessary to take into account the executive committee's enormous responsibilities throughout the whole process, as it was the entity that promoted the monument and had it built, thus having to defend it from the attacks of which it was the target and prevent it being destroyed by any means. Even knowing that some of its members belong to the "group of admirers and friends of Sousa Martins" which is promoting the supposed new monument, as is the case of Casimiro José de Lima, who, according to what his brother Gaspar told him in one of the letters he wrote to Sofia, is the main defender of the idea, maneuvering everything in the background in order to achieve his sinister aims, Aleixo concludes as the train again begins to slow down, about to enter Campolide Station, where it stops for a short while before entering the tunnel leading to Rossio Station. He casts a quick glance through the window at the houses on the Campolide de Baixo hillside, where the public lighting gas street lamps are gradually being turned on, yet he is unable to make out his former studio, which he left shortly before he departed for Sofia. After a few minutes' wait, the train started off again towards the tunnel, which crosses the city for almost three kilometers towards Rossio Station.

To what extent might these articles about his latest work, and the unquestionable international recognition that it implies, allow a *volte-face*, a reverse in the whole process? What would be the reaction from the bulldogs to the photographs of his model published in the *Brasil-Portugal* and the praise for it from Xavier de Carvalho and Silva Lisboa on the news pages? Now added to by the honorable second place he was awarded by the competition jury, news of which he only discovered on the day of his departure from Paris? Aleixo wonders, looking out of the window at the dark walls of the tunnel, as the inside of the carriage is plunged into a darkness that is only not total because of the faint light from a small electric light bulb, miraculously lit up in the middle of the ceiling.

Mr. José de Figueiredo will certainly take advantage of this example to once again vehemently condemn competitions as a form of adjudicating artistic works, in his opinion a veritable plague spreading dangerously throughout Europe.

Major Ribeiro Arthur, even if he acknowledges a certain merit in the model and in the idea underlying it, will nevertheless certainly find, after patient analysis of the photograph with a magnifying glass, some badly conceived anatomical details on the head, on the limbs, or even— who knows?—on the private parts of some of the several nags.

Mr. Fialho de Almeida will suggest when faced with the quality of the making of this new work, that there is no doubt a hidden collaborator who should be awarded the responsibility for such international success. Or, worse than all this, will they toast it with absolute silence and indifference, a sign that they consider that the battle has already been won? Aleixo wonders again, as the train starts to slow down, a sign that the end of the tunnel is approaching, and with it, the end of the journey.

What remains to be seen in the middle of all this is the reaction of the executive committee and even the great committee, principally by those among their members who did not adhere to the initiatives of Mr. Casimiro Lima and his friends, men he considers to be honorable, straightforward and true to their word, like José António Serrano, Hygino de Sousa, Alfredo da Costa, and Miguel Bombarda, or even the Duke of Palmela himself. Might the news of this triumph of his finally open their eyes, making them understand the enormous error, the enormous injustice that is about to be committed with their complicit silence and indifference? God only knows, he thinks. God only knows in his infinite mercy, but he will do everything to the limits of his strength to make them see how wrong they are in their assessment of his Sousa Martins. And once all arguments have been exhausted he will have no solution left but to sue for compensation for damages and loss, even knowing that no moral or material reparation could ever compensate him for the irreparable harm caused to his good name and his artistic career, he concludes to himself, as the train, having finished driving through the tunnel, enters Rossio Station, progressively slowing down until it comes to a stop at the first platform.

"Do you need any assistance, sir?" asks Aleixo thoughtfully, seeing his travel companion trying to take down one of his two heavy suitcases on the luggage rack above his seat.

"Don't trouble yourself for me, kind sir," the other gentleman replies, with the enormous case sliding onto his shoulder, whilst the lady has opened the compartment door and is calling for a porter to carry the baggage out of the station.

"It is no trouble at all," insists Aleixo, kindly, helping him get the two cases down, after which he places his top hat on his head and takes his leave, alighting to the platform.

"Aleixinho! How are you? I started to think you'd missed the train, man," he suddenly hears the unmistakable voice of his brother Gaspar.

"Here I am, finally. Safe and sound. And how are you, lad?" he replies, turning to embrace his brother, among the crowd that almost completely fills the platform, with the arriving passengers, laden with their cases and bags with souvenirs from the World Exposition, and the noisy groups of relatives and friends who are waiting for them all along the train, increasing in size in a direct relationship to their importance and influence in society.

"Never better. I got in from the Minho last night, on the evening train. What about your journey?"

"Rather reasonable, despite the delay."

"Well, even so, it was only an hour and a half, which isn't bad for nowadays. Shall we go?" says Gaspar, looking very elegant in his gray overcoat, white cache-nez, and top hat, after looking at the station clock, with its hands almost on eight.

"By the way, where are you taking me this time?"

"As I didn't know what arrangements you had made I booked you a room at the Avenida Palace, right next to mine. And tomorrow you can do whatever you like."

"Excellent. That way we can spend some more time together. To catch up on things, right?" replies Aleixo, looking at him anxiously.

"That's exactly what I was thinking. Where is your baggage?"

"In the hold of the *Wagon-Lit* carriage. This time I decided to stretch the purse strings and I rented a sleeping bunk."

"Absolutely right. It's much greater comfort," says Gaspar, signaling to the hotel porter to go and get his brother's baggage.

"Wait a minute. Shouldn't we be going that way?" asks Aleixo, suddenly noticing that they are going exactly in the opposite direction to the other passengers.

"No, lad. Further down there is a direct entrance to the hotel. Which avoids us having to go downstairs to the entrance and then come up again," replies Gaspar.

"Really? I didn't know," replies Aleixo, surprised.

"Well? A great triumph in Bulgaria, then? You'll have to tell me all about it over dinner." states Gaspar, taken by enthusiasm.

"How do you know?" asks Aleixo in surprise.

"How do I know? Through the articles that came out in the *Século* and the *Notícias*, how else? Followed by that beautiful article by Xavier de Carvalho in the *Brasil-Portugal*, with a photograph of the model and everything. A stunning conception, your monument. And what perfection of details. Clearly showing that when you want to you can also do just as well or better than the others."

"You mean you don't know about the classification of the competition?"

"Don't tell me you came in first place?" asks Gaspar, stopping walking.

"No, but it was close. I came second. Which, given the circumstances, isn't bad at all."

"Not bad at all? It's excellent, lad. What a great lesson you're going to give the ones from *Baixa*, the *bulldogs*, as Xavier de Carvalho calls them," states Gaspar, radiant with enthusiasm as they come to the end of the platform, always followed at a reasonable distance by the young hotel porter, pushing a cart with the cases. Near to a narrow door with no sign or reference to the hotel, is a butler who welcomes them with a bow. The door, located on the level of the fifth and top floor of the hotel, has direct access to the landing of a beautiful marble staircase that describes a soft arc as it goes down the stories to the ground floor.

"We have a table booked in the restaurant for eight-thirty. But I imagine you would like to go to your room to change, right?" asks Gaspar as they wait for the elevator to arrive, on the left of the door at the beginning of a long corridor giving on to the rooms on that floor.

"After two days of traveling what I need is a good bath," Aleixo replies, at the precise moment that the elevator comes to the landing.

"In that case, I'll go down and wait for you there," Gaspar says, now inside the elevator, after telling the operator to go stop.

"All right, I'll see you soon," replies Aleixo, coming out onto the landing, where the butler and the porter with his bags are waiting for him, ready to accompany him to his room. It is a spacious compartment on the corner of the building, with two high windows on each of the outer walls, decorated with thick *grenat* velvet valance curtain rails. The interior is sober, but comfortable, from the yellow and white striped silk linings of the walls, contrasting with the more intense color of the curtains, to the several items of furniture elegantly distributed about the room: two brass English-style beds, with a chest of drawers and toilet-table next to it, two ottomans and a low table in the corner, and a beautiful, inviting English-style writing desk between two windows giving on to the 1.o de Dezembro street. At the entrance, on the left side, there is a spacious private bathroom, walls, and floor lined in marble, and in the middle, an impressive brass bathtub with a shower head in the corner, which Aleixo orders to run as soon as the butler has finished unpacking his bag.

"So, how do you feel?" Gaspar asks him as soon as he sees him appear at the door to the bar, wearing a starched shirt, white *papillon*, black jacket, and matching striped trousers.

"Like a new man, after a quick but invigorating *bain douche*."

"How do you like the bedroom?"

"Luxury. On a par with the best in Paris. Our brother Luiz was right when he stayed here for the inauguration of the monument to Sousa Martins: compared to this, the old Braganza is a veritable hovel."

"I'm glad. I'm pleased you like it. At the moment it's the best hotel in Lisbon, many pegs above all the rest," says Gaspar, motioning to the butler to fill up another glass of champagne, which he then passes to his brother.

"Here's to you, Aleixinho, for this yet another extraordinary triumph, there in far-off Bulgaria," he toasts, raising his glass and slightly clinking his brother's.

"Thank you very much, Gasparinho, for your good wishes and your friendship and dedication," Aleixo replies, touched.

"Shall we go to the dining room?" asks Gaspar when they have both emptied their glasses.

"Let's go," replies Aleixo, walking towards the glass door that gives on to the restaurant, a spacious rectangular room that occupies almost all of the front of the building facing the Liberdade avenue, lit up by three enormous chandeliers hanging from a high ceiling, made up of worked stucco, walls with mahogany wainscoting panels, covered up to the ceiling in light velvet with floral patterns, contrasting with thick valance curtain rails in old pink framing the high inset windows. The tables, set for four people, are set out in three rows, one in the middle and two along each of the side walls.

"Sir and company, please do me the honor of following me," says the *maître d'hôtel* eagerly as soon as he sees them enter the room, then accompanying them to one of the still empty tables, next to the central window, from which they can see the monument to the Restauradores Square and the Avenue, all lit up.

"Well, for someone who has just come back from Paris, probably you didn't feel like this type of food," Gaspar suddenly realizes, flicking through the menu, made up completely of French cuisine.

"Yes, a roast cod with oven-baked new potatoes in olive oil, or liver and onions might perhaps go down better when recently arriving," Aleixo replies with a smirk. "But these *Filets de Sole à Cherbourg* might be just as good. And it's lighter food as well."

"Do you want soup? I've already tried this *Potage Reine Margot* and it is excellent," suggests Gaspar, immediately obtaining the agreement of his brother, who is busy observing the surrounding tables, full of a distinguished clientele made up in the main by foreigners who were guests at the hotel, added to by some well-known faces here and there, politicians and society people.

"So what are your impressions of the World Exposition?" asks Gaspar, after giving instructions to the *maître d'hotel*.

"An absolutely extraordinary event. Forty-odd million visitors according to the latest figures. And now, with the great influx of the last few days, it is foreseen to be fifty."

"Hasn't it closed yet?"

"It was supposed to close, but it was decided to extend it a few days. So much to see, to visit, you can't imagine. Starting with the pavilions of the several different countries, all located along the right bank of the Seine, on the Rue des Nations, some of which are absolutely remarkable, both in terms of architecture and in what one could see inside them. And ending in the many buildings constructed especially for the occasion, such as the Palais de l'Électricité, all dedicated to showing the extraordinary potential of electric energy, or the Château d'Eau, with its fantastic fountains and jets of water. Or the Petit and the Grand Palais, veritable temples devoted to the arts, and the Rue de Paris and the Vieux Paris, where there is the large amusement park, with its many theatres and cabarets, its restaurants and bars, and I don't know what else."

"What were the art exhibitions like?" insists Gaspar, as one of the waiters comes over with a terrine to serve the soup.

"Overwhelming. At the Grand Palais there were the major exhibitions of painting and sculpture, with the official representation of the different countries present, including Portugal. But while the painting was organized into rooms according to the different countries, the sculptures, given the large size of many of the works present, was all in a single space, corresponding to the central nave of the building, and covered by an enormous glass skylight. In the Petit Palais, there were retrospectives of French art, one covering the last decade and the other one the century. Besides this, there was a pavilion in the Place de l'Alma, totally devoted to the work of Rodin."

"Where were your works in the middle of all this?"

"In the Grand Palais, as a part of the great exhibition of sculpture, along with the works of the other Portuguese artists. And where I could also see the remarkable works by my friend Saint-Gaudens, the great American sculptor I told you about."

"What a pity! What a pity I couldn't go to see all those wonders with my own eyes. I had everything prepared to go in July, but with the unexpected fall of the government it ended up being impossible."

"You don't know what you missed," replies Aleixo, dipping his spoon into the soup, waiting for his brother to finally broach the only subject of conversation that matters to him: the latest news about the monument to Sousa Martins.

"Did you manage to ride on that train that goes across Paris underground? A friend of mine, who came from Paris a short while ago, was absolutely amazed after he took the trip. He says it is the means of transport of the future, at least in the big cities," Gaspar continues, as if nothing else mattered.

"Ah, yes, the *métropolitain*. It is a truly remarkable invention, that is true. Allowing one to go across the whole city, from the Porte de Vincennes to the Porte Maillot, in only a few minutes. Avoiding the traffic problems that are increasing on the surface, aggravated by the growing number of cars and carts on the streets. A fast, modern 'mole', Eça de Queiroz called it the last time I saw him in Paris at the Consulate, very concerned about the disturbance caused by the works that had turned the city upside down at the time."

"Our great Eça. Now he's gone, poor man, this summer."

"True. But what he suffered from must have been an old illness you know? That time I was with him in the Consulate, shortly after I had received my award from Emperor Ménélik, I found him rather weak and run down, convalescing from what he called agues, a swamp fever. Which he must have caught on one of those trips he made to the Middle East. Or during his stay in Cuba."

"Well, there are the most diverse and varied opinions and versions about that. But at least he had the right to a grand funeral, with the presence of the whole government, representatives of the King and Queen, and a lot of people on the streets. But, irony of ironies, when they came to the Oriental Cemetery and went to put the urn, which had come from France, in the crypt… Well, it wouldn't fit."

"You're joking. So what did they do then to solve the problem?"

"They had to leave it in the cemetery chapel, waiting for a solution."

"It sounds like a scene from one of his novels. And it's a good metaphor for our atavism, our narrowness in seeing things. Which he certainly wouldn't have passed up," concludes Aleixo, preparing himself to finally hear the news for which he is so anxious.

"And now, I'm very sorry, but… I want to hear everything about that rousing success of yours in Bulgaria, from the beginning to the end," he says, impenetrable at the end of his *Potage*.

"What can I tell you, lad? The truth is that besides what you have read in the newspapers there isn't much else to tell," replies Aleixo, unable to disguise his frustration.

"Not much else to tell? You go abroad the way you did, destroyed by the attacks targeted at your monument, you cross Europe from one end to the other to Bulgaria, and in five months you create that which is probably your best work up to now; you manage to be applauded by the press and the public opinion of the whole country, you see the most important Bulgarian poets dedicating lines to your work, you have the Prince of Bulgaria lending you his own horse as a model and offering you a position as a teacher at the Sofia School of Fine Arts, and now you come here and tell me—your brother—that there isn't much else to tell me other than that which was said in the newspapers?" insists Gaspar, not giving up easily.

"If you must know I myself am the first to be surprised and to find it difficult to understand what really went on," replies Aleixo, yielding to his brother's insatiable curiosity.

"Cripes, how did you manage to do all this in so little time? How did you get to such a point of trust with the Prince for him to have such attention for you, prepared to let you use his own horse?" Gaspar continues, after tasting the fillets of plaice accompanied by roast potatoes and stir-fried vegetables which one of the waiters had just brought him.

"Well, the letter of recommendation from King Carlos was a great help. As soon as I arrived I went to the palace to ask for an audience to give it personally to Prince Ferdinand, which happened two or three days later. And then I started to be invited to receptions and even to the more intimate dinners, during which I was able to talk at length to the Prince about the most varied issues, from art to politics, including the similarities between Bulgaria and Portugal. Indeed, Prince Ferdinand showed great warmth and appreciation for our country, often recalling his stay in Lisbon during the ceremonies for the wedding of King Carlos and Queen Amélia."

"And what was the business of the horse about?"

"As simple as that. During one of those conversations, I thought of asking him where I could find a horse to use as a model for the Czar's horse. And he told me to go to the Palace stables the next day to see what they could come up with. Imagine my amazement when I got there and they presented me with a beautiful Arab thoroughbred and told me it was *Sultan*, one of the Prince's own horses, given to him by the Emperor of Turkey."

"I bet your colleagues were green with envy, right?"

"When they found out at the Fine Arts School that I was in the Palace stables doing sittings with the Prince's horse, accusations of favoritism started to go around immediately, as all the other competitors had to be content with extremely ordinary horses from the Bulgarian National Guard," Aleixo explains, as the *maître d'hôtel* comes over to ask what dessert they would like. Both of them opt for *poires au vin*, followed by coffee.

"And when did the Prince invite you to teach at the Fine Arts School?" Gaspar also wants to know.

"Towards the end, a few days before I left," Aleixo replies, increasingly convinced that his brother is deliberately avoiding the subject of the monument to Sousa Martins, for whatever reason.

"And you didn't even consider accepting?"

"Yes. Because of the kindness shown me by the Prince and all those people I must confess I hesitated somewhat. But then, thinking about what it would be like to live lost at the ends of Europe, so far from my friends and family, I ended up politely refusing," replies Aleixo, unable not to think about Maria for a moment, who was so close to convincing him to stay.

"It might have been a very interesting experience for you."

"Nothing is stopping me from reconsidering my position someday. But not now, for the moment I needed to come back to Lisbon, to take advantage of this international recognition I have just received to try to stop the demolition of the Sousa Martins. Because if I didn't do so I would be giving my detractors, on a plate, the decisive argument for them to achieve their designs, accusing me of having fled from these difficulties because I didn't have the courage to stand up in its defense," he adds, taking advantage of this connection to introduce this issue he was so anxious to hear about.

"If that was the reason you turned down the Prince's invitation I think you made a mistake," pronounces Gaspar.

"Why do you say that? Is there any news?" asks Aleixo, suddenly restless.

"Yes and it's not good," replies Gaspar, now unable to avoid the subject much longer.

"What's going on then? Can't you tell me?" insists Aleixo, preparing himself for the worst.

"I don't know how to tell you this any other way, Aleixinho, so the best thing is to get straight to the point: yesterday Lisbon Council authorized the demolition of your monument and its replacement with a different one," Gaspar replies uneasily after a few seconds of hesitation.

"That's not possible. The Council can't authorize something like this without the prior agreement of the executive committee. And of the great committee, for God's sake," Aleixo replies, suddenly very pale and with the blood rushing out of his face.

"That's the problem. Those knaves have already given their consent. And, according to today's *Século*, unanimously.

"No, that's impossible. They can't do that," says Aleixo furiously. "Don't they have an ounce of shame in their bodies? Allowing the pure and simple destruction of a work made by public subscription, the making of which was controlled by them in all details, just because some articles came out in the newspapers inspired by the envy and jealousy of those who are not able to bear other people's success? It's a unique case in the whole of Europe..."

"...calm down, Aleixinho, calm down and keep a cool head..." says Gaspar, holding his arm.

"...if they didn't like my design, my monument, they should have said so before it was built, placed, and solemnly inaugurated, not afterwards. Like they did with Rodin's Balzac. They had plenty of opportunities to do so," continues Aleixo, indifferent to his brother's appeals.

"You're quite right, it would have been much more honest and correct of them. But what do you expect? This isn't France. In this country no one ever accepts their responsibilities at the right time," says Gaspar, finishing his coffee.

"I'll tell you one thing. If this really goes ahead they will have to answer for this affront, this attack on art and my good name. Mark my words. The gentlemen of the Committee and the Council."

"Well, if you are talking about a suit for damages and losses then I, as your lawyer, strongly advise you against it."

"Against it? So you think this is acceptable? You think that a supposed group of friends of a public figure like Sousa Martins can go to the Council and without any serious justification ask for the demolition of a monument that they themselves approved and had built for it to be replaced by another one? And that the Council should accept this request without any further explanation?"

"You are totally and absolutely right, it is a complete scandal, from start to finish. But even so, in relation to a lawsuit, I maintain my opinion."

"Why? Can you explain why you think so?"

"Because you are not thinking about one very important detail: in the meantime, the government led by José Luciano de Castro fell and a regeneration party government has since taken office, presided over by Hintze Ribeiro. And that makes all the difference. Because, and don't doubt this for a second, if I were still the Minister of Treasury Secretary and a Member of the Parliament this would never have gotten as far as it has. There would always be criticism, but a demolition? They would never risk going so far. Neither the committee nor the council. If they are doing so it is because they feel protected, because they know that the government supports them, a government that is only happy when it is denigrating and destroying everything that was done or supported by the previous one."

"But what has that got to do with the courts and with the application of the law?"

"Apparently nothing. But in practice everything. There are always commitments and influences, people moving in the shadows, like the sinister Casimiro José de Lima and others. Indeed, what they have managed to do in only a half dozen months is the best proof of what I'm saying."

"So you mean that they could bring about influence over the judges in order to get a favorable decision?"

"Yes. Absolutely. With this revanchist spirit acting at the highest level of government and the testimonies of your many detractors, big-wigs like Fialho de Almeida, Ribeiro Arthur, and José de Figueiredo, you can be sure that the most likely outcome would be for them to win, alleging that you did not keep to your part, that you did not correctly carry out the model that they approved."

"So such an international recognition like this I have just achieved, is of no use in the courts, for the Portuguese justice?"

"Very little use. If Rodin had replied to your letter, defending the quality of your monument, perhaps the tune might have been different, but unfortunately, he didn't, for whatever reason."

"He probably didn't have the time. He's too busy with his pavilion in the World Exposition."

"Your bad luck. Because concerning your success in Bulgaria they will certainly belittle it, saying that they are not at all interested in what happens or happened there, which is a country in the boondocks of Europe. That what matters to them is what happens here. And here your work, which is what is at issue, is no good; it is a veritable monstrosity."

"So you are saying that nothing can be done, that I should shrug my shoulders and accept the idea of the demolition?" asks Aleixo, downcast, his coffee going cold in front of him.

"I think you've got no choice, no matter how hard that is. But above all I think you should make an effort to move forward, not to lose heart, to make the best of this new international success of yours to get new work."

"Who's going to give me work from now on if my name here is ridiculed and mocked every day in the humorous newspapers? If my only work built and inaugurated in Lisbon will be inexorably demolished by the council cavil without anyone raising a finger or saying a single word in its defense—who, tell me?"

"If not here, it'll be abroad, in Bulgaria, in Paris, or somewhere else."

"I don't know. I have to think, I have to reflect very maturely on all this to decide what to do. And now, if you'll excuse me, I'm going for a stroll, I need fresh air," says Aleixo, wiping the sweat running over his brow with a handkerchief before standing up.

"Don't you want me to come with you? We can go to Chiado, to Silva's, and drink a cognac."

"Don't take it wrong, Gaspar, but I prefer to go alone, to stroll around Rossio Square, or even down to the Terreiro do Paço, to cool my head down."

"If that's what you prefer. But are you sure you'll be fine?" asks Gaspar, concerned.

"Don't worry, Gaspar. And thank you again for your advice. And your frankness," replies Aleixo, turning and then walking towards the exit door.

XXI

Ponte de Lima, 17th of December, 1914

"THE BRIDGE MUST BE DESTROYED"—he was dumbstruck as he read the headline of the editorial in the latest issue of the *Comércio do Lima* newspaper, a veritable death sentence for the old monument that gave the town of Ponte de Lima its name and was its calling card image, here considered, right in the first paragraph, as the major factor responsible for the damage caused by the enormous floods that had completely swamped the town and the neighborhood of Além-da-Ponte during the previous week.

"We need a bridge that is built using the modern system, or, if this work cannot be completed now, as it is very costly, the destruction of three or four arches in the existing bridge, replacing them with an iron platform—thus making it much easier for the water to flow out on the occasions of major flooding," he read further on, before coming to the final appeal "to all of the local population, without regard to political tendency and merely for the good and progress of this town, to all of those who have preponderant influence," to use "all their efforts, all their goodwill and all of their energy to achieve the desired result."

How was it possible for a newspaper with the traditions and honors of the *Comércio do Lima*, whose collaborators had included people like João Gomes de Abreu e Lima, João Caetano da Silva Campos, Francisco Teixeira de Queiroz, the great poet and diplomat António Feijó, and his own Uncle Gonçalo, Count of Bertiandos, to quote just a few names, and whose director was Pelagio dos Reys Lemos, the grandson of that great adopted Ponte do Lima citizen who went by the name of Miguel Roque dos Reys Lemos, a man who had done so much for the preservation and divulging of the borough's culture and extremely rich artistic and architectural heritage, to launch such a campaign on its pages, having the effrontery to state that in doing so it was interpreting "the general feelings of the Pont do Lima people"? he wondered indignantly, springing up from his leather armchair near to the fire and pacing up and down with his arms crossed behind his back and staring at the floor of the library, with its plaster ceiling, walls lined all round with austere chestnut wood bookshelves full of beautifully bound books.

Yes, because if the bridge made it somehow difficult for flood water to flow past, this was due to the fact that the riverbed was completely silted up, meaning that when there was a lot of water, as had happened the previous week, the stream came out of its natural path and quickly burst its banks. And that the water level would immediately increase given that the trees, stones, and debris that the stream would inevitably drag with it would end up obstructing a good deal of the arches that supported the bridge. It wasn't necessary to be a specialist in hydraulics or a bridge and paving engineer to understand that the solution to the problem of the flooding would need, not obviously the destruction of the bridge—an idea that could only enter the minds of people who were ignorant and short-sighted—but dredging of the riverbed upstream and downstream, as well as the regularization of its banks from its source to its mouth, thus once and for all avoiding the rise in the water to levels that might jeopardize the safety of the local populations and their belongings. And of the bridge itself, which according to another article he had read in the *Comércio*, had its stone parapet destroyed in several places along its course, he recalled, suddenly stopping to take out his silver cigarette case given to him by his Uncle Gonçalo on his eighteenth birthday in April, now resting on the ebony desk where he kept the paperwork for the administration of his houses and kept up with his correspondence, there in the corner of the library, near to one of the balcony windows. Now, to attribute the responsibility for the damage caused by the floods to a monument that had been there since the first century, in the case of the Roman bridge, and since the fourteenth century, in the case of the gothic bridge, was a sign of myopia, ignorance or simple stupidity, which not even the natural despair and consternation over the damage caused during the floods could excuse. That is not to mention the proposal for its destruction and replacement by "a bridge built using the modern system," or, in a more moderate version, the destruction of three or four arches and their replacement by an iron platform because in this case, the nonsense was bordering on the most complete mental weakness. How could anyone in their right mind imagine a bridge like that, with centuries upon centuries of history and tradition, being destroyed until no trace remained, no memory for the coming generations, to give way to a new bridge, or to have a part of its structure amputated and have an iron platform replace it, in total dissonance and disharmony with the rest of the monument, just so the floodwaters could "flow out more easily"? he asked himself, after lighting his cigarette and looking at the cloud-laden sky through the steamed-up panes of the window. No, never on earth. And if it was necessary to form a popular opinion movement in defense of the bridge he would be there, ready and available for whatever it might take, he decided, starting to walk back and forth in the library again as he started to draw up a plan of action: first to go and see the damage caused on the bridge and nearby, as the previous day, when he had arrived from Coimbra, it was too late to do so, and he had spent the morning finding out about the damage caused by the floods and the bad weather on his several different properties; then a trip to the Café Camões looking for supporters for his cause among those regulars he knew and might be there. And once he had presented and debated the issue with them he could right away start drawing up a manifesto against the demolition of the old bridge, instead of defending the dredging of the river and the regularization of its banks from its source to its mouth. And which would then be sent to the local newspapers, the *Cardeal Saraiva* and the *Comércio* itself, he thought before looking at his pocket watch, its hands showing two-thirty. The ideal time to catch some friends and influential figures locally at the café, where they usually got together after lunch for a coffee and chat, he said to himself, putting out his cigarette in the ashtray before turning around and going out through the door to the beautiful, spacious living room and taking his leave of his aunt Ana, the only permanent resident of that house for several years now, sitting by the fire and busy knitting. From there he passed through the Arms Room, magnificently decorated with shields and swords belonging to the several different generations of first-born sons of the family, who could also be seen in some oil paintings on the wall, from which he came out into the long and wide stairway connecting to the ground floor, the steps of which he descended two at a time, not without previously taking his hat and raincoat hanging on the coat rack, and then finally, almost running, he crossed the enormous vestibule towards the heavy door.

Outside, he raised his face and looked at the clouds, noting the uncertain weather, threatening rain, as he walked down the Vasco da Gama Street, opposite the pompously named Hotel do Arrabalde, a modest establishment with a half dozen bedrooms and a room for meals, the property of a Galician Spaniard called Manolo before he came to the São João square and turned right on the way to the river and the bridge. The thick, brown waters and the great deal of mud and rubble that they dragged with them were still running with appreciable speed, covering a large part of the sandbanks next to the left bank, but now somewhat lower than the level of the bridge, the arches of which were now totally uncovered and unobstructed, he noticed as he walked towards the other bank among a group of people, carriages and carts that were coming and going, until he stopped at one of the places where the stones from the parapet had been destroyed on both sides over several meters. A clear indication that the waters, in their fury, had overrun the bridge, dragging everything they could with them, which to a certain extent explained that outrageous idea that had sprung up in some minds that this was the major cause of the flooding of the banks, he thought as he stooped down to observe the damage more closely. Further on, close to the Church of St. Anthony of the Old Tower, there was another break in the parapet, he noted as he stood in the middle of the platform, unable not to cast a quick, anguished glance to his right, seeking that little pearl of a unique and extremely original monument that was the Chapel of the Guardian Angel, until he finally spotted it in the distance, half-submerged by the flowing waters of the river. Having gone past the Church of St. Anthony, he entered the Roman bridge, which was obviously narrower and rougher than the Gothic one, with its almost nineteen centuries of existence, which he followed until he came to the small Largo de Alexandre Herculano, still, with visible signs of the violence of the waters in the holes in the pavement and the sand all over the place, he noted before he turned round to go back to the town, passing among new waves of passers-by, some of whom tipped their hats to him and greeted him ceremoniously, as if they had known him forever. Once he had crossed the bridge he carried on to the center of the main square, near to the fountain, where, even more than in the case of the Alexandre Herculano square, there were visible effects of the floods, with benches ripped up, large quantities of sand deposited by the river waters, fallen trees, and cobbled pavements raised in several different places, he noted before entering the Café Camões, located more or less in the middle of the line of buildings that closed off the square on the side opposite to the river, its walls coated with framed mirrors over varnished light-colored wood wainscoting, black and white checkered mosaic floors, plaster ceilings from which hung two enormous chandeliers, and square tables with marble tops accompanied by comfortable chairs with red leather seats and backs, made in the same wood as the wainscoting.

"Look who's here! It's Zé Aurora!" he suddenly heard someone shout from one of the side tables, being none other than his dear friend Júlio Pereira Pinto, a companion in evening discussions and parties during the summer holidays, who immediately stood up ready to greet him. "Or should I rather say Count of Aurora?" he added, smirking.

"No, man. It's too soon for that. How are you, Júlio?" he greeted, holding his hand out to his friend, disguising his surprise at hearing his noble title being mentioned out loud in public for the first time.

"Never been better," replied Júlio Pinto, very well dressed in his dark brown suit, round-collared shirt, and modern tie, smiling and pointing to the chair opposite his before sitting down himself. "So, when did you arrive?"

"Last night. Straight from Coimbra," he replied, signaling to one of the waiters to bring him a coffee.

"What's the news from there?"

"The same old same old. What about here? Everyone's still in shock because of the effects of the floods, then?" he asked, as the waiter set down a cup of coffee and the sugar bowl in front of him.

"And shouldn't they be? Have you seen the state of the bridge?"

"I've just come from there now. The power of the waters is indeed impressive, to be able to drag those really heavy stones like that. But to go from there to consider that the bridge is responsible for the damage and destruction caused is a great distance," he stated, staring at his friend, after putting two spoonfuls of sugar in his coffee.

"Ah, so you've read the latest issue of the *Comércio*," his friend immediately deduced.

"Of course. And I'm furious, as you can imagine. How can a serious newspaper with traditions like the *Comércio do Lima* have the effrontery to set off on a public opinion campaign in favor of the demolition of a monument with so many centuries of history as our bridge?" he asked, after first sipping at his coffee.

"And which, for your information, the *Cardeal Saraiva* enthusiastically supports in today's issue," said Júlio Pinto, picking up the newspaper on the table and then reading out loud:

"In its last issue, our illustrious local colleague, *Comércio do Lima*, began its campaign in favor of the removal of that impediment to the fast and free-flowing waters of the River Lima and we second it with pleasure, certain that someone will take the field to defend the higher interests of Ponte do Lima."

"A scandal, a disgrace. And a demonstration of a deep lack of affection and disrespect for our region, its traditions, and its monuments, which deep down is what grants the reason for existence and identity to our souls as Portuguese and people from Minho.

"But the idea is being rather well accepted by the powers that be here. It is said that there have even been contacts made with the Minister for Development, to try to get him to come here and convince him of the advantages of the demolition."

"So now it is necessary to do something to go against that idea, don't you think?" he asked, holding his cup of coffee before taking his final sip.

"You don't say?"

"A manifesto, for example. A manifesto in defense of the bridge, against its demolition that we would give to be signed by the important figures in the area, who cannot be in favor of such an idea. People like João Gomes d'Abreu e Lima, Francisco Teixeira de Queiroz, Francisco de Abreu Coutinho, the Count of Calheiros, and my Uncle Gonçalo, Count of Bertiandos..."

"...and the Count of Santa Eulália, if you don't mind, while you're on the subject. Who, so it seems, is the only person to have openly declared himself against the demolition up to now."

"Really? Where?" Aurora was curious to know, taking his open cigarette box, which he handed to his friend.

"It appears he went to the editorial office of the *Comércio* yesterday, giving a piece of his mind to Pelágio. That it was a disgrace, an outrage, to be starting up a campaign for the demolition of a monument such as this, with so many centuries of history. That is, in other words, exactly what you just said," said Júlio, after taking a cigarette and putting it in his mouth, leaning his head towards the lit match held out to him by Aurora.

"You don't say. Now there's someone with sensitivity and intelligence enough to understand what's at stake. Not surprising though, he's an artist, a man of culture, who knows how to recognize the historic and artistic value of a monument like our bridge. We have to contact him quickly," proposed Aurora, after also lighting his own cigarette.

"Here in the town, it is difficult to find him. Only if we go to his house, Glória."

"Why not? I've got a free afternoon. I've dealt with everything I have to do today," replied Aurora, after taking two or three puffs on his cigarette without a break and without swallowing.

"Do you know him?"

"Hardly. I remember him here a few years ago, in Bertiandos visiting my uncle, one time when he came here with his American wife. In the end, they stayed for dinner."

"What did you think of him?"

"Well, I must have been about thirteen or fourteen years old, if that much, but I remember it like it was today. He was very correct and charming, in his white linen suit, hair parted down the middle, thin upturned mustache, pleasant, a nice conversation; she very elegant in a light colored dress, very tight at the waist, and a beautiful tiara on her head," Aurora recalled, his eyes sparkling.

"Do you think he will still remember you?"

"Probably not, but I'll make myself remembered."

"So it's decided. Let's go," said Júlio, leaving some coins on the table, after which they both stood up and walked along the aisle towards the exit, among the tables already half empty at that time.

"Do you know how to get there?" José Aurora asked his friend as they were crossing the square towards the street that connected to the parish church, where several carriages for hire were parked.

"Yes. We go to Refojos along the Arcos road and then we take the Count's road," explained Júlio.

"The Count's road?" Aurora found this strange.

"Yes, that's what people are already calling the road that he, Santa

Eulália, had recently opened up to there, to Glória. It is a much shorter course and much better laid out than going the other way, through Jolda. And the view is surprising," explained Júlio Pinto, before going to the driver of the carriage at the front, to explain the course for him to follow.

"But how did he, a private citizen, manage to convince the landowners to let him cross their lands with the road he built? Aurora asked curiously, when they were now inside the carriage, going round the Praça de Camões square to the bridge.

"Oh that. By buying their properties. From Cedofeitas to there, to Glória, is all his. Which, added to the monastery estate, they say is about twelve hundred acres."

"That's a giant area, man! they only have properties of that size on the Alentejo plains," said José Aurora, surprised. "What does he do with them?"

"Nothing special. They're run by keepers, whom they say he doesn't even bother charging rent."

"And what happened to the model estate that he proposed to set up in Refojos, on the convent grounds?" Aurora also wished to know, as they were passing over the part of the bridge where the water had destroyed the parapets.

"Well, that's just it. He spent loads of money on machinery and very modern agricultural equipment, which he had sent from the United States, to carry out intensive grain farming, he planted hundreds of vines and fruit trees in orchards. And all for nothing: the corn and the grain didn't take, half of the vines dried up and the fruit trees withered, they don't grow. But he doesn't seem to mind much, because in the meantime he has decided to go back to horse breeding. He says he wants to set up a stud farm as good as anything done abroad.

"Well, with horse-drawn carriages being replaced more and more by cars, it shouldn't be a great business. But even so, it is an interesting idea. And he knows about horses if my Uncle Gonçalo is to be believed."

"Particularly about driving them wildly around these roads frightening everyone. Just the other day I saw him go past here on this road in a carriage pulled by two pairs of Lusitano horses and with two English mares as outriders…" said Júlio, when after passing the place called Além da Ponte they entered the Arcos road.

"At least that means six-horse pulling in the same direction."

"And as the horses haven't been gelded…" added Júlio with a malicious glance.

"You can't be serious! So the poor Lusitanos keep on running to see if they can catch the mares…" Aurora interrupted with a guffaw.

"They get up such a speed that he always has a beater up ahead, a servant in a *charrette*, pulled by four colts. So no one gets in his way, otherwise, it is certain death," stated Júlio.

"And what has happened to the monastery in the end? Hadn't he also promised to restore it?"

"What I have heard is that he installed acetylene lamps in all the cells and connected all the outer walls of the cloister to make an enormous water tank, a pool…"

"A pool? What for?" questioned Aurora, at the same time noting the entrance to the access drive to the beautiful Paço de Calheiros, on the left, a solid eighteenth-century construction with a chapel, veranda, and two turrets, which he could glimpse for a second from the following bend in the road.

"I don't know anything about it, but some people swear they saw him drive by in a gondola, that he brought over from Venice," Júlio replied, with a smirk.

"A gondola? From Venice? I don't believe it. It can't be true."

"I'm just telling you what I was told, nothing else, because I didn't see it," Júlio Pinto stressed as they drove up the São Simão hill, with its very white chapel at the top, standing out against the dense, leafy greenery covering the whole of the hillside.

"So when he is here where does he live? In the monastery or Glória?"

"In Glória, although he goes almost every day to the monastery. It is even said that he has a little something going on there," said Júlio with a twinkle in his eye.

"A nobleman like him, a believer and God-fearing man, married to such a distinguished woman from the highest ranks of American society? I do not believe it," stated Aurora firmly.

"Well, I've been told her name is Branca and she acts as his house-keeper over at the monastery."

"And what proof of this is there? And how on Earth do you know all this?"

"My dear sir, this is a small, tight community. Everyone knows everything, unlike in the city. Don't ask me whether it is true or not. But, as the saying goes, 'where there's smoke there's fire'. Indeed, the same is true about the burglary on Glória last year..."

"What burglary? I don't know anything about this," asked José Aurora, stupefied.

"A very strange case which has yet to be explained. Everything was splashed all over the local newspapers. Several persons traveling in a powerful motorized vehicle, which is very rare to see around here, taking advantage of a time when no one was here, given that he and the American woman had gone to Lisbon and the housekeeper had also gone out, went through the gates and drove up to the house, broke down one of the doors to the kitchen and entered..."

"...stealing everything they could, I imagine..." interrupted Aurora.

"That's where you are wrong because they took nothing. They just broke and smashed up everything they could, including all the many works of art and precious objects that were there, some of which were very valuable, as you might imagine. And then they did the same in the chapel, destroying the altars and ripping out the images, which were spread about the ground and smashed. Having finished their 'work' they left the house, got back into their vehicle, and sped off away," he explained.

"All of this is really, really strange. What conclusion did the authorities come to in the end?"

"None. Because he apparently did not file a complaint. But the word around here is that it was political vengeance, as some people say he donated a lot of money to finance the monarchist insurrections of Paiva Couceiro," said Júlio, to his friend's great surprise, now that in the distance one could begin to see the immense wall of the monastery, standing impressively among the houses of the town of Refojos.

"Look, if he did so it just proves he is a true patriot, who cares about the destiny of his country. Because this, with the republic, is obviously not going anywhere," Aurora let out as he lit another cigarette.

"Here we are finally coming to the road that he opened to the Paço da Glória," said Júlio Pinto, leaning out of the carriage window as it was slowing down to enter a wide, well-cobbled driveway leading up the hillside over Refojos.

"Paço da Glória? Since when has it been a Paço? I always heard my uncle call it House of Glória or Glória Estate, but never Paço. Because for a house to be called Paço a king would have to have slept there at least one night, as you know " Aurora explained.

"Good question. As long as I've known it has always been the House or Estate of Glória. Only just recently, since he's been here, have they been calling it a Paço," Júlio recalled, as they were passing a little hamlet with a half dozen houses before they entered a thick woodland.

"It's probably another of his 'fancies,' added to all the others you mentioned. And that I knew almost nothing about until now. Because in fact the little that I knew was told to me by my Uncle Gonçalo, and only included one or two extravagances. Everything else had much more to do with his career as an artist, as a sculptor," continued Aurora, as the carriage advanced around the bends in the road through the leafy stone pine and oak woods.

"He, a sculptor? I didn't know that," stated Júlio Pinto, surprised.

"Why, yes. He is the author of that statue of the Sacred Heart of Jesus on the Santa Luzia Hill opposite the church being built."

"You don't say! I would never have imagined it."

"And according to my Uncle Gonçalo he had a somewhat auspicious career in Paris, where he studied, with several works exhibited in the Salons, a grand Prix, and very favorable references in several French newspapers…"

"…Well, to listen to you it seems that we are not talking about the same person…" Júlio interrupted, stupefied by what he had just heard, at the moment they were coming out of the wood to start to descend the bends of the slope, passing by the terraces and trellises of the surrounding estates.

"What a view! How stunning!" said Aurora, looking ecstatically at the extraordinary landscape that was now opening up before him, made of steep slopes and deep valleys, with small meadows and fields, plowed and planted, standing out against the deeper green of the woods, dotted here and there by the white color of the houses.

"Everything you see around you belongs to him. That wood down there, they say he bought it intending to cut down all the trees so from his bedroom window he could see the Boavista house, where he was born. Imagine," said Júlio, pointing to a dense green expanse covering a hillock down below on the right.

"You don't say."

"It's true. He only didn't go ahead with his intentions because the groundskeeper managed to make him see the enormous mistake he was about to commit. Over there, ahead on the left, is the Granja estate, with that beautiful mansion. Which has been restored by him, making use of the stones from the Remédios Monastery that he didn't use on Glória," explained Júlio Pinto, pointing to a pretty two-floor construction set on a hilltop and surrounded by layers of terraces down the hillside.

"It's hard to believe that someone could afford to buy all these properties just to open up a road. Which has no other purpose than to save him some time and discomfort when he goes from one house to another, among the many houses he possesses," commented Aurora, pensively.

"And now, from here on we are in the Glória estate," said Júlio, after they passed through a stone gate, followed by a wide, straight road bordered by supports distributed regularly along the route which were the bases for slim iron arches connected by wires and on which grew vines, at the moment without any leaves. Two or three hundred meters ahead the road veered to the right and then to the left again, passing through a beautiful and unusual three round-arched stone portico set on elegant cylindrical columns with capitals and giving on to a further gate. Passing through this, they continued along a stone-paved path to the wide courtyard in front of the house, where a servant, no doubt alerted by the noise of the cart's wheels on the cobbles, was waiting for them. It had not been more than five minutes since Aurora had given his calling card to the boy instructing him to hand it to his employer when they began to hear a sudden and intense pealing of bells coming from the other side of the house, to which they immediately went, in time to see, as they looked up above the seven full stone arches of the loggia that occupied the central part of the facade to see real church bells ringing out, while the Count of Santa Eulália, in his shirt sleeves and wearing no hat, serge trousers tucked into riding boots, was coming down the steps smiling to greet them.

"Our apologies for this intrusion, Count, but the issue that brings us here is serious," young Aurora began by saying a little haughtily, before introducing his friend.

"Not to worry. There's no need to apologize. It's a pleasure to receive you here in this your house," replied Santa Eulália, greeting them effusively. "So? What do you think of my bells?"

"They have an excellent sound," replied Aurora, hardly recovered from the surprise.

"They are from the church of the extinct Remédios Monastery, in Braga. They arrived with the demolition stones, and as I didn't know what to do with them I decided to hang them in the arches on the balcony, to ring every time we have visitors," said Santa Eulália smiling, with a sweeping gesture to the balcony, as the bells slowly returned to silence.

"Good use, no doubt at all," added Júlio as he gave a panoramic glance around the wide yard in front of the house.

"How you have grown, boy. The last time I saw you, over in Bertiandos, you were still in short trousers. And now you are a man. How old are you?" observed the Count, looking José Aurora up and down, as he suddenly blushed at finding himself thoroughly looked over, with his thin, weak body swimming inside his modern mackintosh, bright, very blue eyes, hair parted at the side, impeccably combed with hair cream.

"Eighteen. In April."

"And how are your studies going?"

"They're not going so badly."

"What year are you in?"

"I'm in the third year of Law. At Coimbra."

"Ah, very good. And do you know what career you are going to follow when you finish? A judge, like your father?"

"Yes. It's a possibility I am considering, but I don't know yet exactly. When I finish we'll see," Aurora replied evasively.

"Well, would you like to see the house?" asked Santa Eulália, putting an end to his inquiries.

"As long as we're not disturbing you…"

"Not at all. I'm very pleased to show you," he replied, motioning for them to follow him.

"In that case, thank you. My Uncle Gonçalo never tires of praising the recuperation and restoration work you have carried out here, Count sir," stressed Aurora.

"Not Count. A count never uses a title to another count. Call me cousin," interrupted Santa Eulália.

"Cousin?" Aurora found this strange, unaware of any close or distant relationship between them.

"Yes, cousin. We blue-blooded from Minho are all cousins to each other. If only because we are all direct descendants of King Afonso Henriques," Santa Eulália insisted, ironically.

"The house is indeed very original and different from anything else one sees here in the Minho. And the restoration has been so well done that it is difficult to tell what was added from what was already there," noted Júlio Pinto, who was not a blue-blooded Minho person, after looking at the building carefully.

"For me, the most original aspect lies in the two turrets and the Italianate loggia in the middle. Which are not my work, but by Francisco de Araújo e Amorim, who had the house built in the eighteenth-century after a long stay in Italy as Minister of Portugal," clarified Santa Eulália.

"Hence the loggia and the Mediterranean inspiration for the house. Which curiously reminds me much more of the famous Palladio villas than of the castles of Ludwig of Bavaria, that my Uncle Gonçalo talks about," observed Aurora, not resisting the chance to show his erudition.

"You're right boy, well observed. After all, I did little more than take the lime off the wall to leave the stone showing. And added some elements, like those battlements, for which I used the stones from the demolition of the Remédios Monastery, and the tubes connecting them, which I bought second hand in Oporto, taken from the old acetylene gas piping in the city. Besides the iron guards on the balcony windows and stairways. And a few other little details, but which helped to beautify the construction," concluded Santa Eulália as they walked around the house on the opposite side of the entrance.

"The result is truly magnificent, surprising," commented Aurora, stopping to take a look from a distance, before then rejoining the others.

"Here is the chapel, dedicated to Our Lady of Glory," observed Eulália before opening the door in the side facade of the house.

"A beautiful baroque carved retable. And the statues are magnificent," commented Aurora, now inside the chapel, nodding towards the figures of saints on the retable.

"They came back a few days ago from the restorers, after the damage they suffered at the hands of the band of scoundrels who burgled my house last year," explained Santa Eulália bluntly, while the other two walked around the inside of the room, crossing themselves respectfully in front of the altar. Once he had closed the door to the chapel again, he led the visitors back to the front of the house and from there to the inside, going up one of the stairways to the balcony, at the top of which there was the main entrance. This opened onto a vast hall, with headroom of over four meters, a varnished brown plaster ceiling, and bare stone walls like on the outside, decorated with oil paintings and church carving works. At the end of this hall was the library, a rectangular space, with a ceiling also in plaster and walls lined all round with full bookcases up to the top, including between the French windows giving onto the garden. On the opposite wall, on the inside, a fine fire crackling away inside an impressive granite stone fireplace, in front of which was a broad settee and two armchairs.

"What would you like? Tea, coffee?" asked Santa Eulália, pointing to the settee for them to sit down, while he chose one of the armchairs.

"Coffee, if it's not too much trouble," replied Aurora, seconded by his friend.

"It's no trouble at all," he said, after giving instructions to one of the maids who had in the meantime come to the room. "So, what is the matter that has brought you here?"

"It is the bridge, our beautiful bridge, which gives its name to the town and to the borough. We heard that you have shown your disapproval of the campaign to have it demolished launched by the *Comércio do Lima...*" stated Aurora.

"Don't tell me that you, two educated and intelligent young men, are in favor of such a barbaric act..."

"Not on my life. We are also totally against it. We are even thinking of launching a manifesto in defense of the bridge, against its demolition..." Aurora announced vehemently.

"That's an excellent idea. One must do everything to avoid this enormous foolishness. You may count on my unconditional support."

"We are very grateful, cousin," replied Aurora with satisfaction.

"There's no need to thank me. Indeed, as soon as I found out the bridge had been damaged by the floods I telegraphed the government and proposed to pay for the work to rebuild it. And also to replace the battlements, which were an integral part of it. Which some bright spark, of the same kind as these who want to demolish it now to 'improve the circulation of the water', had removed some dozen or so years ago, God knows why."

"That is a fine gesture. Of great generosity and love for our land..." commented Aurora, touched.

"Even so, they haven't answered me. As I am a monarchist, they must be wary of my intentions..." stated Santa Eulália, at the moment when the maid came in, a fine country lass, in slippers, gown, and petticoat, her right hand uneasily balancing a silver tray with a coffee pot and three cups.

"Well for that it would be necessary for there to be a government. The new ministry only swore office yesterday..." replied Júlio as the maid served him coffee.

"Yes, it's true that in the meantime Bernardino Machado's has fallen, God rest his soul..." said Santa Eulália as soon as the maid withdrew after leaving the tray on the table in front of the settee.

"And as soon as it started, it already caused protests. According to what I read this morning in the newspaper, Machado dos Santos considers the new ministry a veritable affront to the country as it is made up exclusively of followers of Afonso Costa. And as a protest he decided to resign his mandate as a deputy of the Nation," Júlio Pinto recalled.

"He can't complain much, given that he is largely responsible for the 5th of October and all of the mess we have been living through since then. But there is no doubt that a government made up of followers of Costa will only aggravate the climate of permanent tension the country is going through," said Santa Eulália.

"Well, with the appeal that former King Manuel made for the monarchists to abandon their struggle against the Republic and put the interests of the country first while the world war is on, one might expect that at least on that side things should start to calm down," stated Júlio.

"I have my doubts. Couceiro has already shown that he is not prepared to accept the king's will. And the military revolt that took place two months ago in Mafra, in Vila Real, and in some other places, is the proof of this," countered Aurora.

"One more to add to all the others, always with no result," said his friend.

"Yes, but you can't pin all the blame on him. Many good people throughout the country were committed to supporting him and, when it came to the crunch, ducked out," replied José Aurora, defending the monarchist captain Couceiro.

"I did what I could to help him, but the fact is that Paiva Couceiro, albeit being a fearless and brave man, has a great lack of strategic vision. And of leadership capacity," Santa Eulália burst out, greatly surprising the other two.

"Well, if you knew what people were saying at the time about that help," Júlio Pinto boldly put forward.

"I'm sure it wasn't worse than what they were saying in the United States. Where we were even, my wife and I, accused in the newspapers of being behind Paiva Couceiro's campaigns, which we had financed with one hundred and fifty thousand dollars a year. All this with the unconfessable aim of placing myself and her on the throne, imagine," said the Count, with a loud guffaw.

"No one was speaking about amounts here exactly, but everyone said that you, sir, were financing him," Júlio Pinto again risked saying.

"Well my friends, the conversation is very interesting, but time flies. It is almost dinner time. So I will have two more places set at the table and you will then go back to town more comforted," the host suddenly proposed after rapidly glancing at his pocket watch, showing almost 7:00 p.m.

"Not at all, cousin. We have already caused you enough trouble with our visit," protested José Aurora ceremoniously.

"On the contrary, I will be greatly pleased if you dine with me. It isn't every day that I have the privilege of conversing with two educated, aware, and well informed young men. I insist," said Santa Eulália, now standing up and ready to go to the other side of the house to give his instructions.

"Well, if it is like that then we gladly accept. Don't we, Júlio?" said Aurora, turning to his friend who nodded, immediately showing his agreement.

"In that case, you will allow me a moment to go and tell the cook," replied Santa Eulália, walking out of the door.

"So, Zé, what do you think of our Count?" whispered Júlio as soon as the sound of the Count's footsteps on the wooden floor had died down.

"I'm fascinated. He's a veritable figure from a novel," replied Aurora, his eyes sparkling.

"True. He certainly lives up to his fame," said Júlio, after which the two remained silent, waiting until they again began to hear footsteps on the floor.

"Please come with me," said Santa Eulália, again appearing at the library door, and then leading them through the long hall.

"Here is the toilet closet, if you need it," he suggested as they passed the last door on the left of the hall, giving access to a spacious room with a bathtub in the middle, attached to the wall by a rack of thick iron rings, and, above it, a copper water tank with a broad enamel shower head at its base.

"Have you seen this bathtub, Júlio? It's just like a boat," commented Aurora after they went in, staring in amazement at the strange object coated in enamel inside and wood outside.

"True. I hadn't noticed," replied Júlio, while Aurora relieved himself in the W.C.

"It's really the stuff of artists," Aurora said, washing his hands and then combing his hair and adjusting the knot in his tie, after which both of them left the toilet compartment and went ahead through the same door their host had taken, and which led to another room that was almost as long as the first, with the same high ceiling, in plaster, and the same walls with the bare granite showing, along which there were some fine items of Dona Maria and Dom João V furniture along with some more church carvings. At the end, on the left, was the door to the dining room.

"Ah, my dear friends, come in, come in. Please don't notice the mess on the table. But this is where I eat, work and spend most of my time," apologized the Count as soon as he saw them coming in, standing up near to one of the French windows giving onto the balcony, with a sweeping gesture to the enormous wooden table in the middle of the room, one half covered in books and papers, the other half-covered with a white linen tablecloth, where the same maid who had brought them coffee was now busy setting the plates and glasses, taking them out, to great amazement, from inside a Baroque religious carving set into one of the side walls, which was reached by means of a few steps on the floor.

"Excuse me cousin, but…are these drawings yours?" José Aurora could not resist asking, after passing a glance over the papers on the table, among which he could see several pencil and charcoal drawings along with some photographs of sculptures.

"Yes, of course. Some made over the last few days. So I can keep my hand in, given that I cannot make sculpture. Well, shall we sit down?" he proposed, immediately occupying the head of the table as he gave Aurora the right and Júlio the left.

"You mean that despite all your other activities you have carried on your artistic activity…" Aurora deduced, returning to the conversation as soon as the maid had served them a steaming broth with a thick slice of smoked sausage and a hunk of cornbread.

"Indeed, as much as possible. This year I exhibited at the Salon in Paris," replied the Count before beginning the meal.

"I didn't have the slightest idea. I was convinced that you had completely abandoned sculpture. What was the work you presented at the Salon?" insisted Aurora.

"I presented two. One is a stone statue, another a bronze bas-relief, both intended for a monument in homage to a great American sculptor, Saint-Gaudens, who did me the favor of also being my friend. The *New York Times*, one of the most important American newspapers, was fulsome in its praise for the statue, saying that it showed a great resemblance to Rodin's *Thinker*, which is at the entrance to the Panthéon National, in Paris," said Santa Eulália with some pride.

"Which, considering everything, would not be very surprising, given that, according to my Uncle Gonçalo, you would have worked with him, with Rodin, when you were a student in Paris," stated Aurora, just as, with the soup finished, the maid was approaching with a tray full of appetizing cod cakes served with rice.

"Yes, for a while," Santa Eulália replied evasively. "But today I think I have my own style, even though I obviously do not reject the influences of those whom I consider my masters."

"Where will the monument be placed when it is finished?" asked Aurora.

"Well, New York City Council has shown some interest in keeping it, to put it in one of the city parks. We'll see when the war is over, so I can go back to the United States in safety and take up the negotiations again," he replied.

"Whatever the case, it is a pleasant surprise to see that after all, you have not abandoned sculpture and that it seems that you have continued to work keenly all these years. That is, despite the many other activities you have also carried out here in Minho in favor of our land," Aurora stated enthusiastically, as the maid served him the second course, succulent Minho style veal.

"Yes, but if you don't mind me saying so it has not been very easy. With this dispersion over the two sides of the Atlantic, many ideas, many projects, many opportunities have been left by the wayside without me being able to carry them out," lamented the Count thoughtfully, after a long silence." And here in Portugal, the same has also happened somewhat, as my attempts to introduce new crops and new production methods in agriculture as backward as ours demands a great, great deal of attention. That I haven't always been able to provide, as I always spend part of the year in the United States. So my results have not always been the best."

"Even so, you have proved that in our country it is also possible to produce using new methods of tilling and working the land. Now what is necessary is for other farmers to follow your example. And for the government to invest in the training of agricultural technicians, able to drag our farmers out of their ancestral backwardness," proclaimed Júlio, in visionary style.

"Let's hope so, my dear boy, let's hope so. Well, I wish that you might not be too disappointed with the dinner, which could not have been more simple and frugal. But as I get older I am more and more like Jacinto, in the novel *The City and the Mountains*, that remarkable creation by our Eça de Queiroz: the more I know the pleasures of civilization the more I appreciate the good, simple things of our countryside."

"It's true: what better can there be for someone from Minho than crispy cod cakes and tender veal like we have just eaten?" agreed Aurora, seconded by a nod of the head from his companion.

"So we are all in agreement, "finished the Count with a broad smile as, having taken away the plates, the maid was pulling a tray with dessert out of the dumb waiter.

"No doubt," replied Aurora.

"Well, for dessert we have roasted pears, a recipe of mine, inspired by the famous French *poires au vin*. I hope you like them," the Count pointed out.

"Wonderful," commented Aurora, after delighting in a good slice of pear soaked in a delicious sauce of warm wine and sugar with a slight touch of cinnamon.

"Indeed, an excellent delicacy," added Júlio.

"I'm glad you like them," said the Count with satisfaction, before ordering the coffee and cognac. Which they drank as they had a lively chat, after also accepting a Cuban cigar offered by their host.

"Well, my esteemed cousin, the visit and the dinner have been most pleasant, but it is getting late," José Aurora finally said, after looking at his watch, with the hands touching half-past eight in the evening.

"Very good. Do not hold back for me," replied the Count, immediately standing up to accompany them to the exit through one of the French windows to the balcony, which he opened slightly. The evening was cold, and the sky overcast, threatening rain. At the bottom of the steps, the carriage was already waiting.

"Cousin, once again, thank you very much for the reception and the dinner," José Aurora said finally, holding out his hand and immediately seconded by his friend.

"I thank you for your visit. And as for the manifesto about the bridge, count on me. When it is ready send it to me for me to sign."

"Certainly. You'll be hearing from us soon," replied Aurora as the vehicle started off towards the exit.

XXII

Paris, 5th of October 1902

"*MONSIEUR RIBEIRO!*" calls René, the hotel receptionist, as soon as he sees him cross the entrance hall to the elevator coming from the dining room, where he had just taken breakfast.

"*Bonjour, René. Qu'y a-t-il?*" asks Aleixo, as soon as he comes over to the reception desk.

"*Un message pour vous, Monsieur, arrivé ce matin,*" replies René, handing him a small envelope with the hotel emblem stamped on it. "It was left by a short, stocky middle-aged gentleman, with *grosse moustache, avec un tout petit accent.*"

"*Merci, René.*" Aleixo says laconically, looking with intrigue at the envelope with his name, followed by the qualifier of "*illustre sculpteur,*" written on the front, before putting it in his coat pocket and continuing on his way to the elevator.

Who from among his friends and acquaintances would have taken the trouble to come there to his hotel early in the morning and leave him that note? He wonders as he closes the partition grill and presses the button for the fifth floor, opening the envelope without any further ado and taking out a hand-written note that—surprise, surprise!—is signed by Xavier, good old tireless Xavier de Carvalho, one of the extremely rare journalists who never gave in and was never intimidated by the shameless campaign carried out in Lisbon against him and his monument, to top it all by his own newspaper, *O Século*, but who, far to the contrary, right at the height of that campaign, had had the courage to write fulsome praise about his triumph in Bulgaria, Aleixo cannot help recalling as he puts the key into the door to his room. The note is to invite him to accompany Xavier "on the last homage to that great figure in European culture who was Emile Zola," at one o'clock in the afternoon today, proposing, if he should be interested, that he go to meet him at his office on the Rue de St. Georges, right there a few yards from his hotel, at around half past twelve midday. Well, yet another showing of proof of the consideration and esteem held for him by this generous, good man, this educated and superior mind, by inviting him to join him in a solemn demonstration of such great importance and significance for France and for the whole world, as the burial of the departed Zola will no doubt be. Zola whose unexpected death was possibly caused, according to the reports published in the newspapers, due to choking because of the excess of carbon monoxide generated by the deficient working, or even total blocking of a chimney while he was asleep in his bedroom alongside his wife. Could this "deficient working" or even "total blocking of the chimney" had the hand of some irate anti-Dreyfusians or anti-Semitics? And thus, in such a prosaic and stupid manner, one loses a great figure of such importance when so much was still expected of him, unanimously considered to be the greatest living French writer after the death of Victor Hugo, the author of several dozen enormous volumes in which he widely exemplified and developed his ideas, of note among which were the famous *Germinal*, and the more recent trilogy of *Les Trois Villes*. But he was also an intrepid defender of great causes such as the fight against poverty, oppression, and injustice, never being afraid to sacrifice, when necessary, his personal comfort of his successful literary career. As only recently had been the case over the famous Dreyfus affair, when he decided to denounce the hypocrisy and injustice of the high-ranking military hierarchy, in a letter he addressed to the President of the Republic under the title *J'accuse*, published in early 1898 in the newspaper *L'Aurore*, as soon as a court-martial absolved Captain Esterhazy, who had been proven to be the real traitor, the one who had given information to the Germans, and for whose crimes the unfortunate Captain Dreyfus was paying, having been unfairly accused, stripped of rank and deported to Devil's Island. How can he, now, not accept the dignified invitation made to him by Xavier de Carvalho in this note, to accompany him on paying last respects to a figure of such stature, even if this alters his plans for work this Sunday, committed as he is to as quickly as possible finishing the model for the bust of Napoleon on which he has been working since he arrived from Spain in the studio belonging to Maurice, an old companion from his days in the Académie Julian, just up there in the Montmartre neighborhood? He wonders, looking at the hands of his pocket watch, showing five past eleven, before heading to the French window, which he opens slightly, letting in the cool, clear, dry, bright October morning with the sun shining intensely in the blue sky, such as hadn't been seen for some time in Paris.

Oh, what pain, sadness, and grief over these last two years, the first of a new century that at the outset had seemed to be so promising, so full of well-founded expectations in the successes and triumphs of his career as a sculptor, he says to himself, leaning over the railing and looking for a moment at the Place Pigalle, at the top of the street, where one can already see an increasing movement of people towards the Boulevard de Clichy and to the Rue de Bruxelles, where the unfortunate writer's house is. Two years in which, to the contrary, he saw his name continuously insulted and slandered by the humorous newspapers, to the delight of the whole of Lisbon society, splitting themselves laughing at the constant allusions to his name, to his figure—"The eminent sculptor of hipbaths Queiroz Ribeiro," "Queiroz Ribeiro, the distinguished fountain sculptor," "the distinguished and hairy sculptor Queiroz Ribeiro"—without him being able to do anything to stop such torture. But, worst of all, was the brutal beating to which he was subjected one night when coming home alone by a bunch of thugs who said they were medical students and wished to avenge the honor of the person they said was their master, Dr. Sousa Martins, in their opinion seriously offended by his monument, recalls Aleixo, with a feeling of a mixture of sadness and rage, not so much against the feeble-minded individuals who had beaten him and left him lying on the ground, unconscious, but against the others, those who with their articles, writings and caricatures had indirectly encouraged them to commit such a cowardly act. His convalescence from the wounds and the bruises was prolonged, at the Casa da Boavista, far away from Lisbon and its atmosphere of intrigue and gossip, taken care of with the redoubled efforts of his dear sisters Tina and Claudinha, not so much the wounds on his body, which soon healed, but the wounds on his soul, which were much deeper and more difficult to heal. How was it possible that after such a striking success as that which he had achieved between 1898 and 1900, with constant praise and eulogy in the newspapers and public opinion, both in France and Portugal, with demonstrations of approval by the highest dignitaries in the country, from the Church to the Government, including the Parliament and the Royal Family itself, could his reputation have fallen in such a short time, so far down to the point of seeing a work of his being destroyed, with its base and obelisk being reduced to a pile of stones by the city council's hammer, and his statues purely and simply melted down so that the bronze could be used in the new monument, while he himself was attacked and cowardly beaten up in the street in broad daylight? That was the question he could not stop asking himself, silently locked in his room, throughout all those months of reclusion in which he stayed at Boavista until he finally came to the conclusion that he was not the one at fault, but the country in which he had the ill fortune to have been born, where neither the common folk nor the elites had the education and sufficient preparation to understand art like his, he recalls as he absent-mindedly watches the figures who pass by further up in the Place Pigalle in increasing numbers.

So the only solution left to him was to leave, to set off once again for somewhere far afield, where his work could be appreciated and recognized, without preconceived ideas nor fixed judgments. But where? Paris, the City of Lights, the Capital of the World, where he did his studies and had his first successes? No, no matter how much he might like the idea, he was well aware of the enormous difficulties he would have to face in a city like Paris, spilling over with artists of the most varied origins, schools, and tendencies, forced into unbridled competition in order to survive, and above all at a time when his name was now practically forgotten, despite the good reception his works had received in the French newspapers some years earlier. Sofia, where two years earlier he had achieved a great triumph, including an invitation to teach at the Fine Arts School? No, Bulgaria was a small country on the edge of Europe, too isolated for whatever he did to have any influence outside its limited frontiers. And it was then that he remembered the conversation he had some years earlier in Paris with Saint-Gaudens, in the *Procope*, on the eve of his return to Lisbon to begin his work on the monument to Sousa Martins: "America is the land of opportunities. It is a great country, where almost everything remains to be done. And where there is always room for a talented young man with a will to work, as seems to be your case," Saint-Gaudens had said to him, something which he had not taken seriously at the time, then being confident about his future success after having won the most hotly-disputed competition of the last years in Lisbon. But now that this success had ended up in a

glaring setback, why not America, why not the New World, "the land
of opportunities," above all starting with the support of such an influential figure as Saint-Gaudens? That was the question he asked himself
over several days, leaning over the balcony of his bedroom in Boavista,
until he finally decided to write a long letter to Nellie, his dear Nellie,
explaining the situation he was in and asking her how he could get in
touch with Saint-Gaudens to ask him for work, wherever it might be.
The answer wasn't long in coming and could not be more encouraging.
Despite the serious health problems he was suffering, Saint-Gaudens
was preparing to accept responsibilities in the World's Fair in St. Louis, Missouri, in 1904, concerning all the sculpture work decorating the
roads, squares, and gardens, as well as the many dozens of pavilions to
be built in the exhibition grounds, and that, having been contacted by
Nellie, had said he was thrilled at the idea that he could count on him,
Aleixo, to work on his team. Aleixo had already read some articles in the
newspapers about the holding of this new world exhibition, through
which the Americans intended to commemorate the passing of a century on the purchase of the twelve states that made up Louisiana from
the French, in the time of Napoleon, as well as about the grandiose and
unique nature they intended to grant it, and so was immediately won
over by the idea of crossing over the Atlantic to America as soon as possible. However, there was a great obstacle to be overcome: the amount
needed to pay for the trip to New York, and from there by train to St.
Louis, besides the money necessary to cover his first expenses, which he
didn't have, now that his finances had been stripped bare after having
no work or commissions for over two years. Once again, thanks to the
friendship and generosity shown by his brother Gaspar, his guardian
angel, his protecting saint in good times and bad, as he liked himself to
be referred to, everything was solved, Aleixo can't help recalling, before
he again looks at the hands on his watch, about to show eleven-thirty.
Time to get ready for the funeral, if he doesn't want to be late at Xavier's office, he thinks, immediately going back into his bedroom, yet not
without noticing his ticket to America, right there on the sideboard,
next to the dressing table mirror. "*Compagnie Générale Transatlantique,*"
he reads across the whole of the top of the page, followed in bold letters
by the name of the ship, "*LA LORRAINE,*" the class, "*3ème*" and finally
the destination and departure date: "*New York, le 10 Octobre 1902,*" that

is, next Friday. Which means that besides the time he will manage to have free today, after the funeral, he only has two more days to make the final touches to the model of the bust of Napoleon and to pack it up with all necessary care to prevent it from suffering any damage on the journey, he concludes as he takes off his corduroy trousers and then puts on a pair of formal black, striped trousers he takes from inside the wardrobe.

But the good thing for him is that tomorrow and later he can almost certainly count on the help of Maria, who has been so useful over the last month. Indeed, Maria, the young and talented Fine Arts student who was his assistant in Sofia when he was making the model for the monument to Czar Alexander II, and who is now in Paris, attending the Académie Julian, now that her father has in the meantime been appointed the diplomatic representative of the Principality of Bulgaria in Paris. And whom, by a happy coincidence, he met on the Boulevard St. Germain only a few days after his arrival from Portugal, when she immediately offered, with the enthusiasm and generosity typical of her, to support him in carrying out his new project, he recalls as he opens another drawer looking for a white starched shirt and a black *papillon*.

And what splendor of a woman Maria had become in the meanwhile, over these last two years, he says to himself, for a moment unable not to think of the exuberance and agility of that body, now with its shapes completely defined, that angelic face, with that very fair, soft-lined skin, her blond, curly hair tied back over her neck, which she would sometimes let down, letting it hang magnificently to the middle of her back, and her eyes, those eyes of an emerald green, but which, depending on the light or the emotions in her soul, could also take on the color of a sea of deep, clear water. And what a precious help she had been, as was the case only a few days earlier during the complicated process of shaping his Napoleon in plaster and which, not having the finances available to pay a professional, he had decided to carry out himself. What skill, what nimbleness of hands she showed when she helped him cut up the clay work into so many pieces in order to then make the negative impression of each of them and finally pour in the liquid plaster into them. It was a pity that he was unable to have her help at the weekend also, but some family commitment kept her away from Paris until the next Monday, Aleixo laments as he puts on his *papillon* under the starched collar of his shirt.

A nimbleness and skill with her hands that owes a lot to the extraordinary artistic development she had also undergone in the meantime, going from the young and inexperienced apprentice with whom he had started to work at the Sofia Fine Arts studio, who knew little more than how to knead the clay and prepare the plaster, to the applied student he now met again, sharing with her not only a good deal of the various and complex tasks of making the work but also some of the ideas and conceptions at its base. Which also had to be reflected in the way they began to address each other, now no longer the distant *Maître* Ribeiro and *Mademoiselle* Maria that they used in Sofia, but simply by their Christian names, Alexis and Maria, and more so in their relationship of increasing intimacy that had in the meantime been developing between them, cemented over the many days they had spent together in Maurice's studio during the last month, he thinks, sitting at the foot of the bed as he puts on his patent leather shoes and tightly ties the shoelaces.

A relationship which in her case could well possibly be more than that, judging by the intensity of certain looks of hers, or by the way sometimes, when they are carrying out some work that implies closer physical contact their faces become flushed and their breathing is hurried, he recalls, standing up to put on his waistcoat and jacket, which are hanging inside the wardrobe. Well, the things of a romantic, dreamy, Slavic maiden that time will solve, he thinks, given that he, albeit not denying the sincere friendship he has for her nor the attraction he feels for her, is about to leave for America and thus is in no position to encourage romantic liaisons with anyone, and much less so with a naïve young lady who knows nothing of the ways of the world and life like Maria, he concludes to himself as he takes his top hat, white gloves and Bengal cane with a silver knob that are on the chair near the chest of drawers before he leaves the room.

"*À ce soir, Monsieur Ribeiro. Bonne journée,*" René says to him, looking amazed to see him go by dressed *de rigueur* on his way to the door. Outside, intense sunshine floods the facade of the hotel, lighting up the pink marble sign next to the door, with the name of the hotel, and underneath it "*Electricité,*" "*Bains-douches*" and "*Téléphone,*" three major modern commodities for nowadays, fortunately increasingly accessible and widespread, but which until relatively recently were unthinkable in a neighborhood hotel like this one, thinks Aleixo as he walks along the pavement towards the little Place St-Georges, then entering the street of the same name towards Xavier's office. It is a building with a ground floor and four stories, with nothing special to distinguish it from the buildings next to it, with all of them having a wide passage in the middle of the facade giving on to the *cour*, a spacious inner patio around which several offices and shops are distributed, among which is that of the distinguished journalist and man of letters.

"Mr. Queiroz Ribeiro. How are you? I'm glad you could come. Please come in," he is greeted by Xavier, with the usual cheerfulness and bonhomie, as soon as he opens the door, short hair, thick mustache turned up at the corners, glasses slipping down his nose, sleeve guards over his white starched breast shirt.

"First of all, allow me to thank you from the bottom of my heart for thinking of leaving that note for me, my dear Xavier," Aleixo says to him, greeting him with an effusive handshake before entering.

"Not at all, there's nothing to thank me for, Mr. Queiroz Ribeiro. I ought to apologize for my boldness, disturbing you like that on a Sunday morning. But at least it is for a good cause," replies Xavier, immediately ushering him along a little hall towards his office.

"Indeed," replies Aleixo as he casts a quick glance around the office, with its enormous fire lit in the middle, a large African blackwood desk on the left, and two *fauteuils* with a low table on the right, next to the window. Behind the desk, a bookshelf running all the length of the wall, also in blackwood, full of books and magazines, along with stacks of newspapers laid out in a more or less disorderly manner along the several shelves.

"Mr. Queiroz Ribeiro, you will excuse me, but I am just finishing writing an article that has to be sent to Lisbon today. If you wish you may read the latest editions of the *Século*. There is one in particular there that should interest you," says Xavier, pointing to the pile of newspapers on the low table in front of the *fauteuils*. That one on the top, page two, top left corner."

"Ah, thank you very much," says Aleixo, opening the newspaper with curiosity until coming to his host's usual column, "Letter from Paris," in the middle of which he discovers the following reference: "In the last issue of the important magazine *Les Actualités Diplomatiques*, several works by the sculptor Queiroz Ribeiro are reproduced in a full-page photo-engraving."

"Does it have your approval?" asks Xavier, as soon as he sees Aleixo raise his eyes from the newspaper.

"It couldn't be better, my dear friend," Aleixo is pleased to state, touched by the reference made to the recent publication of his works in that important French magazine, about which he had informed Xavier in advance.

"Delivered as promised. And perhaps those simpletons in Lisbon will finally begin to realize the mistake they have made," replies Xavier, before plunging back into his article.

"I doubt it. So, today is Sunday, and you're working as well?" asks Aleixo, watching Xavier dipping his pen in the inkwell and then writing some sentences on one of the sheets of paper in front of him.

"That's true. I have been here all morning gathering information and writing the news that will be out in the morning edition of the *Século* about the funeral. I just needed this one for everything to be ready. Unfortunately for us journalists, when there are events of this importance there are no Sundays or public holidays to be had. Our only concern is to get the news to our readers as completely and quickly as possible," replies Xavier, raising his pen when he gets to the end of the paragraph, then carefully passing the blotting paper over the text.

"Well, the good thing is that it's not every day that an Émile Zola dies, otherwise you wouldn't have time for anything else," jokes Aleixo, as Xavier puts the papers on his desk away.

"True, but this year there has been such a rush of events that it's almost impossible to stop, have you noticed? First, right at the beginning, the death and grand funeral of Queen Victoria, after a reign of over fifty years, taking all the presidents and crowned heads from all over Europe to London, including, obviously, our King Carlos, whom I had the privilege to accompany as the reporter from the *Século* given the task of covering the journey, both in London and then here in Paris on his way back. Then there were the festivities for the coronation of King Edward VII, and once again I went to London to accompany Luiz Filipe, the Royal Prince, in the representation of his father, for it all to be canceled at the last minute because of the king's sudden illness. In the middle of all this, there was also the coronation of King Alfonso

XIII of Spain, with festivities carrying on in Madrid for over a week. But fortunately, I managed to avoid that one, as they sent someone from the editorial staff in Lisbon, which is nearer after all.

"Indeed, that's a great deal of events for one year," interrupts Aleixo, shifting in his chair, not knowing how to call Xavier's attention to the passing time without being rude.

"And that's not to mention the end of the Boer War, with the signing in Pretoria of the surrender of the rebel forces. Or the constant references in the French press throughout the year to the financial situation in Portugal, saying that we are broke, bankrupt. Or, also, the rumors that started about the possible sale of some of our colonies to the British in order to pay our foreign debt to the creditors, as the only manner of solving the problem."

"Well, my good friend, I did not wish to interrupt you, but time is getting on," Aleixo finally says.

"You're absolutely right. With all this conversation I was forgetting about the time. We must get going," Xavier replies, standing up after glancing at the clock.

"The good thing is this glorious sunshine like we haven't seen for some time in Paris," comments Aleixo as they are crossing the courtyard, looking at the back of the building, brightly lit up by the sunlight, before they enter the passage leading them to the street.

"So, Mr. Queiroz Ribeiro, are you determined to go over to the other side of the Atlantic?" asks Xavier when they start walking up the Rue St. Georges.

"Absolutely. I've already booked the ticket."

"When are you leaving?"

"Next Friday. The tenth."

"I must make a note of it, to then put an item in the newspaper. After all, there is no one better than you to assess your situation and know what is best for you. But it pains me deeply to see the departure to such a far off place of an artist whose talent I have seen grow and develop over the years you have spent here. And whose successes I have had the satisfaction to be able to accompany and announce in the newspaper. And all only because of that mean, small-minded atmosphere in Lisbon, that climate of intrigue and gossip at which we Portuguese are so prodigious. And which Eça, our dear Eça de Queiroz, was so good at characterizing," says Xavier, saddened, as they arrive at the Place St. Georges.

"He warned me, you know? During one of the rare times, I had the opportunity to chat for some time with him here in Paris at the General Consulate. But I didn't pay any attention to it at the time, in my presumption and naiveté, being so ecstatic about the reviews and references to my works which were constantly appearing in the Lisbon newspapers at the time. I had no idea of what was coming, you see?"

"What they did to that statue of yours is completely unheard-of. Only possible in a country where ignorance and obscurantism reign. There is always criticism for one reason or another. But to purely and simply demolish a monument, a work of art, the model of which had been chosen in open competition, and above all by public funding? No, nothing of the kind has happened in any European country. At least they could have done what they did with Rodin's *Balzac*, rejecting it when it was still only in plaster, before casting it in bronze and placing it in public."

"My dear Xavier, that is all in the past for me now. A past I want to forget in a hurry because of the amount I have suffered over these last two years. Now what I want to think about is—I won't say my future, as there will be very little relation to what has gone before—but what will come next, there…far from Portugal, on the other side of the Atlantic," replies Aleixo bitterly as they are entering the Rue Frochot.

"And are you taking any contacts, references, letters of recommendation?"

"Yes. Fortunately, I have a lot of work waiting for me in St. Louis. Where, as you know, they are actively preparing for the 1904 World's Fair. With the most consecrated of American sculptors, the famous Saint-Gaudens, who is kind enough to be my friend."

"A sculptor of great standing. I well recall his equestrian statue that became very famous here during the Paris World Exposition. What was it called?"

"The one of General Sherman?"

"That's the one. Magnificent. Opulent. A veritable masterpiece," says Xavier emphatically, as they pass by the entrance to the Hotel Frochot.

"And I'm also taking a project to present to the authorities for the exhibition, on which I have been working here in Montmartre in a friend's studio," Aleixo can't resist saying.

"Really? What project is that?" asks Xavier, with the typical curiosity of a journalist, always on the lookout for news.

"It's a bust of Napoleon, who, as you know, was the person who granted the purchase of Louisiana to the Americans. But it is a giant bust, with several floors inside it, intended to be set up inside the exhibition space itself, all in cement and iron like the famous Chicago and New York skyscrapers. On these floors, served by elevators allowing one to go from the bottom to the top of the bust, there will be halls that can be adapted to the various ceremonies taking place during the event. The height of the bust will be such that the windows that light up the halls, which are on the level of the head, will appear to be hair when seen from afar," explains Aleixo, suddenly enthused by his own project.

"That's an extraordinary idea, my dear Queiroz Ribeiro. It's what I say... Down in Portugal, they have no idea what they are losing by wasting such a talent, a prodigious imagination like yours," says Xavier, genuinely surprised by the description of the work, before they turn into the middle of the great crowd that now completely fills not only the Place Pigalle but also the Clichy and Rochechouart boulevards, respectfully waiting for the parade to begin.

"Let's see if we can get to the front," Xavier shouts to him, pushing through the immense and increasingly compact wall as they advance along the Boulevard de Clichy towards the Rue de Bruxelles, the entrance to which is blocked off by a police cordon. Taking out his journalist's *laissez-passer* from his pocket, Xavier shows it to the police chief, who immediately gives orders to let them pass. Inside the barrier, one can obviously move more easily, as, besides the journalists, there are only some friends of Zola's, public figures, representatives of unions and associations. The entrance to Zola's house is all adorned in black and silver, with shields bearing the letter Z for Zola in the middle, while on the pavement, on either side of the door, lists of condolences have been set out.

"Look, here comes Jean Jaurès, the head of the Socialist Party. And Colonel Picquart, next to him. He was the one who discovered the real traitor was not Dreyfus but Esterhazy. And as a reward the military authorities immediately sent him to Tunisia, preferring to keep an innocent man in prison and deported than to eat humble pie and admit they had made a mistake," says Xavier, as they wait on the left of the door to sign the list of condolences.

"Yes, I remember reading about it in the newspapers," replies Aleixo.

"And the one back there is Mathieu Dreyfus, the unfortunate captain's brother," continues Xavier, as Aleixo looks at the heavy and stern faces of all those figures passing by very dignifiedly in their black coats and top hats, on their way to the house, no doubt to present their condolences to Madame Zola before the cortège begins. Then an army company arrives from further down, moving forward along the middle of the street until it halts outside Zola's house. It is exactly a quarter to one on his pocket watch when Aleixo sees the hearse arrive, followed by two other carriages, slowly coming up the street until they stop at the door to the house. The wreaths are then taken in their hundreds from inside the house to the carriages, leaving Xavier in a veritable frenzy as he tries to identify the names on the respective ribbons, then noting them down on his hardback Moleskine block in a speed writing that only he must be able to decipher. When the wreaths have finally filled the carriages, a third carriage comes from the bottom of the street to take the rest of them. Then it is the solemn moment to transport the coffin from inside the house to the hearse, followed with consternation by all those present, standing either side of the door, whether they are journalists, public figures, representatives of the most varied types of organizations, all sharing in the deep emotion of the moment, in which the body of the deceased writer will forever leave that which was his home and go in a cortège to the cemetery. The figures of Mathieu Dreyfus and Colonel Picquart suddenly appear in outline at the door of the house, shouldering the front of the urn, followed by other figures whom Aleixo does not know, but who were no doubt carefully chosen for that final homage to the great Zola. Once the coffin has been placed in the hearse it is the moment for the widow to leave the house, then going immediately to sit next to it, her head covered by a hat and her face hidden by a black veil, supported by several other ladies. The military honors then begin, carried out in absolute silence, only broken now and then by the orders given by the officer commanding the company, after which the cortège finally sets off towards the Boulevard de Clichy, immediately incorporating all the people waiting there to follow it, among whom are obviously Aleixo and Xavier. In the meantime the police force that had previously blocked off the street now stands in front of the cortège, opening up a path through the crowd, which respectfully bows as the hearse passes by, with the gentlemen removing their hats.

"The number of people here is amazing, isn't it? The last time I recall seeing such a crowd was at Victor Hugo's funeral," Xavier whispers to him as the cortège finally reaches the end of the boulevard before turning upwards to the entrance to the cemetery.

"True. I've never seen anything like this either," agrees Aleixo, impressed, after glancing around at the sea of people stretching off into the distance, from the beginning of the Boulevard Rochechouart to the end of the Boulevard de Clichy, some forming a part of the cortège and other watching it go by from either side of the avenue.

"A while ago a colleague of mine said that the police estimated over 200,000 people in the crowd," comments Xavier.

"It's very probable," replies Aleixo at the moment the hearse with the coffin and the three carriages with flowers have entered the cemetery gates, with some disturbance then taking place at the front of the cortège, which Xavier decides to go to investigate, returning flushed after a short time.

"It's best we wait a little while for things to calm down up at the front. From what I was told, as soon as the hearse and three carriages entered the crowd rushed forward into the cemetery and in the ensuing confusion, several people were injured, trampled on by those coming behind them. Now they are only letting people with tickets or a pass get in," he explains, as he takes his block from his pocket to scribble down a few more notes. When everything seems to have calmed down the two of them push through the sea of people, which gets thicker and thicker as they get closer to the entrance to the cemetery. As soon as they go past the heavy iron gate they quicken their pace until they manage to catch up with the cortège again, now going down one of the Alamedas in the cemetery and coming to a stop next to a large mausoleum, in front of which the coffin is placed for the final homages to be paid.

Someone starts to make a speech up at the front, near to the coffin, whom Xavier identifies as the Minister for Public Instruction, then followed by several other speakers, the last of which is the famous writer Anatole France, speaking in the name of the friends of Zola. As soon as the speech is over repeated cries of *"Vive la France!"* are heard, then followed by the passing of the figures and representatives of the different organizations present in front of the coffin, which Aleixo and Xavier also join. As the many Embassies present pass by they leave wreaths or throw bunches of flowers, at the same time respectfully doffing their hats again. Some people cannot contain themselves, and shout: "Honor to Zola!"; "Honor to he who made justice and truth triumph!"; "Honor to the apostle of justice," phrases that Xavier hurries to write down in his notebook.

"Well, my dear Xavier. Now that I have paid my sincere homage to this refined spirit, I will take my leave to try to still get some work done today. Are you coming or staying?" asks Aleixo, after they have passed in front of the bier.

"You will excuse me, Mr. Queiroz Ribeiro, but I have to stay behind until everything is over: it comes with the territory," replies Xavier, saying goodbye with an effusive handshake and his wishes for good fortune in America, before returning to his notes.

"A quarter to four," notices Aleixo, looking at his watch, when he finally manages to leave the enormous crowd behind, which is still accumulating at the entrance to the cemetery, then going up the street that goes around the enclosure on the east side. "Almost a whole day's work lost," he says to himself as he is halfway up the slope, a little before turning right to then carry on towards the Rue des Abesses, right in the heart of Montmartre. Yes, at best he has two hours, two hours and a half before the sun goes down over the horizon, leaving him without any natural light to work in, he concludes before he starts walking up the steep Rue Ravignan, until he comes to a small, pretty square surrounded by trees and dominated by a long, low single-story building known as the Bateau-Lavoir, occupied from one end to the other by artists' studios. Having crossed the square, Aleixo turns right to finally enter the Rue Gabrielle, where his friend Maurice's studio is.

"Alexis, vous voilà enfin!" he hears, amazed, Maria's unmistakable voice greeting him from the back of the studio as soon as he opens the door. "I've been waiting for you for two hours. I was just about to go, thinking that you weren't coming."

"Maria! *Mais quelle surprise, ma chérie,*" he stammers, as he sees her walking to him, magnificent in her leisure outfit, moss green velvet

jacket and skirt, frilled silk blouse and short-brimmed hat, with a pro-
fuse decoration of feathers and plumes on the top of her head.

"Daddy suddenly felt ill last night after dinner, and so we decided to
come back to Paris at once. Fortunately, he is feeling much better today
and so I thought of coming over here to see if you needed my help,"
she replies, standing in front of him in the middle of the studio, a long,
narrow space with two windows on the street side and a large window
giving onto a small garden at the back, full of canvas both painted and
ready to paint, set on the floor, hanging along the walls or simply on
easels, as Maurice, after having studied at the Académie Julian, decided
to abandon sculpture and devote himself exclusively to painting.

"Yes, I in fact intended to come here to work all day, but early in
the morning, I had a visit from a Portuguese friend, a journalist, asking
me if I wanted to go with him to the funeral of the great writer Emile
Zola, right here nearby at the Montmartre Cemetery. So, I've only just
got away," justifies Aleixo.

"Ah, so that's why there were so many people on the street when
I came here." "Yes. According to the police, there were over 200,000
people." "So, you removed the mold without waiting for me?" she asks,
pouting, after glancing at the extremely white bust of Napoleon standing in the middle of the room on an easel.

"Yes. If I had known you were coming today I would have waited,
especially as it wasn't very easy to do on my own. But as you said you
were only coming on Monday I decided to get ahead with some work,"
he replies, slightly ill at ease.

"Why such a hurry, Alexis? I would have been more than pleased to
help you," she insists, going over to the work.

"The problem is that my passage to America is already booked, you
know? And I'm starting to have little time to get everything ready, too
little," he replies, following her until the two of them are side by side
in front of the model, with the different parts that form it already
attached, but with clear imperfections at the seams.

"When is your passage then?" she asks, after a few seconds hesitation.
"Next Friday."

"So soon?" she asks, as if not wanting to believe in his suddenly so
close departure.

"Yes. Yesterday, after I prepared the plaster and put all the parts together I decided to take advantage of the time and go to the shipping company offices and book the trip. And as there were still some places on the *La Lorraine* for the tenth I decided to take one, as the sooner I arrive the better are my chances of managing to go ahead with this project of mine."

"Which means that the model has to be ready and finished by Thursday," she concludes, unable to contain her growing anxiousness.

"No. I wish it were. Tuesday night at the latest, because on Wednesday I have to send it by ship to Le Havre and I have to go by train in order to complete all the necessary formalities for it to embark on the steamer," explains Aleixo.

"So you mean you're really determined to go. That nothing can dissuade you from this absurd idea of dropping everything and just going off to America like that," she suddenly blurts out, staring at him harshly, her face suddenly transformed.

"Don't make things even harder for me than they are already, Maria. You know how difficult it is for me to leave a whole life behind me, the places and people I love. But what alternative do I have? Tell me?" he says, upset.

"*Mais…n'avez-vous pas compris? Je vous aime, Alexis…*" she suddenly says, in an outburst coming straight from her heart, her eyes welling up with tears.

"How can you say such a thing, Maria? How can you say you love me? Me? I who knew you when you were little more than a child? And who now, two years later, you meet again in Paris, passing through, about to leave, above all in such difficult circumstances as these?" he replies, with all the conviction he is capable of when faced with that sudden but totally unexpected confession.

"I have loved you since the moment I saw you, Alexis, at the Fine Arts School in Sofia, when I went there with my father to be introduced to you. It was enough to look at you once to conclude that you were the man of my life. And since then I have never stopped loving you and thinking about you for a single minute. And I think it will be like that until the end of my days," she replies, a stubborn gaze, tears running down her face, before she hurls herself into his arms, wildly kissing him on the mouth, as she crushes her body against his.

"But what future can you have with me, Maria, when you are only twenty years old and I am almost thirty-five?" he says, when he finally breaks free from her arms.

"What difference does age make in love? Didn't you tell me that your sister has just married a man sixteen years older than her?"

"Yes, but my brother-in-law is a man of means, living off the income from his properties. While I don't have anything. My career is practically ruined and there is nothing left for me except to emigrate to the New World and try to start everything over again," he says sorrowfully, and at the same time wiping the tears from her face with the back of his hand.

"Daddy would help us, I'm sure. He has you in great esteem, as you know," she insists, as if not hearing him. "We could both live here in Paris. And rent a studio so you could work and relaunch your career."

"But what honorable man, with a name and breeding, could accept such a situation, Maria? Tell me? Getting married, forming a family without any means of his own, nor enough work to allow him to support himself. Forced to live off the generosity of his father-in-law..." insists Aleixo, looking at her in the eyes, holding her by the shoulders.

"That would just be in the beginning, *mon amour*, until you managed to get some commissions. Which, with your good connections, would not be very difficult."

"My dear Maria, I have lived in Paris for seven years and I know the difficulties an artist has to face here to be able to achieve success."

"But didn't you recently manage to see several works of yours published in the *Actualités Diplomatiques*, which Daddy says is one of the most prestigious magazines in France?" she insists, not giving up.

"It is true that I still have some friendships here, from the times when I lived here and had some successes at the Salon. But that alone guarantees nothing. While, on the contrary, in America, which is a huge country, there is a lot of work and very few artists with the experience to do it."

"I don't know if it is as easy as you say."

"Have no doubts about it. Just in St. Louis, wherein two years' time the World's Fair will be held, they are going to make hundreds and hundreds of sculptures to decorate the facades of the many buildings that will be built there, the squares, gardens, and streets that will crisscross the fairground. And I have also this project of mine for the bust of Napoleon, which, if it goes ahead, might bring me great fame and fortune. And then indeed I can come back to Europe and relaunch my career here also. And then everything might be different."

"Then can I still harbor some hope that one day you will come back to me?" she asks, her eyes suddenly very open and shining.

"The future belongs to God, Maria. You know what great friendship and esteem I feel for you. And that this month of working together, here in the studio, has contributed to reinforcing it even further. But these are the contingencies of the life I have chosen. For us artists, art is above everything else, no matter how difficult that is for us, no matter how great the solitude and suffering it forces upon us," Aleixo finds himself using the same words that he heard from Nellie's mouth when some years ago she announced to him, without any contemplations, that she was returning to New York.

"Yes. I understand how important it is for you, as an artist, to manage to restart your career, after everything that has happened to you. As it would no doubt be for me if I were in the same circumstances. And although at the moment I am suffering in anticipation because of your departure, I still must admire you even more for your perseverance."

"Thank you, *ma chérie*. Thank you for your understanding," he finally says to her, kissing her hands and then her face softly.

"Well, it must be very late now," she says, suddenly noticing that they are both almost in the dark.

"A quarter to six," says Aleixo, after consulting his watch.

"I have to go. Daddy is at the hotel waiting for me, for dinner," she says, after wiping her eyes and face with a handkerchief, which she takes out of her purse, and after putting a little powder on her cheeks and nose.

"Then we'll leave together. I'm not going to manage to do anything else here today," he says, accompanying her towards the door to the street. Outside there is still a touch of brightness spreading over the sky, while the public street lights are slowly coming on.

XXIII

Ponte do Lima, 22nd of April 1916

SEEN FROM A DISTANCE, the plot could almost be taken for a simple, nameless grave, kept to a large stone slab with a cross on top, which only when seen close up revealed itself to be the covering of a little mortuary chapel, all discreetly built below ground level and only accessible through a folding cover, also in stone, in flagrant contrast with the neighboring vaults on either side of the central aisle of the cemetery, somewhat ridiculous and pretentious in their facades of miniature Gothic cathedrals, he noted as the front of the cortège of which he was a member, along with the other pallbearers, finally approached its destination.

"What a crowd," he exclaimed to himself after a brief look back, at all those anonymous, poor and badly dressed people, who had been joining the cortège as it passed by over the course of the kilometer or more from the parish church, now almost completely filling the access ramp and wide front opening to the cemetery, yet not daring to enter beyond the gates, an area naturally reserved for the members of the family in mourning and the major figures of the land. As soon as the hearse cart stopped in front of the vault the priest began the final prayers and blessings, followed in the utmost silence by those standing by, after which the employees of the funeral company took the coffin on their shoulders and with all due care let it down through the opening to the interior of the underground chapel.

"So Gaspar, what do you say about the declaration of war by Germany?" the Count of Calheiros asked, standing next to him as soon as the ceremony was over when the last undertaker left and closed the trap door to the vault.

"Well, after our government had requisitioned all the German ships anchored in our ports one couldn't expect anything else. Over seventy of them, apparently," replied Gaspar, now that the deep silence that had

415

accompanied the final prayers offered by the priest before the lowering of the coffin had quickly been replaced by increasingly lively conversations among those present, as they awaited their turn to give their formal respects to the family in mourning.

"Your friend Afonso Costa didn't waste any time leaving the government and handing it over to António José de Almeida. With the pretext that the moment demanded a patriotic government, of 'Sacred Union', as he calls it. When what he wants is to put the burden onto the opposition parties in regards to the unpopular measures that our participation in the war is bound to bring about. And then, when people start protesting, the blame won't be on him but the others," João Gomes Abreu e Lima stated as he joined the two of them.

"For a start, he is not, nor ever has been, my friend," a slightly irritated Gaspar was quick to reply. "And secondly, if it were as you say, he would not have kept the most difficult ministries for himself and fellow party members: Finance, War and Foreign Affairs."

"He's not your friend? For god's sake, Gaspar, I've still got that famous speech you made in the Chamber right after the regicide, in which you swore as to his honor and probity, praising him to high heaven," Calheiros recalled with a certain malice.

"True, but at that time no one could imagine what he was about to become: a cruel and merciless man, who would stop at nothing to achieve," replied Gaspar, unhappy about that sudden and untimely evoking of the 'flirting' that he and the dissident progressives, under the leadership of his cousin and friend José d'Alpoim, had carried out with Afonso Costa and several other members of the Republican Party before and after the regicide.

"He should be ashamed to be speaking about sacred union, after not even a year ago, he took his 'democratic' supporters to bring down the government of General Pimenta de Castro, which indeed was a true government of union and national reconciliation. Which didn't just free the monarchists from prison and exile, but gave them effective freedom of expression and association," insisted Calheiros.

"Well, not all of this is bad, now that the Ministry of War is still in the hands of our friend and fellow Minho citizen Norton de Matos. Who, even though he is a Free Mason, is a balanced and sensible man," said João Gomes, to smooth things over.

"And apparently he is doing a good job in preparing our troops to enter the war alongside the British," added Gaspar.

"More cannon fodder is what it is. Which the German artillery will not forgive. When those formidable Big Bertha cannons start to fire over the allied trenches it will be a veritable slaughter. And then it's everyone for himself," commented Aleixo, thinner and paler than the last time, but well-dressed and elegant as always in his black overcoat, high hat, and silver-topped Bengal cane, joining the queue that had in the meantime formed in front of José Sá Coutinho, Count of Aurora and Maria Cândida Malheiro Reymão, Viscountess of the Torre, nephew and niece and closest relatives of the deceased, Lady Ana Cândida de Araújo Vasconcellos Feio, First Countess of Aurora.

"A virtuous lady, whom we came here to bury today," commented Aleixo as soon as they had said their goodbyes and turned towards the exit to the cemetery, passing through all those poor people who were standing around, no doubt waiting for the important folk of the land to go so they could pay their last respects to their protector over so many years.

"Indeed. A kind soul, who always practiced good for the poor, for the underprivileged. It is said that they came by the dozens to knock at her door, up there in the Nossa Senhora da Aurora House. And now they have all come to the funeral to say their farewells to her forever. No doubt grateful for all the good things she did for them."

"I rarely remember seeing so many people in this cemetery."

"Well, lad. It's almost one o'clock. What shall we do?" Gaspar suddenly asked after glancing at his watch.

"So let's go for lunch. It's not every day that I have the pleasure and honor of having my dear, beloved brother Gaspar here with me," said Aleixo, affectionately giving his brother his arm.

"Where should we go? I don't know anything here," the latter asked pragmatically.

"We could go to the Hotel do Arrabalde, which belongs to a Spanish family from Galicia. It's a modest place, but the food isn't bad at all. That's where I have lunch and receive people on market days, like today," replied Aleixo.

"Fine, but in that case, we'll go in my motorcar, man. I've had enough of walking today," said Gaspar, annoyed after the walk from the parish church and pointing to his beautiful *Hispano-Suiza* automobile, Afonso XIII model, parked right there in the square, next to which stood Agostinho, his chauffeur, impeccable in his dark gray outfit, knee-length boots, and peaked cap, awaiting instructions.

"Well, I left my horse-drawn brake down in the town, so I have no choice but to accept your invitation," replied Aleixo, somewhat put out, due to his visceral aversion to automobiles, before sitting in the back seat, with the top down so they could enjoy the warmth and sun of that fine spring day.

"There you go with that mania of yours about horse-drawn carriages. When are you going to stop that? Today's automobiles are nothing like those of fifteen or twenty years ago. They are the safest, most comfortable, and fastest form of transport that exists, you can be sure," Gaspar answered as soon as he sat down next to his brother.

"I've got my doubts about that, my dear Gaspar. Every day I'm always going past automobiles in my carriage. Comfortably sitting there, with no unpleasant noise or smells. And the more they sound their horns the faster the horses run. Sometimes my problem is precisely that of being able to hold the horses back after they hear a few horns honking. So they don't take the bit between their teeth," countered Aleixo, now with the automobile going down the steep slope connecting the access road to the center of the town.

"Well, with the forty horsepower engine of my *Hispano-Suiza* I don't have those problems. Everything is solved with the gears, the brake and the accelerator, isn't that right, Agostinho?" his brother replied good-humoredly, putting his hand on the chauffeur's shoulder, the latter then nodding agreement when they were coming down to the bottom of the slope.

"How is my dear sister Isabel getting on?" Aleixo suddenly asked, referring to his sister-in-law, Isabel Corte Real, whom Gaspar had married years earlier, remarrying after a long period as a widower.

"She stayed in Marco de Canaveses this time, which is where she really feels at home. Lavandeira is a beautiful house. One of these days you must come and visit," Gaspar proposed as they were passing by the parish church, carrying on towards the Largo de Camões.

"I certainly shall," promised Aleixo, looking absent-mindedly at the very busy stalls in the fortnightly market set up there along that stretch of the riverbank.

"There is no doubt that the battlements grant a different presence to the bridge, a greater dignity. A good job you managed to convince them to place them there, Aleixinho."

"Indeed, but you can't imagine the trouble I had, even though I was paying for it all. With the Town Council, the Government, the Heritage Committee. A world of bureaucracy and difficulties. But anyway, now it's done. I just hope they don't start to come down with the next floods, as happened last year with the parapet," replied Aleixo, as the automobile stopped outside the Hotel do Arrabalde, in the Vasco da Gama Street, a modern, good-sized building, with five bay windows all along the first floor, decorated with stone masonry work rounded off at the corners, which was repeated further above on the second floor, but without the windows jutting out. A little further up, on the opposite side of the street, was the Nossa Senhora da Aurora House, with its windows and shutters closed, with the family coat of arms on the corner covered in black cloth as a sign of mourning for the death of the Countess.

"So you come here punctually to have lunch every market day?" asked Gaspar as they went up the two flights of the wide wooden staircase leading from the entrance hall to the first floor where the dining room was, taking up the whole of the front of the building.

"To have lunch and to receive people: housekeepers, neighbors, and people with the most varied requests. Then for a fortnight, until the next market day, I can rest. No one else bothers me," replied Aleixo as they were waiting at the entrance to the room for the owner of the hotel to come and seat them.

"Good Morning, gentlemen," the man greeted them in a thick Galician Spanish accent, bowing low almost down to his feet before pointing out a free table near to one of the bay windows over the street.

"So, Manolo, what do you have for us to eat today?" asked Aleixo, as Gaspar looked at the man. Short, bald, stocky, with a scruffy white apron around his waist, covering his serge trousers almost down to his shoes, unable not to feel surprised at how his brother, who was an artist and man of the world, had settled so comfortably into his new role as a wealthy landowner and farmer.

"Today we have *Arroz de Sarrabulho*, and *Rojões à Minhota*, which are really special. Besides these, we have roast kid with roast potatoes and *Bacalhau à Zé do Pipo*, which are also both excellent choices," replied Manolo, in his ringing tone set somewhere between northern Portugal and Spain.

"Well. If you want my opinion go for the rice and the kid. They're top-notch," suggested Aleixo.

"Excellent. Then that it is. I haven't had *Sarrabulho* for a long time. And then the roast kid to follow, also a great dish."

"And to drink?" asked the Galician.

"There's no need to ask that, Manolo. Bring a carafe of that delicious home-produced *Alvarinho* you have there," requested Aleixo, as he occasionally nodded in acknowledgment to the respectful greetings coming to him from the surrounding tables.

"And what do you do with the rest of the time around here?" Gaspar asked, returning to the issue after Manolo had withdrawn amid bows and 'thank yous'.

"I read, I write, I draw, I go riding in the countryside."

"Don't you get bored with only that to entertain you?"

"Sometimes. But on those occasions, I take a Victoria carriage or a brake and go over to Refojos to see my colts and my horses. Sometimes I stay there for a few days busying myself."

"A few days? Do you have so much to do there?" asked Gaspar with some suspicion, suddenly recalling certain rumors that were going around about a little arrangement between his brother and a woman called Branca, whom he had employed as the housekeeper for the Convent.

"There's always a lot to see, to decide. Not just with the horses, but also the other things I have over there: the orchards, the vineyards, the corn, the grain," replied Aleixo, as Manolo served them the sparkling *Alvarinho* from his native Galicia.

"That goes down quite nicely," commented Gaspar, glass in hand and clicking his tongue while thinking: 'What if it's true? So what? A man isn't made of ice. And above all his wife is so far away, on the other side of the Atlantic...'

"What did you expect? I only bring you to the best places, man. The only place better is the Procope, in Paris. Or our Tavares Rico, in Lisbon," replied Aleixo ironically, after also tasting the wine.

"What do you do with all the produce from what you grow over at the Convent?" Gaspar insisted.

"Well, a lot of what I planted isn't producing anything yet, as is the case of the vineyards and the orchards. And the intensive cereal farming, using American methods, hasn't worked out very well. The labor force is weak, and the people ignorant and untrained. No matter how hard one teaches them how to do things they don't understand. And as soon as one turns one's back they do things wrongly, in their own manner. Conclusion: it is an almost complete disaster," he answered, with some indifference.

"But Aleixo, excuse my frankness, what do you know about these new forms of farming that you can teach them? You being an artist whose main occupation in life has always been sculpting?"

"What I've read in books, lad. And what I saw being done in the United States, on the giant properties that the Stetsons have in Florida and in California. And on other great estates I visited over recent years to see how it was done."

"And you honestly think that enables you to come here, to such a backward place as this, where things have been done in the same way for centuries and centuries, and so radically change these people's mentality? Because what you are proposing is a real revolution, lad. In the farming and production methods."

"I was convinced I could, that I would do it, but unfortunately the practice has shown me the opposite. Without base training like what is taught there to farmers, one can achieve nothing other than disappointments and setbacks. So that what I'm left with now are my horses, my stud farm. Today, before you go back to Gondarém, you must go and see it. You'll be surprised," replied Aleixo, suddenly enthusiastic, as Manolo came over with his *Arroz de Sarrabulho,* made with blood and pork, beef and chicken, all in an earthenware pot, which he immediately began to serve.

"Fine, as long as we don't finish lunch too late, because I don't want to travel at night."

"You won't need to. Come and see it with me and then you can carry straight on," Aleixo proposed.

"We'll see. Because there's no doubt that you know about horses, it always has been one of your big passions. And good quality grooms must also be easy to find around here. The problem is that in the future, with the expansion of the automobile industry, horses will be used less and less. Only for recreation and bullfights, nothing else. So I don't really see the point of having a stud farm here in the Minho when there are plenty of them in the Alentejo, with much greater tradition and quality," said Gaspar skeptically as he opened up space in his rice to let it cool more quickly.

"It's worth the trouble just for the pleasure of seeing the young being born and growing up to an adult age," his brother replied before taking another drink.

"Frankly, Aleixo, it breaks my heart to see you here alone in the middle of these dull backwoods with your young colts and horses. And the failure of the intensive crops on your model farm. You are a first-rate artist, above most others, capable of remarkable works like the *Christ* in Santa Luzia, or that *Vasco da Gama* you have over there in Philadelphia. You have a wife who admires and esteems you so much, to the point of satisfying all your whims, no matter how absurd they are. And you are, after all, a man of the world, who lived a large part of your life in major cities like Paris, Chicago, and New York," Gaspar stated indignantly, before tasting his rice and stew.

"What do you want me to do, man? Sail off now on a steamer across the Atlantic, subject to being sunk by some German submarine, like what happened last year with the *Lusitania*?"

"No, it's not that, but…"

"…My favorite steamer. I used that dozens of times on my trips between New York and Paris. Plunged to the bottom of the sea in less than twenty minutes…. Almost one thousand and two hundred lost souls, Gaspar. A disaster only comparable to the sinking of the *Titanic*," Aleixo recalled, horrified.

"Yes, but it appears that it was carrying weapons and munitions sent by the Americans to the Allies. Which obviously went against its status of neutrality."

"Even so, nothing justified such a vile and cowardly attack as that one, without any forewarning, against a passenger ship. On which only innocent civilians were traveling, who had nothing to do with the conflict."

"No doubt. An abject act. And of enormous cruelty."

"So I'm not risking the journey until the war is over. Despite the half-baked excuses by the Germans concerning the Lusitania and their promises not to get up to the same thing again, it is still very dangerous to cross the Atlantic."

"What's the matter? Aren't you eating? This *Arroz de Sarrabulho* is a specialty," said Gaspar, noticing that his brother had not touched his food.

"I haven't had much of an appetite lately," explained Aleixo, taking his fork and somewhat uninterestedly putting a little rice in his mouth."

"On the subject, a little while ago you said that when at Glória, besides reading and writing, you are also drawing. So what drawings are they?" asked Gaspar, totally off the subject.

"Well, ideas for sculptures, what else? That I sketch out in charcoal, in their different details, I don't really know for what purpose. Perhaps out of professional habits, or because I don't know how to do anything else. Because after all, who is to say that I will feel like going back to sculpting when I can finally return to the United States?" he finished, now definitively pushing away his plate after two or three more forkfuls.

"Don't you still have that studio in New York?"

"No. After the sinking of the *Lusitania*, when I realized that I wasn't going back to America so soon, I decided that the best thing was to get rid of it. And so I asked Isabel to deal with the matter."

"And what has she done with the things you had there?"

"She has had everything put into storage in New York, waiting for better times: unfinished works and ones to finish, models, tools and I don't know what else," said Aleixo glumly, as Manolo cleared away the plates.

"Why don't you set up a studio here in Glória in the meantime? Or over in the Convent, where you have more room?" asked Gaspar, wiping his mouth with his napkin, now more consoled.

"I've thought about that on occasion, but it is all very complicated. Sculpture is very demanding, not like painting, or poetry, which you can do anywhere. You need materials like clay and plaster, you need stone and you need people to help and are trained for the purpose. You need easels and daises, or even scaffolding for the larger works…"

"But all of that should not be so difficult to get, Aleixo. You could have it sent from Braga or even Oporto…"

"Yes but then you know what it is like. I'm always waiting for the war to end at any moment and then I can finally go back to America. The only place where, when one looks at it properly, I can still see myself working as a sculptor. Because here hardly anyone sees me as one anymore. And the few who do think I have completely abandoned the activity after my marriage to Isabel. For them, deep down, I am no more than an extravagant landowner who goes around throwing money about on fantastic projects that are wildly absurd," said Aleixo, somewhat acrimoniously, as Manolo was approaching with the serving of roast kid.

"Another jug of *Alvarinho*, gentlemen?" he asked.

"And perhaps, just between the two of us, they might be right to an extent, Aleixinho. After all, instead of using the money that Isabel has so generously granted you, enabling you to concentrate on that in which you truly have real talent, in which you are unique and irreplaceable, your sculpture, you are wasting it by buying land and more land and doing agricultural experiments for which you definitely do not seem to be suited to do," stated Gaspar.

"My sculpture, my sculpture. Come on, who is interested in it nowadays, Gaspar? Tell me."

"A lot of people. At least judging by what you told me about the works you presented two years ago at the *Salon* in Paris, in homage to your friend Saint-Gaudens, just before the war broke out. Which had good references in the French and American newspapers and that the New York City Council was interested in having to put in one of the parks in the city.

"Yes but that was long ago, good grief. And in the meantime I had the bad, the terrible idea of coming to Portugal, and what if I can never leave again?" asked Aleixo, dejected.

"Perhaps the war will end sooner than is thought and you'll still be in time," said Gaspar optimistically, enjoying his first taste of roast kid which had just been served.

"With my luck lately I doubt it very much. It's always the same thing. When I'm one step, one simple step from getting the recognition I aspire to so much, something always comes along…something that stops me from getting there. And it's always been like that throughout these over twenty years of devotion to art," replied Aleixo, looking at his plate with boredom, undecided about trying the kid. "Sometimes I find myself thinking that the only true glory I have really achieved until now is a house, over there in Jolda, in the borough of Arcos de Valdevez, which in a twist of fate, is exactly called Glória. And even so, I had no other choice but to buy it. And then to have a new road built in order to get there more quickly. To Glory," he added sarcastically.

"I think you are exaggerating, Aleixinho. It's not that bad. Your career is full of successes. Which have made a lot of people envious."

"Really? Whom? Tell me," said Aleixo disdainfully.

"Well, to start there is the enormous triumph you had at the *Salon* with your *Êxtase Religioso* when you were still a simple student of sculpture in Paris. And which almost earned you a medal…"

"Exactly, 'almost'…"

"…followed by the *Heart of Jesus,* which was praised by most of the Lisbon newspapers and critics. And which is still there impressively in Santa Luzia…"

"Yes, but how often have they wanted to take it down to melt the bronze in order to get some more money to pay for that horrible temple by Ventura Terra that they are building?" Aleixo pointed out after taking another long swig of *Alvarinho.*

"Well, there are plenty of stupid and ignorant people. Which doesn't mean it isn't a work enjoyed by the others, those who are neither ignorant nor stupid. And the same thing happened with the *Vasco da Gama,* which received the highest praise in the French and Portuguese press of the time…"

"Even so, I never even managed to win the first prize in the Centenary sculpture competition, despite there only being two entrants…"

"But at the time you won the one for the Sousa Martins monument, which was much more important…"

"Yes, the more the worse for me. If I for one moment could imagine what would happen after, then I would never even have entered the competition…" insisted Aleixo in the same tone, nodding to Manolo to bring more wine.

"…And you almost won the one for Czar Alexander II, in Bulgaria…"

"Yes, almost. By a whisker… But the truth is that once again I didn't win. Despite having the almost unanimous support of the Bulgarian press, the Prince and the greatest intellectuals in the country. But once again I didn't win. I came second…"

"Well, the truth is that you didn't have much luck either with the bust of Napoleon you took to the World's Fair in St. Louis…"

"Oh! I had almost forgotten about that one. A grandiose, magnificent project. Which I took with me as a model, set out in all of its details: a giant bust of Napoleon to be built inside the fairground in iron and cement, the same height as the Statue of Liberty, on the inside containing huge halls that could be adapted to the different ceremonies of the fair, illuminated by windows set out in such a manner that from below they would give the impression of being hair…"

"A remarkable idea. And so original…"

"But as soon as I got to New York I fell ill with Typhus which almost left me at death's door. When I finally recovered, the opportunity to present my project to the authorities had gone, because all the decisions about the fairground had already been made," recalled Aleixo.

"Well, being so bitter and pessimistic as you are, I won't even dare to mention the statue of Queen Amélia… A work of genius, according to what I could see from the photographs you showed me at the time…"

"Which is rotting over there in the warehouse in New York; because I finished it too late…. The monarchy was already on its last legs by then. Everyone thought it was excellent but no one would risk putting it in a square in Lisbon. Or in one of the royal palaces…"

"And that beautiful statuette of Dr. Cook, the discoverer of the North Pole, of which you sent me the photograph printed on a postcard, what happened to that?"

"It's best not to talk about that. When the *Arctic Club of America,* who commissioned it from me, were ready to cast it in marble to have it placed in one of the parks in New York at the request of the City Council, in homage to the person then considered to be the Vasco da Gama of the modern age, the man falls into disgrace, having been accused of being a charlatan. And of never having reached the North Pole at all. Result, he was expelled from the *Arctic Club* and, once again, everything was called off…" said Aleixo, concluding, holding his fork over his plate and seeming to have lost the little appetite he still had.

"Well, when you look at things there is no doubt that you haven't had luck on your side, Aleixinho. If I believed in witches I would even say that someone put the evil eye on you," said Gaspar, after finishing his second course.

"Perhaps you are right. Who knows?"

"But after hearing you describe all these setbacks of yours I have to think that perhaps it all would have been different if instead of going to America, you had stayed here and fought, replying to your detractors with the quality and originality of your work, without ever being intimidated by them. Until you were finally recognized and accepted. Doing things differently, like all of those who dared innovate throughout the centuries. Isn't that right?"

"Who? For example."

"Your Rodin, without having to look too far. He always laughed scornfully at all the criticisms of him throughout his career—and there were lots of it—as he was so convinced of his path, of his truth. Even going so far as to present his *Balzac* at the *Salon*, straight after it had been rejected by the Society that had commissioned it. You told me that yourself. Or Van Gogh and Gauguin, who never let themselves be intimidated by the insults and criticisms directed at them and their works. Until they ended up being recognized as the great artists that they are today. Or poets like Baudelaire, sued because of his *Fleurs du Mal*. And writers like Flaubert, also the target of a process because of his *Madame Bovary*. And it wasn't because of opposition that either of them stopped writing or publishing."

"But none of them saw their works being destroyed after having been solemnly inaugurated, as I did, Gasparinho. No matter how many criticisms and insults they might have faced. And just that fact makes all the difference..."

"Yes, that's true, but..."

"...because I was ready for criticisms and setbacks, they always exist, especially when one tries to do something new, something different. But not to see a monument of mine demolished with total impunity, like had never been seen before in any country in civilized Europe, and without anyone raising a finger to defend me. Nor to be insulted and humiliated in public, made a laughing stock in all the humorous newspapers for over two years. Until I was cowardly beaten up by a group of wild madmen, like I was," blurted out Aleixo bitterly, then drinking all the wine in his glass in one gulp.

"Yes, you're right. It is a situation that really has no parallel with anything that might have happened in other countries that are certainly more educated and civilized than ours, where coarseness and ignorance still reign. But if you had perhaps managed to hang on a little longer, to see whether things calmed down, to then go back to your work…"

"Who would be interested in giving me any work at that time? After everything that had happened?"

"And what would you like for dessert? We have rice pudding, *leite-crème*, jam with cheese…" interrupted Manolo, taking advantage of a pause in the conversation.

"If you want my advice, go for the rice pudding. It's delicious. Almost as good as we had at home," advised Aleixo.

"Rice pudding it is, then," agreed Gaspar, before getting back to the thread of the conversation. "But you realize that when you went to America you ended up leaving yourself open to your detractors?"

"Yes, but if you recall I had no intention of going there to stay. My original idea was to go and present the model for the bust of Napoleon to the authorities at the St. Louis World's Fair and, if things went well, stay there for a while until things calmed down here. It was only later when there was the possibility of being named Consul in Chicago, that I decided to settle there. As that gave me an albeit modest base for subsistence and at the same time, being consul, I had access to the rich and influential people in the city, through whom I could get some work as a sculptor.

"But that was now another type of career, different from the one you had before. In which sculpture was added to by another type of concern and obligation, as a diplomatic representative of Portugal…"

"You know, many years ago, in Paris, there was someone who said something to me that I will never forget as long as I live. And which I have been thinking about a lot lately, particularly since I received the sad news of her untimely passing…"

"Who was that?"

"Nellie, Nellie Mears. The American sculptor on whom I had a crush when I was studying there, remember?"

"Yes, I have a vague idea."

"She died two months ago. She wasn't even forty, imagine. Single, living in New York with her sister, who was a writer, in a house that was also her studio."

"What did she die of, being so young?" asked Gaspar again, visibly enjoying his rice pudding, unlike his brother, again holding his spoon dangling over his dish as he spoke.

"It was sudden. According to the New York Times, it was heart disease."

"So what did she say to you that was so important that you never forgot it?"

"That artists cannot have a life like other people, a bourgeois, stable life with all the comforts and commodities. That for them their art is above everything else, no matter how hard it is for them, no matter how much solitude and suffering they are forced to accept."

"A beautiful philosophy of life, no doubt about it. But who are the artists who can follow it nowadays?" asked Gaspar, after finishing his dessert.

"She did, to the end. Without ever waiving or making concessions. Living on the edge of subsistence, from the little she could earn from her works."

"And would you have been able to live a life like this, made up of solitude and suffering, just out of love for art?"

"At the beginning, when I was in Paris, I thought so. But after everything that happened in Lisbon I realized I couldn't, I wasn't able to—that I had to take advantage of other opportunities that came my way. Like the case of the consular position in Chicago. Or, later, my marriage to Isabel," replied Aleixo, after a prolonged silence, as Manolo came with the coffee and brandy.

"So we come back to the same thing: if particularly with your marriage, you finally managed to get the financial stability that you desired in order to carry on with your art without great sacrifices, this also gave you the means to occupy yourself with other things. Like the farms you decided to start to buy. Or the agricultural experiments you have been devoting yourself to over the recent years. And which have ended up distracting you from that which was your main vocation, sculpture."

"That's true. Without the means given to me by my marriage, I would never have been able to do any of what I have done here..." interrupted Aleixo, a cup of coffee in his hand, before taking two small sips.

"...if you had invested all that capital and time working hard in your studio in New York you might have had more bad luck like you had with the statue of Dr. Cook, or of Queen Amélia. But you certainly would have had other opportunities of equal or greater value, through which you could have built a much more solid and consistent career. And which, when you think about it, you still have plenty of time to do as soon as you can get back," stressed Gaspar optimistically.

"Perhaps. Perhaps you are right. Perhaps it is not too late to rethink my life, my aims, and my priorities. And start over. After all, I'm still only just forty-eight. If God gives me life and health I can live another forty-eight…"

"At least until ninety, lad, like the venerable lady we came here to bury…Well, it's time for us to be getting on, don't you think?" said Gaspar, noticing that the room was now completely empty of other customers.

"Yes, but to go to Refojos, to the Convent to see my colts, my foals, right? I insist," stated Aleixo, with a slight stutter in his voice.

"It'll have to be a quick visit. It's almost four o'clock, and at half-past six it is dark," replied Gaspar after looking at his watch.

"Don't worry. In your powerful *Hispano-Suiza* you'll be in Gondarém in a jiffy," said Aleixo, slightly swaying as he walked to the door after having generously paid Manolo without even looking at the check for the meal.

"Yes, but even so we have to hurry," replied his brother as they went down the stairs after Manolo had ordered one of his stable boys to bring the Count's carriage to the front of the building.

"How shall we go? Do you want to go ahead, or shall I?" asked Aleixo, taking the reins from the stable boy before stepping up into the brake, with two pairs of powerful Alter horses at the back and two elegant English mares upfront.

"You go on. I'll catch you up. First I have to go over to the Café Camões and buy a box of cigars," replied Gaspar, walking towards his *Hispano-Suiza*, parked a few yards further down.

"We'll see about whether you catch me or not," Aleixo said as a challenge, immediately setting off down the road to the Largo de S. João, then carrying on towards the bridge, while the car went on to the square.

"When you see the Count's brake, slow down and follow behind him, do you hear Agostinho? But no honking the horns, or the horses will get frightened," Gaspar shouted to his driver as soon as he started the car up again on the way to the bridge.

Hopefully, the conversation may have been useful. And he might finally learn some sense, he said to himself as he lit his cigar, unwittingly recalling what he had just told his brother about the way he was wasting his time and squandering money instead of investing them in the only thing that he really knew and was good at: sculpture. Perhaps he had been a little too tough on him, he thought, but truths were there to be said, and he, as a brother and a friend, could not carry on for much longer watching that slow but inexorable destruction of a life and of a career, just like that. And was she, Elisabeth, aware of the harm she was doing to her husband, making limitless amounts of money available to him to satisfy all his whims, all of his fantasies? He wondered, looking distractedly at the beautiful facade of the Paço de Calheiros on his left, half-hidden by the vegetation. Probably not. She would probably be doing it with the greatest of intentions, convinced that this would be the way he felt satisfied and fulfilled when it was exactly the opposite. The truth is that since the days after the destruction of his monument in Lisbon he hadn't seen him so unhappy and unprotected as now, but perhaps his talk might produce some effect and he might be convinced to set up a studio in the Convent, in the old monks' refectory or somewhere. Where, little by little, he would recover his path again, that which was truly his vocation, until he could return to the United States and take up his career again, he said to himself when, after a tight bend, they began to climb up to the São Simão hill.

"The Count's brake is taking its time to appear, Sir," Agostinho suddenly said, turning back worriedly.

"Don't worry, man. It's because he had to stop off somewhere on the way," replied Gaspar, used as he was to his brother's fancies, as his stop at the café was very short and the car went at over twenty miles an hour, a lot faster than a brake can achieve, even when pulled by two powerful pairs of thoroughbreds enticed by two English mares. On his left side, glancing through the thick woodland covering the top of the hill, there appeared the little chapel of São Simão, a short while before they finally began their descent to Refojos, a green and fertile valley protected by mountains and hills, stretching along the right bank of the River Lima, in an extensive reticule of meadows and fields of corn, divided by rows of trees and trellises, in the middle of which rose the impressive figure of the enormous monastery with the parish church next to it.

"Sir, there are some people down there. Wouldn't it be best to stop to see whether they have seen the Count's carriage go by?" Agostinho suddenly asked, seeing a group of villagers standing shouting and waving their arms on the road further ahead, near to a bend.

"What is that? What's going on over there?" Gaspar hardly had time to say, his heart beating wildly, not wanting to believe what his eyes were seeing as the car came closer: a smashed-up brake lying in the ditch on the left, at the entrance to the road that his brother had built up to the Paço da Glória, and a little further ahead, surrounded by the group of villagers, what seemed to be a body lying lifeless on the ground.

"It was an accident, sir. It was an accident," said one of the locals, his face tanned by the sun, his hat pulled down to his ears, as soon as the car stopped at the edge of the road.

"It is the nobleman from the Convent. He was driving so fast that when the horses turned this way the carriage couldn't hold on and turned over, releasing the horses. And the poor man was thrown out into the ditch, God help us," added another man, taking his hat off while talking to the elegant and well-dressed gentleman who was rushing towards the fallen body.

"Aleixo, Aleixinho! Can you hear me?" asked Gaspar, trying to remain calm, kneeling at his brother's side, after putting his ear to his chest and sensing that his heart was still beating. He then undid the knot in his tie, unbuttoned the front of his shirt, and raised his head, putting his folded overcoat under it. "Aleixo, Aleixo. Come on, wake up," he insisted, slapping him lightly on the cheeks, which were stained by the blood flowing profusely from a deep gash on the top of his head.

"Eh? What happened? What's going on?" Aleixo finally replied, opening his eyes for moments.

"You had an accident, lad. Don't you remember?" asked Gaspar, staring at him.

"Yes. An automobile, a damn automobile…started honking its horn at the exit to the bridge…and the horses got frightened…. They took the bit between their teeth…I couldn't control them anymore…until the bend, the bend to my road…"

"They wanted to go home, the rascals. It always happens when they get frightened and take the bit between their teeth," explained Gaspar.

"They must be getting there by now, the speed they were going," said the local villager who had spoken first.

"What about your legs? Can you feel them? Are they hurting? Can you move them?" asked Gaspar, helping him to bend his knees, bleeding under the tears in his trousers.

"Yes. I think so…more or less," babbled Aleixo.

"At least it looks like nothing is broken, thank God. Let's see if you can stand up," said Gaspar, putting his arm behind his back, and at the same time signaling to Agostinho to do the same on the other side. "So, how do you feel?" he asked as soon as his brother was totally standing up.

"It could be worse," he replied, trying to put his feet firmly on the ground.

"You're a lucky man. With a fall like that, you are lucky not to have stayed where you fell."

"The worst thing is my back…. It hurts me a lot…. And here in front, on my belly," said Aleixo, suddenly contracting his face in a spasm of pain as he touched his abdomen.

"One or two broken ribs and some bruises. Nothing that one or two weeks' rest won't solve," suggested Gaspar, looking at his thin back after lifting up his shirt.

"Do you think so?" said Aleixo, not very convinced.

"Well, let's see if you can get to the automobile," proposed Gaspar, nodding to Agostinho to help him, as the villagers attentively watched the development of the operation. Then Agostinho opened the back door, got into the automobile, again holding Aleixo behind his back, until he got him to sit on the seat with the aid of Gaspar from the outside.

"Oh, Hell! I lost my wig," Aleixo suddenly noticed as he ran his hand over his head after the automobile had started off towards the Convent.

"It must have fallen off when you fell. Don't worry. When you are better you'll have another one made," replied Gaspar, next to him, only then noticing that sudden, drastic change in his brother's appearance, who was now totally bald, without a hair on his head, which, added to his bloodied face and disheveled appearance, made him look ten years older.

"Where, good Lord? That one was made in Paris…" replied Aleixo, suddenly upset.

"Look here, lad. Rather your wig than your head. And give thanks to God that it wasn't anything worse," blurted Gaspar, as they were turning right, going up the road that passed among houses and huts on their way to the square in front of the parish church, and from there into the Convent estate through the main gate, then parking near to the door leading to the cloister.

"Oh, my Blessed Virgin Mary! What a calamity, what a calamity," a pretty young girl cried out tearfully as she came running out of the building to the automobile, as she realized the awful state that Aleixo was in, with his head back and eyes closed as if he were dead.

"Calm down, girl, it's not so bad," said Gaspar, now outside the car, seeing that sudden, unusual explosion from the girl, who was no other than Branca, the much-talked-about housekeeper that his brother had brought from Viana do Castelo to look after the Convent. And for who knew what else.

"What happened to you, my poor thing?" she asked, looking at her boss in distress.

"The horses got the bit between their teeth and the carriage turned over," Gaspar explained dryly, looking the girl up and down, unable to notice in her a certain elegance in her deportment and dress, with very bright clear eyes, harmonious features, blondish hair up at the neck and well presented in a silk blouse with flesh-colored frills and a brown serge skirt.

"So it was this time. I've been afraid it would happen for a long time, Sir. The Count goes around so fast on these roads," she replied, after a long sigh, as Aleixo straightened up his head and opened his eyes, looking at her for a brief moment and then closing them again.

"Well, now we have to take him inside and put him in bed, to see if he gets some rest. Please send for an armchair and some pillows so we can carry him as comfortably as possible upstairs to his bedroom," ordered Gaspar, before going back into the car to see how his brother was reacting, after Branca had gone inside along with two servants, then appearing again with a Blackwood armchair full of pillows, which they set down next to the car. Following this, Agostinho, aided by one of the servants, picked up the wounded Aleixo and sat him down as comfortably as he could on the chair, then, led by Branca, they carried him along the entrance hall to the cloister, and from there to the stairs up to the top floor, to the quarters that Aleixo had set up and furnished for his stays in Refojos as soon as he bought the monastery. At the end of the corridor, Agostinho and the servant went into the bedroom, following Branca, lifted Aleixo from the armchair with the same care that they had sat him down, and laid him on the large four-poster bed that occupied the center of the vast room.

"Poor thing. We have to take care of him right away, clean up his wounds," said Branca in a faltering voice, then immediately sending one of the servants to fetch a bowl of hot water, compresses, and towels.

"Yes, but the most important thing is to send someone to Ponte do Lima straight away to bring a doctor. The idea I got was that there probably isn't any major injury except for some broken ribs and some bruises and scratches. But just to be safe the best thing is for him to be seen by someone who knows," said Gaspar, glancing casually around the whole room, occupying the whole breadth of that wing of the building, with a bay window to the south, from which there was a stunning view over the river and the nearby lands. Next door there was a little room, also with a bay window, but facing west, and a bathroom with a WC.

"Of course, Sir. I will give the orders right away," replied Branca as Gaspar went over to his brother, who in the meantime appeared to have fallen asleep.

"And tomorrow I wish to have news. In the morning send me a telegram from the post office in Ponte do Lima, do you hear?" he said, on his way to the door, precisely when the two maids were arriving with the bowl of hot water, the compresses, and the towels.

"Of course, Sir. And wouldn't it be best to send a telegram to the Countess as well, to tell her what happened?" suggested Branca, accompanying him along the corridor.

"Yes, but I'll take care of that. Don't worry. Now go and take care of your patient, I know the way out," said Gaspar finally, looking at his watch, showing almost five. 'With a bit of luck I'll still get to Gondarém before nightfall,' he thought, rushing down the steps and then stopping for a moment to look at the "swimming pool" that his brother had ordered built in the center of the cloister: a vast water mirror inside the little wall supporting the pillars, which he had connected and cemented all round, leaving the old granite fountain in the middle, emerging from the water. "Artist's things," he said out loud, shaking his head, before turning and walking towards the exit. "Artist's things."

EPILOGUE

ALEIXO DE QUEIROZ RIBEIRO DE SOTTO MAYOR D'ALMEIDA E VASCONCELLOS, COUNT OF SANTA EULÁLIA, DIED ON THE 6TH OF MAY 1917, AT THE RIPE AGE OF 50, "having been tortured over about three months by an incurable disease," as was stated in his obituary in the *Comércio do Lima* newspaper. Popular legend states that his dog was found dead on the following morning at the door to the room where his body was laid in a mourning coffin.

His funeral took place on the 10th of May in the Refojos do Lima Cemetery, and according to the newspapers of the time, over eighty ecclesiastical figures were in attendance, as well as a large number of people from Ponte do Lima, from Viana do Castelo, from Arcos de Valdevez and from Ponte da Barca, in that which was considered by the *Jornal de Vianna* newspaper as an "eloquent demonstration of the loss felt by the departing of such an eminent citizen."

His widow, Sarah Elizabeth Stetson, Countess of Santa Eulália, arrived in Refojos do Lima four days after the funeral, on the 14th of May, having come from the United States of America, "from which she departed, despite the enormous risks involved in the journey, to come to accompany her husband in his illness, as soon as she had been given word of it," according to the *Aurora do Lima* newspaper.

In 1922, John Stetson Jr, the eldest son of Elizabeth, made a donation to the University of Harvard, where he had studied, of a holding of about nine thousand books in Portuguese, in memory of his stepfather, the Count of Santa Eulália, a grant which was completed over the following years with further donations, all of which may still be consulted in the university library.

Elizabeth died in 1929 due to an attack of pneumonia when she was visiting her younger son, G. Henry, on his *Sombrero Rancho* estate in Pasadena, California.

ACKNOWLEDGEMENTS

FIRST OF ALL, MY THOUGHTS must go out to Lewis Stetson Allen, without whose help this book would probably never have been written, at least not in its final form. I will never forget the way Lewis welcomed me to his house in Boston, and how he immediately set me at ease so that I could research the documents and objects that were in his possession relating to the marriage of his great-grandmother, Sarah Elizabeth Stetson, to my great-uncle, Aleixo de Queiroz Ribeiro, Count of Santa Eulália. Just as I cannot ever forget the prompt way in which, over the five long and thrilling years that have seen the writing of this work, he always dispelled my doubts in the many emails we exchanged, as well as during his increasingly assiduous personal visits to Portugal.

I must also mention his mother, Elizabeth Stetson Allen, whom I visited in Washington, in the company of Lewis. At the ripe old age of 102, she was the only survivor among those who knew or who spent some time with Aleixo, according to the personal information she shared with me about him and about her grandmother.

I must as well recall my father, Ernesto, and his brother, Gaspar, who shared with me, since my childhood, many stories and legends about this extraordinary figure, introducing in me bit by bit an increasing need to write this book.I want to thank also Luiz de Azeredo Vaz Pinto and Joaquim Queiroz Ribeiro de Sousa Coutinho for having granted me access to Aleixo's artworks and documents existing at Casa da Boavista and Casa da Loureira.

I remember as well the sculptor José Rodrigues and José Maria Tavares da Rosa, for the useful information they gave me about the techniques and processes involved in the art of sculpture; Luís de Castro Vaz Pinto, for his medical advice about the way the death of the protagonist of this novel probably occurred. All my thanks to Father António Vaz Pinto, for the information he granted me about certain aspects of the liturgy of the Catholic Church; Francisco de Vasconcelos, for helping in the research of issues relating to titles of nobility and the granting of honors; Professor Jacinto Rodrigues, for his useful advice concerning historical research and the enthusiasm he aroused in me about the extraordinary figure of Father Himalaya, a unique scientist, and inventor; and Rui Viana, Chief Librarian of the Viana do Castelo Public Library for his precious help during my regional newspaper research.

Finally, all my gratitude to Paula Mendes Coelho, my wife, for the infinite patience and enthusiasm with which she accompanied me throughout the long process of gestation and creation of this book, of which she was the first, tireless reader. Above all, however, I must thank her for her literary intelligence, her critical spirit, and insight, without which the final result of my work would have been indubitably weaker.

As far as the American publication is concerned, I want to thank Dr. Philip Eggers, Professor Emeritus and Former Chairperson, English Department, Borough of Manhattan Community College of the City University of New York, for his precious editing suggestions and remarks; Dr. Maria do Carmo Eggers-de Vasconcelos, for all her encouragement and support about the process of publishing this novel in the USA; and Lauren Grosskopf for her dedication, professionalism, and hard work, both as editor and graphic designer.

This novel was published in the USA with the support of the General Directorate for Books, Archives and Libraries/DGLAB and Camões, Instituto de Cooperação e da Língua I.P/ Camões I.P. - Portugal.

The translation of the text to English was supported by FLAD's Alberto Lacerda Translation Program.

WORKS CONSULTED

IN ORDER TO SET this narrative in historical terms I have used, among other works, the following: *Portugal da Monarquia para a República,* coordinated by J.A. Oliveira Marques (Presença, 1991), *História de Portugal em Datas* (C. Leitores, 1994), *Memórias, de Raul Brandão* (Relógio D'Água, 1998), *Um Herói Português Henrique Paiva Couceiro, de Vasco Pulido Valente* (Aletheia, 2006) and *Memórias da Condessa de Mangualde* (Quetzal Editores, 2002).

In order to have a better knowledge of the Portuguese art scene at the end of the nineteenth century, and particularly in relation to the reception of the works made by Queiroz Ribeiro, I consulted *A Arte em Portugal no Século XIX,* by José-Augusto França (Bertrand Editora, 1990), (in which I discovered that the statue of the *Sagrado Coração de Jesus,* a full body pose, over four meters in height, is a bust, after all…), *Dicionário de Escultura Portuguesa,* by José Fernandes Pereira (Caminho, 2005), *Arte e Artistas Contemporâneos (3.a série),* by Ribeiro Artur and *À Esquina,* by Fialho de Almeida, etc.

In relation to Rodin's works I have used, among others, *Cher Maître, lettres à Auguste Rodin 1902-1913,* by Rainer Maria Rilke and Kitty Sabatier (Paris, 2002), *Rodin à Meudon La Villa des Brillants,* by Antoinette Le Normand-Romain and Hélène Marraud (Musée Rodin, 1996) and *Rodin,* by Raphaël Masson and Véronique Mattiussi (Flammarion, 2004); about works by Saint-Gaudens, *Augustus Saint-Gaudens, 1848—1907, Un Maître de la sculpture américaine* (Paris, 1999); about Denys Puech, *Denys-Puech, 1854-1942, Catalogue,* (Musée des Beaux-Arts Denys-Puech, 1993).

For the historical and geographical setting in the Ponte de Lima region I mainly used the *Roteiro da Ribeira Lima,* by Conde d'Aurora (Ponte de Lima, 1996), but also the *O Mistério da Estrada de Ponte do Lima, António Feijó e Eça de Queiroz,* by A. Campos Matos (Livros Horizonte, 2001) and *Subsídios para a História do Convento de Refóios* (Ponte de Lima, 1988), among others.

On nineteenth century Lisbon and the Chiado area in particular, I mainly based myself on *O Chiado Pitoresco e Elegante*, by Mário Costa (Lisboa, 1987) and *A Lisboa de Eça de Queiroz*, by Marina Tavares Dias (Quimera, 2003); on nineteenth century Paris I used, among other works, *Paris au Fil des Jours Dans la Carte Postale Ancienne, 1900, by Yves Bizet* (Gerfaut, 2003), *Paris*, Archives de France, (Paris, 1993) and *Le nouveau Montparnasse, de la Porte Océane à la Seine* (Paris, 1990).

On Sousa Martins I consulted *Sousa Martins e suas Memórias Sociais, Sociologia de Uma Crença Popular*, by José Machado Pais (Gradiva, 1994), and *Sousa Martins (In Memorium)*, (Lisboa, 1904); for the chapter including Eça de Queiroz I used information taken from *Eça em Verdemilho e a Sua Vida*, by António Lebre (Livraria Borges, s/d), *Os Eças, Memórias*, by Maria Augusta d'Eça d'Alpuim (V. Castelo, 1992) and *Eça de Queirós*, by Maria Filomena Mónica (Quetzal, 2001), etc.; for the references to António Nobre I mainly based myself on *António Nobre, Correspondência*, by Guilherme de Castilho.

Besides all these works, it was fundamental for me to consult the pages of the Portuguese newspapers of the time, particularly *O Século, Diário de Notícias, Aurora do Lima, Comércio do Lima* and *Cardeal Saraiva*, where, besides articles and news items of general and specific issues, I found these remarkable predecessors of the society magazines that were the social columns of the newspapers, with such suggestive names as *Ecos da Sociedade, Registo Galante, Vida Elegante, High-life*, in which society-life was analyzed down to the root; but also so in the American newspapers, mainly those that appear in the book of cuttings made by Miss Beach, besides others I was able to access on the Internet and on sites such as *Ancestry.com* and *ProQuest Historical Newspapers*.

MANUEL DE QUEIROZ was born in Porto, North of Portugal, and lives in Lisbon where he works as a writer, architect, and urban planner.

For several years he has been a member of the Portuguese PEN Club Board, the Portuguese Order of Architects National Board, and the Architects Council of Europe Executive Board.

He was 19 years old when he started publishing poems and short stories regularly in several Porto and Lisbon newspapers and magazines, followed by a first book of poems, *Encontro* (1969).

His first novel, *O Dedo na Ferida (The Finger on the Spot)*, published in 2001, won the 2002 Portuguese PEN Club Award for First Novel.

In 2008, he published the novel, *Os Passos da Glória*, selected for the Fernando Namora Award shortlist. In 2020, this novel won a grant from the Portuguese Government for its publication in the USA, under the title, *My Art and My Stetson*.

A new novel, *O Lado Negro do Vermelho (The Dark Side of the Red)*, and a volume of short stories, *No Verão de '68 e Outras Histórias de Viagens (In The Summer of '68 and Other Travel Stories)*, will be published in 2021.

CPSIA information can be obtained
at www.ICGtesting.com
Printed in the USA
JSHW040825110421
13408JS00001B/1